HIGHLAND HAVEN

Maurice Duffill

 www.trafford.com

North America & international
toll-free: 1 888 232 4444 (USA & Canada)
fax: 812 355 4082

May the
Scottish Highlands
flourish

and thanks to the Highlanders
for accepting this
Sassenach author and his wife
so readily for so many years

Also by Maurice Duffill

View of Life
End of Term
The Link – from Before Big-Bang to Brain and Beyond

Highland Haven is a work of fiction;

Although the locations, historical background,
fauna and flora, are real,
all characters, apart from Doug Grant and his wife Dorothy,
are the inventions of the author;
any similarities to actual persons, or assumed implications due to
actual residences coincident with locations used in the story,
are not intended as reflections on their character.

The inclusion of Doug Grant as the padre is a mark of respect for
a dear friend, now departed; however, he never was a padre.

Highland Haven

CHAPTER 1

"Darling; look at this advertisement." The excited voice from the kitchen was that of Sue, Sam Jackson's wife; he was in the bathroom still with his face masked by shaving soap.

With a groan he came through, to join her at the breakfast table. Leaning over her shoulder, he deliberately daubed soap on the side of her face while trying to read the item in the paper.

"Now, what's all the panic?" he enquired.

With a splutter from her toast-filled mouth, she exclaimed, "You rotten husband you - here's me trying to satisfy your great desires, when all you can do is ruin my beautiful complexion with that foaming muck you call soap."

"Never mind the soap, let's get down to satisfying my great desires. We haven't time to go back to bed, I should be thinking about preparing for the office; why do you choose moments like this to be amorous, you gorgeous thing?"

By the time he'd finished squeezing her it was difficult to tell who was supposed to be shaving.

"Get off, you clown! I was referring to the paper. There's a job for you."

"What do you mean - a job for me - when I'm up to my eyes with it, on this Tewkesbury project?"

"I don't mean for now, I was thinking of the future. You always said that you didn't want to stagnate and, recently you remarked that it would be difficult to find a challenge comparable to this mill job you're on."

"That is true, my learned one," he mockingly replied. "But, where is this leading?"

"Wipe your face, sit down, eat your toast and, for heaven's sake, read this ad."

Maurice Duffill

He dutifully did as he was bid; and read:-

WANTED

ENGINEERING MANAGER

Must be youthful in spirit
but have had years of experience
in many engineering disciplines.

A lifelong project
of unique character
awaits the successful applicant
prepared to re-locate
to a rugged highland glen
in Northwest Scotland.

The faint-hearted need not apply.

Send C.V. to Box 152 Daily Telegraph.

After a long pause, he murmured "Well, I don't really know what to think."

"Have a go," she urged. "At least apply and find out what it is all about."

"You seem mad keen to go leaping off to the frozen north," he retorted.

"Well, it sounds different, and you always said that once the kids had grown up and left us, you'd like to try something out of the ordinary. Where's your adventure?"

"O.K., I'll give it a whirl tonight when I come home," he relented.

"That's what I love about my daring, darling husband; he's so impulsive, he makes wild, venturesome decisions without need of wifely consultation."

"If," he replied quickly. "I was not so pressed for time; I would show you how impulsive I *can* be while keeping you to your promise of satisfying my great desires."

"Oh, get along with you and hurry home." She said, giving him a cuddly kiss as he went out to his car.

Highland Haven

And so it was, that evening after dinner, they settled down to the task of composing a letter of application, laying great stress on Sam's many years of varied engineering responsibility.

Unnoticed by Sam and Sue, that day's paper also carried advertisements, written in similar vein, for Commercial Manager, Estate Manager, Personnel Manager and an Accountant.

That evening, and one or two following, saw many people dotted about Britain expressing their enthusiasm for the various positions offered, whilst at the same time, wondering what they may be letting themselves in for.

Some ten days had elapsed when, at the Jackson's home, the telephone rang. It was early evening and Sue could be heard singing in the kitchen as she cleared away the dinner pots and loaded the dish washer. Sam lifted the receiver.

"Mr. Jackson?" asked a female voice.

"Speaking."

"I am Miss Fitzroy, telephoning with regard to your application to fulfil the position of Engineering Manager in the Scottish Highlands. Mr Jackson! Can you allocate next week-end to come up here for an interview?"

"Well," he pondered, "it's a bit short notice but....yes! I'll manage it somehow."

At this point Sue came through from the kitchen to check who Sam was talking to but could only establish 'its them', as he hurriedly covered the mouthpiece.

"I should point out that the invitation is also extended to your wife." Miss Fitzroy continued. "It is important that her acceptance is also established."

"Well yes, she will be able to join me."

This remark caused Sue to prick up her ears.

"Please," went on Miss Fitzroy, "be at Rufforth airfield, outside York, at 11 o'clock on Friday morning. A private aircraft will collect you. Bring clothing and personal toiletries for the week-end. We dress for dinner, but include stout walking shoes or boots. You will be returned to York on Monday afternoon."

"Please tell me, who we are to meet and where we are being taken."

"All will be made quite clear on your arrival." She haughtily retorted.

"Very well then; we will both be at the airfield at eleven on Friday." Sam conceded. "I trust we shall meet on arrival?"

"Yes! That is correct. Goodbye."

As Sam replaced the receiver, Sue could hardly contain herself. "Who are they; what airfield; where are we going?"

"Hey, hang on lass. Let me get my breath back.... That, my dear wifey, was a pompous twit of a female-type secretary glorying in the name of Miss Fitzroy.

She, apparently, was speaking on behalf of the people to whom we wrote with regard to that job in the Highlands."

"But, who *are* they and what's it all about?" pleaded Sue.

"That's the point, I don't know. She wouldn't say. Actually, it's all very peculiar. We've both been invited to an interview, in Scotland, this week-end. There's a private plane picking us up on Friday at Rufforth."

"Hey!" cried Sue, "you don't think it's a plan to kidnap us, do you?"

"Don't get your whatnot's in a twist. Somebody who can sport a private plane would find no profit in hijacking *us*. No, there must be some reason for keeping us in the dark, but I don't know what. Anyway let's not worry about it; just look forward to a week-end away at someone else's expense. We are to go prepared to dress for dinner, so it doesn't sound too bad."

"Oh, what should I take for evening wear?"

"Nothing too fancy; how about your white cocktail dress; that looks smart."

"I'm all excited; I can't wait for Friday, to see what it's all about. I hope I don't let you down."

"I'm sure you won't. But you will just have to be patient."

It was 10.30 when they motored through the entrance, giving ample time to find out where to leave the car. Rufforth is not highly organised like a normal commercial airport, it is a semi-retired wartime R.A.F. base used by a gliding club and odd people flying in to York races. Having parked the car alongside a hanger, Sam and Sue went in search of somebody; anybody.

"Let's try the control tower," suggested Sam, after twenty minutes' fruitless effort. "There must be someone up *there*, the R.A.F. use the runway as a satellite to Linton-on-Ouse, for practice landings."

They both climbed the stairs, conscious that time was running out; their 'personal wings' would soon be here.

"Ah", uttered Sam, as they entered through the doorway; "there is life here after all."

A female human being could be seen at the control desk, reading a paper-back book. She spoke. "I'm the controller, can I help you?"

"Well, I certainly hope so. You're the first person we've seen since we arrived. Are you expecting a private plane at 11 o'clock?"

"Yes! Let me see, it's a Grumman Widgeon coming from Luton and routed on to North West Scotland."

"That'll be it. We are to join her for the rest of the trip north. A Widgeon," Sam added wistfully. "Isn't that an old amphibian?"

"You've got me there. It's a new one on me." The controller confessed.

Highland Haven

"More likely *before* your time; if I'm not mistaken. It is, I think, an American wartime communications aircraft used in the Philippines for Island hopping. It could land either on rough airstrips or on the water in quiet bays or rivers."

"It sounds as if you know quite a bit about aeroplanes," she commented.

"Well, I was an R.A.F. pilot," Sam admitted. "But that was after the war, in the early jet era. I was a night-fighter pilot."

"RUFFORTH, FROM HIGHLAND LASSIE. DO YOU READ? OVER." It was a voice on the radio.

"STRENGTH 5, HOW ME? OVER," replied the controller

"FIVE ALSO. APPROACHING FROM THE SOUTH ABOUT 10 MILES. REQUEST JOINING INSTRUCTIONS. OVER."

CLEAR TO JOIN. RUNWAY TWO FOUR. QNH 1009, WIND; LIGHT AND VARIABLE. VISIBILITY; SLIGHT HAZE. OVER."

"ROGER. BE WITH YOU IN THREE MINUTES."

"By heck!" exclaimed Sam. "That bit of dialogue takes me back."

In no time, the radio burst into life again. "HIGHLAND LASSIE - DOWN WIND."

"CLEAR FINALS." She replied.

As the aircraft turned and let down towards the runway, all three in the control tower could see the design was certainly unfamiliar, being half plane and half boat with wheels.

"FINALS. UNDERCART DOWN AND LOCKED."

"CLEAR TO LAND." She confirmed, "AFTER LANDING, APPROACH THE TOWER. YOUR PASSENGERS AWAIT."

"ROGER, WILCO," came the reply.

"He sounds very much like an ex-RAF type." Sam observed, as they both bade farewell, leaving the controller to her book

They arrived on the tarmac just as the plane came to a halt. As they approached, two figures emerged; one, a well-built fellow who was obviously the pilot, with his peaked airline type hat and shirt sleeves, the other being a slim young college student.

"Mr and Mrs Jackson?" enquired the pilot. "I'm Ted Evans your winged chauffeur."

"Evans from the heavens," joked Sam as they shook hands.

"Ignore my corny husband," chided Sue, as she greeted him.

"Take your seats on board, I'll stow your bags. I must report to the tower, and Mr Codling here has a weak bladder I'm afraid; he's seeking the necessaries. I'll be with you shortly; introduce yourselves to Mr and Mrs Fraser, the other passengers."

Alan Fraser was a smallish man, a little over-weight through good living.

About three or four years older than me thought Sam. His wife, Mhairi, matched him well, being a little shorter, a little slimmer and a little younger. Genuine friendliness was apparent as they shook hands all round.

"What do you know about this set-up?" Alan Fraser anxiously asked.

"Not a thing," Sam answered forcibly. "Miss Fitzroy, who spoke to me on the phone, wouldn't tell me a thing."

"That was the same with us," agreed Alan.

"It's a bit worrying, don't you think?" added Mhairi.

"I'm glad somebody else feels the same," replied Sue.

Their hesitant conversation was interrupted by the return of Mr Codling, whose handshake felt appropriate to his name, like holding a wet fish.

The pilot's return soon cut short any further talk as he re-started the noisy engines.

It was a good day for flying, no cloud and still air, although a slight haze impaired vision towards the sun. As the aircraft climbed away, the high wing of the Widgeon gave the passengers a clear view of the Vale of York, a lush green valley between the heathery brown of the moors to the east and the Pennines to the west.

The pilot advised them, over the intercom, that the flight would last 1 hour 40 minutes, give or take a minute or two, which should bring them to their destination nicely in time for lunch. For information, he added that their cruising speed would be 150 knots at the safe height of 4500 ft, to clear the mountains to the north.

As the aircraft reached its cruise height, the pilot eased back on the throttles, giving a considerable reduction in noise level.

"That's better," breathed Sue. "I can hear myself think, now. I don't know how you could stand all that noise every day when you were flying."

"Jet aircraft are a lot quieter," assured Sam. "The pilot of a Meteor can hardly hear the engines, bearing in mind that he is wearing ear pieces to his helmet. Anyway, it's a lot quieter now he's throttled back."

Mhairi turned around from the seat in front. "The pilot's quite forthcoming with information, isn't he? But he still hasn't said exactly where we are going. Did you notice?"

Sue was pleased she had an ally, someone who shared her fears. "I can't imagine," she confessed, "why they won't tell us. They must be up to something illegal or immoral."

"For heaven's sake," pleaded Sam. "Let it drop. Stop worrying about the 'whys and wherefores', treat it as an adventure. And enjoy it!"

"My sentiments exactly," interjected Alan.

Highland Haven

Conversation ceased, the passengers contenting themselves by admiring the superb view as their flight took them north-west, diagonally across the fells of the northern Pennines, and so into Scotland.

It was approaching 12.30 when the pilot announced that they were nearing Ben Nevis, which would be on their starboard side, as they turned up the Great Glen. Turning over Fort William, using Britain's highest peak as a corner stone, the aircraft began to lose height.

"We're going down," observed Sue.

"Yes," agreed Sam, "it looks as if we're to follow the glen. Our mystery rendezvous can't be too far away."

A few minutes later the plane banked sharply left, over a loch on the Caledonian Canal, to cross the ridge into Glen Garry. The flight continued, still losing height until, as they passed over the head of Loch Garry, the engine note changed noticeably.

"He's selected fully fine pitch," commented Sam. "We must be going to land, but I'm blowed if I know where."

The aircraft banked, first left then right, weaving between the mountains until, quite suddenly, a large dam appeared ahead. Beyond was a large loch, with extensions probing the minor glens between the surrounding peaks. Descending parallel to a single-track road which was clinging to the hillside on the northern shore, the amphibian gently touched down on the mirror-like surface.

"Don't unfasten your lap straps until we are at rest on the shore," instructed the pilot. "We will taxi up a ramp, after first putting the wheels down, so as to keep your feet dry."

The aircraft - or was it now a boat? - continued to the far end of the loch where could be seen the ramp, alongside which, a mini bus awaited. With a final surge from the engines, the amphibian came off the water on to the dry concrete ramp. Ted Evans shut down the engines, bringing peace and quietness once more to this remote glen; not a building could be seen.

As they climbed out of the aircraft, voice was given to pent-up feelings.

"I'm glad that's over," Mhairi admitted. "I thought we were going to hit one or other of those peaks."

"Wasn't it worth it though?" observed Alan. "Just look at the fantastic vista. What magnificent mountain grandeur. Even I could be inspired to write poetry. It really is beautiful."

A tall slim woman, with rather peaky features, was waiting by the open door of the small bus. "Welcome!" She said formally. "I am Miss Fitzroy. If you will board the vehicle, your baggage will be loaded for you, so that we may proceed without delay."

"A right punctilious person," remarked Sam, to nobody in particular.

"She's just as I imagined her," observed Alan.

The driver and the pilot joined them, having transferred the baggage.

"Proceed, Mr MacDonnell," their aloof guide commanded.

The five mile journey was as scary as the latter part of the flight; travelling in the bus, albeit a mini-bus, along the narrow single-track road didn't make for a relaxing trip. The vehicle and the road were the same width, making it difficult to negotiate the tortuous twists and turns. To add to the tension, humps in the road were so severe it was at times impossible to see the road ahead until the crest was reached.

As they rounded a bend, with a rock-face like a wall on their left, the road plunged steeply, keeping pace with a tumbling burn on their right.

"You'll not forget this excursion in a hurry," commented Sam. "It's a thrill a minute."

"I'm not the only one who'll remember this," observed Sue; "Mr Codling looks a bit green."

"I wondered why he was so quiet," mused Sam. "I must say he doesn't look to be the adventurous type."

The bus ride finally became calmer as they arrived on level ground at sea level, and turned along the driveway to a large detached house overlooking a sea loch.

As Miss Fitzroy led them to the imposing front entrance, the door was opened by the housekeeper, Mrs Pat Evans, wife of the pilot. They were shown into the drawing room to take drinks, while having the opportunity to freshen up before lunch. However, a surprise awaited them. There were many more people in the room and it soon became obvious that lunch was to be the moment when the mystery would be unveiled.

CHAPTER 2

"Gentlemen - and Ladies;" It was Miss Frosty Features demanding immediate attention; "Will you please take your places at the lunch table, through in the dining room; each seat is annotated."

Everyone obediently filed into the spacious room, which boasted illuminated ancestral portraits upon the walls. At the far end, a grand piano awaited the fingers of some maestro to tickle the ivory keys, but the centre-piece was an enormous oak table set for over twenty lunches. Each place-setting was labelled by a boldly written name on each side of a folded card; this way everyone was able to identify all others.

As the inquisitive guests took their places, Miss Fitzroy announced the entrance of the long-awaited host. "May I present Sir Richard and Lady Dorothy Blaisdale."

Of average height, they both looked to be in their early sixties; she, two or three years his junior. Grey, with a ruddy complexion, he gave the impression of an outdoor man; shooting and fishing probably. Her glowing cheeks and weathered forehead suggested she was a 'horsey' woman.

"Ladies and Gentlemen," he greeted quietly. "Please be seated and enjoy your lunch. I'm sure our bracing air will have generated an appetite."

Whilst the soup was being served, Sir Richard continued from his seat at the head of the table. "No doubt you are all somewhat intrigued as to the secrecy surrounding your visit and the apparent rudeness of my secretary by refusing to explain the motive. Let me re-assure you that nothing underhand is envisaged. I have very comprehensive development plans of a unique character and before revealing them, I seek your written assurance that nobody here will divulge any of the affairs of the week-end. This undertaking must apply, whether or not you are ultimately successful with your application."

"Accordingly," he continued, between spoons-full of soup, "I have prepared a formal document declaring your sworn confidentiality which requires the signatures of everyone in this room. It will be passed round the table. Please oblige."

The soup was followed by a generous portion of roast venison accompanied by roast potatoes, green peas and sumptuous, wine-laced gravy. A bold red wine, Chateaneuf-du-Pape, was proffered to further enhance the meal.

"With a meal like this, he could convince us of anything," muttered Sue.

"You're still suspicious, aren't you?" Sam retorted incredulously.

The meal progressed with small talk, through the dessert of fruit salad immersed in brandy cream, to the cheese and biscuits.

The efficient staff cleared away the debris, and then returned with cups and trays bearing large pots of coffee, hot milk and brown sugar, together with a number of carafes, and glasses for all.

The host waited until the staff had left the room then drew attention to himself with a little cough. "Please help yourselves to coffee. The content of the carafe is not brandy but, as you might expect, a fine malt whisky. Be my guests; savour it while I deliver my explanatory speech."

There was the expected clatter of cups and saucers by the ladies, and the clink of glass on glass by the men, until all were primed with liquid refreshment.

"Over recent years," he commenced. "I have acquired substantial acreage in these mountains and now, having realised my assets in the Far East, am in a position to commence fulfilling a long standing ambition. The objective is to re-populate this area."

"Many years ago, as most of you will be aware, the glens supported hundreds or even thousands of people, but the selfish attitude of the major land owners of the period replaced them with sheep during the infamous Highland Clearances. I intend to redress past injustices."

"You can imagine that the conditions in which the previous inhabitants lived were far from ideal. Existence is all that could be claimed. It most certainly is not my intention that 'peasants' should grovel for an existence on this land. Quite the contrary, my aims are far higher."

Pausing for effect and to take a lingering sip from his whisky glass, Sir Richard continued, "I believe, with the aid of modern technology, that we can create, in these Highland glens an environment that is conducive to enjoyable, profitable living. I must stress the use of the word 'enjoyable'. My philosophy is that life is to be enjoyed, not simply endured; enjoyment that stems from achieving goals rather than from extravagant pursuits."

"Let me also dwell on that word 'profit'. Profit is necessary for any business to remain viable, as you will all be fully aware. However, the need to be efficient must not be allowed to overrule consideration for all those affected. We are all on this planet for the betterment of mankind; let's use our particular talents to bring out the best in others, not to ride roughshod over the less able."

After a short pause, during which a mumble of conversation could be heard from his intrigued audience, Sir Richard pronounced, "I make no apology for being rather pedantic on this question of business morals. It is my philosophy of life and the underlying reason for this project. Any of you that feel unable to conduct their affairs whilst adhering to this principle are advised to withdraw now."

"He knows what he wants," breathed Alan Fraser across the table, "and I think he has the strength of personality to make quite sure he is going to get it."

Highland Haven

Before Sam had the time to reply, their host continued, "Since nobody has chosen to leave, the implication is that we are, fundamentally, all in agreement. I do not propose, at this juncture, to go into great detail regarding this long-term project. It is sufficient to say that the objective is to build a community here in this quiet corner of Britain that will demonstrate a social order based on teamwork, rather than the more traditional 'rat-race'."

"Do not misunderstand my intentions; this is not to be a village of cranks, this new township is to be built up on sound, but forward thinking principles. We will have many fights on our hands, objectors will seek to prevent this alternative use of mountain regions; there will be many technical difficulties with construction; the climate will be a major stumbling block to re-population; and income must be generated at an early stage in order to finance further progress. All these, and more, are obstacles to be overcome."

"If you thrive on problems and your wife is also prepared to accept a worthwhile challenge, since she too will need to take an active part, we will proceed with the next phase."

As Sir Richard rose from his seat, he half turned to 'frosty features', then to the assembly he announced, "Miss Fitzroy will advise you of the rest of the programme." Without a chance of comment or question, he and Lady Blaisdale left the room.

The immediate rise in noise level, as everybody started talking at once, gave the impression of 200+ occupants rather than 20+.

"Gentlemen, GENTLEMEN!" Miss Fitzroy endeavoured to gain attention. "Gentlemen - and ladies - tomorrow Sir Richard and Lady Dorothy will be conducting joint interviews in the study. I have posted a schedule in the hall so that you can ensure availability at the appropriate time. You will notice that, when I said 'joint interview' - I meant joint in both senses; your hosts will interview each candidate simultaneous with his wife."

Quelling further chatter with a sweep of the hand, she went on," Between now and your appointed time, you are free to take in the scene, but I would point out that in the library are many books and maps of the area which you may find of interest. Dinner is formal, 7.30 for 8p.m."

"Let's get some air," Sue gasped. "After that lovely lunch and the verbal afters, I feel like a diver needing fresh oxygen."

"I do too;" came the voice of Mhairi as they rose from the table;" Would you mind if we joined you for a stroll?"

"Be our guests," replied Sam with an exaggerated magnanimous gesture.

"We are most honoured;" whimpered Alan as he mockingly bowed to his new found friend.

"Give over, you two;" interjected Sue. "I think these grand surroundings have gone to your heads."

Outside, the foursome deliberately moved away from the main group by taking a path hugging the rocky loch side. Even though a granite cliff rose dramatically from the very edge of the water, birch trees and rowan miraculously found a foot-hold in the crevices to form a droopy canopy over the perilous walkway which had been hewn out of the mountain.

Rounding a bend they came upon a grassy 'oasis' where a waterfall tumbled from a sizable cleft to form a busy stream rushing under a plank bridge to the freedom of the sea loch.

"I'm glad to be off that narrow ledge," breathed Mhairi with relief. "I didn't like that at all. It was as if the steep rock-face wanted to push us into the water. Oh - but isn't it beautiful here?"

"Fantastic;" agreed Sue. "Let's sit on that knoll over there, so that we can hear ourselves think. The stream is very pretty but it does make a lot of noise."

"*Burn*", Alan corrected Sue.

"I beg your pardon?" Sue queried, somewhat taken aback.

"In Scotland, a stream is called a *burrrn*", explained Alan with an exaggerated roll on the 'R'.

"Oh yes, I'm sorry. I had forgotten that your surname was Fraser. Do you originate from these parts?"

"Not really. My ancestors come from the south side of Loch Ness, but I was born near Glasgow. However, I reckon I'll be able to keep you right if we all work together."

"That brings us to a leading question." Sam declared. "Are you and I in competition?"

"There's a point," admitted Alan. "We don't yet know very much about each other."

"Let's get it over with." Sam forcibly suggested. "I'm an Engineering Projects Manager - what's your line?"

"Well, that's alright then. My engineering knowledge is limited to building services, drains and all that sort of thing," conceded Alan, adding "My field is property. I'm currently managing a large estate consisting of half a dozen farms, a small hamlet and, would you believe, a castle!"

"That sounds jolly interesting." Sue declared. "Why are you considering a change?"

"I've been with this family 'empire' a good many years now and I felt the need to explore new possibilities before I was too ancient. Having spent many happy holiday hours in the region of my ancestors, this project could fulfil my desires, and I know that Mhairi would just love to live hereabouts."

16

Highland Haven

"My case is much the same." Sam volunteered. "It would be good to take on one last big project that, after a few years, becomes less demanding as one becomes decrepit. Although there are lots of questions to be answered, it does seem as if Sir Richard's ambitious brainchild has all the necessary ingredients."

"I wonder why they insist on interviewing wives along with husbands," pondered Sue.

"Alan used to do that, didn't you?" Mhairi said.

"Yes! If the job involves living in amongst it, so to speak, then it is important that the wife should become settled in order to properly support the husband in his work. I suspect there is a bit more to it in this case, though."

"How do you mean, dear?" enquired Mhairi. "You've got me worried now."

"Well, I think they are looking for willingness to help build a close knit community, not just a soul-less conglomerate of activities."

"You're probably right," agreed Sam. "It's just as well that Sue and I have some experience in that quarter. We used to run a charity trust, committed to organising social events as well as raising money for local needs. We were also, amongst other things, members of a drama group and a small choir singing anything from 'Moon River' to 'The Messiah'."

"Oh, hark at our community spirited comrades, then;" joked Mhairi.

"O.K. then, since we are showing off community credentials; Mhairi and I are not without experience I would have you know;" said Alan haughtily. "We were both on the management committee of our local Boy Scout group. My dear wife was co-founder of an old people's club, and I surveyed an old canal for a preservation society."

"If you two are at least half as capable at your work as your mutual claim to social consciousness, the jobs are yours for the asking," mocked Mhairi.

"Do you both think you would take to living here, starting off with a raw development project; bearing in mind that initially, facilities such as shops, beauty parlours, theatres and the like are, no doubt, many miles distant ?" Sam challenged.

"Oh, but it's beautiful; surely anyone could be happy here amongst these stupendous peaks and placid lochs. We're very lucky to be given the chance," interjected Sue in total naivety.

"Sue, you are just like my wife," declared Alan; "you can only see today. Why do you think that this area is so sparsely populated? It may be idyllic at this particular moment but, make no mistake it can all change very quickly. Howling gales and torrential rain can arrive with very little warning. Those stupendous peaks become awesome when capped with dense, overpowering clouds. These placid lochs become fearsome oceans, eager to gobble up the little boat from which an unsuspecting angler had lazily been casting for trout five minutes before.

"Oh Alan," pleaded Mhairi. "Don't be so dramatic.   You'll frighten off Sue and Sam."

"I'm not trying to be dramatic. I've seen it happen on a number of occasions. Bear in mind, this is the wettest and windiest region in the U.K., facing, as it does, the open Atlantic. I certainly do not wish to paint a rotten picture, quite the contrary; it can be most exhilarating and the source of inspiration to artist and writer. No, don't be put off; just consider the motto of the Royal Observer Corps 'forewarned is forearmed'."

"The weather factor is certainly going to be a major consideration in any development plan," observed Sam. "Both from the point of view of the engineer required to carry out any form of construction work, and from the point of view of attracting people to make their homes here."

"Well, I don't care what you say. I would like to come here," declared Sue. "And the idea of building a completely new, socially integrated, community in this unusual environment fascinates me."

"Here, here," chorused Mhairi.

"That seems to settle the basic question then," admitted Sam. "All we've got to do now is to convince the powers that be that we are the right people for the job."

"Do you know, we've been chatting here for ages?" Mhairi challenged. "We'd better get back; we haven't even established where our rooms are."

Reluctantly, they stirred from their beauty spot and set off across the burn and along the perilous pathway back to the lodge.

Entering the magnificent home by the front door, they came directly to a blackboard set on an easel. The names of all the guests were listed, giving room numbers and interview times for the following day.

"Here we are;" commented Alan. "Mr and Mrs A. Fraser - room 11 - interview 10.30 am Sat."

"And here we are; Mr and Mrs S. Jackson - room 13, that's very appropriate," remarked Sam, and then read on. "Interview 12.00 noon Sat."

"Why is room 13 so very appropriate?" enquired Mhairi.

"Well, we had two attempts at getting married, the 13th September then the 13th December." Sam replied. "I was called up into the R.A.F. prior to the first date and the Queen refused me leave to wed. The next opportunity was during leave at the end of my officer training course, before starting flying training; so we say - Sue was lucky the first time, because she escaped me, but I was lucky the second time. So we consider '13' to be lucky for both of us."

"Oh, isn't that a lovely tale Alan?" Mhairi said, giving him a cuddly squeeze.

"It sounds a bit Irish to me," he scoffed jokingly.

Highland Haven

"You've no romance left in you." Mhairi retorted pushing him away, discardedly.

"Let's get up those stairs and find our room," suggested Alan. "Then we'll see if there's a spark still left"

"Get away with you. You've got a one track mind."

"All men must be the same," interjected Sue.

After a pleasurable evening of fine food, good wine and interesting but light conversation, all settled to a comfortable night in well-appointed rooms, the only drawback being the apprehension for what tomorrow's interview might hold.

CHAPTER 3

Breakfast was a further example of highland hospitality: fruit juice, followed by steaming hot porridge or a choice of cereals. The main course was a generous plate of bacon, sausage, tomato and egg, accompanied by toast and butter. To finish, there was highland oatcakes with heather honey or, if preferred, a choice of two marmalades, coarse or fine shred. With a constant supply of piping hot tea or coffee, this made an ideal start to the day.

"This way of living suits me fine," commented Sue. "I just wonder whether this indulgence at the meal table is normal around here, or is it all specially laid on for our benefit."

"Perhaps," said Sam, "One needs all this good food to combat the elements."

Alan, who, together with Mhairi, had just joined them at the table, took up the topic. "The usual thing up here, for those that can afford it, is to have a good breakfast and a good evening meal with just a snack lunch in between. I think this comes about because, in the summer most are working long days out on the hill: stalking, forestry planting, felling or fencing. It's too far to return for a meal so they take with them a piece - a packed lunch."

"Your husband is a mine of information," Sue commented to Mhairi.

"Well, he has spent a bit of time up here, particularly as a youth."

"What happens in the winter, Alan?" Sue enquired, "Aren't the days much shorter?"

"Very much so," Alan agreed. "This is something you would have to get used to. Summer days up here are very much longer than down in the south of England. In fact, on clear nights, in midsummer, it doesn't darken completely at all."

"We're not above the arctic circle, are we?" interjected Sue.

"Not quite, but the sun sets north of north-west and rises north of north-east so it doesn't drop much below the northern horizon. A great hue of bluish light can often be seen due north at midnight."

"Oh! Is that the northern lights?" Sue asked.

"No - that is something quite different. That is a phenomenon caused by the Earth's magnetic field which is concentrated at the poles. Occurrences are quite random."

"As I was saying, whereas in the summer it doesn't really get properly dark, in the depth of winter there is a period of only about six hours that can be called daylight. For that reason, people do not waste valuable sunlight having fancy meals. Conversely, the long dark nights are made more acceptable by lingering over the evening meal."

Highland Haven

"You do seem to be particularly aware of such matters." Sam observed.

"Well, climatology is my hobby, and I'm particularly interested in human relationship to varying climatic conditions. In fact, I've developed a simple device I call my exposure meter, which enumerates human feeling of combined wind, rain and sunshine."

"That could be useful in connection with this project." Sam declared.

"Quite so," Alan confirmed. "Not only does it relate to human experience, it is an indicator of growing conditions for vegetation."

"Never mind all that technical chat," Mhairi insisted. "It's too early in the day. Let's go into the library and grub up on the district before we have to convince them how keen we are. It will be expected of us."

"I hope you have time for a chat with us after your interview," Sue said, "so that we will be pre-warned what to expect. I'm scared to death about being questioned."

"There you go again," Sam moaned. "You're always finding things to worry about. Just be yourself. If we get the job you can't keep up any pretence for long, so act natural."

"But what if I let you down?"

"If you are your normal self, you'll do for me. That's why I married you."

"Oh, isn't that nice?" said Mhairi. "Alan never says such things to me."

"No! I've got to keep you on your toes. We mustn't have you becoming complacent."

"Isn't he a beast? These Scotsmen never realise that to have sweet nothings whispered in our ears, does work wonders to we members of the fair sex. Still, I wouldn't swap him for all the haggis in the Highlands."

"There's a thing, Alan, what is a haggis?" Sue asked.

With a sideways glance at Sam, he explained that it was a rather plump bird, something like a pheasant, but unique to the Highlands since it had one leg longer than the other enabling it to walk easily on the hillside.

"But what if it wanted to walk the other way?" Sue queried after having pondered for a while.

"I'm afraid there is no time for further explanation," Alan said. "It is time for our grilling. We must go."

"The best of luck;" Sam declared. "We'll see you back in here."

Sam and Sue took advantage of the library facilities, he studying a large-scale map of the area, while she absorbed some of the local legends, such as that of the Water Kelpie - half fish and half beast, who had great taste for taking innocent children down into the depths of the loch.

A short hour passed when they were surprised by the return of their new friends.

"How did you get on? What are they like? What questions did they ask? "Burst forth Sue excitedly.

"Hang on," said Alan. "Let us catch our breath."

"They are very nice," volunteered Mhairi. "You needn't worry. They just talk easily with you, slipping in the odd question, but mainly giving you the chance to ask anything you want. I'd like to work for them, or with them, as they would have it. It seems to be a very exciting project, never before attempted."

"Well, you are obviously taken with it, Mhairi; how about you, Alan?" Sam asked.

"Let's put it this way, I'll be very disappointed if I don't get the job."

"Fair enough; anyway it is time for us to find out for ourselves." Sam said, shepherding his wife through the door.

Somewhat apprehensively, they entered the outer office manned by Miss Fitzroy; the time was 11.55.

"Good morning," she said formally. Pressing the intercom switch, she immediately reported, "Mr and Mrs Jackson are here, Sir, five minutes early; are you ready to receive them?"

"Please show them in;" came the voice of Sir Richard.

"Very good, Sir;" she replied; then to Sam and Sue, "please step this way," leading them through a substantial oak door into a heavily-panelled room. A deep pile blue carpet covered the floor, wall to wall, softly absorbing any sounds. Massive matching blue drapes were drawn back, either side of a deep bay window revealing a superb view of the loch. A large brass telescope mounted on a tripod was positioned to scan the coming and goings of water-borne traffic.

"Mr and Mrs Jackson," the secretary announced.

As they stepped forward to accept the outstretched hands of both Sir Richard and his wife, Sam could not resist passing comment.

"What a marvellous room with such a fantastic view. It must be inspiring to work here. It would make a pleasure out of any paper work."

"I'm glad you like it; it pleases us too," Sir Richard acknowledged. "Please sit down and make yourselves comfortable."

As they took their seats, their hosts came from the desk to join them in comfortable chairs. In this informal atmosphere, Lady Blaisdale opened the evaluation.

"Do you know this area at all, Mrs Jackson?"

"No, my Lady, I regret to say. It is only now that I've discovered for myself the wondrous beauties of the highlands."

"Have you made friends with anyone in the party?" enquired Sir Richard, more to Sam than his wife.

Highland Haven

"We certainly have. The couple who came up on the aircraft with us, Mr and Mrs Fraser, have proved to be good companions and he, being a Scot, has been educating us on matters concerning the area."

"Do you think you could work together on this project?"

"I'm sure we could," Sam confirmed, "although I am, as yet, a little in the dark as to what would be expected of me."

"The air of secrecy is unfortunate but necessary at this stage. Sufficient to say that if you were successful, as Engineering Director, you would be required to solve any technical problem arising. For instance, this new community will need better physical communications than the one road existing at present, but it would not be satisfactory to have a network of roads totally dominating the scene."

After a pause, during which time he offered and poured Sherries for all, Sir Richard continued, "New industries need to be established here, to make the scheme commercially viable, but it would be unacceptable to allow factories or offices to be the main feature of the skyline. These are the sort of problems you will be required to deal with, along with routine matters of power supplies, rainwater drainage, sewage disposal, telecommunications and many other special problems that I am not prepared to discuss at present."

"That, if I may say so, Sir, sounds to be quite a plateful. However, I would love the challenge. I am well used to tackling new problems," Sam declared.

"Yes, I am well aware of your background, Mr Jackson. It is because you have an innovatory mind that you were selected for interview. However, it is noted that your formal qualifications are somewhat lacking, and I must tell you that I will be making a choice between you and a more academically qualified candidate. Equally, I must admit that he has less proven experience than you"

"I am frequently up against this problem," admitted Sam. "My answer is that where greater specialist knowledge is needed then it is up to me to consult the appropriate authority. I have found though, that in order to be safe, most experts seek solutions in conventional practices and as a result, opportunities are missed for progressive development."

"This is very true," agreed Sir Richard. "However, we'd like to know more of your non-technical background."

"Yes," his wife continued, "I hope you realise that the building of a community does not depend on concrete and steel. It is more a question of communication, not the electronic variety, human communications. It is important that every effort will be made to involve the inhabitants in development here. This way it becomes their township, not just a place to live and work."

"I take your point," Sam conceded. "This is something I too feel quite strongly about. Because of this, I recently extended my ancillary responsibilities of advertising and publicity of our company's activities to include the publication of a house news-sheet. The objective was to draw everyone together by showing the end result of their labours, indicating how problems were overcome and highlighting benefits to the client. This has brought about a greater understanding between staff and work-force, thereby speeding up agreements which have led to greater satisfaction and improved efficiency."

"Perhaps I should declare, at this juncture, my managerial methods," stated Sir Richard. "It is my intention that the project will be subjected to a 'Dictatorial Democracy'. What I mean by that is that I will dictate the fundamental objectives for the management to resolve, in a democratic manner. At all times I will retain the power of veto which I shall exercise should I believe that progress is going off track."

"Your intentions I can understand," Sam affirmed, and then asked. "What would executive management comprise?"

"An accountant and four directors; personnel, commercial, property, and engineering, would form the board under my presidency. I envisage that the Engineering Director would take overall responsibility for project management by heading the management committee."

"The social aspect would be my concern," Lady Blaisdale proclaimed. "Whereas management is expected to consider social implications at all times, any redress will be channelled through me. Additionally I, with the help of some of the wives, shall organise social events, craft hobbies and see to the establishment of voluntary work. I'm sure that the experience of Mrs Jackson would be of considerable value."

"Thank you, Ma'am," replied Sue shyly, adding "It all sounds very exciting."

"If you have no further questions at this stage, I will specify the proposal." After a short pause, Sir Richard continued, "If successful, you would be offered a salary of £40,000 fixed, regardless of inflation, for the next five years. A company car would be provided but you would be expected to make your own personal arrangements regarding pension and the like. How does this appear to you Mr Jackson?"

After a pause for consideration, he replied, "I am most keen and interested in the project, but I would ask that a suitable free house be included in the offer."

Sue blinked in startled disappointment that her husband should risk throwing away this remarkable opportunity to start a most satisfying new career.

"Why do you consider that so important?" asked Sir Richard, not believing that he was simply being 'screwed' for more.

"If a house was provided free of charge, I would then invest the proceeds from the sale of my existing property. This would act as insurance against failure of this project for whatever reason. If that, perish the thought, were to happen, you would still have the land. Without a nest-egg, I would have nothing."

24

Highland Haven

After a thoughtful pause which, to Sue, seemed interminable, Sir Richard replied, "we'll give thought to your request when considering your application, and now, if you have nothing further, we'll terminate the interview by offering our hospitality for what remains of the week-end. You will be flown back on Monday morning. A formal communication will be posted to you without delay, as soon as everyone has been interviewed."

Rising from their seats, they both thanked their hosts for the courtesy afforded to them, then left through the great oak door, wondering whether or not they had been successful.

"Oh, I do hope we get it," Sue sighed. "I'd be so disappointed if we didn't."

"So would I," Sam admitted. "Sue, don't mention anything about the salary, or the matter of the house, to Alan or Mhairi. If we both get the jobs, it could be that I may have secured a better deal than he. It sounds from what was said, that I may become Managing Director, so we must be careful not to upset them before I've had chance to establish myself."

"How did you get on? What do you think about it all?" Mhairi said as soon as they entered the library. "Let's go into the dining room and have a chat. They've prepared a buffet lunch."

Having selected their gastronomic wants from an abundant table, the foursome settled at a table with a view of the sea loch below, through a truly picture window.

Sam and Sue gave a summary of their interview which turned out to be quite similar in form to that of their friends.

"I don't think I can contain myself till we get home," admitted Mhairi.

"We must find something to occupy us," Sam pronounced. "I experienced a similar situation at the end of my officer-training course, in the Isle of Man. After our final examination, all pupils were sent on a treasure hunt, covering the whole island, whilst the results were worked out. By the time we got back, about three days later, the pass list was posted on the notice board. It saved a lot of nail biting."

"This afternoon," declared Alan, "there's some skeet shooting, if you're interested."

"What on earth is a skeet?" asked Sue, "some kind of bird? If it is, I want nothing to do with it."

"No," assured Alan, "skeet shooting is firing at clay pigeons."

"Oh, that's alright then," said Sue, "but we haven't got a gun with us. In any case, I don't know about Mhairi, but I've never fired anything other than a fairground air gun; pinging those little darts into paper targets."

"I imagine it will be somewhat different," mused Sam. "It'll be a twelve bore, won't it Alan?"

"What is a twelve bore? Or shouldn't I ask?" queried Sue, in total ignorance.

"That's a gun which fires cartridges filled with hundreds of pellets. The idea is that the spread helps you to score a hit, but it isn't as simple as that."

"I wouldn't know what to do," Sue pleaded.

"That's ok," Alan assured her. "Ted Evans, the pilot, is to give the necessary instruction. There is nothing to worry about. It will just be for fun."

"Alright then I'm game, if you all want to go."

"There's a sport."

"Sport, my aunt fanny; it was the mention of the handsome pilot that swayed her."

"Get away with you." Sue retorted.

"I don't wish to plan your lives for you." said Mhairi, "but shall we put our names down for the pony trekking, tomorrow?"

"That's more my cup of tea," declared Sue. "Will there be enough mounts for all four of us?"

"Well, apparently there are about ten, so, it's first come first served."

"With shooting today and pony trekking tomorrow, it'll make a splendid week-end, whatever the outcome," Sam declared.

"Oh don't talk like that dear, think positive! You are going to be selected."

"Hark, at my dear wife. It's amazing what good food does. It was only five minutes ago that she was pleading to a higher authority to forgive all her sins and grant her latest wish."

"Oh, you do exaggerate. Anyway perhaps that higher authority has already indicated to me that the job is yours."

"That's just wishful thinking," Sam asserted.

An hour later found them on the open moor, receiving basic instruction on the use of firearms, from Ted Evans.

Having established that none of them was experienced, he explained about the device secreted in a protective bunker which hurls out the clay discs. On the command 'PULL', his assistant in the bunker, would release the spring-loaded mechanism to fling out the target.

His attention was then turned to the gun, in particular, the safe handling thereof. "It is not funny to lark about with a gun," he declared in a forceful manner, so that no one would mistake the seriousness of the matter. "At all times, unless actually firing, the gun will be carried 'broken', empty of cartridges, like this," drawing attention to the way in which shot guns are hinged in the middle, making it impossible to fire.

"When called upon to shoot, you will step forward, load with the cartridge provided -so- close the gun, keeping the barrel pointing forward -so- and then give the command 'PULL'.

Highland Haven

Immediately, a black disc spun through the air from a point just behind a small hillock. A loud report preceded the disintegration of the target as he pointed the gun and fired.

"You will then 'break' the gun and discharge the spent cartridge case -so- and say 'CLEAR'. There is no danger as long as this procedure is rigidly adhered to and everyone else remains behind the shooter."

"Now then, who is going to shoot first?"

"You go," Sue said. "I'm afraid of doing it wrong."

Sam stepped forward.

The instructor showed him how to hold the weapon firmly but lightly against his shoulder so that he could quickly respond to the appearance of the target. "Don't attempt to sight it." He said, "Just point; as soon as you see the target, point the barrel at it and squeeze the trigger."

Sam was given a single cartridge. He stepped forward, loaded the gun, raised it to his shoulder, and then called 'PULL'. He fired and, much to his amazement, the target went into a shower of pieces. He unloaded the gun, and stepped back.

"How about that then?" he proudly asked.

"First time lucky;" his wife jokingly needled him.

"We'll soon see about that," he retorted, as he accepted a second cartridge from Ted Evans.

He stepped forward, loaded, 'PULL' he commanded, BANG; another clay was shattered.

"'Top shot Sam', they call me," he boasted, as he prepared to take his third and final shot. 'PULL', but this time after the bang, the target continued to glide, unscathed, through the air to land in one piece on the soft peat.

"Pride goes before a fall," Mhairi tendered gingerly.

"Very true," admitted Sam. "I've been guilty of that before."

Although the women, by nature being more timid, made a poor start to their first attempt at skeet shooting, as the afternoon wore on, they gained confidence, whilst the men seemed to deteriorate. By the time they called a halt, the gentle sex had the edge. So it was that Sue and Mhairi walked into the lodge with their heads held high in contrast to the men following behind, in mock submission.

There, on a display notice, ahead of them in the hall was the announcement -

TONIGHT,
AFTER DINNER (7.30 for 8.00)
A TRADITIONAL CEILIDH

"What in heaven's name is a SEE-Y-LID-H?" asked Sue incredulously.

Maurice Duffill

"That - my cockeyed friend is pronounced KAYLEY," explained Alan, with a giggle. A Ceilidh is a highland party where, traditionally, the entertainment is provided by those attending; professionalism is not expected, just the willingness to have a go; singing, dancing, recitations, the playing of any musical instrument, anything to amuse others. Of course, there's bound to be an abundance of highland dancing."

"We're rather keen on dancing but we are not familiar with the highland variety," Sam declared.

"Och, nay worry laddie," replied Alan laying on the accent, yu'll sooon be picken it up."

"Good heavens!" cried Sue, "have we got to learn a new language as well?"

"I just wish I'd brought my kilt," Alan moaned.

"Never mind, darling; when we move in, there will be plenty of opportunities to show off your hairy legs," Mhairi suggested.

With that, they all went to their rooms to bathe and change.

Having an aperitif, followed by wine with the splendid dinner, and a powerful malt whisky to finish mellowed the tension created by interviews past or pending. Pretty well all present were ready to let down their hair at the forthcoming 'shindig'.

As they rose from the table, willing hands re-arranged the furniture, while staff cleared the table, which was then dismantled and removed. While all this was going on, a small band, consisting of drums, fiddle and accordion, were arranging themselves by the grand piano.

Ted Evans stepped onto the small rostrum, "Good evening everyone, as your master of ceremonies for the evening, I would like you to welcome the music makers - 'THE THREE GEES' - or more correctly, 'The Great Glen Group.' who will start us all off with a Canadian Barn Dance."

Leading the dancing himself with his wife Pat, they were soon joined by others to fill the floor with guests and estate staff mixing in a general 'get to know you' session. This was followed by a Scottish waltz and then a Schottische – a rather intricate and energetic speciality of the Highlands.

Exhausted, Sue flopped into her chosen seat. "Well, that's got the blood moving in my veins." Turning to Alan, she panted "The first two were fair enough but that schottische thing had me tying my legs in knots."

"I must admit that it takes a bit of practice to get that one right," admitted Alan. "You see, we all learned this kind of dancing at school, while still very young and receptive."

"Even the boys?" chimed in Sam

"Oh yes, most of the male partners of the girls were the boys," he replied sarcastically.

"Tha' knows what I mean," said Sam. "In our school it would have been considered 'sissy' to have dancing lessons with girls."

"Perhaps we Scots develop more quickly. It was considered a great excuse to get our hands on the lasses."

"He hasn't changed," cut in Mhairi. "He still finds any excuse to maul me, Scottish beast that he is."

"Nationality doesn't seem to have any bearing on the matter," Sue observed. "My fella is just the same."

"Ladies and Gentlemen," the MC called. "While you catch your breath we have a volunteer to entertain you with a Gaelic song. Please give a big hand to Mrs Anne Slater."

The non-Gaelic speaking audience listened attentively to the pleasing sound of her voice without understanding a single word.

"What a peculiar language," Sue commented. "It's a bit like German with Welsh mixed with it. I could never learn that. It's not like French or Italian where you can often guess the meaning, because we use some of their words in our language. I've no idea what that was about."

The evening continued with dancing the Eight-some Reel, the Dashing White Sergeant, the Gay-Gordons and an energetic affair called Strip-the-Willow. These were punctuated by a variety of entertainment ranging from somebody's impersonation of George Formby with the plinkety-plonk of his Ukulele to the Highland-Fling performed by two waitresses accompanied on the bagpipes by the Laird himself.

Shortly before midnight, the guests climbed wearily up the stairs to their beds for a well earned rest.

CHAPTER 4

Sunday morning was a sunny morning; beautiful streaks of light radiating from behind the mountains to the east.

"I don't know where all this vicious weather can be that Alan was telling us about," Sue commented, "We've had nothing but good since we came. Mind you, I'm not sorry, particularly today, since we are going pony trekking."

"Yes," agreed Sam. "When the sun is fully awake, and those wispy bits of cloud have 'burnt' off, it looks as if it's going to be a sweltering day. Ah, here's Alan and Mhairi - good-morning!"

"Ciamar a tha thu?" Alan said, in greeting.

"He's swearing again, in the presence of ladies," declared Sue.

"Oisach - I merely asked - how are you? Your reply should be 'Gle Math', pronounced GLAY VA, which means - very well."

"Here endeth your Gaelic lesson for today," Mhairi suggested, not being too keen on words she couldn't get her tongue around. "What time are we due to start playing cowboys?"

"09:30," Alan muttered, having been cut short while airing his knowledge. "By the way, the lassie that is taking us is the wife of the chauffeur. It seems that all the wives take an active part in affairs."

"Well, I suppose," offered Sam, "there is nothing else available, and I would imagine they will not be paid a great deal."

"True," agreed Alan, "but what about the pilot? His wife is the housekeeper."

"I was talking to him yesterday, at the shoot. It seems he couldn't stand the monotony of airline routes and took this job for variety. His wife apparently was a hotel manageress and, in her present capacity, is responsible completely for everything to do with the house and the well-being of all its occupants. He told me that they'd never been so happy and our hosts are excellent employers, firm but considerate."

"That sounds alright then," Alan agreed. "I wonder what the snag is; it all seems too good to be true."

"Sceptic," declared Mhairi, "anyhow, never mind that; it's time we changed our clothes for the riding gear they provided."

"Riding gear, you call it?" Alan retorted; "Just an old pair of pants and an anorak."

"Well, I think it was very decent of them to avoid spoiling our own clothes. They knew we would not be prepared for pony trekking."

"As usual, you are quite right," Alan conceded, as they trotted up the stairs.

Highland Haven

They were soon 'togged' up in their borrowed clothes and heading out to the stables, which were situated to one side of the driveway, not far from the lodge."

As the four of them made their way into the stable yard, a voice behind them attracted their attention.

"Would you all be going on the ponies?" The tousled haired fellow called. Receiving an affirmative acknowledgement, he went on to introduce himself. "I'm Hamish Gordon, and this is my wife, Sylvia."

"Pleased to have you join us," welcomed Sam. "Are you both experienced with ponies?"

"Not at all; we've never before had any riding except for donkeys on the beach at Blackpool. I thought we'd take this opportunity to remedy that omission."

Hearing their voices in the yard, Ann MacDonnell appeared and introduced herself. "My husband and I have already saddled up your mounts, as you can see," she said, pointing to the group of ponies tethered at one side of the yard.

A loud shriek, from the 'blonde-bombshell' Sylvia, caused everyone to look around.

With an alarmed expression on her face she said, "Surely we are not riding those huge beasts; they are horses not ponies."

"Give over darling," muttered her husband, in obvious embarrassment. "They are ponies."

"They're not like those little shaggy things I've seen on the pictures," she persisted.

"Those are Shetland ponies you're thinking of. They are far too small. Suitable only for children, I imagine."

"She'll be alright sir," their leader insisted, reassuringly. "I'll give her Dolly, she's very docile."

"However will I get my legs either side of that fat belly?" Sylvia pleaded with her husband.

Turning away in disgust at the way this 'towny' was making the fair sex appear stupid; Ann MacDonnell advised them all that the trip would last all day. She said that they would have frequent opportunities to stretch their legs during the twelve mile trek.

"Where are we going?" enquired Alan.

"To the far side of Sgurr a'Mhaoraich, by going up Allt Coire Sgoireadail to Wester Glen Quoich and then to Alltbeithe; there we will be met by my husband with the mini bus."

"Are you any the wiser?" asked Sue of Alan.

"Certainly; Sgurr a'Mhaoraich is that large pointed mountain to the east of us - Sgurr means high, circular, precipitous hill. Allt means burn or stream to you. So we are to go up one stream, or burn, along another round the back of that large mountain until we arrive at the pick up point."

"Before mounting up," commanded their young leader," ensure your girth straps are really tight. When you think it is tight, put all your strength into gaining an extra hole on the belt."

Stupid Sylvia turned to her husband whilst pulling on her trouser belt. "Why do we have to do this? It's killing me."

"Not yours! The pony's! You dumb cluck," exclaimed Hamish. "Look, she's showing you; the big strap that goes right under the pony's belly."

"But what if I hurt him? He might kick me."

"Stop greetin' and just do as you're told."

The command came to mount up, and a fair sight it made; inexperienced riders, or potential riders, were slithering and sliding all over the place in an attempt to climb astride their mounts which seemed ten feet tall.

Progressively, by helping each other, the ragged party was ready to sample forward motion. Sam agreed to bring up the rear, towing the pack horse with their lunches and wet weather gear. This enabled Ann MacDonnell to lead whilst having her eye on the barmy blonde.

She led the string into the wood directly behind the big house. Climbing very steeply, the ponies scrambled their way up to a small rocky path running off south-east, to their right.

Even at the rear, Sam could hear the shrieks of Sylvia Gordon as her mount was persuaded, by whacks on the rump from the guide, to push-on regardless.

They emerged from the wood to find themselves on a steep slope, about four hundred feet above the loch, now behind them. Progressively, their route curved north-east, around the shoulder of the hill, until they were alongside a burn tumbling down the gorge towards them.

The narrow path clung to the hillside above the rushing waters until, after approaching the head of a waterfall, they found themselves more or less on the same level. The string of ponies forded the burn, and then continued for about another hour to forge on even deeper into the mountains; just prior to what seemed like an impregnable wall of rock, the party reached a pleasant green area alongside the burn. Their leader, much to everyone's relief, declared this a rest point, not apparently, so much for them as for the ponies. However, everybody gladly dismounted to exercise ill-treated parts of their bodies.

Relaxing there, free from the unfamiliar strain of sitting astride the heaving body of a horse, they all admired the panorama presented to them from this vantage point half way to the heavens. "This is awe inspiring," observed Mhairi. "To see such rugged peaks at such close quarters takes the breath away. It seems as if there is nobody else on this planet; we are totally disconnected from humanity."

Highland Haven

"I agree," Sam interjected. "But not from all living things. Ranging up and down that burn was a very peculiar looking pair of crow-like birds," he said to their guide. "What would they be?"

"They're Hoodies." She replied. "Hooded crows - so named because of the black head and neck on the otherwise grey body."

"Are they carrion, like the common crow?" he asked.

"Yes! But they do eat all manner of things. They are considered as vermin, and are hated by most."

"Why, particularly?" Sam queried.

"Well, they have been known to attack even a cow. If a beast were to become trapped in a bog, a hoody might peck out the eyes."

"Oh, how horrible;" exclaimed Sue, who had been listening to the conversation.

"Strangely though," continued Ann MacDonnell, "there used to be a gamekeeper living in the glen who made a pet of one and even taught it to talk, so they can't be all bad."

"Do Golden Eagles live around here?" Mhairi joined in.

"Yes, they certainly do." she answered. "You're more likely to see one on the next stage of the trek, after we cross that ridge. However, if you are interested in the bird life of the region, keep your eyes open for the ptarmigan. That's a game bird, something like a grouse. It frequents the bleak mountain peaks, living off heather shoots mainly. It is the only British bird that changes colour with the seasons, becoming white in the winter."

"Did I hear you say we were going up there;" wailed Sylvia, pointing at the rock wall ahead? "You must be joking, it's impossible."

"Mrs Gordon, you shouldn't get yourself in such a panic," retorted the guide. "I've done this route many times in the past without difficulty. Trust me."

"There's always a first time," she moaned. "It's alright for you, you're used to riding; this is my first time on a 'real' horse."

"Well I'm sorry, but we'll nae be turning back now. The more difficult parts will be done dismounted, so you'll have nothing to fear." Ann MacDonnell tried to reassure her, although signs of calm forbearance fraying at the edges were beginning to show. "Anyway, we must get on. I'm not too happy about the weather outlook."

"Why is that?" Sue wondered. "This fluffy white cloud, all in little squares, looks lovely. Surely that's not going to give us any trouble?"

"That innocent looking cloud is called Alto Cumulus and forewarns of a front. If you look to the west, you can see a change taking place. Normally, a warm front takes time to develop, but the way that build up is occurring, it looks as if a cold front has caught up with it to form an occlusion which will bring with it unstable squally conditions; best not to hang about."

"You obviously know your weather signs," observed Alan.

"Anyone living in the country has an eye for the weather." Ann replied, as they all started to re-mount, "but in the hills, an outdoor person is particularly conscious of any changes because of the speed with which they can occur."

The party moved off, up the ever steepening slope, to the rocky ridge ahead. As the path became a narrow ledge climbing acutely, they each dismounted once more and led their ponies, in single file. These difficult portions were very short, interspersed with rideable sections, so the riders became quite proficient at getting on and off. Even 'Blondie' seemed to cope, but not without a lot of verbal protest.

Eventually, the gradient began to ease to a gentle slope as they neared the summit of the saddle between two peaks. There, before them, over a small rise, was a calm pool or small loch which turned out to be their lunch stop. It transpired that all small lochs are called 'Lochans' and that this one gloried in the name of 'Loch Bealach Coire Sgoireadail'.

"What a mouthful," commented Mhairi.

"But - what a beautiful view," noted Alan. "Just look how far we've climbed."

"It really is marvellous," Sue agreed, as they eagerly consumed the contents of the hamper carried by the pack horse. "There is no sign of human life at all. We are in a world of our own."

"That," interjected Ann MacDonnell, "is what Bonnie Prince Charlie thought in 1746 when he was escaping from the English soldiers after the battle of Culloden. He crossed these hills oblivious to the fact that sentries had been posted on the slopes of Sgurr a'Mhaoraich, over there. Fortunately, mountain mists had closed in; they didn't see him nor did he see them. In his ignorance, he succeeded, finally reaching the coast of Morar beyond those peaks behind us."

"Tell me," said Alan, with his mind on estate acreage," does all this land belong to Sir Richard?"

"Yes, and much more," she confirmed. "As soon as we move off, which we must do now if we are to beat the weather, we'll breast that final rise. A dramatic view will present itself across Wester Glen Quoich. The very sharp ridge opposite as we start the descent, forms the northern boundary of the Laird's territory."

"You were certainly right about the weather," admitted Alan. "Those dark clouds to the right are building ominously."

"Yes, we had better get on with it. I don't want to be caught up here." Then as an instruction to all, she announced, "Just over that rise is a steep descent into Glen Quoich. We must endeavour to complete it before the weather strikes. BUT, do not rush your ponies. We don't want any accidents. Let them find their own pace;

they are very sure footed and will follow me as quickly as they can. They too, know bad weather is coming."

With everyone remounted, she enquired if Alan would bring up the rear and presented him with a whistle. "If anyone is delayed, blow me a warning," she commanded, now assuming a serious posture. "We must not become separated."

As soon as their guide led the party over the rise, a scream was heard from the front. Sam, accompanying Alan at the rear couldn't imagine why Sylvia was refusing to go on. Ann had to drag her forward by taking the pony's head.

Only when they got to the same point, could they realise what all the fuss was about. The 'steep descent' seemed almost vertical. It looked, at first, as if they were about to walk out into space but the tenuous path angled off to the right, reducing the gradient slightly.

"I can appreciate why she told us not to rush down here," Sam admitted. "One could soon lose control on this loose surface."

The ladies in front of them were very quiet, not liking this part at all, but they were both determined not to show themselves up as the blonde bombshell had.

Some very heavy raindrops started to fall, causing Alan to look behind them. To his amazement, the ridge they had so recently left was already obscured by cloud. It was looking very black beyond. He touched Sam on the arm and, without saying anything, simply pointed behind.

Sam looked round "Good-night! This is going beyond a joke. I see what you mean about the weather changing quickly in the Highlands."

The words were hardly out of his mouth when the heavens seemed to open. Not just rain, but hail came pelting down, stinging their hands and the exposed back of their necks. Simultaneously, a wind sprang up from nowhere driving the pellets of ice through their trousers.

Their leader pulled up behind a large boulder. It didn't provide much shelter but it was the only protection on the otherwise barren mountainside."

"We'll put on the waterproofs," she declared," but keep a tight rein on your mounts. They don't like this anymore than you do. Take it in turns to shelter the ponies behind others until the worst of this has passed."

"What happens if it doesn't pass?" asked Sue.

"Now Sue," pleaded Sam. "Don't you start worrying Mrs MacDonnell; she's got quite enough to think about."

The day had turned to night, the other side of the glen could not be seen and the howling wind was already creating drifts with the hail-stones.

"It doesn't look as if it's going to ease," declared the young leader after a while. "We mustn't stay here any longer."

"Oh, we should never have come," wailed Sylvia, with actual tears starting to trickle down her cheeks. "Surely somebody will come for us?" she sniffed.

"Get a hold on yourself," Ann demanded. "What can others do that we can't do for ourselves? We could rustle up a helicopter, I have a radio, but they'd never find us in this."

"My husband will initiate a search party if we are long overdue at Allt Biethe, but that won't be for hours yet. No, the best help in these circumstances is self help. We've just got to put up with the weather and press on before we lose sight of the path."

"We must get down into the glen bottom," she stressed. "So please mount up, but do keep the person in front of you in sight. I repeat - we mustn't get split up."

"Oh, Hamish," Blondie whimpered.

"Now come on dear," her husband replied, "we must go on, or we might be in real trouble. I'll have words about this when we get back."

"*If* we get back," she snivelled.

The waterproofs did reduce the discomfort. The hail wasn't so painful on the hands. Capes had been provided, but peering through the icy precipitation was both difficult and agonising. First one, and then another of the ponies would stumble in the appalling conditions, giving rise to a startled gasp.

To stagger blindly down that interminable trail was an awesome experience. They never knew how much farther there was to go except that, once they reached the glen bottom, they would still have about two miles to go in this wretched weather.

In the poor visibility, they waded across a burn and then linked up with another path to the south-east. Proving that they were, indeed, off the mountain-side, there was a noticeable easing of the gradient to a shallow decline, seeming to be quite flat in comparison.

"We'll carry on to an old ruin, about a mile on," shouted their guide through the shriek of the wind.

At least the wind was completely behind them; that is, when it wasn't swirling round from the side. The track was more prominent, allowing the ponies to amble along on their own with the riders shrinking into the protection of their large capes.

Finally, the dishevelled group was led into the puny shelter, three and a half walls, no roof, but a welcome hovel in which to gain respite from their ordeal.

"How on earth did you manage to find this place when we could hardly see the person ahead?" Sam asked Mrs MacDonnell.

"The ponies and I are very familiar with the area. It was the natural reaction," she explained, then instructed all to secure their mounts in the lee of the ruin.

Whilst hopefully waiting for the line of squalls to pass, they gladly took refreshment, hot soup cannily held in reserve for just such a moment. Miraculously, half bottles of whisky appeared from nowhere to help recharge their batteries. Even those not normally given to imbibing, took a 'pull'.

Highland Haven

Discussing their situation while huddling together for protection, they discovered that the objective, Allt Biethe, was approximately one mile further on. Not having spent long with their ridge-top picnic, as had been intended, they were still ahead of schedule even though they had been extra cautious coming down.

Another half an hour in their inadequate shelter could show whether or not an improvement was forthcoming, without causing any unnecessary alarm.

"What's at Allt Biethe?" Sam asked.

"It's just a convenient meeting place to be picked up," Ann replied. "There is an unsurfaced road to a cottage, along which the mini bus can run without difficulty. There is also a byre where we can leave the ponies."

"I suppose a byre is what we would call a barn?"

"Yes, Mr Jackson, you're learning. Well everyone, it doesn't look as if it's going to improve so we'd better brave the elements once more; it is quite straightforward, but please continue as you were, in single file, keeping each other in sight.

The rest and refreshment had done them a power of good for, although the weather was no better, they seemed to get along without too much difficulty. Whether this was due to their growing experience or the numbing effect of the whisky wasn't known. Nevertheless, all breathed a sigh of relief when a couple of stone buildings complete with roofs, appeared out of the white curtain in front of them - and there was the mini bus, waiting. They rode, without dismounting, into the byre to gain sanctuary at last.

"I won't be sorry if I never see another horse for the rest of my life," declared Sylvia, as she slid out of the saddle into the arms of Hamish. "My legs are like jelly, my hands are freezing, my back is aching and my head is pounding. We must have been mad to do that – for *fun*."

"Never mind, dear," he soothed, "we'll soon be back now. We'll have a hot bath and a good meal; then you'll feel fine again. I must admit, it was quite an experience."

Sam, who had been listening to the outburst, took up the theme with Alan. "It has certainly driven home to me that the climate up here must not be treated lightly. I know you warned us of how quickly it can change, but there's nothing like personal experience to convince a person."

As if the weather man in the sky had been listening, the hail stopped, the wind dropped and the clouds started to break. Within five minutes, the sun was streaming down from a large blue clearing in the 'heavens'.

They all went out to soak up the warmth, discarding their oilskins, and were treated to a remarkable sight. The mountains were clothed in white, giving them a preview of a winter scene, in mid-summer. The south facing slopes were already beginning to 'steam' as the sun evaporated the drifts of hail-stones. It wouldn't be long before the resulting mist would obscure the peaks, although the sky was now crystal clear.

"I know we've just had a very unpleasant couple of hours," declared Sue, "but I feel exhilarated. That living picture is fantastic and I believe I know it personally. Does that sound daft?"

"Not at all," conceded Sam. "I know what you mean. We've just had an experience never to be forgotten and yet it resulted in a strange but beautiful vista."

They re-entered the byre to tend their trusty steeds. Ann's husband, Jock the chauffeur, was already preparing feed for them. They soon had the saddles off, together with the bridles, giving the animals freedom to feed and roll about in the straw.

Their chores completed, and with great stiffness, the newly initiated riders clambered aboard the four-wheeled transporter as a welcome alternative to the four-legged variety. There were many oohs and ahs as they sat down.

"Horse riding would be a lot less painful if the seat was softly upholstered, instead of those hard leather saddles," commented Sue, as her posterior sank into the foamed cushion.

"You'd find difficulty staying with the pony when doing anything other than a slow walk," Ann assured her. "I can't imagine what it would be like taking a gallop in an armchair," she mused.

As they were being driven back to the lodge, Sam turned to the subject of safety in the mountains. "If the weather was anything like that when the Bonnie Prince was traversing these hills, it's no wonder the sentries didn't see him," he said. "Mind you, it's obviously a perilous trip alone. Only a fugitive would try it."

"You'd be surprised," countered Ann. "Many a person, who should know better, goes walking alone in the hills; all too often putting their lives in jeopardy, and those of the mountain rescue teams who come to their aid."

"I suppose two or three should go together," suggested Sam.

"Ideally, the minimum should be five," cut in Alan." Should one member of the party have an accident, say he breaks a leg; then two can stay with him while two go for help," he explained. "Obviously it isn't always practical to have five in a party. This means for every one less, additional precautions should be taken."

"What sort of precautions?" Sam quizzed.

"Correct dress - protection from cold and wet - is the prime consideration."

"That's obvious," interjected Sam.

"You might think so, but did you imagine being caught in a blizzard today? The climate can be quite different a couple of thousand feet up," Alan insisted. "When we flew in, you saw how close Ben Nevis is to the sea shore at Fort William. This causes a constant problem; tourists see Britain's tallest mountain so close to hand and are tempted to walk the path to the top. Ladies in summer dresses

Highland Haven

and unsatisfactory footwear set off into an environment totally different than the high street of shops. Not only does the temperature drop as height is gained, the wind is likely to strengthen giving an increase in the wind-chill factor. Add to this the fact that it requires great effort to climb over 4,000 feet – particularly if one is not fully fit, resulting in exhaustion. The body is then weak just when maximum resilience is called for."

"Another *must* is a compass. To the unfamiliar, it might seem totally unnecessary when just going to the top of that hill," he suggested. "What happens though, when the cloud base suddenly drops and the luckless hikers are on the peak? All directions seem the same; all are downhill. They climb up from the road and, inadvertently, descend into a remote, uninhabited glen, miles from anywhere. It's like being at the north pole; all directions are south."

"I see what you mean," confirmed Sam. "One doesn't realise that dangers are so close. I suppose a whistle is a good thing to have along?"

"Essential!" Alan confirmed. "Modern technology has provided another useful aid, the foil survival bag; well worth having one or two in your car at all times. They take up little space and could save a life. Maybe yours if you run into a snow drift. "

"The most important precaution that all should take in these parts, at all times, is to let someone know your plans," Alan continued. "Even travelling in a car on these remote roads a person can be in serious trouble if he breaks down, particularly at night. If somebody knows you are overdue, search and rescue teams can be set in motion."

"That is a sensible tip," agreed Sam, as the mini bus stopped in front of their weekend residence.

Sir Richard was on the step to greet them, obviously quite relieved that nobody was any the worse for the harrowing experience.

After hot baths and another delightful meal, during which their host made a gentle parting speech, the evening was spent in light conversation over occasional drinks. Those who had experienced the pony trek retired early, somewhat exhausted; tomorrow was departure day.

CHAPTER 5

Very much refreshed, Sue and Mhairi, at breakfast the following morning, agreed that it was a pity to be preparing for return home. Notwithstanding yesterday's trial, they had enjoyed themselves and fallen in love with the area. They both very much wanted their men-folk to be successful with their applications.

"Well, you'll just have to be patient," Sam declared, in reply to the various comments regarding future careers. "Let's take a gentle stroll down the other side of the loch," he suggested.

"A good idea," agreed Alan. "It will be an opportunity to savour our last hour or two here."

"Just in case either of us is not successful, I've written our address and telephone number down, so that we can keep in touch," Sam said passing Alan a piece of paper.

"Great minds think alike," parroted Alan, asking his wife to search her handbag for his scribbled note. "We do seem to get along together fine, don't we?"

"We certainly do, socially," agreed Sam; "but would we accept each other in business, at different levels?" he finished, not very subtly.

"If you mean - would I work for *you* - the answer is yes! You're in for the big job, aren't you? Sir Richard asked me how I felt about you in such a manner as to imply that I wouldn't be top dog. Well, I didn't admit it to him but, I'd rather somebody else had the associated headaches. Let me stick to estate management as it relates to agriculture and forestry; you are welcome to the problems of trying to coordinate this lot"

"I reckon that's cleared that little problem out of the way," Sam said gratefully. "I must say it did come as a surprise when he intimated that I might take on the whole thing but, I must admit, it suits me. You see, I'm a jack-of-all-trades and can relate one discipline to another. In other words," he added jokingly, "I'm a bit of a scatter-brain."

"So long as your scatter-brain does the right thing with regards to the Property Director, that'll be all right by me, but I must warn you, I don't like to be ignored. My professional opinions are based on sound experience and I would expect them to be considered."

"My, we are getting serious," Mhairi declared. "It sounds as if you have both got your jobs."

"It does, doesn't it?" Alan admitted. "I just got carried away."

"Well, I hope you have," Sue asserted, "got the jobs I mean. Mhairi and I have our side of it all worked out."

"What do you mean?" Sam asked wonderingly.

Highland Haven

"Lady Blaisdale made it quite clear that we wives are expected to take an active part in this venture, and we intend to do just that," she retorted.

"Oh, pardon me for questioning your intentions," Sam muttered, humbly.

"No need to scoff," said Sue. "You'd soon complain if we didn't do our bit and, I've no doubt; it would be frowned upon by his lordship if we sat with our feet up, basking in *your* glory."

"O.K., you've made your point. So, what *have* you in mind?"

"Did you know, Mhairi is an expert on herbs and perfumes? Well, we thought we could perhaps develop markets for "Highland Herbs and Remedies" blended with "Scottish Scents"." Sue put forward with confidence, then added, "I would help her with that, learning as much as I can as we go along, but my speciality is on the secretarial side, both for the business, and related to the formation of clubs."

"Well, I must admit, you've had experience as secretary of the Carnival Charities Trust, The Women's Institute, and that senior citizens' club you started with Lady 'Whatnot'."

"The Evergreens", Sue recalled. "Yes, but it would be a while before there was sufficient population to start forming clubs or societies. In the meantime, Mhairi can be establishing her wild plant business to help bring some income."

"I don't know if suitable plants will grow in these wild parts," Sam contended.

"Just look there," Mhairi insisted, "that yellow flower is wild Goldenrod. Now, that plant used to be valued for its curative properties, either drunk as a hot beverage to combat kidney trouble or as an ointment for treating wounds."

"Well, what do you know?" Sam commented, a little sceptically.

"And that one there," she went on, ignoring the remark, "is Devil's-bit, made famous by Nicholas Culpepper. The root of the plant is used in the preparation of a remedy for throat infections."

"Nicholas *who*;" retorted Sam?

"Culpepper; he was a herbalist, back in the 17th century."

"Well we live and learn," conceded Sam.

"Actually, Mhairi *is* quite an expert," Alan declared. "As wife of an estate manager, she had plenty of opportunity to study wild plants and read of their ancient uses."

"Do you think herbs and scented plants could be grown in the area?" enquired Sue.

"Well some certainly, as shown by the presence of these wild plants. I have noticed some oddities about. Look across at the lodge, where we are staying, and you'll see evidence of semi-tropical plants in the garden."

"I wonder if the Gulf Stream runs into this sea loch?" suggested Sam. "The Isle of Skye, just off the entrance, might funnel a warm current right up here."

"It could be," agreed Alan. "That would certainly influence the climate. We'll have to look into all this if we get started."

"One scented plant that certainly does grow up here is the Bog Myrtle," Mhairi asserted. "In years gone by, beer was made from its leaves, instead of hops, to flavour the liquor."

"There's something else then," propounded Sue, with over-eager enthusiasm, "we could build a brewery."

"Oh good-night!" exclaimed Sam. "Let's get back before this crazy wife of mine takes over the commercial development of the whole area."

They started back, still enjoying the serenity of the situation when, without warning, two loud blasts followed by an ear-splitting roar made all four of them physically start.

"MY GOD, WHAT WAS THAT?" Shrieked Sue, in obvious terror.

Sam pointed, almost breathless with shock. Two powerful jet aircraft were disappearing, in a steeply banked turn, between the peaks behind the lodge. A smokey exhaust trail showed their track had been from low over the water, behind them, to skim the ridge and enter the small glen, up which they had trekked the day before.

"TORNADOES," he shouted, above the din. "By crikey, they were low; and going like a bat out of hell with their re-heat power on."

"I'd forgotten about that," Alan declared, "this is a training area where low flying is practised."

"I don't think these blokes need much practice." professed Sam. "They must have pulled a lot of 'g' to fly between those crags the way they did."

"I nearly had a heart attack," Mhairi admitted. "I never heard them coming."

"They were just showing off, at our expense," Sue moaned "they don't need to fly that low."

"Oh yes they do," asserted Sam; "the idea is to keep below the sky line to avoid radar detection and to hide their exhaust heat."

"The radar I can understand, but why trouble about their exhaust?" asked Mhairi, recovering her composure.

"Modern missiles often employ heat-seeking infra-red guidance systems to 'track' the target, explained Sam, recalling his R.A.F. training. "The most sophisticated make use of a mixture of radar, infra-red, ultra-sonics, lasers and television, all linked by a micro computer to the flight controls of the missile to steer it to the unfortunate intruder. All of these techniques need 'line of sight', so if the pilot can keep mountains between him and them, he has a chance."

"It sounds gruesome," Sue declared. "Here we were enjoying the peace and serenity of this marvellous place and now we're brought back, literally with a bang, to the harshness of modern life."

Highland Haven

"It's probably a good idea to be reminded from time to time of the hard facts of life," suggested Alan. "The tranquillity of an out-of-the-way locale, such as this, could easily lull a person into a falsely serene state of mind."

"Why can't life be serene? That's what I want to know," asserted Sue, quite despondently. "If mankind wasn't so cruel and selfish, there wouldn't be any wars; no need then for your noisy Tornadoes to disturb our peace."

"Talking of noise," interrupted Sam, to change the difficult subject "we'd better put our best foot forward or else Ted will be taking off without us."

"Let's run," Sue agreed. "We need time enough to enjoy our last meal here. I'm sure they won't let us down with the final lunch."

"We fellas will give the wee lassies a ten minute start and still beat you to the Laird's Table," Alan challenged.

As they trotted off chattering, he added to Sam, "*Now* we have peace. Lasses don't seem to be able to walk quietly along, truly soaking up the aura of relaxation. We'll have to persuade them to take up smoking a pipe; that should make them tranquil."

"You have a point there, Alan. But where would we be without them? Their often crazy notions bring a spark to life. It would be deadly dull if only the serious matters were discussed. Their very femininity makes a man feel like a man, if you follow my rather cockeyed comment."

"I know what you mean and, I must admit, I wouldn't be without Mhairi for all the haggis on the hill."

"That reminds me," Sam declared. "Sue asked me last night if the Highlanders have haggis shoots as they do with grouse."

Before Alan had time to curb his laughter to answer, they'd arrived at the lodge to be greeted by a supposedly irate Sue. "It's not fair, you didn't run. You sent us off so you could have a secret man-talk. Now we are all sweaty for nothing."

"Ladies don't sweat," retorted Sam; "pigs *sweat*, ladies *glow* and, of course, men *perspire*."

"Never mind all that clever chat, Sam Jackson, let's go and eat."

As they entered the dining room, they realised from the few place settings that most of the other candidates had already left. The majority, having travelled from other parts of Scotland or Northern England, had made use of their own cars or the train. Their other travelling companion was, however, already in the room waiting.

Mhairi tactfully opened conversation with him. "We didn't see much of you over the week-end, Mr Codling?"

"Well er, no; I wasn't feeling too well the first evening, and then I spent most of the time in my room reading a book from Sir Richard's library."

"Do you think you would enjoy working here?" She enquired, trying to sound him out.

Maurice Duffill

"I don't think so," he confessed. "I didn't spend my years at University studying engineering to become a mountain goat. I want to create a new harbour in the Middle East, or great highways across China; something worthy of the title 'Engineering'."

Sam, hearing this, had to make comment. "I suspect you are trying to run before you learn to walk," he said, a little testily. "I can visualise many substantial problems here; but maybe you are looking for something closer to text book situations.

"Obviously this is your field," he replied angrily. "Well, you are welcome to it." At that, he turned away to terminate the conversation.

"You weren't very nice to Mr Codling, dear," Sue asserted.

"Well, he made me a bit mad. Fresh from college; thinks he knows it all. He's never had his hands dirty but feels he's God's gift to engineering," Sam propounded.

"It's peculiar, the different concepts people have of engineering," he continued; "on the one hand, some consider the man who repairs the TV. to be an engineer. While on the other hand, some look upon engineers as if they are conjurers, creating great wonders. In my experience, an engineer is a satisfier of 'wants'. He uses scientific knowledge and practical experience, to overcome life's physical problems."

"The Americans call an engine driver 'an engineer'," observed Alan.

"I suppose that illustrates the origins of the problem. The very word means to do with engines. I'm no literary expert but, I think the word has developed wrongly. You see, an engine was a solution to a particular technical problem of the past. This could have led to the use of the word for those who solve technical problems."

"We'll have to dream up a new word," suggested Sue. "How about 'genius' or 'mastermind'?"

"Does *your* wife resort to sarcasm when faced with superior intellect?" asked Sam, himself employing great sarcasm.

"That pre-supposes Alan can exercise superior intellect," Mhairi was quick to point out.

"Before this battle of the sexes develops further, I suggest we eat," proposed Alan, taking his place at the table.

After their lunch, they soon found themselves, complete with luggage, being driven in the mini bus up the steep climb from the sea loch to the crest of what seemed like an unassailable rock wall. Had they not previously come down this same tortuous route, the passengers would not have believed it possible.

"I wouldn't fancy driving up or down here in the depth of winter," Sam confessed.

44

Highland Haven

"It does cause a few problems," conceded Ted, sitting behind them. "It all adds to the excitement of life, though."

"I'd have thought you had excitement enough, flying your aeroplane in and out of these mountains," Mhairi advanced, remembering her raised heartbeats as they approached to land on the calm waters of the loch.

"Flying becomes second nature as one gains experience. In that respect, it's like driving a car. When you're learning, the prospect of another drive excites you but later, when you have been a qualified driver for some reasonable length of time, you drive automatically. It's only when circumstances are extraordinary, such as bad weather or faulty brakes, that you once again, become aware of your detailed actions and the blood starts to run a little quicker."

"How much like driving a car is flying an aeroplane?" Mhairi asked. "You don't have a steering wheel, do you?"

"We don't have a gear lever either. The basic difference is twofold. Firstly, unlike in a car, if you are in trouble, you cannot stop; if something goes wrong, a pilot can't just pull over onto the verge to repair it, or wait for the breakdown truck. Similarly, he can't stop and ask the way if he gets lost."

"The second major difference," he continued, "is that the aircraft is moving freely in a fluid. In a car, turning left usually means the vehicle goes left; slowing down is simply a matter of less throttle and perhaps some brake; however, when flying, each action has definite side effects."

"How do you mean - it's not like taking medicine, surely?"

"Not really. Then, on second thoughts, if you don't take the appropriate action, you will certainly need a doctor - or an undertaker. What I really meant was that if, for instance, a pilot attempted to turn left by simply operating the rudder then he will be in big trouble. In fact, the aircraft will go into a spiral dive."

"A spin, presumably," Sue suggested, trying to air some knowledge gained from her husband.

"No. That is something a little different. In a spin, the aircraft is stalled. That means not really flying, sinking without proper air flow over the wings. A spiral dive would be the result of using rudder alone. You see, as the turn started, the outer wing would be going faster than the wing on the inside of the turn and therefore develop more lift, tipping the aircraft over, which, if nothing was done to correct it, would develop into a dive. Thinking of diving out of control, a common misconception about flying, often aggravated by Hollywood films, is that, if the engines fail, one immediately goes into a screaming dive. Whereas, even modern jets can glide for some distance, depending on how much height is available."

The verbal flying lesson was brought to a sudden halt as the minibus braked to a standstill. A herd of dangerous looking Highland cattle was straddling the narrow lane. The largest of the beasts was staring straight at them with front legs planted firmly astride the roadway and its enormous horns appearing to span from verge to verge.

"A little caution is indicated here," suggested Jock, the driver. "She's guarding a clutch of wee ones who are just learning what life is all about."

"Isn't it dangerous to allow such wild animals to wander freely?" Sue enquired with a little nervousness in her voice. "I'm certainly glad to be inside this bus rather than walking unprotected."

"I know they look fearsome but they are normally quite forgiving," Jock explained; "it's just that, with the calves so young, she is feeling protective. It would certainly be unwise to leave the vehicle just now. If you want to take pictures, better to shoot through the window. I shall just push by slowly and she will treat us like some inanimate object not worthy of her wrath."

As the bus eased by, the great beast gave the side a warning nudge with her overweight rump.

"I bet there are a few steaks in that," mused Sam; "Scottish beef at its best."

Their bit of excitement over, it wasn't much further before finding themselves alongside the amphibious aircraft sitting on the concrete ramp. They all disembarked and assisted with transferring the luggage from bus to winged boat. A stiff breeze was whipping up the surface of the loch to substantial waves. They were all quite pleased when the door of the aircraft was closed behind them, keeping out the chill draught.

A few moments passed while the pilot checked over his cockpit then; first one then the other of the two piston engines was started. After a period of warm-up, the passengers felt the release of wheel brakes and the aircraft began to roll slowly backwards into the water. The breeze carried them away from the ramp until Ted Evans opened up the port engine to swing them around and, bringing up the power on the other engine, sped downwind across the loch.

"He's never going to get up enough speed to clear those mountains," said Sue, somewhat alarmed.

"Don't panic", assured Sam. "He's only taxiing to the other side of the loch. He will take off into the wind."

"Won't that slow him down and make it more difficult to get into the air?" Mhairi asked, turning round from the seat in front.

"You're forgetting; it's speed through the *air* that matters. If that wind is blowing at twenty knots, then as soon as he turns towards it, the air-speed will be twenty knots. If he needs eighty knots to fly, then he only has to go at sixty knots over the water before he can lift off."

"That's clever," declared Mhairi. "I wonder who thought of that."

"*Birds;*" Alan said simply.

46

Highland Haven

As the aircraft neared the shore along which the narrow lane clung to the hillside, Ted used the engines to turn about until, facing into wind, both engines were brought to maximum power steadily accelerating the 'Widgeon' to take-off speed.

Over the roar of the engines, Sue shouted, "We're going at an angle to the way we landed."

"The mountains ahead of us don't seem so high," Sam called in reply.

The overpowering noise was suddenly reduced as the pilot settled the aircraft in level flight just above the peaks. The intercom crackled into life.

"We'll stay at this height for a little while," the pilot announced; "firstly, because we have to, owing to military aircraft in the area. Secondly, you will get some nice views of the west coast of Scotland. We shall cross the coast, very shortly, slightly south of the fishing port of Mallaig. Further to your right, you will see the Isle of Skye."

"Oh yes! There it is," Sue exclaimed. "What are those red-coloured mountains across the middle?"

"The Cuillins," volunteered Alan.

"Ahead, and to your right, are the islands of Rhum, Eigg, Canna and Muck," the pilot advised over the speakers.

"What funny names," Sue commented.

"Yes," agreed Alan. "They all mean something. Canna has something to do with porpoises. Muck is Pig Island. I can't remember the others."

The aircraft banked to port.

"We're turning over the island of Coll," Ted advised his passengers. As the aircraft levelled from the turn, he continued; "Further out, on your right, you can see Tiree. On your left is the comparatively large island of Mull."

"Mull of Kintyre, Mull of Kintyre," Sue sang out loud.

"Wrong!" interjected Alan. "Mull of Kintyre is not an island. It is the name given to the point of the large peninsula forming the west bank of the Firth of Clyde."

"Ahead is the famous Iona - that small island just off the tip of Mull', Ted's voice over the intercom advised. "St. Columba, from Ireland, came here in the sixth century to bring Christianity to Scotland. Since then over forty Scottish kings have been buried there, including Duncan, you know - the one slain by Macbeth. Before we go too far, look close down on our left and you will see the tiny uninhabited island of Staffa, made famous by Mendelssohn with his Hebridean Overture - Fingals Cave."

"Look! I can see the rock columns forming the entrance to the cave," Sam claimed. "I'd like to visit there - and Iona. History and legend abound in these parts."

47

Maurice Duffill

"As we leave Mull," Ted continued, "we see the small island of Colonsay, with Islay beyond and Jura off to the left. Islay, you may be aware, is famous for its malt whisky."

"I never realised how many islands there were off the Scottish coast," Sue admitted. "Just look over there, over to the left, off the end of the island of Jura. There's a whole cluster of small islands; I wonder if they are inhabited?"

"Some are. The very small ones are used for grazing sheep." Alan informed them. "The strip of water at the end of Jura, between it and the rocky island beyond, is very famous. Perhaps I should say infamous. At certain tidal conditions, a massive whirlpool is formed capable of taking quite large vessels. It is called Corryvrecken."

"Oh, I've read about that," Sam recalled. "Isn't there a legend about somebody luring a poor unfortunate victim into the current so that he was sucked down?"

"Yes, but I can't remember who," Alan admitted. "I read a story where it was used as a means of escape by someone being chased by a high speed boat. The 'hero' skirted the most severe vortex knowing his pursuers would be unaware of its presence. Being at night, the 'villains' went blindly to their doom."

The airborne guide, Ted, spoke again over the intercom. "The land you now see ahead is the peninsula of Kintyre. The small island just before it is called Gigha - God's Island. The bottom end of the peninsula has been made famous by the ex-Beatle, Paul McCartney, with his song 'Mull of Kintyre'. Apparently, he made his home there after the group split up."

"Ahem!" coughed Alan, as his previous exposé was confirmed.

"All right, clever clogs," commented Mhairi. "We know your knowledge of Scotland is impeccable. There's no need to rub it in."

"Beyond Kintyre," continued Ted, "we can now plainly see the island of Arran."

"It's no wonder that the well known Aran wool is thick and coarse," noted Sue, "look at the rugged hills the sheep have to graze on."

"That's the wrong Aran, silly Sue, "Alan interjected "The Aran the wool comes from is off the west coast of Ireland."

"The water we are now crossing," continued Ted," is the Firth of Clyde with the mainland shore coming up ahead. The wee rock about ten miles off the coast is the island of Ailsa Craig - commonly called 'Paddy's Milestone', because it is roughly half way between Glasgow and Belfast."

"I thought Ailsa Craig was an onion," Sue confessed. "Isn't the Clyde wide? If that little rock is ten miles off the shore, it must be about twenty-five miles across from Kintyre."

"About right," confirmed Alan. "You realise that it is further than from England to France?"

48

Highland Haven

"I'm rapidly coming to the conclusion that there's more to Scotland than I ever imagined," Sue admitted.

"Och aye, it's a fair land," Alan declared, with pride.

Their fascinating airborne journey continued, over the Galloway hills and then, across the Solway Firth to England.

"We are now crossing the Lake District," announced Ted, sometime later, determined to maintain the travelogue to the end. "Close on our right, is England's highest peak – Scafell; at three thousand two hundred feet, it is almost a thousand feet less than Ben Nevis."

"It won't be long before we are at Rufforth," Sam declared. "As an experienced pilot, albeit military flying, I must say I can't recall a more interesting flight; a superb day for a superb trip. I'm certainly tempted to explore the Scottish islands at the first opportunity."

"As we cross the Pennines," Ted's voice, once more informed them, "the area on your right is Howarth country, made famous by Emily Bronte with her book 'Wuthering Heights'."

"There's no end to this pilot's knowledge of Britain," maintained Mhairi.

"Well, everybody has heard of Wuthering Heights," Alan commented.

"Yes, I know - but he seems to know where everything is and the tales behind everything. I bet there's a lot more that he didn't have time to tell us."

Assuming the tone of a major airline captain, Ted made an announcement. "Ladies and Gentlemen, we shall soon be arriving at Rufforth, where our passengers for York will disembark. Please fasten your seat belts and extinguish any cigarettes until the aircraft comes to a standstill. Your captain and crew, one-and-the-same, trust that you have had a pleasant journey and hope the airline will be of service to you on a future occasion."

No sooner were the words out of his mouth when the engines changed tone, flaps were lowered and the undercarriage was extended, all ready for landing. Ted eased the throttle back as the aircraft 'greased' on to the runway.

It was almost with a sigh that the machine stopped vibrating, as the propellers finished whirling round at the chosen parking position in front of the control tower. The pilot left his seat to hold open the door whilst Sam and Sue alighted.

Having said their farewells to their new-found friends, the Jackson's shook Ted's hand and thanked him for a most enjoyable journey, expressing genuine hope that they should meet again.

Standing there together, watching the old amphibian take off and fly away south, Sam and Sue became very thoughtful. What would the future hold? Was this the turning point in their lives; or had this most enjoyable, most unusual week-end been - just good fun?

Maurice Duffill

It was in this frame of mind that they drove quietly home, hardly speaking a word. The next few days would be agony, waiting for that fateful envelope containing Sir Richard's decision.

Sam declared, "I vote for an early night to the land of nod. Tomorrow, we both must get stuck into our work, to keep our minds off Scotland.

So it was, later that evening, they climbed the stairs to bed, Sue clinging to Sam's arm saying, "I hope, I hope, I hope."

CHAPTER 6

Sir Richard Blaisdale, busy in his study signing letters to the candidates for his new projects, was interrupted by his secretary.

"Your visitors have arrived, Sir," announced Miss Fitzroy.

"Take these; they are all finished," he instructed, passing the pile of correspondence to her. "Send them in!"

The deputation from down the glen was expected as a result of a previous telephone call. The inhabitants of Glengarry, downstream from Quoich, already hard pressed to make a living from the meagre land, were concerned about the proposed developments they had heard about.

"Miss Morag Matheson and Mr Robbie McIntosh," announced his secretary, as the two were shown into the room.

She was a tall broad-shouldered woman of a rather domineering nature, although obviously well educated. He was slightly shorter, a slim wiry person whose ruddy skin indicated his outdoor activity as a crofter.

Miss Matheson who it turned out, was the secretary of some national association, felt that she was well informed. Adopting a superior attitude, she led the approach forcefully. "I'll come straight to the point, Sir Richard," she declared. "We would like to know what your intentions are. What *are* you proposing to do around Glenquoich?"

Sir Richard took an instant dislike to this person's attitude but, more importantly, he wondered how much she knew. After all his attempts at secrecy, how did she know anything at all?

"My intentions, Miss Matheson, are a personal matter. What leads you to believe they are any concern of yours?"

"Well, for one thing, you have applied for permission to take over the maintenance and 'any future development' of the road to Kinlochhourn from Quoich dam." she replied.

"That is true," he admitted but still not elucidating. "Why does this trouble you?"

"If you privatise that road," she conceded, "we shall be denied access."

"That is an erroneous assumption," Sir Richard declared, a little annoyed at her arrogance. "I can assure you that residents of the glen will have free access to Loch Hourn, as they always have."

"Why then are you taking over the road?" burst in McIntosh, "it'll cost you a lot of money. We are not stupid. You must have an ulterior motive to take over what the country can do for nothing."

"I have no intention of revealing my detail plans until I am ready. All I am prepared to say at the moment is that, God willing, the benefits to the glen will be considerable and that you, along with other residents, will be given every opportunity to participate."

"What you don't realise," maintained McIntosh, "is the difficulty we crofters have, supporting our families on the meagre ground still available to us. It's landowners like you that have sold off great tracts for forestry, depriving us of grazing and our hay meadows."

"I'm not responsible for the policies of past landlords," replied Sir Richard, in defence.

In support of her colleague, Miss Matheson retorted, "It's just like The Highland Clearances all over again. It was sheep that ousted the crofter before; it'll be trees this time."

"I repeat - I am not responsible for the forestry down Glen Garry, as you well know. My proposals concern land well away from your croft, Mr McIntosh, and your home, Miss Matheson. I fail to see what grounds for concern you have."

"You are hedging," Insisted McIntosh angrily. "You've not had all those people up here for fun. You are up to something."

"Whom I have up here, is no concern of yours. I do not intend to discuss the matter further and would be obliged if you would leave," Sir Richard said with finality as he pressed a button, calling his secretary.

As they were being ushered out, Miss Matheson fired her parting shot. "We shall do all in our power to prevent you subjugating the people of this glen."

Later, over coffee, Sir Richard discussed the encounter with his wife. "I just don't know what is worrying them," he said, "I've no intention of ruining their life style. Quite the contrary, I'm going to a lot of trouble and expense to avoid spoiling Scotland's most beautiful glen."

"Yes - but darling, don't you think you could set their minds at rest, by explaining what you have in mind? You know how jealously they guard their independence. Highlanders' hospitality and their unrivalled generosity evaporate if their means of earning a livelihood is challenged."

"I know they are unwilling to be open about their activities, and so am I. If I was to reveal my basic concept at this stage, profit-seeking parasites would swarm like vultures. By keeping quiet, I am actually helping them."

"Do you think they know more than they admit?" she asked.

"I'm not sure. If they do, somebody has talked. I do think there is more to this than has yet been revealed. Their outburst was quite panicky. It didn't seem reasonable in the circumstances being discussed. They accuse me of holding back, of 'being up to something'; I'm beginning to think that perhaps they are up to something and are afraid my plans will interfere with theirs."

"What sort of thing do you think it could be, poaching; an illicit whisky-still, perhaps?"

"I really don't know," he admitted. "Whatever it is, it's going to give us trouble until we get to the bottom of it."

Driving back down the glen, Miss Matheson assured Robbie McIntosh that, in her capacity as Secretary of the National Association of Rights, she would bring pressure to bear on the reticent Sir Richard. She would have people come and poke around until they found out just what was going on.

If she hadn't been concentrating on driving along the narrow, single track road, Miss Matheson would have observed a dramatic change in her companion's facial expression. As it was, his voice betrayed his sudden nervousness.

"Oh, er - I shouldn't get too involved," he blurted out. "Let's wait and see what happens. We'll just keep a canny eye on things without involving others."

Not realising that she had merely been used because of her overbearing manner, the roused committee woman was taken aback.

"I have contacts with people in high places," she declared. "Let's use them to stir it up. That'll get to the bottom of this business. Why hold back now? He virtually threw us out. Do you realise that?"

"Yes, but it might cause more trouble than we bargained for," he weakly attempted to dissuade her.

"I think you've suddenly gone yellow," she scorned.

"Promise me," he said, in a vain attempt to keep her in check, "don't do anything until we discuss matters some more and agree on a course of action."

"I just don't understand you," she said. "You were full of fire when I first mentioned his application to the regional council. You had all sorts of devious theories to explain his motives, none of which you were going to let him get away with. Now, suddenly you've gone all cold. I intend to use my influence to find out what he's up to, regardless of what he said. I'm not afraid of him, we have our rights."

"Morag; ease off - please. Let's see what time will tell," he pleaded, wishing he'd never inspired her to challenge Sir Richard.

"I will not. Nobody's going to accuse me of giving up at the first hurdle."

It was with trepidation that he climbed out of her car at the end of the track to his croft. He had insisted she should not take him all the way. He wanted the walk. He needed to think.

As he approached his humble cottage, head bowed in deep thought, he was startled by the sudden appearance of Malcolm Ferguson, a rough-and-ready character, renowned for his brushes with the law.

"How did you get on? Did you find out what the sassenach is up to?" he hastily asked.

"We've got problems," he confided. "Let's go inside and share a bottle. I need it."

Indoors, over numerous drams, Robbie told 'Fergie' what had transpired and the way their 'tool' had become a 'weapon' against them. Depression crept over them as the facts of the matter soaked further in, assisted by the scotch.

"What are we going to do?" Fergie asked. "We should never have got 'loud mouth ' involved."

"I know, I know!" retorted Robbie, annoyed that his confederate should criticise *him* when he was too thick to plan anything. "I've been thinking. I wonder if there's some way we can distract her."

"How do you mean?" Fergie queried.

"Well, you know how excited she gets over anything. I was wondering if there was something we could do to give her something personal to get uptight about. Then she wouldn't have time to be bothered about Blaisdale."

"What, like assaulting her with my deadly weapon?" he clownishly suggested, his eyes dancing at the thought.

"Fat chance you'd have," Robbie replied. "She'd soon sort you out, big as you are. But, it's a thought. Supposing she started to receive obscene telephone calls. She'd certainly get worked up about that."

"That's up my alley." Fergie stated. "I'd like to hear her reaction to randy suggestions."

"Right then, that's what we'll do." Robbie confirmed. "I'll leave it to you to make the calls and I'll keep in touch with her to see if it has the desired effect."

"I'm going down to the Garry tonight. I'll make the first call from there, at the booth."

"Good! She's expecting me to get in touch after 'sleeping on it'. Don't over do it though; and make sure she doesn't recognise your voice. She'd link you with me straight away."

On his way to tend his sheep, the next day, Robbie McIntosh called in to see how their 'victim' was coping with her new problem.

"I've been thinking, you were right," Robbie lied. "Perhaps we should get your people involved."

"Oh, I can't think about that, just at the moment," she wailed. "Something terrible happened last night and it really upset me."

"Why Morag, I'm sorry to hear that. Whatever was it? Do you want to talk about it?"

"I must talk to somebody. I really don't know what to do," she confessed, obviously quite shaken.

"Come on then, sit down. You can confide in me," he cajoled. "Can I get you a drink; you need to calm down."

"There's some sherry on the dresser, over there," she indicated. "Have one yourself."

Highland Haven

She slumped into a soft armchair whilst he poured the two drinks and presented her with one.

"It may seem silly," she commenced, "but it has made me feel dirty. Last night I had an obscene phone call. A man! He rang me at about 10 o'clock. He didn't say much at first, just murmuring to himself, if you see what I mean. Then, after I'd asked who it was, he started to say terrible things about what he would like to do to me. At first, I was so shocked I didn't know what to do. I just listened to him, until I was shaking all over. I managed to slam the phone down and then almost went into hysterics."

"My God!" Robbie exclaimed, in mock concern, delighted at the success of the first attempt. "Tell me, did he know who you were? Or had he just picked you at random?"

"I don't know," she said.

"Did he use your name, at all?"

"I don't know, I can't be sure," she started to snivel. "What should I do? Should I call the police?"

"Try not to upset yourself too much. You may have been unlucky. He may never call again. There are these cranks that get some sort of perverted delight out of ringing up just anybody. If you have another call, let me know and I'll contact the police for you."

"Thank you," she sobbed. "You are kind. It's nice to know I've a friend to turn to, but you will understand that I don't feel like ringing people over that other matter, just yet."

"That's alright," he assured her. "There's no rush. We can attend to that when you've got over this business."

"I think I'll go and work it off in the garden," she said, as he started to leave.

Robbie continued up the glen to Fergie's cottage, to congratulate him on his first effort the previous night.

"I right enjoyed it, "the rather obnoxious character admitted. "You should have heard her screaming at me."

"Eh now look, Fergie. I don't want things to get out of hand. Miss Matheson's welfare is nothing to do with me but I wouldn't wish any harm to her."

"Come off it. You wanted to give her something to think about," Fergie shot back at him. "I'm quite looking forward to repeating my performance, tonight."

"No! Leave it a while, "Robbie commanded." If you go at it too madly, the police will be brought in and we'll have to give up. We've got to drag it out so that she'll go cold on the other thing."

"I suppose you're right. You give me the nod then, when she's sweat a bit," Fergie agreed, with reluctance. "Do you know when the next trip is?"

Maurice Duffill

"There's one due, but I don't yet know when. I'm expecting a call any time now. Get your fishing gear ready."

It was that very evening, the coded call came.

"The next meeting will be held at the usual place on the 16th at the usual time," the voice specified vaguely.

Knowing the form, Robbie didn't require further clarification and, accordingly, acknowledged the message.

As soon as the caller had rung off, he dialled a number at Corran, near the mouth of Loch Hourn. "Please let Angus MacGilvery know that our next meeting is on the 16th," he said to the person at the other end, adding in confirmation, "that's the day after tomorrow."

"I must remember to let Fergie know," he muttered to himself. "At least his 'Lordship's' plans won't interfere with this trip, whatever he has in mind."

Midnight, just over a day later, saw silent activity at Fraoch Eilean, a tiny island just off the rocky south shore of Loch Hourn. Angus MacGilvery eased his boat away from the mooring, in a familiar manner. The fact that it was a dark night presented no real problem since he was constantly piloting the 'Heather Queen' between his isolated boathouse and the village of Corran three miles or so down the loch, on the north shore.

Tonight, as on other 'meeting' nights, he was not headed for his drinking haunt at Corran but beyond, out to sea. With the powerful engine held down to a low throb he skilfully guided the ruggedly built fishing boat past the cluster of rocks and islets opposite Barrisdale Bay. He didn't want to attract anyone's attention to his activities; not that there was likely to be a human being around these remote parts, but one couldn't be too careful.

The tide being well down, he had to steer towards the south shore to avoid the 'Ellice' shoal, awkwardly sited in mid-loch. Timing of the trip always had to be to give him high tide on his return. He would need the extra depth then.

About three miles further, and he was opposite the village; it would be unlikely for anyone to notice him at turned midnight, with a dark, moonless sky. He was keeping fairly close to the south shore and the loch is a mile wide thereabout.

Another three miles and he could vaguely make out the beacon sitting on the rocks known as 'Sgeir Ulibhe' which heralded the widening of the loch into the Sound of Sleat. Keeping well to port of them, roughly half way to the south shore, he progressively opened up the throttle to three-quarters, giving him about twenty knots.

As the 'Heather Queen' surged forward with her new found energy, Angus steered gently port to a southerly heading down the sound. His change of course

56

formed a long sweeping curve as he maintained a more or less constant distance from the lonely shore, by sighting the silhouette of Knoydart's rugged mountain peaks.

Now on a steady course, he presently came in sight of a few remaining street lights and a beacon which indicated the position of the west coast fishing port of Mallaig. From here the protection given from the Atlantic winds by the Isle of Skye diminished, as the 'Point of Sleat' was rounded to enter the Cuillin sound.

Although the air was not particularly cold, the increase in wind strength brought added chill to the exposed wheelhouse, as the boatman applied more effort to the helm; the rising waves, now and then breaking into a fine spray, made it quite hard work to steer in a steady manner.

As his starboard turn brought the vessel around the point onto a north-westerly heading, Angus held the course steady, to run seawards between Skye and the isle of Rhum; soon, neither coast could be seen, and he relied entirely on his compass.

Thirty-six minutes later, without sight of anything, he made a ninety degree turn to port. Fifteen minutes of blind running, into the teeth of the stiff breeze, brought the tough little boat into the Sound of Canna, the waters between Rhum and the Isle of Canna.

He was able to confirm his rough position by the vague outline, square off to port, of the mountains of Rhum. Angus eased a little closer to the shore. It was important to get an accurate sighting of the westernmost point, which gloried in the Gaelic name of A'bhrideanach.

His 'target' was due at a position of precisely 57°N 7°W at 0400 hours GMT. This location, south of The Minches, is in the midst of 'The Sea of the Hebrides'; out of sight and earshot of the many Western Isles. The nearest being Eriskay, some ten miles distant, would not be witness to the early morning rendezvous.

Angus checked his watch; it was 0255. If his well practised plan was on schedule, he would see the point very shortly. There, right on cue, he could just see the end of the land mass. Steering even closer to the rocky shore, he set an accurate course and checked his engine revolutions to be sure his speed was correct. Now was the time for precise navigation.

Leaving the point close on his port side he looked at his watch once more - 0300 exactly. He would maintain this course accurately for 30 minutes, and then turn starboard 90 degrees to a heading of precisely 300 degrees. If all was well, 'the ship' would appear thirty minutes later.

Although Angus was a 'loner', he always felt a little apprehension at this stage in the sortie. On the very first trip, he felt positively nervous. It wasn't the navigational problem that worried him, although special care was necessary; it was the clandestine meeting. To be setting off, alone, in the dark waters of the Hebrides, to meet a total stranger, for an illicit purpose, would raise the heartbeat of any man; particularly, when it turned out that the man, and the ship, were Russian.

Nothing had been explained to him; it was not for him to know, but after a number of 'meetings', Angus had gradually discovered the legitimate business of the vessel. The Russians were bringing soda-ash to a seaweed processing factory near Oban in return for a load of their product. He had also found out that, as the ship entered Scottish waters, a message was transmitted to the Russian fish factory ship anchored in Loch Broom. A crew member would then go ashore at Ullapool and telephone the rendezvous to the Glengarry number - simple and safe.

Turning onto his north-westerly heading after the thirty minutes, Angus switched on his hydrophone equipment. Although really intended to locate fish, a tuning device had been added to synchronise with a special underwater signal emitted by the Russian ship. It now acted both as a homing device and a means of identification. Deliberately, it only worked at short range.

For a while the earphones were silent, but then a faint signal could be heard. Progressively, the sound gained strength until Angus's peering eyes were able to discern the slightly fluorescent glow of the 'target's' bow wave, topped by the navigation lights.

He swung the little boat away, then curved back round to a matching course parallel to the ship. A slight adjustment to the helm caused the 'Heather Queen' to track across her stern, about a hundred yards aft. Angus could clearly see the name, 'Ivan Boronovich', just below the rail where two men were watching his manoeuvre.

There, amongst the foam of the wake, was what he was looking for. An erratic splashing was the clue to the whereabouts of his 'booty', trailing behind the ship. A quick flip with the boathook landed the package on board. Angus slashed the towline with his knife. The pickup was complete.

With a wave of acknowledgement, he backed off to port then opened up the throttle to separate as quickly as possible. The dark silhouette was soon lost in the murky night and Angus throttled back to cruising revs. He could now steer due east, until the island of Rhum appeared, then follow its coastline until he reached the sound of Rhum, between it and the island of Eigg. Backing a few degrees to the north would then ultimately bring him back into the sound of Sleat.

It was about 0630 as the sturdy little boat passed the lights of Mallaig, apparently returning from an overnight fishing trip. 'Nicely timed for the 8 o'clock pick up', he murmured to himself.

An hour later, he was back in Loch Hourn approaching the anchorage where he started. Rounding the rocks and islets off Barrisdale Bay, he passed by his boathouse, then continued eastward up the ever narrowing loch.

Highland Haven

Another half hour negotiating the familiar hazards of this lengthy intrusion into the Highlands and he arrived, now with reduced speed, at the eastern end - Loch Beag and Kinlochhourn.

Nosing over to the pier on the south shore, opposite the big house, he could see the figure of Malcolm Ferguson putting away his fishing tackle, in readiness to help him refuel from the bulk tank ashore. This was the routine designed to cover up the hand over of the package, still wrapped in its waterproof cover.

The task complete, Fergie bade farewell to Angus, then watched as the boat sped away at the head of its foaming wake, a night's work carried out to plan.

Fergie, anxious to be rid of the compromising package, was soon in his 'banger' of a car, lumbering up the steep climb from Kinlochhourn. His function as errand boy was to deliver the goods to Robbie McIntosh at his croft.

Robbie, waiting for his arrival, had a quick chat over the telephone with Miss Matheson.

"No," she said, "there had been no further calls from that horrible person. It must be as you said, just a random call."

"Oh that's good, I hope you'll soon forget about the filthy things he said to you," lied Robbie, thinking, 'we'll soon alter that'.

As soon as Fergie arrived, Robbie concealed the package until the fertiliser representative could call to collect.

"No doubt you will be going down to the Garry for a dram," Robbie perceived. "It's time to liven up Miss Whatsits again."

"Great!" exclaimed Fergie, "that'll make the day."

"I've been thinking," Robbie declared. "Don't use her name, unless she gives it to you, which is unlikely. If you do, she will be suspicious of someone local. Keep her guessing completely."

That night, the obscene call really shook her. The following day she called on Robbie to tell the sorry tale, expressing sickness that the respite had been short lived. It was agreed that he would phone the police, there and then.

He was anxious that he be fully aware of the police response, so willingly took this duty upon himself. They said that someone would call within the hour to take a full statement.

"Are you busy, Robbie?" she asked, "because I'd like you to be there."

"Alright!" he agreed, trying desperately to hide his delight.

Having taken a full written statement of matters so far, the Sergeant from Fort Augustus claimed she had two choices. The telephone people could give her a new, ex-directory number or, if she was prepared to help the police to catch the man, she could agree to a phone tapping connection being used.

After a lot of thought and no small amount of persuasion by Robbie she agreed to the phone tap.

When, the next day, Robbie told Fergie of the outcome of his call, he couldn't understand Robbie's intentions.

"You're trying to drop me in it, "he claimed.

"No, you dim nut. If she takes an ex-directory number, we'll have to pack it in. But, if you are careful and keep the calls short, we can still harass her."

"Oh, I'm with it now," he agreed.

"If you can make a call from away, somewhere, this will make it more difficult to trace."

"I'm going to Inverness in a couple of days," Fergie informed him. "So I'll make the next call from Garry, then one from 'Ness."

After a couple of weeks intensive 'treatment', Morag couldn't take any more and announced she was so upset and sick of it all, she was accepting a long standing invitation to visit the U.S.A. She would be away for at least two months, possibly three.

"We've succeeded," Robbie eagerly informed Fergie.

"I'll miss my bit of fun," he replied sorrowfully. "But I suppose our money-making racket is much more important."

"You can say that again," Robbie confirmed. "I just hope 'His Lordship's' plans don't interfere in the future."

CHAPTER 7

A few days had passed since the Jacksons had returned from their Highland adventure, yet they were still in an unsettled frame of mind - hoping and wishing.

Whilst preparing breakfast, Sue heard the postman drop the mail through the letter box slot. With more restraint as each day dawned, she stopped what she was doing to collect from the hall carpet, the daily incomings.

Drinking his fresh orange juice, Sam watched her as she returned.

"Your name has been entered in another £50,000 Readers Digest competition," she announced, as she flicked through the assortment of mail. "There's a telephone bill, a letter from my mother, and one from INVERNESS! - IT'S COME! Oh, open it quickly. I can't wait to know."

"Well... I think we'll finish our breakfast first. Then I'll open it, or maybe I'll leave it until I come home from the office. It'll be something to look forward to," he teased.

"There'll be no breakfast in this house until that letter is opened and read out loud," she assured him.

"Ah well, under the threat of starvation, I'll succumb to your wishes," he conceded, hardly able to contain his own eagerness.

Dear Mr Jackson,

I am pleased to inform you that your application for the position of Engineering Manager has been successful. However, as discussed, you will be required to assume full responsibility to me for the development of all aspects of the project. Accordingly, your position is raised to Development Director at a salary of £50,000 per annum, fixed for five years.

It is agreed that your house will be provided free of charge for the term of your engagement.

This is a permanent appointment, provided you agree to the special conditions imposed by the Board of Directors, under the chairmanship of myself. Although these conditions may be considered radical and have yet to be finalised, with your help (as

Development Director), it is necessary that you agree to the following:-

FIRSTLY - your appointment can, in the event of serious misdemeanour, be terminated by a tribunal of fellow directors chaired by myself.

SECONDLY - in lieu of income tax and national insurance contributions, which will be paid for you on a corporate basis, you will be obliged to invest in the project, half of your salary. This obligatory share will not be transferable.

THIRDLY - notwithstanding the fact that your house is to be provided free of charge, you will be required to pay a modest ground rent for all land attributed for your personal use. This will be in lieu of any rates.

If you, and your wife, accept the aforementioned, please notify in writing at your earliest convenience the date you propose to take up the appointment.

On receipt of your confirmation of acceptance, details will be sent of proposed modifications to existing property to become your new home. Your suggestions or approval would then be solicited. In the meantime, temporary accommodation awaits your occupancy.

I look forward to your reply.

Yours sincerely,

Sir Richard Blaisdale

"Oh darling," exclaimed Sue, flinging her arms around him to give a loving hug. "You've got it! But I don't understand those conditions. Why do you have to invest so much of your salary, it's like giving back half of it? You may as well take only half in the first place."

"Oh no, that would be no good at all," Sam replied. "I don't know what's behind it, but somehow, for reasons I don't yet understand, he's paying my tax for me if I invest in his project. Since my tax and national insurance is greater than fifty per cent, I can't lose. I'm intrigued though, as to why he should make this arrangement."

"From what he says in the letter, it sounds as if you will be drawing up the rules with him," she suggested. "That's odd, isn't it?"

"Well, not really under the circumstances. You see, we are starting off a new company and although he knows what he wants to achieve, the details still have to be worked out."

"If, as he says, this is a permanent position, why does he talk of terminating it - before you've even started?"

"That's fair enough. He must protect himself from an unscrupulous misuse of position. It also means my appointment is secure unless I seriously misbehave myself. Regardless of all your questions, I'm quite happy and intend to accept. Ok?"

"It's fine by me, in fact I'd be very upset if you didn't," Sue stressed. "It was just that I didn't understand those funny clauses. How much notice are you going to give?"

"Three months. I've already been thinking about that problem," Sam admitted. "I've no intention of blotting my copy book here. This mill project is at a critical stage but another couple of months should see it over the hump. One more month to tidy things up and hand over; then I'm sure I've left in good order. I might need to turn to them one day so it will be time well spent. Besides, we need adequate time to sell this house to get the best price."

"I suppose you're right," Sue murmured. "But I don't think I can wait that long. I'm too excited."

"It'll soon pass when you get stuck in to making all your plans, seeing everyone before we go and generally getting organised."

"Can I ring Mhairi?" Sue asked excitedly. "I'd like to find out if they've got the job as well."

"I don't think that's wise. It might cause embarrassment if they haven't yet heard when in fact the letter could be in the post to them. Let's leave it a little while. I was thinking," Sam continued, "In view of the three month lag before moving up there, I'll offer to pop up for a week-end meeting so that plans can be progressed without waiting too long."

"Oh that's a good idea," Sue agreed. "I would willingly accept another basinful of that highland hospitality."

"Forget it." Sam said firmly. "If we do go up for a meeting, it'll be strictly business. There'll be no time for shooting or pony trekking."

"No, I don't expect that," Sue conceded, "but we could see where we're going to live, both initially and the property that has to be altered."

"Alright then, we'll reply tonight, after our evening meal."

A few days after Sam's written acceptance was sent off, Sue answered an evening telephone call. "It's Miss Frosty," she called to Sam in the kitchen, brewing some coffee. "She wants to know if next week-end would be suitable for a meeting but points out that, to be picked up by plane again, we'd have to set off Friday and return Monday, because Rufforth air traffic control is not manned at weekends."

"That'll be alright," agreed Sam. "So long as departure can be say seven o'clock in the evening. That is 1900 hours; returning as soon as possible on Monday morning."

Sue relayed the message to Sir Richard's secretary who said she would have to check with the pilot.

"Why stipulate seven o'clock?" Sue asked.

"This will give us time to have something to eat before we leave," Sam explained. "Otherwise, they would have to provide dinner for us and I don't feel like starting my new career sponging on the boss."

"We'll be given nice meals the rest of the week-end, I'm sure," Sue suggested.

"That's OK, but I don't want to appear to be milking it."

It wasn't long before Miss Fitzroy confirmed the suggested flight time for Friday.

"Here we go again," Sue said, like an excited schoolgirl. "I could get used to this style of life; having a private aircraft to wing us about our business."

"Once we're settled up there, it'll be back to the old bike again," Sam said. "Just think of it, puffing your way up hill from the one and only shop twenty miles away, with torrential rain pouring down your neck, and the howling wind trying to blow you off the narrow single track road down the bleak rocky slope into the icy loch, way below."

"Oh give over, you pessimistic person you," Sue snapped. "For one thing, I'll have our car because you will use a company vehicle. I must admit though, I don't know where one does the shopping."

"I asked about that," Sam revealed. "Ted Evans said that the nearest shop was at Invergarry, twenty-seven miles from the lodge house where we stayed."

"However does one manage for milk and bread? Do they deliver?"

"At the moment, a post van - a Landrover, comes every Monday, Wednesday and Friday bringing, not only the mail, but newspapers, groceries that have been ordered by phone, and even passengers. It's a bus as well."

Highland Haven

"The newspapers will be out of date," Sue observed. "Still, I suppose we get all the actual news on the television these days."

"Oh, didn't I tell you? Television doesn't reach up there. The mountains blank out the main transmitter, near Inverness. A slave transmitter aimed up the glen, from the Great Glen doesn't have enough power to reach that far."

"You've been keeping things from me, haven't you?" Sue challenged. "You were determined to go and didn't want to put me off, you sneak."

"Guilty!" Sam admitted. "While I'm confessing, I should tell you something else. There's no mains electricity either."

"Now you're kidding. There must be; the lodge has electric light, remember."

"I'm not kidding. They had a small hydro-electric generator in an outhouse, fed from a mountain stream."

"Well - you're the engineer. You'll have to do something about it."

"That is true but, things take time - and money. This is one of the reasons I want a meeting before we go up there; to sort out priorities. Perhaps we can organise a start on some of those problems beforehand. At least, I'll be thinking about matters in advance so that, when we arrive, I can get stuck straight in."

"Do you know, you've really taken the edge off this move; it suddenly doesn't look so rosy," Sue muttered.

"It's better that you are aware of the facts. Anyway, think of the pleasures to come as matters improve. In years to come, you'll say - 'I remember when we had an old generator to produce our electricity or, when we couldn't have television or, emptying the loo in a pit every night before going to bed'."

"I hope you don't mean that." Sue shrieked. "That would be going too far."

"Don't panic my delicate one. We'll have our own treatment plant," Sam assured her. "By the way, you realise there is no mains water? Each place, or group of places, takes water direct from the mountain streams. Sorry - BURNS."

"Is that why the water tastes so nice and is so soft to wash with?"

"The softness is due to the lack of lime. The mountains are mainly granite overlain with peat, so you get that whisky colour due to the rain filtering through the dead vegetation. Of course, there is no chlorine, or alum, or lime, or fluoride, added so there is a pure chemical-less flavour. Mind you, your teeth will fall out in a couple of years."

"Oh you; you always have to spoil things," Sue moaned.

Friday soon came, and they eagerly prepared to depart on their second airborne jaunt to the Highlands. Ted Evans was already there, on the ground, when Sam and Sue arrived at the airfield.

Having said their hellos, they climbed aboard the now familiar aircraft as if they had been used to this mode of travel, all their lives.

"I'm afraid the weather isn't going to be as kind as it was on your previous flights," the pilot announced. "There's a depression moving in from the west, bringing a lot of cloud and strong winds. We'll have to keep at a safe height; so most of the way, we'll be out of sight of the ground."

An hour or so later, they were flying in and out of increasing amounts of cloud as they progressed over southern Scotland.

Ted Evans advised his two passengers that he would be seeking some help from Air Traffic Control at Prestwick and, if they were interested, he could switch the radio on to the intercom so they could listen in.

"Oh, that would be fascinating," Sue declared, as Sam gave the thumbs up to the pilot.

"HIGHLAND LASSIE - PRESTWICK CONTROL - DO YOU READ? OVER."

"WE READ YOU STRENGTH 5"   came the reply.

"REQUEST WEATHER IN AREA OF GREAT GLEN - OVER."

"QNH 996.4, FALLING - WIND SOUTHWEST 25 to 30 KNOTS -
VISIBILITY 3 to 6 MILES DETERIORATING IN SHOWERS –
CLOUD BASE 3000 FEET - OVER "

"What were all those letters and figures, at the beginning?" asked Sue. "The rest of it made sense but what was that 'Q' thing?"

"The 'Q' code is a simple way of saying standard things," Sam explained. "QNH is code for 'air pressure at sea level'; Ted needs that to set his altimeter correctly. The instrument on his panel that indicates the height works in proportion to the air pressure. The higher one goes, the less the pressure."

"What has that got to do with the weather?" Sue persisted.

"As the weather changes the pressure at sea level changes; to be correct, it is the other way round. It is changes in atmospheric pressure that cause weather. That's what the weather man on TV means when he refers to 'High' or 'Low'. So, if the pressure drops, Ted's altimeter will falsely show a higher altitude; Ted will then come down a bit to maintain height and - PRESTO - we fly into a mountain."

"There's a cheerful thought," commented Sue.

Highland Haven

"HIGHLAND LASSIE TO PRESTWICK - REQUEST CLEARANCE TO LET DOWN FOR VISUAL   FLIGHT UP FIRTH OF LORNE TO GREAT GLEN – OVER"

"LASSIE - GIVE ESTIMATED POSITION AND HEIGHT – OVER"

"PRESENTLY 10 MILES SOUTH WEST OF YOU AT 4500 FEET - HEADING 300 DEGREES AT 140 KNOTS – OVER"

"ROGER HIGHLAND LASSIE - MAKE PORT TURN FOR RADAR IDENT"

"What does that mean?" quizzed Sue.

"On the radar they will be able to see a number of aircraft, at various heights; so now, they will watch to see which one does a port turn. That one will be us. They probably know already but are just making sure."

"WE HAVE YOU CONFIRMED - HIGHLAND LASSIE - CALL STEADY ON 240"

"They'll bring us down over the Clyde estuary." The pilot told them, over the intercom, as he straightened from the turn.

"HIGHLAND LASSIE STEADY ON 240," he called.

"ROGER - COMMENCE LET DOWN TO 2000 AND ADVISE"

Ted eased back the throttles and the Widgeon started to descend.

"It beats me," Sue declared, "how he knows which way he's going or what he's doing at all. I can't see a thing in all this cloud. We might be upside down for all I know."

"You might at that," confirmed Sam. "That's what the instruments are for. Some tell the pilot about engines, revs, temperatures, pressures, that sort of thing. The main group in the middle are his flight instruments which indicate speed, height, direction, amount of turn, rate of climb and, see the biggish one in the middle? That is the artificial horizon; it's like a small model aeroplane; it banks, dives and climbs just the same as we do."

"The mind boggles," Sue commented.

Progressively, the cloudy darkness diminished until, quite suddenly, they broke through underneath.

Maurice Duffill

"We are the right way up," Sue observed. "There's the sea and look, on our right, that mountainous island pokes right up into the cloud."

"Yes, that'll be the Isle of Arran," declared Sam. "That's why Prestwick control had us let down over the Clyde. So we wouldn't prang on one of the bumps."

"Some bump!"

"HIGHLAND LASSIE VISUAL AT 2000 FEET," called Ted.

"TURN NINETY DEGREES STARBOARD AROUND MULL OF KINTYRE," instructed control. THEN CONTINUE VISUALLY TO ISLAY THEN RIGHT AGAIN INTO THE FIRTH OF LORNE - YOU ARE CLEARED UP THE GREAT GLEN"

"WILCO," Acknowledged their pilot.

"WE'LL MONITOR YOUR PROGRESS - GOOD LUCK - PRESTWICK OUT."

By now, it was quite murky, but they could clearly see the headland as the plane banked to the right. It was only about half a mile off the wingtip. Soon, the Kintyre peninsula was left behind as they headed out, in the new direction over featureless sea.

"I'm glad he's got all those dials and things to tell him what to do," confessed Sue. "I can't see a thing - except cloud above us and sea beneath us. Even that I'm not sure about; I'm not sure where one ends and the other begins."

"That's usually the case in conditions like these," confirmed Sam, remembering his many hours as an 'All-weather' fighter pilot. "Now you know why he needs the artificial horizon. Although we're not in cloud, there's no natural horizon to be seen. If, under these conditions, a pilot did not make use of his instruments, he could very easily become disorientated."

"What does the pilot do if his artificial horizon breaks down - crash?" Sue asked nervously.

"No. Don't worry. All R.A.F. pilots are trained to cope with that, and I can tell, Ted's ex-R.A.F.," Sam assured her. There are other instruments, which are non-electrical and therefore unlikely to break down at the same time. Some of these can be viewed collectively to act as a substitute."

"They think of everything, don't they?" said Sue, re-assured.

"That's why flying is safer than most people expect," Sam professed.

"Oh look!" observed Sue. "There's some land coming out of the gloom."

68

Highland Haven

"That'll be the island of Islay," Sam declared. "The controller said we were to fly on to here, then turn right again."

The pilot continued as if he wasn't going to turn. Then the passengers realised the island coastline consisted of two prominent peninsulas. As the aircraft passed the second, the starboard wing dipped and the plane followed round the line of the shore until they were heading in a north-easterly direction.

The intercom crackled into life. "We're now heading into the Firth of Lorne," Ted announced. "The small island you see on your left is Colonsay, with Jura on your right. When I flew you home, we passed overhead about here, but at right angles to our present track."

"I remember those names," admitted Sue, "but I don't recognise them again."

"No, you won't," agreed Sam. "The visibility is a lot poorer; we are lower than when we were going home; and we're heading in a different direction. This is part of the fascination of non-airline flying; one sees features from all sorts of angles and under a variety of conditions."

"It's getting darker now," observed Sue. "The cloud is lower and it's starting to rain. What are all those lights coming up on the right hand side?"

As if he had heard her, Ted informed them that Oban was lit up early because of the murky weather.

Now, as they flew up the firth, land was to be seen on both sides while they flew over an assortment of small islands and rocks. Fishing boats could be seen scurrying for the shelter of Oban harbour, as the white-topped waves grew with the increasing wind.

"It looks a bit grim down there," commented Sam.

"It doesn't look too bright up here!" countered Sue. "Are you sure we are going to be alright?"

"I've every confidence in Ted," Sam asserted, but he too was beginning to wonder, knowing they were heading into a mountainous region below peak height.

"That was the island of Lismore," Ted announced, referring to the thin strip of land passing beneath them. "This is Loch Linnhe. We'll soon see the lights of Fort William, beyond the Corran Narrows where the car ferry crosses."

As they flew up the loch, the hills on either side closed in to form the steep-sided Great Glen. Ted had reduced height by 500 feet to keep below the dense, black, nimbo-stratus cloud overhead, now disgorging continuous torrential rain. Visibility had worsened to such an extent that they were alongside before they saw the street lights of Fort William.

"I'll not be attempting to land at Quoich," Ted declared over the intercom. "It would be too risky to fly up Glengarry in these conditions. There is a small grass landing strip at a farm near the castle at Invergarry. I use that occasionally when the loch is too rough. I'll see if I can raise them on the radio."

Maurice Duffill

"HOME FARM - FROM HIGHLAND LASSIE - DO YOU READ? OVER"

"- - - - - - -"silence.

"HOME FARM - FROM HIGHLAND LASSIE - DO YOU READ? OVER"

"- - - - -ER HELLO - I HEAR YOU – OVER" a female voice replied.

"I NEED TO USE YOUR LANDING STRIP - IS IT CLEAR OF CATTLE AND SHEEP? OVER"

"WOULD YOU WAIT A MINUTE WHILE I CHECK WITH MY HUSBAND? "

The wifey was obviously not used to the radio which, combined with the prospect of animals littering the landing strip, didn't help to quell the growing nervousness of Sue. She tightened her lap strap, partly as an anxious gesture, but also to combat the increased bumpiness, now the sea loch had come to an end and they were flying low over land.

"ER HELLO - THE FIELD IS CLEAR BUT MY HUSBAND SAYS IT IS VERY WET - ER OVER"

"ROGER" Ted acknowledged. "WE'LL BE WITH YOU IN FIVE MINUTES - IF I CAN FIND YOU" He added.

"MY HUSBAND SAYS HE WILL TAKE THE TRUCK AND SHINE HIS HEADLIGHTS DOWN   THE STRIP TOWARDS THE CASTLE"

"THAT'S GREAT - THANK YOU" Responded Ted.

"Don't be alarmed," warned the pilot. "But we are approaching from the wrong direction relative to the wind. As soon as we pass by the field, I'll have to make a steeply banked turn to keep between the hills. The engines will be a bit noisy."
"Oh Sam, I'm frightened," declared Sue.
"Don't worry, love," Sam said reassuringly. "He's done it before, by the sound of it. It'll soon be over."

70

Highland Haven

"That's what they say when one is to have a tooth out, but it doesn't make it any easier," she wailed.

The engine note changed as the pilot adjusted the pitch of the propellers.

"Here's Loch Oich," he said as he eased the aircraft down, low over the water. "There's the strip, on the left," he added a moment later.

Ted pulled the noisy twin engined plane sharply up and to the right, towards the steep hill slope to the south of the loch. Just as Sue felt sure they must crash, the wings banked, equally steeply the other way, turning the aircraft back the way they had come.

As they straightened out, the noise of the undercarriage being extended could be heard. Their pilot eased back the throttles to descend steeply over the trees by the ruined castle, aiming for the 'green postage' stamp which served as a landing ground.

Now flying into wind, visibility was even worse than before, with the rain driving straight at them. The two passengers peering forward through the pilot's compartment could hardly discern the lights on the pickup truck facing them until they felt the bump and the following rumble, indicating they were down. It seemed then, as the lights became clear, there was insufficient space to stop.

Sue shut her eyes, convinced they would run straight into the truck. She just hoped the driver had the sense to get out. Then, the rumbling stopped. She opened her eyes to find they were alongside.

Ted shut down the engines and, in the sudden quiet, Sue burst into tears. "Thank God," she cried.

The door was soon opened, to welcome the cheery face of Willy McLeod. In no time at all he'd loaded their luggage into the truck, assisted Sue into the passenger seat, and set off for the sanctuary of the farm with the two men riding on the open back.

"You'll be having a wee dram?" Willy McLeod suggested as they entered the dry of the cosy cottage. "Then I'll run you up the glen in the car - not the truck."

"If that's an offer of something short," Sue said, "I'd be most grateful. I'm shaking all over."

After the whisky had calmed frayed nerves, they set off up Glengarry, being chauffeured by Willy McLeod in his car. The rain continued to cascade from the heavens as much as to say to the two newcomers, 'Now you've committed yourself, I'll let you know what you are in for'.

Even though the weather was appalling, Sam and Sue, riding in the back seat, still could appreciate the grandeur of this most beautiful glen.

The first few miles were heavily wooded with birch along the roadside, backed up by plantations of mixed larch, fir and spruce. As the car turned off the road to

Skye in order to follow the loch side on the single track road to Kinlochhourn, groups of mature trees were found; Oak, ash, willow and beech amongst others.

Nearing the lonely Hotel at Tomdoun, the woods, now containing lovely Scots pine, thinned to a more sparse scrub-like nature with new plantings filling the open spaces.

Passing the mainly wooden hamlet of Kingie, they came in sight of the great rock-filled dam holding back the waters of Loch Quoich. In the wet, blustery conditions, with the light now failing, it looked rather awesome poised above them.

"I wouldn't like to live there," Sue declared as they passed the uninspiring cottages. "I'd always be afraid the dam would burst."

"You are always worrying over something," Sam declared. "I'm sure it's plenty safe enough."

The road brought them to the dam top, and then continued along the uninhabited loch-side to the semi-familiar area of their previous visit. It then didn't seem long before they were descending the dramatic route to the sea loch and the welcome of the lodge.

The warmth of a blazing log fire began to dispel the fears generated by their recent unorthodox arrival but, after a brief social drink with their hosts, Sam and Sue eagerly climbed the stairs to indulge in a soothing hot bath followed by much needed sleep.

CHAPTER 8

The following morning, with their adrenalin flow back to normal, the Jacksons came down to breakfast well rested. Torrential rain was to be observed, through the great picture window, dragging the clouds down to meet the turbulent waters of the sea loch.

Whereas on their previous visit the view was one of scenic beauty, now it was of dramatic tumult. No longer could they see well down the fiord-like cleft in the mountains; the heavy rain and low cloud restricted vision to the immediate shore, giving the visitors a shut-in impression.

"Good morning! Did you sleep well after your ordeal?"

The voice of Sir Richard startled them. He was sitting in a corner sipping coffee whilst their attention had been taken by the sight through the window.

They having returned his greeting and assured him regarding their state of rest, he expressed his regret about the weather and his relief at their safe arrival.

"Unfortunately," he continued, "the climate here leaves a lot to be desired. I just hope that you don't find it too difficult to acclimatise to highland 'monsoons'. It's not so bad when you get used to it," he added. "At least the rain keeps the air fresh; it's rarely dry and dusty."

Over breakfast, it was agreed that the morning would be spent first of all looking at the plans for their home and then by visiting the cottage to be converted into their Highland Haven. On the way back they would have a look at the accommodation that was being prepared as their temporary residence .

Lady Dorothy joined them and commented about the period of notice Sam had chosen to give. Whereas she complimented him on his loyalty shown to his present employer, she expressed concern that the restraint displayed might indicate a lack of dash.

The direction of her conversation took both Sam and Sue by surprise. It certainly appeared that she was the power behind the more cogitative Sir Richard. Maybe this project was of his conception but she was going to see that it all happened. Already this was putting a fresh complexion on matters. She would have to be treated with care.

Sam was quick to point out that he was only too eager to get to grips with the many problems the project would present, as could be witnessed by this very meeting which had been arranged at his suggestion.

Sensing conflict so soon in their association, Sir Richard rose from the table suggesting they should pursue the matter of housing in his study in fifteen minutes.

When Sam and Sue settled themselves in the study, a quarter of an hour later, they were relieved to find that Lady Dorothy was not to join them. They needed time to reassess her role in the venture.

Maurice Duffill

"We propose to extensively modify an existing cottage," commented Sir Richard, as he spread architects drawings on the table. "You, I believe, went pony trekking to Alltbeithe during your previous visit?"

"We certainly did," agreed Sue. "Like the bad weather trip of yesterday, we'll not forget that in a hurry."

"I remember; you were caught in a hailstone squall. Most unfortunate; you finally sheltered in the byre with the ponies, did you not? The point is, the cottage alongside is the one we propose to convert to your home."

"That is a lovely, tucked-away situation," Sam declared; "and this looks basically a nice design." he added, referring to the drawings before them.

"As you see, we've extended the cottage rearwards to provide, out of the ground floor, an entrance hall with lounge to the left and kitchen with adjoining pantry, to the right. Beyond the stairs at ground level, you'll have the master bedroom, bathroom and private study."

"I see," said Sue, struggling in her attempt to understand unfamiliar plans and elevations. "But why do we need the stairs if everything is to be on the ground floor, like a bungalow?"

The two men glanced at each other, Sam expressing an unspoken but highly visual apology for the technical inadequacy of his wife.

With an amused smile, Sir Richard continued. "Up the stairs we have arranged two guest bedrooms, a second toilet - this time with shower - and a linen store. Keeping the main part of the house at ground level will, we feel, help to make it cosy in the winter. It is probable that guests will restrict themselves to the warmer seasons; that is why we have put a door at the bottom of the stairs – to retain warmth at ground level."

"Will the cooking and heating be all electric? queried Sue.

"No, to reduce the load on our limited electrical supply, we have planned to install a gas instant water heater and a gas cooker fed from a bulk tank. Heating in the lounge will be by an enclosed wood burning stove. This diverse energy use has the advantage that failure of one can temporarily be covered by another."

"That seems like a good idea," declared Sam. "I see the cottage is angled to give sun to the kitchen and study in the morning whilst reserving the evening sun for the lounge."

"That is so," agreed Sir Richard. "But I must warn you, except in the high summer, you'll experience considerable cut-off due to the terrain."

"I'm not sure I understand what you mean by that," Sue admitted.

"Alan talked of this," Sam reminded her. "When the sun is not at its height, it passes behind the mountains so that we don't receive direct benefit."

"It's not too bad in this case," Sir Richard explained. "The southern aspect is down a limb of Loch Quoich. It is actually quite pleasant. You'll be blessed with more direct sun there than we are here. Tell me, Mrs Jackson, do you like gardening?"

"Well yes, I'm no expert but I like to see a nice lawn for sitting out, surrounded by flower beds interspersed with attractive shrubs and perhaps a small rockery."

"Good! What we had in mind was to protect the area with a tall deer fence, but to avoid this being too much of an eyesore we'd position it downhill to the south and to the west. The north side will be bounded by the existing buildings which will be converted into a double garage for your use and a business office where all the planning and draughting can take place."

"The byre in which you sheltered," he continued, "will be left with access from outwith the fence so the pony trekking parties can still make good use of it without disturbing your privacy."

"I must say," commented Sue, "you do seem to have thought of everything. I'm really looking forward to moving in. How long do you think it will be before it is ready?"

"I'm afraid it will be six months. We'll start as soon as you've seen the site, this morning, and you formally approve the layout, but the winter is nearly upon us. It is hoped that, before the bad weather sets in, we'll complete the main structural alterations; then it depends on the severity of the winter."

"Where is the temporary accommodation?" enquired Sam.

"At the farm across the water from here. Work is already well in hand to modernise the cottage and convert the associated buildings into a series of flats. These can be used as temporary homes when needed, then subsequently, let out for holidays."

"May we have a look round on our own?" Sam suggested.

"Certainly; my Range-Rover is at your disposal for the morning. Take these plans and the large scale maps and go up to the site. Nobody will be there but you will find marker posts setting out the proposed fence line and pegs indicating the extension to the cottage. If you call in at the farm on the way back, one of Andrew MacPherson's men will show you the farmhouse which is almost ready for you. Lunch is between one and two. Oh by the way, there are two sets of waterproofs and Wellington boots in the car. I hope they will keep you dry."

Leaving the house, they dashed across the drive to the waiting vehicle in an attempt to defeat the efforts of the cloud-borne spray-nozzle. As they set off up the tortuous hill, they realised that this was the first time they had been alone together on the estate; and it would be nice to be able to pass comment on what they saw without first choosing their words.

One advantage of an area such as they were travelling through was the ease with which one could follow a chosen route; there was virtually no alternative.

Twenty-five minutes from starting they were drawing up in front of their future home.

"Oh, it looks very small," Sue declared disappointedly.

"Hang on, lass. You are looking at the original cottage," Sam pointed out. "Wait while you get this wet gear on so that we can brave the elements for a closer look."

After sorting out his and hers, they donned the borrowed clothing.

"Eeee, you do look a duck in that outfit," Sam teased her; "It's far too large."

"That's because I am slim and petite," she boasted in reply. "Anyway, the weather is only fit for ducks, so I am appropriately attired."

"Here are the pegs showing the extensions," Sam pointed out as they went round the back. "Now let's see. That is the lounge, that's the downstairs bathroom and there's the study."

"Oh that's all right then. That'll make it a whole lot bigger," Sue admitted, "so more or less half of the existing cottage will be kitchen. That's nice. I do wish I could understand drawings. I'm beginning to see how it will be now. I couldn't before."

"Well," teased Sam, "it wouldn't do if everybody was a genius, like your husband."

"Be off with you, slave, and show me where this horrible fence is going to be, then."

"Right down there, look. There's the marker posts he mentioned."

"Surely, that's not going to interfere with our view," she suggested.

"No, I wouldn't think so. It's far enough away and, being down hill, we'll see right over it. Mind you, I wouldn't want that view spoiled," Sam said, as he realised the rain had stopped and the visibility cleared. "I think the weather-man in the sky is playing games with us. That is just beautiful, even with the wind whipping up the loch."

"I agree," said Sue. "We are lucky to be coming to a place like this. I just hope her ladyship doesn't spoil the situation; she seemed very severe this morning.

"Perhaps she just got out of bed the wrong side," Sam suggested. "Don't let it worry you. Just be wary of her until we've sized her up."

They returned to the Range-Rover, stripped off the cumbersome protective clothing, and drove back the way they had come. Now that the rain had stopped and the clouds were already lifting, they enjoyed the steep descent to the farm. Busy waterfalls abounded on both sides, their beauty compensating for the drenching they had briefly suffered.

Andrew MacPherson, who turned out to be a local contractor as opposed to an employee, was himself at the farm. He gave Sam a genuine welcome handshake

Highland Haven

and insisted he be called Andy. He showed respect to Sue by doffing his well-worn peaked cap.

The red faced, broad shouldered boss was delighted to hear they approved the proposed work in the cottage. He would be given the contract. Eagerly he showed them around the farmhouse to display the quality of his workmanship; obviously aware that, in due course, Sam would be the one authorizing sub-contract work.

The farmhouse, although not as pleasant as their future home, was quite roomy, with all mod cons and, Sue decided, very satisfactory as a home for three months. In fact, she would have been happy to live there on a permanent basis had they not been offered Alltbeithe.

"What about electricity?" Sam asked Andy. "There's no mains supply here, is there?"

"Och no, we'll be installing a diesel generator in that building across the road," the big fellow replied, as they went back to the car. "His 'Lordship' has some idea about a hydro-electric scheme to feed all of Kinloch Hourn but we are to fit the 'genny' for now. If you're the engineer, maybe he wants you to sort it out."

"Maybe so," Sam agreed as they drove away to seek lunch.

"Do you know anything about hydro-electric schemes?" Sue asked.

"Not a lot," Sam admitted. "Like all engineering problems, it has to be tackled with logic. What do we know? What do we need to know? Do we have contact with someone who can advise? Having basically surveyed one's own resources, then the problem is examined, bearing in mind what we are trying to achieve. Reviewing basic physical laws; considering whether or not the objective is possible. If yes, then examining the practical problems. Having decided on one or more possible solutions to the overall requirement, it is then necessary to investigate cost and the time it will take to complete."

"Ask a simple question and I get a lecture", groaned Sue. "I must say though, it all sounds very complicated, particularly if you're not familiar with that sort of work."

"Not really, let's look at this hydro-electric scheme, as an example", Sam suggested. "You know, without any engineering knowledge, that a high rainfall is necessary. We've seen plenty of evidence of that. Of course, actual data would be needed, but that we can get from the Met Office. The next thing is height; we need mountains to hold the rain so that it can be fed by pipe to a much lower level, creating sufficient pressure to drive the turbines. We've certainly got plenty of mountains hereabout; we can see them."

"Now, we must look more closely," he continued. "Using contoured maps, can we find a valley or gorge where water has been collected for us into a stream? There are many around us. So", declared Sam, "it would seem quite reasonable to build hydro schemes in this area. But - wait a minute, there's a snag. The rain

77

Maurice Duffill

doesn't fall continuously and the demand for power varies considerably. What if we all want electricity and the stream has dried up through lack of rain?"

"Can't you build a dam?" Sue interjected.

"Certainly; that is the obvious answer. We can't store electricity - but we can store water. So we move to phase two of our problem. We need to dam up the stream to form a storage reservoir. Dams are obviously very expensive to build so we must look for a situation where a small dam will hold back a large amount of water. Our contour map will show us where."

"We are now at the stage where we can do some preliminary basic calculations. Isaac Newton taught us how to calculate the energy stored in a situation like this. We must now assess if this is sufficient for our needs."

"Eh, hang on," Sue pleaded. "You are confusing me with all this technical talk."

"But you do see, my pretty one, without any specialist knowledge, one can make big inroads into the task by simply using logic?"

"Ah, you're trying to make it sound all very simple and straightforward," Sue said, "but I'm sure you are over simplifying. It can't be as easy as all that or we wouldn't need engineers at all."

"Of course; that was just an outline; there are many other matters to look at. These will bring their own problems, making the final decision quite complex. Is the rock in the area of our chosen reservoir impervious to water? Is it suitable to take the strain of the dam? These questions need the specialist knowledge of a geologist. What size generator should we install? This depends on how much power will be demanded. Will there be high demand for short periods or low demand for long periods? Should the power be transmitted at high or low voltage? This depends on how far it has to travel. There are, of course, many more."

"Ok, ok; you've convinced me," Sue conceded. "Your technical lecture impresses your technically ignorant wife; I just hope you *can* solve all your problems with your brilliant logic."

"Well you did ask," Sam said humbly. "I can't help it if my enthusiasm runs away with me. Let's go and eat. I'm starving. All this fresh air has given me an appetite."

"Voted unanimously," agreed Sue.

The afternoon was spent in the study, with Sir Richard, delving into the objectives of the project, both physical and philosophical. Then, having received verbal approval of the plans for the Jackson home, Sir Richard asked them both to sign a formal document to that effect.

"I have a policy of documentation," Sir Richard explained. "If a matter is important, then it should be committed to paper. It can then be referred to, or

78

checked up on, or amended; having said that, we mustn't become bogged down with paperwork. If there is no use for it, don't write it."

"I'm glad that you take this approach," Sam concurred. "I also find that, should an important question arise or a strong point needs to be made, it is best dealt with in writing; it assists the writer to put over the point, by choosing his words correctly. It also enables the recipient to consider the whole question before taking any action."

"Yes, I agree, which brings me to another point, that of confidentiality. I think, Mrs Jackson, that you have some secretarial experience?"

"Yes Sir," Sue replied. "My typing is not very fast and I don't take regular shorthand, but I do know how to set out a good letter or report."

"The request I make, is that all confidential matters should be handled between you. Any other staff, that may subsequently join the team, should be used for technical and general business purposes. I need a confidant, and as Development Director, your husband shall be that confidant."

"I take it, from those remarks, Sir, that you have no objection to my wife being party to confidential matters." Sam proffered, "discussion with another can often clear an obstacle from the mind."

"Quite so," he confirmed. "The point is, I desire that you should ultimately understand and support my motives in pursuing this venture, so that we can attain success. However, from now onwards, information should be passed only on a 'need-to-know' basis."

"I can understand that Sir, " Sam asserted. "However, that being the case, do you agree that I may ask any question without appearing presumptuous?"

"So long as it is relevant to the project, I agree absolutely. In fact, I encourage it. Do you have an immediate question in mind?"

"Yes Sir, finance. Firstly, how much capital is available at the outset?"

"The quick answer to that is fifty million pounds has been allocated for the initial development period. However, we will need to discuss, at great length, where priorities lie. That capital will not be sufficient to complete all that is in mind. We must, in general, pursue schemes that will bring returns in preference to those that don't. Before you go on," he added, "I must stress that here is an important point of policy. Whereas it is accepted that profitable business is essential to progress, we must not chase the tail of profit to the exclusion of amenity. That would defeat my objective."

"That I can appreciate and I must say, it will be a pleasure to promote a project where financial gain is not the prime motive," Sam enthused. "However, my second question concerns your second condition imposed on my acceptance. How are you able - and why should you wish, to over-ride income tax?"

"I'm glad you raised that because it opens up a whole sphere of policy. There are three reasons. Firstly, after much negotiation and canvassing at the highest level I have secured agreement, for a temporary period at least, that income tax shall be superseded by a 'double' profit tax on a corporate basis; all gross profits will be taxed as they are made and then the gross annual profit will be taxed at the end of each financial year. Whereas this may seem like a penalty, the lack of personal tax is an aid to development in these parts by being an incentive for people to repopulate the area, and acting as a magnet to keep them here."

"I must say, Sir," interjected Sam, incredulously, "you must have some very powerful allies to achieve that."

"Shall we say, it didn't come easily," Sir Richard replied. "My second reason is that it will give all participants an opportunity to have a financial share as an inducement, or reward whichever is preferred. All will be encouraged to invest in either the scheme as a whole, or in support of individual projects within the scheme."

"My third reason must be treated in the strictest confidence, since it involves the aspect of my ambitions so far kept an absolute secret. In order to illustrate, to the powers that be, that there are alternative ways of managing a whole country, it has been agreed that we shall be allowed to put my principles to the test of a long term experiment. This concession regarding income tax is an essential first step."

"This is an amazing and exciting revelation," Sam admitted. "I am beginning to appreciate the magnitude of your aims."

"I believe," went on Sir Richard, in further explanation, "that the ideal political state is a delicate balance between capitalism and communism, not a wishy-washy half way house, a recipe using the best ingredients from both systems. Involvement of the whole population, at all levels of society, is essential for the development of a close knit community. Similarly, firm direction by experienced management is necessary in order to guide all the energy to a fruitful conclusion which is financially self supporting."

Sam couldn't contain himself. "Sir, these ideals are marvellous but what is the ultimate aim? What if we are successful?"

"That, for the time being, will remain a secret, even from you. When we have worked together for some while, and developed a close understanding, all will be revealed. In the immediate future your prime task is to generate the necessary atmosphere of purpose; it will be up to you, as the Development Director, to ensure that maximum possible involvement of all concerned is achieved."

"It would appear," declared Sam, "that I have unwittingly, accepted a massive responsibility to you Sir. However, I hasten to add, it is a challenge I willingly accept."

Highland Haven

"Don't let the prospect overawe you," Sir Richard stressed. "I've grown into this thought pattern over a number of years, you are just being introduced to it. Let me, by way of example, divert the topic to religion. No, I don't propose to burden you with a sermon; sufficient to say that my religious beliefs might properly be described as non-conformist. However, the need for a church in this developing community is evident."

"The church should bring together the whole populous, not divide it by differing rituals of service. A Minister, of no rigid religious trait, as is the case of a military padre, would have to be appointed. The church itself should be built by voluntary effort. If the architectural team design the building to meet an agreed form, and the cost of materials is met by the project, then everyone should be encouraged to assist in building it. This then would truly be the church of the community."

"This is something the ladies can involve themselves in," volunteered Sue. "It would tie in nicely with any social groups that are formed. We could assist with the actual construction as well as working on decoration. Perhaps we could create a great tapestry."

"My wife tends to run before she can walk," Sam propounded, a little embarrassed at the vision of her competing with Bayeaux.

"Point taken," Sir Richard replied. "Don't forget though, without enthusiasm we'll get nowhere. It's your job to direct it into useful channels rather than dampen it down."

"However, I think that's probably enough to dwell on for the moment. Tomorrow, I'd like to go into some of the physical schemes I have in mind and hear any thoughts and ideas you may have so far."

They left the study bursting with excitement, deciding to go out for a walk - if weather permitted - before changing for dinner.

After the night and morning of rain, it was very pleasant in the late afternoon, proving their friend Alan Fraser to be correct when he warned of sudden changes. This change was definitely for the better, so it worked both ways.

"Oh, Sam," said Sue as they strode out arm in arm, "it's all so exciting, it's positively frightening. I'm overwhelmed."

"I must admit, it's a bigger project than I imagined. Not so much from the engineering point of view but this political or humanistic aspect I never contemplated," Sam confessed. "Mind you, it seems to be a great idea. It's awesome though, like creating a notable moment in history. It'll either go down as a failed attempt at political reform or be signposted as a great turning point in the husbandry of a nation."

"You make it sound even more important. I don't know if we are competent for such worldly affairs," Sue contended.

Maurice Duffill

"Don't forget, great statesmen and other world renowned figures are only people, human beings who have applied themselves successfully to a task. They were inexperienced children, once upon a time," Sam propounded. "Regarding the degree of importance, it is incalculable. If the project is successful, politicians of all colours must take note. It would be bound to affect future thinking - the world over."

"I think we should leave the discussion at that for now. It seems to be getting more frightening," Sue pleaded. "Do you know what I would like to do? Have a vicious game of tennis to knock all of this out of mind for a while."

"Well, we've just about got time before dinner. ABOUT TURN." demanded Sam, setting a brisk pace back to the lodge.

At breakfast, Sam reflected on the marvel of physical exercise combined with sleep. The awesome tensions of yesterday had completely left him and, evidently Sue. They were keen to resume discussions with their new chieftain.

"I think we should start the session this morning by explaining the basic organisation as I see it," Sir Richard declared. "Obviously as Chairman of 'The Quoich Development Corporation', I head the board. I already have a staff which in general terms should be considered private, or at least not under direct control of the directors. This consists of my housekeeper, Mrs Evans, who is in charge of the whole house, garden, stables, including the Chauffeur/Handyman. Her husband, the pilot, answers directly to me. Then of course, there is my secretary, Miss Fitzroy who, incidentally, has sight of confidential matters but is not a party to such discussions, and finally, my accountant Mr James Donaldson. He will shortly resign from his partnership in Inverness, to be solely concerned with our affairs."

"As Development Director, you - and you alone, apart from Mr Donaldson, will have full access to all project accounts but not, of course to my personal accounts. In keeping with the policy of self containment wherever possible, all personnel should be encouraged to make use of Mr Donaldson's services for their private affairs under his sworn guarantee of confidentiality."

"Do I take it Sir, Mr Donaldson will also be available to the directors to carry out cost analysis exercises regarding various project developments?" Sam enquired.

"Certainly; to all intents and purposes, he will be working for you. The reason for my maintenance of direct control is simply sensible protection of my funds," Sir Richard explained, adding, "No offence intended."

"None taken Sir. No wise person would give such open access to his capital without some safeguard."

"Quite so; now then, as previously stated, you are totally responsible to me for all aspects of the project and I promise, on my part, not to interfere without consultation with you. You and I shall have frequent discussions on progress, future plans, finance and all matters relevant, in addition to the more formal directors' meetings."

"You will have three co-directors responsible to you for – respectively, Personnel - Mr Stewart Slater, Commercial - Mr Hamish Gordon, and Property - Mr Alan Fraser, whom you already know."

"Oh, we are very pleased about that," interjected Sue. "We formed an instant friendship with him and his wife, and my husband has already established Mr Fraser's willingness to work with him."

"I'm pleased to hear that, but please do not let your friendship weaken your resolve to keep our objectives confidential," he warned. "They have already been notified of the commencement date, February 1st, just a month after you move up here. Initially, they will be accommodated in the farm apartments, alongside the house acting as your temporary home."

"Most functions will automatically fall into one of those three categories, or engineering, which is my concern," agreed Sam. "But there will also be an overlap in some cases which, I presume, you will leave me to decide who will be responsible?"

"It is entirely up to you, but you must draw up 'Terms of Reference' for each position so that everybody knows where they stand. I shall prepare just such a document covering your responsibilities - and powers. You will of course need engineering staff quite soon, since a considerable amount of your time and effort will be directed to general matters. Choice of staff I leave entirely to you but again, I have a policy I wish to be pursued with regards to rates of pay. We'll discuss this at greater length some other time."

"Sir, might I suggest a further meeting in one month's time to cover that point, so that further selection of staff can proceed? This will also give me time to consider a basic programme of development and, if possible, I feel that my co-directors should have the opportunity to meet me and decide on their future boss before they commit themselves."

"That is quite a point," he conceded. "It wouldn't do to have incompatibility. I'll have my secretary telephone them and make the arrangements."

"Now then," he continued," regarding specific schemes. On the commercial side, high on the list we have tourism; I envisage self catering chalets, a hotel and restaurant, sports centre and craft workshops. More use can be made of the land, so agriculture and forestry must be developed in spite of the poor climate. To that we must add fish farming, both freshwater and in the sea loch. Do you have any suggestions at this stage, Mr Jackson?"

Maurice Duffill

"Obviously, I will have to rationalise my thoughts since learning of your ultimate objective, but one or two matters are worth mentioning. It occurs to me that it is most important to keep abreast of modern methods and ideas to make this whole venture viable. As a result, I believe an adequate mainframe computer is essential. This would not only be used for accounting but for general project management, the accumulation of data regarding our activities and environment, and for access to other national and international data banks. Having installed this expensive equipment, we would then sell time to other concerns, we could carry out research, for a fee, we could write programmes for sale, and we could arrange training courses. These are all potentially profitable activities which can be carried out in a Highland situation since they do not depend on the state of the environment."

"That sounds plausible." Sir Richard commented. "I must admit, I too felt a centralised computer would be desirable but hadn't realised its potential. That's encouraging."

"Allied to that, we have a communications problem both within the estate and to the outside world. It is not reasonable for instance, in these modern times, that people should not have the benefit of television and its associated facilities. To overcome this, I think a communications tower will be necessary. This would avoid the unsightliness of pole mounted wires everywhere and the wild assortment of aerials common to present day towns. Accepting this as a solution, then make a feature of it. Build it as a mountain top viewpoint with cafe/restaurant and an electrified funicular for access to the base."

"Do you know, I think you've got something there," conceded Sir Richard, "but I must remind you that it will be necessary to initiate the more profitable schemes first, so that they can be used to finance other projects. However, this conversation reinforces my belief that two minds are better than one. We can build on each other's thoughts."

"I'm grateful for your confidence in me, Sir," replied Sam, "but I do need more time to consider other ideas as well as learn more about the area before making further suggestions."

"I do appreciate that, I was really attempting to discover how your mind worked and I see there is plenty of inspiration. When considering a priority list of schemes, we must not lose sight of non-commercial services. Progressively, we will need to establish medical services, security corps to deal with minor infringements from within and to protect people and property from without, and eventually we'll need a school, entertainment facilities, and, of course, there is the church."

Highland Haven

"Yes Sir, then one can add basic needs such as water supplies, sewage disposal, access roads and power distribution. It will be difficult to strike the correct balance. There is a lot of 'chicken and egg' situations."

"You've obviously got a full appreciation of the overall problem. I think, at this point, we'll break for lunch. My wife will join us afterwards, but we'll keep it fairly short; a lot of ground has already been covered."

It was with some apprehension that Sam and Sue entered the study for the afternoon session.

Lady Dorothy opened conversation. "My husband tells me you are full of bright ideas Mr Jackson. It is gratifying to know that we appear to have made the right selection for the position of Engineering Director, but I would remind you that your status has been raised to Development Director - responsible for the whole project."

Sam, getting very hot under the collar, felt he had to say something but was afraid he might be too impulsive. "I'm somewhat at a loss to know where this is leading, Ma'am."

"The point is a town, no matter how large or small, is not just bricks and mortar, or computers and communications; it is a living entity. People are like food, they make it grow. Like a magnet, a town with a good beginning attracts people but then it needs to pulsate. Take away the people and the town dies."

"I understand your viewpoint Ma'am, but unless we provide basic amenities to a standard compatible with modern expectations, we'll not be able to attract anyone."

"That is true. However, I earnestly ask you that in all your plans, you endeavour to bring colour to this community. Colour can be added architecturally, either garishly or subtly. Colour can be added by variety in function, as well as in appearance. All I ask is that we must avoid the pitfalls of modern new towns."

"To further stress my wife's comments," Sir Richard added, "there is, these days, a considerable amount of discussion regarding 'The Standard of Living'. But what is 'The Standard of Living'? Is it measured by what we can buy? Does the number of visits to a show or the local pub have any bearing on the matter? We suspect that what people are really seeking, but don't usually realise it to be so, is an improvement to 'The Quality of Life' rather than their standard of life."

"I know what you mean," volunteered Sue. "This is something *I've* thought about. A countryman, on comparatively low income enjoys simple pleasures of natural beauty, fresh air and the freedom to think. On the other hand, the city dweller rushing about trying to make money gets little real satisfaction from material things and suffers the falseness of the concrete jungle."

"That about sums it up," he conceded. "What we are attempting to do is blend the attributes of the express train and the walker. The express train gets on with the job, keeps to its chosen path, but in dashing here and dashing there it misses a lot of life. The walker, on the other hand, observes most and tends to enjoy what nature has to offer - but takes a long time to get anywhere. He wanders all over the place with very little purpose. It is not for you or me to decide how people shall live, but our aim is to provide the environment in which the *quality* of life can be raised - for those who choose to accept it."

"Mr and Mrs Jackson will be thinking we are bigoted moralists," Lady Dorothy declared. "However, at the risk of confirming that impression, I would have you ponder this: the silent majority are usually led by the vociferous few, simply because it takes a certain amount of theatricalism to make one's self be heard. Here, at Glen Quoich, we aim to quietly pursue a different way of management, no hard-sell, just persuasion; but by inviting involvement and providing the opportunity, we believe the strong can help the not so strong develop a more congenial way of life."

"Well, I think our attitude has been laboured enough; we'll call a halt," asserted Sir Richard, then turning to Sam, "I've arranged for my secretary to provide a set of large scale maps of the area for you to take with you. These will have the estate boundaries boldly marked. Additionally, there is a copy of the plans of your new home. Oh, and she will give you some data from the Meteorological Office regarding rainfall and snowfall in this area. You may find that of use when considering development schemes."

"Before departing, Sir, I wish to say a few words on behalf of both of us," Sam announced. "It has been a revelation to us to discover the extent of your aims and can fully understand the need for so much secrecy. We are honoured to be the ones chosen for the driving seat, and assure you that absolutely every effort will be made to guarantee success."

"May I add," joined in Sue, "your hospitality exceeds any of our past experience and we hope that, someday, we may have the opportunity to reciprocate."

As they left the study Sam confided in Sue, "I hope that speech-making by us didn't sound too condescending. I presume they realise that all this has come as a bit of a shock when confronted with it at one go. No doubt that was part of the 'treatment'; shock us into the main idea, then expand the detail points later, as the project progresses."

"Ah well", muttered Sue, "That's it for this week-end. The next session will be in a month's time."

"Yes, but that will be a bit different. I'll be in the chair, some of the time. Here's hoping the other directors respond favourably to the challenge and that they accept my approach to managing such a project. I'm going to need their full support and a bit more besides."

CHAPTER 9

For the Jacksons', the month passed quickly. They were both kept busy making arrangements for the sale of the house, visiting friends and relatives for the last time, and attending to the thousand and one matters affected by their imminent departure to inaccessible Scottish regions.

It was as if they were preparing to hibernate to a lost world on the other side of the earth. They knew that, besides the basic remoteness or at least, out-of-the-wayness, neither of them would welcome visitors for quite some time; they would be too busy.

In any case, most of their friends thought they were mad. Throwing away a good position to go and live in the wilds, where everyone knew it always rained, except when it was snowing; a definite sign of being unhinged. It would be unlikely that anyone would be keen to visit, with the exception of those who would seek to gloat over the Jackson's foolhardiness.

So it was that, amidst their preparations to sink themselves into their chosen new life, another week-end flight to the haven in the Highlands came as a pleasant break. This was particularly so since, this time, it would be shared with their new friends, the Frasers.

During their uneventful flight in the now familiar amphibian, Sam and Sue recounted the events of their previous trip north, in particular the horrors of the flight. Sue then excitedly described the proposed accommodation whilst Sam sounded out Alan regarding their relative positions - now confirmed.

It was quite evident that Alan was pleased the top job had gone to Sam since he had not wanted total responsibility but, on the other hand, felt confident in the relationship with his boss-to-be. Everything seemed to be too good to be true. Sam was very relieved that his Property Director was already a close ally. Next to his position this was the most important post, and they would have to work very closely together to ensure success of the project as a whole.

This being just a short week-end visit, the flight had been timed to arrive convenient for lunch which, as they took their places at the table, reminded them all of their first 'mysterious' visit. Again, Sir Richard sat at the head of the table but this time he made his introductory speech while they were still enjoying their aperitifs.

"Welcome once again, ladies and gentlemen, to Quoich. Although, with one exception we have all met before, I suspect that your thoughts previously were not directed to each other so I shall do the honours and introduce everybody."

"On my left, we have Mr and Mrs Jackson. He is to be the Development Director and, as such will be my right-hand man to whom you all will be directly responsible. More about that later," he added, as a general mumble of surprise rumbled around parts of the table.

Sam was quick to notice a particularly sour look from across the other side, just a little further down. 'That didn't please him' he thought, as he recognised the pompous fellow from the pony trek, complete with his blonde bombshell of a wife.

"Next to Mrs Jackson," continued Sir Richard, "Mr Fraser, our new Property Director, together with his wife, Mhairi. At the end of that side, we have our prospective young civil engineer, Mr Mackay and his school teacher wife who, we hope can be persuaded to teach the way of the world to all the children of our scheme."

"That's the young man I was telling you about," whispered Sam into Sue's ear. "He gained a lot of experience with me straight after university. He's quick to learn and has got guts. That's why I suggested he should take this job. Knowing each other's ways will be a tremendous advantage too."

Sue peered down the table to glimpse this well built, rugged looking fellow with a generous crop of hair, both on his chin and his head. 'He's not spent all his time in an office', she concluded. She could hardly see his wife but judged her to be tall with long flowing auburn hair.

With a sweep of the hand, their host continued his introductions. "On my right, the newly appointed Personnel Director, Mr Slater, with his wife, Anne."

This caused agreeable nods and smiles all round as each guest sized up his future colleagues. 'Looks alright', thought Sam provisionally.

"Further down that side, Mr and Mrs Gordon. Mr Gordon is the Commercial Director," announced Sir Richard.

"So, that's who sour face is', thought Sam, 'I'll have to watch you' he murmured to himself. 'I don't trust your wifey either, she's certainly not suited to the rough outdoors.'

"Last but not least, we have our accountant, Mr Donaldson, with his wife completing the sitting. I've made use of Mr Donaldson's professional services for a number of years, through his partnership in Inverness. As of 1st of January he will be joining the team to devote his full expertise to the project."

Each person, knowing he would sooner or later, cross swords with the holder of the purse strings, paid particular attention to this last introduction. Sam noted that he appeared to be the oldest, by far, and wondered whether he would be too set in his ways to adapt to new requirements. 'I wonder if his quill has been sharpened lately', he thought sarcastically.

At this point, Sir Richard rang a hand-bell to summon the soup. "Enough for now," he declared, "enjoy your meal, and then afterwards each will rise in turn to give us a potted autobiography so that we all become acquainted."

"Oh, I don't fancy that," muttered Sue quietly under her breath, intending that only Sam should hear.

"I should point out," added their host, "wives will be excused the ordeal of declaring their innermost secrets to us."

Sue flushed at the realisation that he must have heard her and gave a sheepish half grin in acknowledgement of his announcement.

As the meal was drawing to a close, with the inevitable glass of pure malt, Sir Richard brought everyone's thoughts back in line by suggesting that Sam should set the ball rolling with his exposé.

Rising to his feet, Sam felt the pressure of many pairs of eyes as they all focussed on him, sizing him up, deciding whether or not they liked what they saw.

"Good afternoon everybody; my name is Sam Jackson and my wife here is Sue. I am an engineer who started my working career in electrical switchgear, you know, the equipment for controlling high tension power lines. That was until it was decided that the nation needed me to assist with the potential defence from the communist threat in Korea, rather than the 'potential difference' of the current flow in cables."

"So, 1952 saw me in Royal Air Force blue, to begin my training as a fighter pilot. I gained a commission, but by the time I was qualified to join a squadron, the Korean War was over. Instead of becoming an intrepid air ace, shooting down North Korean Migs, I became one of the unseen night-fighters, chasing away the Russian Bears."

"Late in 1956, I returned to earth but switched my engineering interests to aircraft. After a spell in a design team, I branched out to electrical components, missile transporters, agricultural equipment, machine tools and automation. This wide variety of design disciplines stood me in good stead when I later moved north to assist a prominent company in its transition to modern methods. This was in the field of materials handling and process control."

"Subsequently moving to an old established engineering company, my newly developed expertise was put to the test by the formation of a totally new division. This caused me to be deeply involved with a very wide variety of industries ranging from the manufacture of glass, to flour milling, and from fertiliser production, to putting the batter on fish fingers. I'm afraid my enthusiasm for the variety of problems dealt with is in danger of boring you to tears, so I'll just leave to your imagination the complexities involved."

"I feel that my varied experiences gained whilst managing many projects, both small and large, will serve as a useful reservoir for this most challenging and exciting venture. My wife, Sue, will ably assist me as my personal secretary. Most sincerely, we both hope that together with the rest of the team we can make this project a great success."

Highland Haven

As Sam resumed his seat, the silence of the room was broken by Sir Richard. "Thank you, Mr Jackson. I think you gave us all a good insight into your career and hope we all agree that you seem to have had the right experience to lead us on. Now perhaps Mr Fraser will enlighten us regarding his past endeavours."

Alan followed Sam's example and stood to deliver his biography in brief. He explained his training as a surveyor in a rural community in the south of England, and how he joined the management team of a large estate. Having been with the one employer most of his working life, his standing grew until some years ago he became the General Manager.

Not only had he many years experience of building maintenance even including the restoration of a castle, his sphere had extended into farm management. With six successful farms to his credit surrounding the estate-owned hamlet, which was also his responsibility, he felt himself well prepared to manage the property and land development for this project. He did concede the need to clue himself up on hill and fish farming. He concluded his summary by highlighting his wife's experience with herbs and other wild flora which she would be able to convert into perfume, health creams, and other medicaments.

As Alan sat down, their host jokingly commented that Mrs Fraser was the first female witch doctor he had ever come across.

Not waiting for a cue, the rather suave Hamish Gordon now rose to his feet determined to create a good impression in front of his new colleagues - or at least their wives.

"We've just been hearing of noble achievements in engineering and property management but, without a demand for services or products, they would have nothing to do. It is this realisation that caused me to go into salesmanship as soon as I left college. I tried a number of fields until I found my niche with a large brewery group."

"It was as a result of my experience in that field that I developed an interest in hotel management and took over one of the group's larger hotels when the opportunity arose. This, in turn, led me to the holiday trade and back to salesmanship."

"Prior to accepting this position as Commercial Director, I was area manager for a large holiday company responsible for anything from package tours to tourist gimmicks."

"I've great plans to develop tourism based on water sports, hill walking, shooting and fishing. This will lead to all manner of commercial opportunities ranging from hotels and restaurants to shops and garages. I just hope the engineers and builders can keep up with my needs."

"Does he really," whispered Sam down the table to Sue and Alan, "I can't see me enjoying working with this opinionated character."

"No - but he's handsome," chided Sue.

God's gift to commercial enterprise sat down, then immediately stood up again, to say, "Oh, by the way, this is my wife - Sylvia," promptly sitting down again.

This caused Mhairi Fraser to observe. "She obviously comes low down on his list of priorities."

"Thank you, Mr Gordon," acknowledged Sir Richard. "Perhaps Mr Slater would follow?"

The tall, comparatively slim Personnel Director designate, sitting opposite to Sam rose slowly, gathering his thoughts.

"In my previous capacity as Personnel Manager I've often subjected candidates to this technique of having a talk-in, one can learn so much. Now the boot is on the other foot - it's my turn."

This caused some sadistic smirks around the table.

He continued, "I started my career as a solicitor and for a few years soldiered on with no real spark. It happened that I had a series of cases having a common aspect, which caused me to consider a change. A claim of 'wrongful dismissal', followed by a contractual dispute, and then an industrial accident claim, all occurred within a twelve month period."

"I found it most interesting to investigate the background to each case, trying to assess the opposing views. I realised that such matters were close to human concern; lives would be significantly influenced by the outcome. This was what was lacking in the bulk of my work, conveyancing, routine wills and dry formal agreements were devoid of personality."

"The turning point came when a company of some standing, for whom I had acted on many occasions, was looking for a new Personnel Manager. After considerable heart searching and discussion with my wife, Ann, I applied for, and subsequently secured the position; I've never looked back since. My investigative approach supported by my legal experience seems to be a good combination. Disputes have been minimal and I have enjoyed helping along the future of the company as well as many of the employees. This project offers me the opportunity to build relationships right from square one. I just hope I can support the team satisfactorily. Thank you."

"I like him," commented Sam. "That's the first time I've met a personnel bod who wasn't a jumped up clever dick, like handsome Hamish over there."

"His wife looks very pleasant too," agreed Sue as they gazed across at a fair, bespectacled rather naive looking young person. "She sang in Gaelic at the Cali, I mean Cayli or whatever. Do you remember?"

"The word is Ceilidh and I do remember," admitted Sam. "I must say she had a very nice voice but what she sang about I wouldn't know."

Highland Haven

"Our accountant will now introduce himself," dictated their host.

James Donaldson demonstrated his overweight stature as he struggled to his feet and surplus skin was set flapping about his cheeks as he stuttered his opening remarks.

"I - I don't re - really know how to b - begin. I've not had an exciting career such as those we've been hearing about; qu-quite the contrary - that's why I decided to accept the challenge offered by Sir Richard. You see, I've been with the same firm of accountants ever since I qualified. The high spot was when I was made a partner."

"It seemed to me that, if I had to re-learn my trade to keep up with this computerised electronic era, I would be well advised to make a fresh start. All the records would have then been stored in a compatible form removing the need for tedious transposition. I had been discussing, with my wife Morag, the feasibility of breaking away from the partnership to go-it-alone, when this project settled matters."

"Sir Richard and I have, over many years of association, built a firm trust in each other. This is highly valued and makes a good foundation for new beginnings. I look forward to working with you all on this most worthwhile venture and hope you will entrust me with your personal affairs as well as the business. I - I do assure you absolute confidentiality, e - even from our mutual boss."

As he sat down, most of those at the table looked for a reaction from Sir Richard and observed a nod of approval supported by an acknowledging wave of the hand.

"His appearance belies his character," Sam commented. "He's more alive than he looks."

"I think," Alan interjected, "this project is what he needs to get him out of a fatal rut. It'll make him, or break him."

"Our newcomer, Mr Mackay, is the only one left," noted their host, "but since he hasn't yet agreed to join us, it is up to him whether or not he wishes to 'expose' himself to us."

"I think," said Angus Mackay, as he rose to his feet, "having heard everybody else's potted history, it is only right you should hear mine - particularly since it is such a small pot."

"After leaving university, I joined Mr Jackson, your Development Director, for some post graduate experience. I found this introduction to industry most useful but then sought work having a greater civil engineering content. This I found with the North of Scotland Hydro-Electric Board. Dams, power stations and roads I found most interesting but, by the time I joined them, there was little new work, it was mainly routine checking and maintenance."

Maurice Duffill

"A project out in the middle-east provided the solution. I succeeded in gaining an Assistant Engineer's post supervising the construction of a complete new town on the Persian Gulf. This was most challenging, but my new wife Fiona, and I, felt this was not the place to start a family and jumped at this opportunity to come back to the U.K."

"Mr Jackson offered me the chance with this project when he discovered his own position was rather more than just Engineer. I hope to convince Sir Richard that I can handle the job and trust I shall not let any of you down. My wife is a qualified school teacher and would be happy to run the proposed primary school. Thank you for your attention," he concluded as he sat down.

"Thank you, Mr Mackay. Your short career sounds most interesting," declared Sir Richard, as he prepared to leave the table," and now I propose you all take this opportunity to become better acquainted with each other. I wish to have further discussion with Mr Jackson. If the men will gather in the library at three o'clock we'll have a further meeting, this time chaired by your Development Director. My wife will join the ladies in the study at that time for an informal discussion."

Sam left his wife in the company of Alan and Mhairi as he hurried after Sir Richard to his office.

As he closed the door behind him Sam found his new boss already seated behind his large oak desk. Sir Richard wasted no time.

"There are two or three matters I wish to discuss with you," he began "Firstly, I must say, your choice of Mr Mackay for the engineering work seems most suitable. Young, keen and yet with appropriate experience. However, the choice is entirely yours. Although I will be most pleased to chat with him I have no desire to interview him. This goes for any other appointments - they are your responsibility."

"This leads me to a most important point of principle; that of salary scale. I believe most strongly, that disputes and jealousy will be minimised if a carefully balanced scale is adopted. Each person should be rewarded in direct proportion to his worth, whether he is a boffin or a buffoon. The difficulty is in making the appropriate evaluation."

"I agree Sir, it is a universal problem," agreed Sam.

"Well, I have given considerable thought to this matter, over a number of years," Sir Richard continued, "and I think the answer lies with a system of points. It is this system I wish to put to the test now. Ideally, as each youth leaves school, a log-book should be issued showing his or her attainments. A credit of points is then given, in proportion."

"I see, Sir, instead of claiming so many GCEs, or similar, a number of points would indicate the standard." Sam acknowledged. "But, wouldn't that be too general? It wouldn't indicate in what subjects the pupil had been proficient."

94

Highland Haven

"That is true, but this is only the start. It simply shows the ability, or otherwise, to learn. It shows the willingness to advantageously use what is offered - tuition and experience. The youth now has the opportunity to increase his points allocation by going on to college, or taking a special course such as an apprenticeship, or attending evening classes or even completing a recognised correspondence course."

"Specialist training, of little value generally, would have points allocated in that particular category. As years of experience are gained, regardless of further training, recognition is given by further credits. This then strikes the balance between academic accomplishments and the wisdom generated by involvement. Higher levels of responsibility generate annual points at a greater rate."

"What about work involving danger or discomfort?" Interjected Sam.

"Whilst any person was engaged in such work, temporary bonus points would be added which are withdrawn once that condition ceases to apply. A coal face worker would receive bonus points for danger, dirty conditions and for unsociable hours. A deep sea diver would receive an even greater danger bonus together with a substantial inconvenience bonus for having to be away from home, but he would not have the benefit of dirt bonus."

"This approach may seem terribly rigid to you, but it does have substantial advantages. If such a scheme was adopted nationally, it would be necessary to negotiate the level of points for each new activity - once only. Thereafter, if a particular person seeks to improve his standing, it would be up to himself to raise his points level. This can be achieved by further relevant education, added experience, assuming greater responsibility or changing to a more hazardous or inconvenient job. He knows, at all times, where he stands."

"This seems reasonable, but who decides the relationship between points and pounds? How is the actual pay settled?" Asked Sam.

"Beside the scheme being a means of establishing a relationship between skills, it acts as an incentive to do more and it also serves as a means of controlling the economy."

"You see," he continued," it is the government of the day that decides the value of a point. Now, just consider the usefulness of that authority. Suppose the nation was having difficulty gaining exports, by declaring a reduction in the value of a point everybody takes a cut in salary; this reduces costs and so making us more effective. Everybody suffers proportionately. Similarly, if the country is enjoying buoyant balance of payments, the value can be raised giving a benefit to all."

"Isn't this like changing the value of the Pound?"

"Similar; but with one distinct difference; if the Pound is devalued then all material values drop relative to world rates. Consequently, imports are dearer causing adverse effects on the economy. The only material change associated with a change in points value is personal purchases abroad, such as holidays."

"That does seem to be the case, I must admit. This whole concept needs time to soak in. It comes as a totally new idea to me," conceded Sam. "There is one thing though; given two people carrying out the same function, one would normally be found a better employee than the other. The system tars everyone with the same brush."

"I agree; we've covered my rather revolutionary proposal somewhat hurriedly. There are many details we have not yet covered. My written thesis here will help you gain further insight. However, in answer to that particular point, merit points are available for special credit, where due, perhaps at year end, in lieu of the traditional salary review."

"What I ask you to do is to apply the principles laid down in those documents, the board of Directors acting in lieu of the government to set the value. In order to establish a starting point for the allocation of points, analyse your own qualifications and experience, apportioning points where appropriate. Regarding our agreement to provide your house free, treat that as a merit award. I'm sure, with your mathematical knowledge, you'll be able to work backwards to establish suitable allocations of points to your fellow Directors as well as the common points value. Here are summaries of their attributes and the agreed salaries. Please keep me informed of any difficulties with the scheme."

"Certainly, Sir," Sam breathed, as he tried to catch his breath.

"Now it is approaching three o'clock, so we'd better get over to the library. I want you to take the chair, I shall sit to your side as adviser, should that be necessary. If you explain the immediate plans the way you see them, your colleagues will quickly taste your authority and respond accordingly. This I feel, is necessary, so that you do not appear to be tied to my apron strings. I also need confirmation that I may go about my other affairs leaving the project in capable hands. My ultimate objective must, I remind you, remain a secret between us."

"I must say, you are really throwing me at it," admitted Sam, "but I give you my assurance that everything within my power will be done to realise your ambitions."

Precisely at three o'clock Sam Jackson took his place at the head of the library table, while Sir Richard took a seat to his side. All the directors and the engineer, Angus, were already seated in readiness at the table, diplomatically leaving the head vacant for whoever was to chair the meeting.

Taking the hot seat, Sam started cautiously. "Gentlemen - colleagues, as you are aware, this project is about the creation of a community here in the highlands. A new community designed to bring back vitality to this currently sparsely populated region. The difficulties before us are numerous, not least of which is

Highland Haven

striking the right blend. We are looking for a menu of development which combines the traditional with the modern; one which re-appraises the land use to give a greater beneficial output whilst, where possible, preserving the character of the hills and glens; a menu which enables more people to have the benefit of the joys of wild terrain."

"This is a very tall order and we are the team charged with the job of ensuring that these aims are achieved. To realise this balanced mix we must, first of all, effect a jell between ourselves. We've just been hearing, at the lunch table, of our varied skills and experience. My job, as I see it, is to make the best use of these assets by generating harmony and close association between us all. Here, I need your help."

"Before you go on," interjected Hamish Gordon, "why you? As I said at the table, unless a market is created - a need generated, there is no purpose in doing anything. It seems to me that the lead should come from the commercial sector."

"It is true that, unless anyone 'buys our product', the project will fail - simply from the lack of finance. Similarly, if our product is poorly put together nobody will want to buy. This is the whole point, without 'playing to the crowd'; we've got to create that subtle blend between supply and demand."

"You see, Mr Gordon, none of us is any more important than another. My job is to plan and co-ordinate, to persuade and cajole. On the other hand, it is your job to promote commercial potential. Although we have adequate finance to 'get the show on the road', the funds won't last forever. We need you to ensure we receive the highest income into the kitty by directing us towards the more profitable pursuits. Having aided in the process of deciding our priorities, it will be up to you to publicise and sell what we have available.

"Likewise, we look to Mr Fraser to guide us in the best use of the land and water resources. Should particular areas be used for farming or fun? Where can the tourist trample and where best should the inhabitants inhabit? These are just some of the obvious areas of consideration."

"Who decides on priorities?" persisted Hamish. "I may propose a sports complex and Mr Fraser objects to the interference with his beloved deer or sheep."

"This is a combined project managed by us working as a team. Whereas ideas are most welcome, and in fact are sought, we all must be prepared to consider other aspects. We shall engage in frequent meetings to discuss the interface between different disciplines, to avoid the tendency of becoming a cluster of separate cells. We must work together, and confide in each other. There is no competition between us, no reason for jealousy. If a decision goes against you, it should only be due to greater priorities - to the benefit of the project as a whole. That, in turn, is to your benefit."

"Whilst on the subject of meetings, all formal meetings will be minuted and will be preceded by a written agenda. This does not mean they should be stiff and totally inflexible. The object is to serve as a memory aid in an endeavour to ensure that each director is au fait with what is going on in other spheres. This way, each is given every opportunity to take advantage of another's actions or, if necessary, raise objections."

"Well, gentlemen, if there is nothing urgent to be raised by anyone else, I'll close our first get together by advising you that every effort will be made to provide permanent homes, in agreed locations, as soon as the weather improves towards the summer. However, apartments are in an advanced stage of readiness and will certainly be available for your commencement date of 1st February."

"This evening after dinner, we shall be presented with a slide show by Mr Ted Evans who, besides being the company pilot, is an accomplished photographer. The subject will be *'This Area - the Topography and the Wild Life'*. I'm sure we shall all find it most interesting as well as useful background information. Tomorrow morning will be devoted to viewing your new accommodation."

As they left the room to rejoin their wives, Sam drew young Angus Mackay to one side. "While the others visit the flats tomorrow, I'd like you and Fiona to join my wife and me for a short drive. That will be the opportunity for me to fill you in and see if we can firm up a definite offer."

"A good start," commented Sir Richard, as he and Sam left the room. "You dealt with Mr Gordon's objections quite smoothly, I thought. I hope I didn't make a mistake in selecting him; he does seem to be a little too full of himself. Mind you, many sales orientated types seem to have that trait. I suppose it is a necessary characteristic."

Rejoining Sue in the lounge, Sam heard that Lady Blaisdale had led a discussion to find out who were the committee types and who were the practical hobbyists. She'd explained that this project was going to be very demanding for the men and that it would be wise for the ladies to work as much as possible on the social side of the development. This would have the dual advantage of keeping them occupied whilst their husbands were busy, and making a positive contribution to the whole venture.

"How did the blonde bombshell, Mrs Gordon, respond?" Sam asked.

"Do you know, she never said a word the whole time; she seemed to be totally preoccupied with her nails," Sue reported. "I thought she was very rude. I know it is really her husband who is employed here, but she should take more interest - particularly when the boss's wife is doing most of the talking."

"Let's change for dinner," Sam suggested. "I'm hungry."

CHAPTER 10

During the customary fine evening meal, conversation was moving freely between all present in a generally relaxed mood. One contributory reason was the absence of Sir Richard and Lady Dorothy; they were on their way south, to business in London. The combined effect of not being 'watched' and knowing that their futures were opening up to interesting, potentially profitable new horizons was almost euphoric.

The lunchtime exposé session had been most useful in breaking the ice; nobody felt threatened and all were keen to learn more of each other. Mrs Gordon, however, seemed to limit her sphere to discussion of the fact that she would have to find a new hairdresser now that she was moving away from the only man that could satisfy her whims.

Hearing her exaggerated chatter from further down the table reminded Alan they had first come into close proximity during the traumatic pony trek. "That lassie is never going to settle up here," he commented to Sam. "I wonder if her husband, Hamish, will find excuses to take her off with him by arranging 'business' trips to wherever."

"Quite likely," conceded Sam. "Whatever happens, I can't see her becoming involved with these social committees that Lady Dorothy is so keen about."

"You never know," interjected Sue, somewhat sarcastically, "she may give talks on fashion and put on mannequin parades."

"Enough of her," Sam demanded. "It's time we took ourselves off to the slide show." Rising from his seat he addressed all the guests. "Ladies and gentlemen, let us repair to the library so that Mr Evans can entertain and educate us with his slide show. Bring your drinks; further supplies will be available with the coffee."

"Quite the little boss-man, aren't we?" chivvied Sue, quietly.

"We'll have less of that," retorted Sam. "I've enough to contend with from the commercial cowboy. I don't want dissension from you as well."

"I was only joking. Don't be so jumpy. What's happened to the Jackson sense of humour?"

"I'm sorry, but I don't think you know what it is like to be in charge. It is very lonely to be out in front - at the sharp end. When one is getting started again, with a new team, it is particularly ticklish. I've got to establish authority - that which is felt to be reliable, but no way do I wish to brow beat; everyone must be given maximum scope to do their own thing."

"Come off it love, we are only going to watch some slides."

"Just bear with me. Anything I say or do at the moment is being noted. I'm on trial. Sir Richard has decided I'm the man for the job, but the others haven't; they are still assessing me. Give it time and I shall convince them; all except one, maybe.

"Good evening all," greeted Ted Evans, as everyone settled into comfortable armchairs. "I hope you find my slide-showing of interest. It is intended as a brief enlightenment of the area so that you may understand it, appreciate it, and enjoy it to the full. I shall begin by showing a slide taken of a model of the immediate district so that you may become oriented with the geography."

"As you see, this glen lies west to east - from the sea to the massive geological fault known as 'The Great Glen' or, to quote the Gaelic - Glen Voor, spelt M H O R - M & H together are pronounced as a 'V'. Mhor means 'big', so we have Glen Big or 'The Great Glen'. So much for an introduction to Gaelic words which you will find attached to all the mountains and streams - or more correctly 'burns' - in the west highlands."

"As you have seen, the mountains of the western end rise to the north and to the south of the loch outside this house - Loch Hourn, The Loch of Hell, so called because, except in summer, it does tend to be rather dark due to being overshadowed by the steep rock faces. At twelve miles long, it is the furthermost incursion of tidal waters into the mainland of Britain."

"The centre section of the district surrounds Loch Quoich, the large expanse of water on which we landed some of you in our amphibious Widgeon. This lake, or loch, was made very much larger than nature had intended by damming the out-flow from the original in order to feed a hydro-electric power station. In fact the water level has been raised approximately one hundred feet, submerging a very fine shooting lodge in the process."

"The water from Loch Quoich, instead of flowing west into the sea, now flows east and passes, via the power station at Kingie, into the River Garry. Incidentally, if you look at a map, you will not see the hamlet of Kingie. In its place you will find Coillie Mhorgil – I'm not sure why; there is a Glen Kingie with its River Kingie merging with the River Garry but the Ordnance Survey do not seem to recognise Kingie as a place to live. A possible explanation is that it was built as a contractor's temporary village, but some of what was temporary has become the permanent residence of stalkers and gillies"

"Moving further east, the Hydro-Electricity Board of the 50's dammed up the salmon and trout-laden river at its down-stream, eastern end to develop Loch Garry which feeds a power station on the shore of one of the Great Glen lochs - Loch Oich, at Invergarry. The terrain to the north and south of Loch Garry is less rugged than that around Loch Quoich but is still very exposed and uninhabited. Be very cautious before contemplating any hill walking; never go alone."

Highland Haven

"We'll leave our picture of the topographical model and run through a series of slides of a more visual nature. Most visitors, including the salmon, approach from the east - out of The Great Glen. Our selection of slides does the same, starting with the ruined castle at Invergarry. This was the gathering place of the McDonnells, the hardy highland clan of Glengarry. There are many bloody tales surrounding the activities of the inhabitants, particularly as a result of their support for Bonnie Prince Charlie who stayed at the castle on more than one occasion."

"As can be seen by this next view, the village itself is quite small, boasting only one wee shop, a petrol station, two hotels, and one and a half churches."

"How can there be one and a half churches?" Hamish Gordon scathingly interjected.

Quite unperturbed, Ted continued with his talk - giving reasonable explanation for his comment. "The Parish Church, shown here, is Church of Scotland which holds frequent services and serves as a social as well as spiritual anchor for the whole glen. However, there is another church, quite small, which is Roman Catholic but this is only occasionally used, since at Fort Augustus just seven miles along the Great Glen, there is an active Benedictine abbey where most Catholics prefer to worship."

"When we came by car through Invergarry," Sam observed, "I noticed a football field on the left-hand side which had very small goal posts but it was a large pitch. Are the locals midgets that can run fast?"

"I can answer that," countered Hamish - eager to put one over Sam. "Civilised games such as soccer haven't penetrated these parts. It isn't a football field, it's a Shinty pitch. Shinty is a variation of hockey - played dangerously with curved sticks which are triangular in section so that the ball can be lifted for very long shots."

"Yes," confirmed Ted, "it's a game for the hardy that have no regard for bodily pain; bruises and gashes are normal, broken limbs common. However, it isn't quite true to say that soccer isn't played up here; there is a Highland League, but the glens tend to favour Shinty."

"I mentioned salmon earlier; they come up to Invergarry via the famous Loch Ness and then enter the River Garry just by the power station."

"If there is a dam to make the water come through the power station, how do the salmon swim up the river?" Cut in Sue, "surely they don't swim up the big pipe; they'd get chopped up by the generator."

"I suppose there is a fish ladder, similar to the one at Pitlochry, where they climb from one tank to another", suggested Alan.

"No, there isn't room enough in the gorge for that arrangement. A special lift has been provided which the fish operate themselves".

Maurice Duffill

"Oh, come on, pull the other leg", retorted Sue. "I suppose the salmon go in through the door, press a button with their flippers to select the penthouse, and then cheerfully emerge when the lift arrives at the top."

"I'm not joking; the Bourden lift is quite ingenious. There are two chambers in the dam, one at the top and one at the bottom. A stream of water is arranged to flow down an interconnecting pipe and out into the river. The salmon swim up the stream into the lower chamber. When fish are inside, a detector automatically closes a door at the bottom so that the water floods up the pipe allowing the eager egg layers to emerge at the top. As they swim out, a sensor counts them and when the number out agrees with the number that came in at the bottom, the lower door opens again to await new arrivals. So we have an automatic lift - operated by the fish."

"I'm sorry," admitted Sue, "I didn't believe anyone could be so inventive. Mr Bourden is to be congratulated."

"So it is that here we have a subtle mixture of man's achievement and the natural beauty of nature," continued Ted, as he displayed a slide of Loch Garry. "This tranquil view of the loch, taken from the dam raises the controversial question as to whether or not man-made dams are an eyesore. Personally, I believe they enhance the beauty of the glens by providing a dramatic contrast between the level surface of the water and the rugged peaks on either side. On a windless day, the reflections can be an inspiration to both artist and poet."

"On the north side, a lonely, single track road branches off the main road to the Isle of Skye, to hug the shore of Loch Garry and continuing right up the glen to where we are now. Those of you who came by car will already be familiar with its windings and twistings. Across the water, on the south side, a range of uninhabited mountains begin with the very peaky, 3,000 foot high, Ben Tee - sometimes referred to as The Fairies' Bowling Green."

"I can't imagine that the mountain is flat enough to play bowls," declared Sue.

"No. Quite the contrary," admitted Ted. "It gained that nickname because it is so steep, with a pointed summit, such that boulders often roll down the slopes - like as if there is someone up there playing bowls - fairies perhaps."

"I suppose you're going to tell us that there is a monster sitting in the loch at the bottom, tossing the stone bowling balls back up," interposed Hamish, displaying total disbelief.

"No, but if it makes you happy I will tell you of the legend of the Water Kelpie who lived further up Loch Garry."

"What next?"

"Look, Hamish," Sam angrily retorted, "we are all enjoying this insight into local culture. It could well help those of us who wish to integrate with the traditional way of life here in the Highlands. If you are not interested, I suggest you go and find yourself a quiet corner elsewhere and reconsider your position".

"You're not going to let him talk to you like that", shrieked his wife as she got up from her seat. "Well I'm not", she added as she stormed out of the room.

"I'm damned if I am, I didn't come up here to take orders from the boss's sidekick." The door slammed shut behind him.

"I'm sorry about that." apologised Sam.

"Well we're not", countered Sue. "We want to enjoy the evening, not listen to petty quibbles. Please Mr Evans, tell us about the beast of the loch".

"In a book entitled "Place Names of Glengarry and Glenquoich", which was written by a Mr Edward C. Ellis who used to own the whole of both of these beautiful glens, is the legendary tale of the Water Kelpie. It seems that eight children were left to play on an island in the River Garry while their parents collected hay from the meadow. The children were delighted when a strange animal – with the front half of a bull and the rear half of a fish, came out of the water to join them. Seven of them climbed on his back for a ride but the eldest was more cautious and found that when he touched it, his finger became stuck to its hide. Quickly realising the implication, he reached for a sickle lying nearby and cut off his finger. The beast was so annoyed that he roared off back into the water – taking the seven children to their deaths."

"Oh, how horrible," cried Sue; "I wish I hadn't asked you to tell us about it."

"It may only be a story concocted by parents to frighten their children into behaving themselves; but you never know," added Ted.

"Quite near to where the Water Kelpie is reputed to have lived, there is now a Bailey bridge giving access to crofts across a narrow neck of the loch at Torr na Carraidh. Actually, there is an ancient burial ground there containing the remains of many of the past residents."

"Further up on the right-hand side, you will discover the traditionally built Highland hotel at Tomdoun; it used to be a staging post for horses on the old route to The Isle of Skye. It is 10 miles from a similar one at Invergarry, and another hotel 10 miles further on along a now closed road across lonely Loch Loyne; this is the Cluanie Inn, on the Glen Moriston to Glen Shiel road. Ten miles was about the norm for horses before they needed a rest; so the hotel was really a stopover for our four-legged friends rather than us humans. The Tomdoun Hotel is now mainly frequented by stalkers, fishers, hill walkers and bird watchers."

"Just beyond, is this lovely little church; still used once a month by about a dozen parishioners. We then come to the hamlet of Kingie that we have already mentioned, lying below the great rock dam which has lifted the level of Loch Quoich. The wild, uninhabited country surrounding the loch is the main area of your concern."

Maurice Duffill

"For all this area is, to the unfamiliar, a wilderness; it is full of life. A great variety of animals live hereabouts ranging from the obvious deer and highland cattle to pine martins and wild cats – not domestic cats gone wild but a much larger beast, recognizable by the black and white rings around its tail. Of course birds abound, the lordly golden eagle and peregrine falcons can be seen soaring from the ridges while the red legged oyster catcher strolls along a shallow shore, and black-throated divers cruise the waters. In the winter, whooper swans can be heard chorusing as they circle again and again to keep ice from forming on the surface of their domain."

"I could talk for hours on the subject of wild life in the Highlands and I have drawers full of slides but I think I had better leave you to absorb this quick sample as an introduction. Later, when you have all settled in, I would be only too happy to go into more detail for those who are interested." Then, as a finale, "I thank you for your attention."

"Thank *you* Ted," Sam replied. "I think that deserves a big hand from us all."

As they dispersed, Sam went in search of the renegade Commercial Director, Hamish. Finding him in a corner of the lounge with a half empty bottle of whisky, Sam broached the difficult subject of their business relationship.

"Hamish, we must deal with our mutual problem," Sam opened, "we leave tomorrow and we need to get things settled between us."

"Don't waste your breath," Hamish retorted, "I'm not having any part of your scheme; I thought I was going to be working for a gentleman, not a jumped-up mechanic."

Ignoring the deliberate insult to his status, Sam demanded confirmation of his intentions. "Are you resigning your appointment before we even get started? If so I will need this in writing."

"I shall be writing to Sir Richard – not to you, as soon as I get home," Hamish sneered angrily.

"Don't forget," insisted Sam, "you signed a confidentiality statement. Nothing you have learned here must be discussed elsewhere. This is not to protect *me*; it would be Sir Richard and his vision for the future, which would be compromised should you do so. Rest assured, he would hound you if you violated that commitment."

"Don't fret yourself, big man; I have no intention of lousing up Sir Richard's plans, I don't know what they are anyway. It's you I can't stand. Just leave me and my bottle alone and you'll not hear from me again."

Sam did exactly as requested; he left him to sink himself in a pool of whisky and joined Sue and the others across the room. Having recounted the set-to with Hamish, he added, "I know who I will invite to take his place." Turning to Sue he added, "do you remember meeting Bill Bates from Wetherby? He had good communications skills and could sell anything to anybody. I'll give him a ring as soon as we get home."

"I'll bet you'll not be sorry to see the back of horrible Hamish," offered Alan.

"You can say that again. Anyway, let's discuss more exciting matters. Have you had any thoughts about your domain, Alan?"

"Yes, I have. I don't yet know what the requirements will be for corporate buildings but I had a notion about the housing. What would you think to creating a sort of alpine village by introducing houses made from a combination of timber and stone, the roofs having large eaves and no gutters except at points of entry?"

"It's an interesting suggestion; the style suits the mountain environment, but what leads you to that proposal; sell it to me."

"The benefits," replied Alan, "are that both the timber and the stone are Highland materials readily available; and the style, whilst befitting the area, avoids the alternative of trying to make everything look old – as if they are overgrown crofters' cottages. To combat the difficult climate, I envisaged low level under-floor heating, backed up by a wood-burning stove, and the windows would be double, double glazed."

"What do you mean, double, double glazed?"

"Each window would have a pane of glass on the inner and outer of the frame, and each pane would be of the Pilkington sandwich type which has a sealed void between two sheets of glass. I know this sounds expensive but the saving in fuel will be considerable and the comfort level will be at a maximum."

"I must say, your concept is interesting and worth pursuing. I'd like to see a proposed design and costing as soon as you can, after we get started. Regarding the corporate buildings, these do present a challenge. Quite a variety will be required, yet we don't want to clutter the hillsides with inappropriate modern constructions. An essential need is that of a communications tower carrying microwave dishes, radio aerials and the like; I envisage this would be a computer centre and telephone exchange, making a comprehensive communications centre. Typically these days, a restaurant is incorporated, giving dramatic views whilst dining; this could appeal to tourists and conference visitors, but the thought of a garish monstrosity on a mountain top revolts me. We also need a hotel able to cope with conferences; this, I feel, would be a good income earner. I'll let you dwell on that over the next month to see if you can come up with any bright ideas."

"Quite a problem," conceded Alan. "There will, of course, be the need for a small supermarket, a church, administrative offices and the like. I shall endeavour to be appropriately original with my forthcoming solution," he said, with exaggerated confidence, aware that their two wives were listening with some awe at what was being called for.

"While thinking of future plans," Sam said, turning to direct his comment to Angus, the young engineer designate. "Do you know anything about mountain railways? We need a small gauge link from the loch-side to the regular line between Fort William and Mallaig. This would be a more reliable route for goods and passengers in the winter, and would reduce the pressure on the single-track road from Invergarry during the tourist months."

"I was involved in some railway working in the Middle East but it was neither narrow gauge nor situated in mountains but, if the appointment is mine, I'll get right onto the job of increasing my education."

"Didn't I tell you? The job was yours as soon as you accepted my invitation to come up here. I also know that Fiona is keen to join us and wouldn't let you turn us down. I'll fix you up with some large scale maps to plot the best rail route. We already have outline planning permission, subject to detail approval."

The young couple gave each other an agreeable hug of delighted excitement as they murmured their acknowledgement.

"Before we depart, I must have a natter with Stewart Slater, our new Personnel Director", Sam said, as he left the group to seek out the remaining member of the new executive.

"Ah, there you are Stewart. I'm not sure how much detail Sir Richard discussed with you, so thought it would be a good thing to review expectations before you depart."

"Well," Stewart replied, "all I know is that because my background was in law, he thought my experience could be beneficial to the company and to the personnel employed."

"I think you may be in for a bit of a shock, but hopefully prepared to widen your experience still further. As Personnel Director, not only will you be responsible for providing suitable staff and maintaining a good relationship between them and the company; your sphere of activity will include the establishment of medical services, a college, a primary school, Glenquoich's own church, emergency services, security, and providing entertainment facilities. This, of course, is as well as arranging suitable housing, and being a legal adviser to anyone needing help in that direction."

"Phew! Sir Richard did say the appointment would be challenging, but I had no idea it was to be so all-embracing."

"All the directors have multiple responsibilities which overlap. You will not be left unaided in attempting to achieve your objectives. Coordination of all the different functions is my responsibility, as is the allocation of the available funds. It is important, therefore, that you keep me advised of progress but you must also consult with me if you are in doubt about any particular problem. I hope that we can work together in a companionable team to achieve success in meeting the aims of Sir Richard."

"Well everybody," declared Sam to all in the room, "I'm sure we have all got plenty to think about and, after breakfast we will be dispersing to our homes for the last time. I look forward to our coming together in one month to start on the tasks within this great venture. When you return, you will need to spend time settling in, so I will not expect dramatic action from you during the first week, but I would value an individual meeting with each of you; then we shall start the next week with a full executive meeting to review the state of affairs. Have a safe journey home and I bid you goodnight – au revoir."

CHAPTER 11

While all the participants of Sir Richard's project were dealing with their immediate problems of relocating permanently to the Highlands, events unusual to the area were unfolding. It all started innocently enough by the arrival at The Tomdoun Hotel of four bird watchers armed with high powered binoculars, night glasses, and cameras having long telephoto lenses. This occurrence was not in itself unusual; the region was, after all, a great area of interest to ornithologists; however, something was amiss.

Ted Evans happened to stop off at the bar that evening, on his way home from Fort William. As a keen photographer of Highland wild life and seeing all the equipment, he thought to engage in conversation.

"You certainly seem to be well geared up," Ted offered.

"Yes, we hope to get some good shots," one volunteered.

"Are you hoping for something particular?"

"Yes, we are particularly hopeful of picking up on the pine marten; do you know what area they are nesting?"

"Nesting? They don't live in nests."

"Oh, 'err, 'err, I am not familiar with rare Highland birds myself but understand there are some pine martens in this area."

"They are rare, and there are some in this area but they don't fly."

"How do you mean they don't fly?"

"They are four legged animals, something like a squirrel."

"Err, err, I think you are pulling my leg, like those who say a haggis is a bird with odd legs"

"That's for sure," said Ted in order to minimize the fellow's embarrassment; but it was obvious to him that he was not an ornithologist, or a twitcher as amateur bird watchers are called.

It was just as well Robbie McIntosh wasn't in the bar; he might have had a nervous breakdown. As it was he had just taken another coded phone call from Ullapool and was busy arranging for Angus McGilvery to take his boat to a meeting in The Sea of Hebrides. He then had to go in search of Malcolm Ferguson to arrange the pick-up.

About midnight the supposed ornithologists slipped out of the hotel and drove away in two cars. One car with two people stopped a short way from the hotel where a little used lane branched off towards lonely Loch Loyne. It was driven a little way up, turned around, then parked with lights off. The second car continued all the way past Kingie, past the dam, around Loch Quoich and down the narrow winding road to Kinloch Hourn. Once there, it was driven part way up the drive to the big house then parked facing down the loch with the lights switched out.

Highland Haven

Hours passed then the two men at Kinloch Hourn, hearing the sound of a car descending the hill, watched as it was driven to the pier, parked and all lights extinguished. With their infrared equipment they saw Malcolm Ferguson climb clumsily from the car and retrieve fishing tackle from the boot at the rear. He set it up on the pier but then retreated to the comfort of his car to have a tipple from a whisky bottle.

Another couple of hours passed, with the temperature dropping noticeably but nobody daring to start engines for fear of discovery. The monotony was broken by the sound of a powerful marine diesel followed by the sighting of a bow-wave appearing around the bend of the sea loch.

Immediately, Malcolm Ferguson leaped out of his car, collected his fishing gear, stowed it, and then prepared to catch a line from Angus on the Heather Queen. Long lensed cameras were clicking furiously in an attempt to catch every detail as the mysterious package was passed from boat to shore. Knowing that Malcolm would have to return up the hill, the phoney bird watchers made no attempt to interfere; they wanted his contact.

As soon as the boat was refuelled, it returned the way it had come and Malcolm set off up the hill in his old car. The two watchers followed at a discreet distance, struggling to keep on the difficult road without lights. The passenger made repeated attempts to contact his waiting colleagues by radio but the terrain was not in favour of their transmissions and the calls remained unanswered.

It wasn't until the following car reached the dam that contact was made and the message passed that the target car was approaching them from the west. Alerted the occupants of the second car strained their eyes to gain early warning of the approach. Suddenly, over the brow of a hill, headlights could be seen; they started their engine in readiness but the target never came. They called on the radio to the following car who confirmed that the target had turned off the lane. The waiting vehicle moved forward, just in time to see the target approaching a croft cottage then, dousing his lights, Malcolm got out to be greeted at the door by the expectant Robbie McIntosh.

Both pursuing cars retreated as the two unsuspecting men disappeared indoors. The car that had been following backed off to a secluded lay-by while the other went back to where they had waited before. They got out of the car to watch from a nearby vantage point and saw their colleagues – on foot, checking around the cottage for means of escape, then settle to wait.

Eventually, Malcolm Ferguson was seen to come out of the house and then drive out in his car. He turned down the lane and drove past the concealed onlookers who immediately followed in their car, still with the lights out. They saw Malcolm park at his own cottage a couple of miles down the lane.

Maurice Duffill

Malcolm got the fright of his life when, just as he went in through the one and only door, a car screeched to a halt as the two occupants leaped out to burst into the cottage and hand-cuff him.

Robbie McIntosh didn't fair much better; he was surprised by a knock at the door but before he had chance to answer or do anything, the two men flung open the door and came straight in.

"What the devil is all this demanded Robby," as he leaped up from the table.

"Her Majesty's Customs and Excise," declared the leader, "you are under arrest.

"What the hell for?" Robby indignantly retorted.

"For the illegal importation of substances." Replied the official and then proceeded to give him the official caution.

"What substances?"

"The substances in this plastic parcel." He said grabbing it from the table where it lay between empty whisky glasses – discarded after the usual celebration of another successful sortie.

"There are no substances in there."

"Oh no; then what are all these manoeuvres for, at dead of night?"

"I'm saying nothing."

Disturbed at the thought that they may be on the wrong tack; one of the officers ripped open the parcel, expecting to find drugs, only to reveal computer discs.

"You got these from a Russian ship;" he declared. "This could be treason – that means life."

"I'm saying nothing." Robbie repeated as the blood drained from his face at the thought of the seriousness of his situation.

He was taken roughly out to the car and driven away, just as dawn was breaking. Further down the lane they saw the bulk of Malcolm Ferguson being pushed into the second car to follow them down the glen and away to Inverness for interrogation at the HQ of the Highland police force.

Leaving them sweating in separate cells, the team of four; which were made up of two customs investigating officers and two detectives from the police force, set about furthering their enquiries. About six months previously, a Nimrod aircraft of the RAF had been returning from patrol over the North Atlantic and, running in from the isolated island of Rockall to their base at Kinloss, observant airborne radar operators had noticed a small craft leaving a ship in the middle of the Sea of Hebrides, then weaving a course through the inner isles to the Sound of Sleat. Being at dead of night, or rather the small hours of the morning this seemed somewhat odd; as a result they reported the sighting.

Highland Haven

Coastguard enquiries subsequently revealed that the ship had been a Russian vessel on its legitimate course to Barcaldine to deliver soda-ash and collect alginates. The appearance of the mystery boat raised concern regarding national security; the cold war being at its peak at this time. During the Herring season, a Russian fish factory ship was allowed to anchor in Loch Broom, near the fishing port of Ullapool, a little to the north of the Isle of Skye, but activities surrounding it were closely monitored; was there any connection?

When another shipment was due, security observations were stepped up; the RAF monitored the whole track of the ship as soon as it entered British waters and, besides additional observers around Loch Broom, all public telephone booths in the area had their calls recorded. It was as a result of checking all calls that a link was made to Robbie McIntosh in Glen Garry; this brought the teams of pseudo-ornithologists to the Tomdoun Hotel. Meanwhile, the crew of the RAF Nimrod was able to observe not only the passage of the Ivan Boronovich but they noticed a small, high speed boat leaving Loch Hourn and, after weaving its way through The Sound of Sleat and around the isle of Rhum, it briefly met the Russian ship at exactly 57°N 7°W; it was then seen to return back to Loch Hourn. They continued to monitor the activity even after it had berthed at the head of the loch. Just as the airborne radar operator was about to conclude that the boat had terminated its journey, it moved off from the pier. They followed the boat's track down the loch until it finally berthed at the tiny island of Fraoch Eilean. All this activity was reported, via the coastguard to the police at Inverness.

It was a very surprised Angus McGilvery that was disturbed from his much needed sleep by the arrival of a coastguard patrol boat. Two policemen leapt ashore to arrest him at his cottage just by the boat-house, while a couple of the crew boarded his boat and piloted it away as evidence. Exploding with pleas of innocence, Angus was taken by boat to the Kyle of Lochalsh where he was transferred to a police car for the journey to Inverness; he too was placed in a separate cell awaiting the outcome of further enquiries.

The customs investigators being surprised to find that the parcel that had been the object of so much subterfuge did not contain drugs, were bemused by the result of trying to read the discs when put in the police computer; they contained only gibberish. "It must be in code;" stated one of the investigators, rather obviously. After much discussion, it was decided to send them to the Ministry of Defence decoding centre at Bletchley Park in Buckinghamshire; they had heard how successful the boffins there had been in solving the problem of the Enigma machines during WW2.

After repeated grilling of the three prisoners, it became obvious that Malcolm Ferguson knew nothing; he was merely the messenger boy acting simply on the instructions of Robbie McIntosh. Angus McGilvery, although taking a much bigger part by making the rendezvous with the ship, was also working to the instructions received from Robbie. All that he knew was the parcel did *not* contain drugs; drug smuggling was something he would not have been a party to. The main attention was then focussed on Robbie; they knew that he was contacted in a prearranged manner from Ullapool by someone with a heavy Russian accent. They also knew that he passed on his instruction to Angus by telephoning the same message to the pub at Corran but what they wanted to know was where the parcel was then sent.

With threats of charging him with treason, Robbie revealed that he was to post the parcel to a London Post Box number, addressed to a Mr Reece. A message was immediately sent to the Metropolitan Police at New Scotland Yard, to have the renter of the box checked out. It was already too late; the mysterious Mr Reece had got wind of the arrests and had disappeared without trace.

It didn't take long for the boffins at Bletchley to unscramble the coding of the computer discs which were then passed on to engineers to evaluate. One disc revealed technical details of a new kind of aircraft; one that, by making use of the ground effect when flying low, could carry an enormous payload. This would be potentially of great use in the battlefield, ferrying tanks and other heavy weapons to the front line. The other disc had a new twist to an old idea. During WW2 the Hitler regime had the idea of putting into earth orbit a giant parabolic mirror; this would then be directed to send a concentrated sunbeam down on London and other targets to set the buildings on fire. At the time of the proposal, they – nor anyone else, had the ability to put anything into earth orbit. Of course, with the dramatic technological developments of recent years, orbiters have become part of modern life and so Hitler's idea could be a realistic threat. However, this disc was not proposing a weapon of war but suggested that such a mirror could be used to overcome major drought problems in Africa and Australia. It showed how, by directing the beam into the ocean off the west coast of Africa or the west coast of Australia, a massive increase in evaporation would occur; the prevailing air movements would bring that moisture over the parched areas of those nations with the potential to relieve the drought.

These revelations caused a great stir in security circles but the conclusion drawn was that the whole nefarious scheme had been a matter of importing the results of international industrial espionage with the intention to sell them on to interested parties; British Aerospace, NASA, or perhaps the European Space Agency.

There was no way that the contents of the previous packages could be assessed unless 'Mr Big' – the mysterious Mr Reece, could be found; this would take a lot of detective work without having any guarantee of success. The matter was hushed up pending further enquiries, for fear of creating an international incident; all three rogues being given nominal suspended sentences. The Highland Queen was returned to Angus, and he, together with Robbie and Malcolm, returned to their normal lives somewhat shaken by their close call. The rest of the glen was none the wiser; just bemused by bogus bird watchers that had stayed only one night.

CHAPTER 12

During the final weeks before commencing their challenging new phase of their lives Sam, besides completing the sale of their house and making the multitude of arrangements necessary for the move, had also ensured that he had his new Commercial Director on the team. He had persuaded Bill Bates and his wife Janette to join him – site unseen, by imbuing him with exciting thoughts as well as a financial incentive; he was now serving one month's notice so would follow up one week later.

The big day came, not only for the Jacksons but the other couples destined to form the vanguard of the Glenquoich development project; they arrived, followed by removal vans, at their new accommodation in the Highlands. The Jacksons were the only newcomers to be housed in their proper home since further housing development awaited the team's own arrival.

Having driven up in their own car for the first time, Sue was less than pleased when they pulled up at Alltbeithe, their new home to be. "Oh, look at the mess; there are all sorts of builder's paraphernalia and rubbish everywhere – it's not finished!"

"Don't get your underwear in a twist;" Sam replied, consider yourself lucky - we only have to move once; this is our new home."

"Home, how can you call it home; we'll need wellies instead of carpet slippers. I just hope the inside is better than the outside."

"What a way to start your appreciation of our brand-new abode. Don't you realise that free mud packs have been provided for the next few months. Let's get indoors and see how the design has worked out; I see a door mat and attendant scraper have been provided in an effort to keep the inside clean-ish."

Walking in through the front doorway, they immediately noticed warmth although the house was devoid of furniture. "Oh look; somebody has been very thoughtful, they've lit the wood stove and I do believe the floor is warm"

"That'll be the under-floor heating;" replied Sam, "I suppose it was put on to help dry out the paint and plaster work."

"Well, I like to think it was put on to make us feel welcome."

"It certainly seems to have changed your mood for the better – which is good," added Sam. "Since we will be sleeping on the floor tonight; until the furniture arrives tomorrow, we'll really appreciate the heated floor."

"We should have stayed at the Tomdoun Hotel for the night, like Mhairi and Alan" Sue moaned, "It would be a lot more comfortable."

"Our van driver promised to be here by 7 o'clock in the morning so I thought it best that we don't delay them – we should be here when they arrive. I have arranged for us to join our new friends for dinner to save you having to prepare my usual seven course banquet," he sarcastically commented.

"I shall let you off then," she conceded. "Let's unpack our sleeping bags and toiletries then go down to the hotel and have a pre-dinner drink."

After a relaxing evening with Alan and Mhairi, Sue went into moaning mood again; "We've now got to go back to sleep on the floor while you both enjoy the comfort of a feather mattress."

"We have another day to wait for our van which had much further to travel than yours. And then," added Alan, "we'll have to move a second time when our house is built. You should count your blessings."

"You two men always gang up against us members of the fairer sex." Commented Sue as they left for the drive to the place they loosely call home.

The morning dawned, and right on schedule the van arrived, while they were rustling up a hot cuppa. "It always works," Sue said to the removal men, "the smell of a cup of tea must have wafted right down the glen."

By lunch-time, all was unloaded and the major pieces of furniture were in place; it would probably take forever to empty all the boxes of crockery, cookware, nick-knacks, photos and souvenirs from their worldly travels, together with domestic and business files, tools, spare bits and bobs, and other paraphernalia that makes a house a home; but at least they were in and could make a start at making Alltbeithe theirs.

Sam's first official task was to contact Sir Richard on the telephone to report their arrival and to request the use of the large dining room for the forthcoming project meeting. Sir Richard welcomed them to their new home and said that he would ask Miss Fitzroy to arrange the furniture suitable for their needs. He then added, "I would ask you to invite the ladies to attend – not to participate but, to be silent observers; this way they will have some insight into the part their husbands, or partners, will be playing and may be encouraged to rise to the occasion with their own social contribution. It is also possible that they may, in private discussions at home, offer some tit-bit – some suggestion, which might further improve some angle of the scheme."

Somewhat surprised by the suggestion, Sam remarked that he had never before heard of such a notion and that wives were usually kept at arms length from business. However, he commented that it would be an interesting experiment.

"By the way;" added Sir Richard, "now that the scheme is about to start I have given the go-ahead for the purchase of a helicopter. I feel, very expensive as it is, this will be an essential tool to give ready access throughout the project area and a most desirable emergency vehicle. Bearing in mind the high running costs its use should be adequate but not excessive. Ted Evans is qualified on helicopters as well as fixed wing aircraft and is currently on a familiarization course for the Sikorsky Spirit. When he returns, he can brief you on the details so that you can best judge its use. I promise you that this is my last act without conferring with you."

As arranged, a week was allowed for settling in during which time Sam had a one-to-one natter with each member of the team. Alan was first on his list since he was anxious to get underway with the building programme.

"I have prepared basic drawings for houses and other accommodation units along the lines I suggested a month ago," said Alan, producing plans and elevations for Sam's comments.

"You've certainly been busy – along with everything else you needed to do ready for the move."

"I must admit, I paid a few quid for someone else to actually do the drawings to my specification; in fact, the same fellow is standing by down south to carry on with the detail drawings if you are happy."

"That's the ticket; we need to crack on, there is much to be done."

"As you see, not only have I prepared designs for three different individual houses, some bigger than others, but we also have apartment blocks for single persons and newly weds – all to the basic Alpine theme."

"My initial impression, Alan, is that these are first class; but I'd like to consider them further before our first project meeting next week. Have you got any costings?"

"Yes, but they may need a general adjustment when I learn more of Highland costs for materials and labour."

"Fair enough. Have you had any thoughts about the corporate buildings?"

"Yes I have; taking your point that you wanted to blend everything with the landscape, and that a tower was a necessary feature for the communications building, led me to think of building a castle."

"Oh, my giddy aunt!" Sam exclaimed.

"It's not as crazy as it sounds;" Alan persisted. "I'm not proposing to build an actual fortress but if the style was that of the medieval period we could have aerials and dishes mounted on the turrets and the buildings beneath would contain the transmitters, receivers, computers and the personnel to operate them. Sit the whole edifice on top of Sgurr a' Mhaoraich and you can go one stage further; build in a restaurant with the resulting magnificent views and you will have a major tourist attraction. You might like to include your conference hotel in the concept to complete the speciality."

116

Highland Haven

"Do you mind if I catch my breath?" Sam spluttered; "this certainly is a radical notion which needs more than a moment to absorb. I must say, the idea does have appeal; a castle on a mountain would not be out of place and it could, as you say, be a draw to our potential clientele. Well, Alan, you have given me plenty to think about so I think we'll call it a day. The project meeting will be at 9 o'clock Monday morning; we'll have to hold it in the big house pending the completion of the project offices behind our cottage here. Sir Richard would like all wives to attend as silent observers but stress with Mhairi that, no matter what, they may not intervene." He then explained the reasoning lying behind the idea.

"This might cause some interesting conversation over the dinner table." Alan replied.

Sam's next target was Angus, the young civil engineer. "How has your railway education expanded over the last month?" He challenged.

"Not too bad;" Angus asserted, I found that it mostly followed fundamental civil engineering practices regarding slopes of cuttings and stability of the ground which, of course in this region will vary from a granite under-base to that of a peat bog. The main aspects I concentrated on were radius of curvature and slope of climb and descent. With these in mind I have proposed a provisional route from Quoich to the Mallaig line at Morar and then, with British Rail permission along the same tracks right into the sea-port."

"Why not run alongside Loch Nevis direct to Mallaig; surely the terrain from Loch Quoich is easier?"

"It is, but we would have great difficulty entering the town of Mallaig because of the contours and the existing buildings; this way we take advantage of the existing rail corridor. I did consider just terminating at the existing rail-line but felt it would be important to us to have direct access to the pier for the shipment of raw materials and for the benefit of the tourism aspect."

"Fair enough; your first priority is to consult with British Rail; they should be cooperative since the proposal will bring increased activity to the area, making the Highland Line more viable. If they are agreeable you can press on by having a detailed survey carried out to finally establish the route. In the meantime there are two other rail related problems for you to consider. Firstly, Alan Fraser is proposing a major building on the summit of Sgurr a' Mhaoraich, will you assess the feasibility of getting staff and visitors, as well as supplies, up there by funicular, cable-car, or any other means you might think of.

The second requirement is a tramway around Loch Quoich. Most of the housing and some other enterprises will be sited on the loch-side so I visualise a computerised – operating-on-demand, electric tramway as being an eco-friendly means of commuting without the intrusion of cars. I don't want to see overhead cables for the power supply nor, for safety reasons, can we have live rails; but I remember seeing some years ago the use of gyros as a means of storing energy on road vehicles. If, at each stop there is a charge point, the vehicle mounted gyros could be taken back up to best speed before moving off. For emergency use, battery power would need to be available; in fact it may be that the gyros should be used simply to keep the batteries charged."

This is a new one on me;" admitted Angus, but how do you envisage these trams should be computer controlled, electronics is not my strong point?"

"Think of the trams as if they are horizontal lifts; you press a button and the nearest vehicle comes to your station. On board, the passenger selects the destination and the vehicle moves off in the appropriate direction. If someone else, further along wishes to travel in the same direction, their button press will cause the vehicle to stop at their pick-up point so as to allow them on board. Although normally single track, for economy of space and cost, each stopping point would have a double track to allow passing. The controlling computer would ensure that no two trams were travelling in opposite directions on the same stretch of track."

"It all sounds very straight forward;" Angus commented with tongue in cheek, "but you are certainly throwing me in at the deep end."

"You wanted a challenge; so a challenge you have got. Don't worry about the control system or the details of the power supplies; other staff will deal with those problems – you concentrate on establishing the route in conjunction with Alan Fraser who is to develop the housing settlements and commercial centres. By the way, we need these projects under-way yesterday."

A couple of days later it was the turn of the Personnel Director, Stewart Slater, to have a one-to-one with Sam. "Welcome Stewart;" opened Sam, "we haven't had much of an opportunity to get to know each other so far. I hope we find we are on a harmonious wavelength."

"I hope so too; I suppose, as the Personnel Director, the onus is on me to demonstrate good inter-relationship skills so that we *do* have a good relationship."

"Well, we all should try and see matters from each other's point of view; it does help to understand difficulties and find solutions. The last thing we want is petty disputes through being entrenched in one's own mind-set. Considering others' views, what do you think of Sir Richard's ideas; don't you think his salary regime is a bit communistic, setting everyone on a rigid ladder?"

"Well, I must admit that I did feel that way at first but then, thinking more deeply about it, I realised that with everyone correctly related on that ladder, there would be much less cause for dispute. Envy regarding another's salary scale would be pointless since that person's superior attributes would be recognized. A lot of energy is frequently expended stirring up jealousy-related trouble when the means of improving one's own position should be identified and then that energy used to initiate improvements to one's own standing; the carrot to do better is dangled before everybody. Sir Richard's further policy of encouraging everyone to make use of what would have been taken in income tax to invest in the project, either generally or in some specific enterprise, is also likely to improve relations. When employees have a proper stake in the company it becomes *their* company; this reduces the us-and-them syndrome, increasing the incentive to be efficient - to be effective. It is only in this situation – where everyone wins or loses with the fortunes of the company that the second element of the salary policy based on relative points could be expected to work. With the value per point rising or falling with the financial relationship of the community to the rest of the economic world, it is in everyone's interest to work towards the very best result even if that means – in difficult times, taking a cut across the board. The end result: we shall be working truly as a team, warming to the success of each and every element."

"That was quite a lecture; you certainly seem to understand Sir Richard's view on this matter so I presume you will be happy to set it up."

"I most certainly will. I'm sorry if my enthusiasm got the better of me; but I find the prospects of working together in this way so exciting and, potentially, so fulfilling."

"Please don't let any of my remarks dampen your enthusiasm;" said Sam, encouragingly, "I hope you can inject that corporate spirit into everyone; this we need. Your first task in setting up the appropriate relationship between all members of the staff from Development Director to the tea lady is to draw up formal terms of reference – making sure that there is a proper link to superiors and to those under their umbrella. While doing this I ask you to arrange an overlap at both ends of the person's responsibilities so that, in the event of their non-availability, others can fill in to keep the wheels turning. Take my own case, for instance; should I fall ill or, perish the thought, meet with a serious accident, policy decisions will be taken by Sir Richard; while ongoing planning, activation and monitoring would be carried out collectively by the directors of the appropriate sphere of activity. Nobody should feel that they are being made superfluous; in fact it should be stressed that their responsibilities are extended upwards and downwards. We can all take advantage of this situation since we will then always have someone to whom we can turn to discuss a problem. Discussing ongoing problems with those in the appropriate chain of command automatically keeps them informed of the state of the game so that they can, in an emergency, make the necessary decisions. As you mentioned earlier, it helps to bind all into an effective team."

"Now I've given *you* a lecture," commented Sam. "Is there any matter you wish to raise at this stage?"

"Well yes; I've found the perfect man for the position of Community Padre. I have asked him - and his wife, to come up this weekend to talk with you with a view to engaging him. Although he would not directly contribute to the profitability of the project, I feel it would be a good thing if he was available at the outset to help create a harmonious society here at Quoich; this would, in turn lead to greater efficiency and, subsequently a more effective outcome."

"What is so special about your candidate that makes you think he is right for the job?"

"Although he was brought up as a Church of England boy, later in life – witnessing the conflict in Northern Ireland and the Middle East, he began to realize that, rather than bringing harmony, hard-line religious teachings were creating conflict with other beliefs; instead of uniting the peoples of the world, the different religions were dividing nations and setting nation upon nation. From this he has developed a philosophy based on personal aura"

"Personal aura;" mused Sam, "Could you explain?"

"He will, of course, explain it more fully himself; but, in essence, he believes that each of us develop a unique electromagnetic aura which is transmittable to those close to us – either close physically or close emotionally. This unique aura, or characteristic, is developed initially from the combination of aura from parents then developed by experience; this leads to the entrenchment which occurs due to contact with others of like mind. His maxim is 'consideration for others' which – as we both mentioned earlier, is appreciating alternative points of view. You will notice that this policy does not object to any particular religion nor does it suggest how one should commune with God – it is a matter of personal preference."

"From what you have just told me, he does seem to be just the fellow we are looking for; somebody with a refreshing view of life for this refreshing community project," agreed Sam. "Would he be prepared to teach his philosophy at our yet-to-be-established college?"

"I'm sure he would. He is about ten years older than you or I and gently carries authority born out of wisdom and, I might add, is ably supported by his wife. He would be a good candidate to chair a tribunal to deal with disciplinary matters; I understand that Sir Richard would prefer that transgressions be dealt with in house rather than involve the police and regular courts in our affairs. By the way Doug was an engineering draughtsman in the aircraft industry; so you will probably find much common ground for conversation."

"Mention of a tribunal reminds me to draw attention to your other responsibilities; we need a security team to guard against interference from outside our domain and, as you have alluded, to any violations of our internal rules of conduct. It would seem logical to give this team a multi-purpose by using them as our emergency service for fire, accident or any urgent medical crisis; this would make for greater efficiency since such duties tend to involve much time on standby. On matters of education, besides a primary school, we intend to develop a system of secondary and tertiary education based on the personal application approach – similar to the Open University with an element of Australia's School of the Air. Although it is not expected that you would directly be involved in any teaching, it will be your responsibility to initiate and monitor the setting up of the necessary facilities – particularly a comprehensive library for study and for relaxation. This leads to your final domain – that of entertainment. It is most important that we do not let our remoteness, further aggravated by frequent bad weather, be a cause for any drop in morale; we must, therefore, see to it that there are many social activities available from which members of our community can choose. The communications engineer will assist by providing TV and interactive services to every home; but we do need the setting up of communal events such as film shows, talks, games evenings for chess or bridge and the like as well as sporting activities; perhaps the ladies can assist in much of this."

"I have a few ideas regarding the social programme;" offered Stewart "and have already discussed with Sir Richard the use of the big house – if at least temporarily. He says that he and Lady Blaisdale normally confine themselves to the east end and that the rest of the house could become a Community Club where these events, as well as business meetings and special events such as weddings – or whatever, could be held. He has even agreed to the establishment of a commercial bar lounge which could become the ad hoc meeting place for anyone."

"This is excellent news; the sooner that little project is initiated the better. Well Stewart, I think we have covered much ground together; we'll leave it at that for now. I look forward to meeting our prospective Padre at the weekend; if we like him, he could sit in on Monday's meeting to meet everyone else while getting the feel of what the project is all about. Oh, by the way, I have settled on two more positions; although I shall be directly responsible for electrical engineering matters, I shall be delegating communications, computing and any automation projects to Harry Shaw, and all general electrical matters of supply and distribution to Arthur Brown; they will be with us very shortly."

"Apart from the departed Hamish, Sir Richard's selecting process has brought together some very keen and able directors who have now been supplemented by others in critical positions", Sam confided in Sue later that day, "with their support, my task will not be so onerous."

"I'm glad of that;" Sue commented, "I don't want my hubby to come to the end of his working day about midnight – all tense and irritable, I want him for me."

"To quote a song 'You Got Me Babe'," he retorted, adopting the technique of a love-sick octopus.

"Get away, you beast from fifty fathoms; I'm trying to prepare the evening meal."

"That's striking below the belt – straight to my stomach."

"Have you finished your programme of natters?" Sue enquired to change the topic.

"No; besides a session with Bill Bates on Saturday and the Padre designate, appropriately on Sunday, I have yet to confront the accountant, Sir Richard's long-standing associate; I'll be seeing him tomorrow."

"I'll be glad when you've done so that you can help me to make this house a home."

"Things are going to get a whole lot busier so I reckon my best plan is to do as I do with all my tasks."

"What's that?"

"Delegate;" Sam said with some finality. "It is always best to leave jobs to those most competent."

"That's not fair; you are taking advantage of your position."

"Yes, I'm power crazy." confirmed Sam.

"Get back to your managerial machinations." She said resignedly.

The morning of Friday, Sam arrived at the big house to find James Donaldson already waiting for him.

"I was not sure why you asked for this meeting." Donaldson admitted, as if he had some objection to being summoned for interview.

"I have been having a one-to-one talk with each of the directors in order to establish our business relationship and to ensure everybody is fully aware of the range of their responsibilities while, at the same time, I hope to learn something of the attributes of each member of the team."

"I see;" was the curt reply, "but I have been working with Sir Richard for many years and he has never found it necessary to probe *my* attributes."

"Look James, this is not an interrogation, I'm looking for your friendship in business. If we can establish an amiable, as well as a professional relationship between the executives of this unique, very demanding project, we will work more effectively together."

"I'm sorry;" Donaldson replied, "perhaps I have jumped to wrong assumptions."

"This is exactly the purpose of this meeting between us; to arrive at an understanding of our business relationship and your relationship with other directors. Unlike in the past, you will not only be dealing with Sir Richard but directly with me and the others. For instance, Stewart Slater – the Personnel Director will need your full cooperation regarding the application of the special salary structure that has been agreed together with the rate of exchange mechanism."

"I don't understand;" Donaldson admitted, "what is this rate of exchange mechanism?"

Sam explained the manner in which salaries will be related to the points value of each employee and then went on to answer his question regarding rates of exchange. "To obtain maximum benefit from one's salary, internal trading will be done directly from the individual's accumulated credits by using an in-house account card – there is no need for money; we are creating a cashless society – well, as far as possible. But, should the particular person wish to carry out some transaction out of Glenquoich then a conversion to £ Sterling will have to take place. This rate of exchange will be set by the board according to the fortunes of the company."

"But I have already agreed my salary with Sir Richard."

"As have all of us;" Sam assured him, "however, the initial task before Stewart is to set the initial points value in proportion to all our salaries; this benchmark will then be used for all new staff and workers."

"Why go to all this complication instead of simply paying in £ Sterling in the first place?"

"This firstly, is in order to prevent the direct application of income tax; which, of course, gives us all a tremendous financial advantage; if an employee converts some of his credits to cash, taxes will apply. The second aspect is that the changing of exchange rates gives the company some control over costs; it will work in the same way that exchange rates between nations influence values of imports and exports."

"I must say, as Sir Richard's accountant for many years I would have thought he would have discussed it with me."

"I imagine he wished to keep this radical notion close to his own chest until the project was launched; it is cooperation between you and me that is going to make this work so, if there is something creating difficulties, we must resolve it between us. Allied to this tax concession is the need to encourage employees at all levels to invest in the project, either in the grand plan or in particular projects within – or both, if they so choose."

"How do you mean, 'particular projects within'?"

"There will be specific projects such as; a communications centre, a narrow-gauge railway to Mallaig, a conference centre, and many more; these will all have to be separately funded and managed to generate a profit as if they are separate companies; this is the only way we can prevent the gross fund flowing into an unidentified black hole. Although Quoich Development Corporation will always hold at least 51% of the capital in any sub-venture, the investment offered by the employees will release funds for other work thereby speeding up the process and strengthening the push for success."

"I suppose the details of this internal investment scheme will have to be worked out between myself and Mr Slater." Donaldson conceded.

"That is so," confirmed Sam. "Another member of the board with whom you will be particularly associated will be the Commercial Director, Bill Bates. He will be setting up a Community Bank so that everybody has a point of contact with regard to their financial affairs. He will arrange with the Property Director, Alan Fraser, for the building, the Personnel Director for the acquisition of suitable staff and you for the banking expertise. In turn, you will need to establish a relationship with one of the major banks for their support."

"Well, I must say, I thought the salary being offered was rather generous and Sir Richard did state that my duties would be rather wider than hitherto, but I never envisaged such a diversion from the traditional accountant's duties. However, if as you say we all cooperate amicably, I'm sure we can make this project workable."

"I'm pleased to hear you say that; early on in this discussion, I thought you were about to raise objections. Just for the record – we are all being pushed into unfamiliar territory; this is the biggest challenge in the lives of every one of us. Welcome to the team"

The weekend was punctuated by two more interviews; on the Saturday, Bill Bates, the newly appointed Commercial Director and past colleague, arrived for his briefing.

"Welcome Bill to the wet and windy West Highlands," Sam began, "I think the best thing I can do to introduce you to your new task is to review your responsibilities; so we'll get straight down to it. Besides selling to the outside world whatever the Glenquoich Corporation may have to offer, you are responsible to me for two branches of our organisation: Sport and Tourism which will be under the immediate management of Farquhar Henderson, and local trades. Tourism will include a hotel having conference facilities and chalets for family lettings while sporting activities will include fishing, stalking, water sports such as water skiing & simple family boat hire, hang gliding, perhaps motor sports such as hill climbing for cars and scrambling for motorcycles, mountain biking, hiking, pony trekking, climbing and some skiing in the winter. Trades will be under your direct control since they will all be separate enterprises such as a community bank, a post office cum stationers & newsagent, a small supermarket, specialist shops such as tourist trappings and gifts, a hairdresser, hardware, a chemist, a garage & service station and a printing and publishing house. Although that sounds like a tall order, you will also be expected to have general control of marketing expert services such as computer programming, and engineering expertise, together with the sale of fresh produce, the output from fish farms, forest timber output and perhaps stone products from our own quarry."

"Phew; you never said there was so much to this appointment when you convinced me to join this happy band." Bill retorted, jokingly adding "What is there to do in my spare time?"

"Don't worry too much; the Property Director, Alan Fraser, has an overlap with you regarding the hotel, chalets and other commercial buildings as well as agriculture, fishing and forestry; the personnel Director, Stewart Slater, will find all the staff you need and prepare terms of reference for each appointment; Harry Shaw will look after the technical output regarding computing; the quarry will be under the control of Angus McKay, the civil engineer; James Donaldson will provide any accounting service you require including the arrangements for the Community Bank."

"That all sounds fair enough," conceded Bill. "I'm glad that you intend developing our own printing and publishing house because I would like to get started in that area during the period needed for the rest of the developments to get under way. I thought we would start with a house journal, perhaps called 'Highland Highlights', which follows the growth of this enterprise while, at the same time, giving an insight into the wild life, the beauties and the history of the region. This could help sell our tourist facilities; keep the employees informed; make a modest profit and prepare us for a much more ambitious publishing project which I have had in mind for some time."

"So you have been giving some advance thought to ways of making money in this remote glen; don't keep me in suspense, tell me more of your publishing ambitions."

"For some time now I have grown increasingly frustrated by interest magazines that don't follow through," Bill pronounced. "What I have in mind is a well researched journal covering a wide spectrum of topical as well as historical, geographical, and biographical articles. By forward planning, each feature would be linked to others in previous or subsequent editions. Take, for example, a biography of Sir Richard; his interests in Malaysian palm oil and rubber could lead to a geographical feature of Malaysia; together with explanations of the processes involved in bringing raw rubber and palm oil to marketable branded goods; his holdings in the gold mines of Australia can be pursued in a similar manner. These articles will be cross-linked to others stemming perhaps from political topics. My frustrations stem from reading some feature in a magazine which generates further interest that cannot be pursued within those pages. It also often happens that some topical matter is reported in the media while it is considered newsworthy, but then it fades from the limelight without a final, properly considered conclusion. In the haste to publish sensational material, attention to accurate detail is frequently overlooked by the press; I would ensure that all facts are correlated and therefore become reliable. What ultimately will develop," Bill continued, "is the development of an active encyclopaedia containing reliable topical material the content of which can be followed down different paths according to the reader's preferences."

"This sounds like a worthy publishing project but will it generate advertising potential to help support the costing?"

"Yes; this leads to another important feature of the proposal. A disciplined approach to the acceptance of advertising would be applied so that only relevant copy would be approved. Referring back to this hypothetical biography of Sir Richard, we would accept tasteful adverts for rubber products – particularly if they further explained some aspect of their production; similarly, soaps and other toiletries based on palm oil would be appropriate. Associated with mention of the Australian gold fields, jewellery adverts, or even suitably worded ads on financial management, might be appropriate. Since advertisements of this sort are more likely to be read, they should carry a higher premium. In order to complete the concept of an encyclopaedia, a comprehensive index would be produced to enable research into the total content of articles and advertising; this would be published at the end of each year."

"With the format you have outlined," Sam commented, "you would need a massive staff to cope with the world spread of content."

"Firstly, my intention was to limit it primarily to British content yet giving links to wherever the feature may lead – as with the biographical example mentioned earlier. I thought we would call it 'British Scene'. The nation would be divided into twelve natural regions so that the centre pages could feature an area of each region in turn, month by month; the Highlands would be an obvious area to look at when it was the month to feature Scotland."

"How would you gather the information in?"

"Having decided on a topic, we would solicit articles from professional journalists throughout the UK; we then would carry out a check on the accuracy of the material submitted – in accordance with the fundamental policy of the end result being a reliable source of reference. This way we keep the overheads down to that sufficient to cover the basic editorial staff and artwork design."

"Talking of that, you should have a chat to Ted Evans, the pilot here, he is a first class photographer and a historian; he could certainly help with matters concerning Highland life, particularly the wild life. However," Sam continued, "I think you have a well thought out proposition; please put this all down on paper with some hard facts regarding costs and potential revenue so that we can enter it in our budget plan. At Monday's meeting, I want you to introduce yourself, summarize your responsibilities and give a brief outline of your immediate proposal; this gives others an opportunity to learn something of you and see how you fit in to the scheme of things. So we'll see you then – thank you Bill."

Relaxing briefly at home – as much as Sue would allow, Sam confided "I really think we have the makings of a great team, they all seem enthusiastic and ready to take on the challenges of all the duties I have been heaping their way; it is just up to me to coordinate all their efforts and guide them to a good end result."

"Good heavens darling, don't start talking about the end already; you are only just getting started," Sue challenged.

"Yes but, whenever you start on a journey you should know where you are going; one gains little satisfaction from aimless meanderings – other than perhaps peace and tranquillity. Ah well, one more to go – the Padre tomorrow, and then it is 'open the flood gates' come Monday's meeting."

Sunday morning was a notable morning – the first visitors to Sam and Sue's new cottage. Stewart Slater had brought the prospective Padre and his wife for their discussion session. He was a tall mature person, although greying slightly; he seemed to be quite fit as if he engaged in regular sport. She was of similar age, also quite sprightly for her years.

"Doug and Dorothy Grant," announced Stewart, formally.

"Welcome to Alltbeithe," Sam replied. "May I introduce my wife Sue. I suppose Stewart has filled you in about what is happening here."

"Well, very briefly; he said he was not free to talk about it until I'd met you."

"Good for him. I hasten to add, there is nothing untoward going on; it is just wise for business and political reasons that all and sundry should not be ahead of us. The world will know all in good time why we are doing what we are doing. Tell me about your relationship with the church."

"I was ordained as a Church of England Minister but my views have changed and I no longer preach. I now feel that one should not preach – one should lead or guide people along a path towards our maker – God. Ritualistic dogma appears to be a means of brainwashing rather than offering alternatives from which to choose. In recent years I have thought back to absolute physical fundamentals and then worked from there through the creation of inorganic matter, the conversion to living plants, to animals and finally to us humans. From this I have developed a philosophy regarding human behaviour. I believe I now understand what makes us tick, how we learn, how our characters develop – good and bad, what truly causes conflict leading to war, and much more. It might seem strange to you, since I was trained in theology, that it is only now that I truly understand how God can be 'in' all of us and what is really meant by us humans being created in His image; He does not look like us, but we **are** made of the same stuff as He. With these fundamental differences to the traditional religious teachings in my mind, I can no longer carry on leading a congregation in the accepted manner. However, I would dearly love to explain the basis of my philosophy and to use it to lead people to a better life. I hasten to add that no way am I advocating some new crank religion; since what I now believe appears to be the link between everything, physical and metaphysical, cosmic or quantum, even the spiritual world of the soul; it does not require doctrines to be established – it just requires understanding. It matters not to me if the listener is Christian – Catholic or Protestant, Buddhist, Muslim, Hindu or even atheist; we all have the same root."

"Quite a speech," Sam asserted. "We are looking for a caring person with leadership qualities who can bind together this new community as it is being established. His outlook must bridge across the potential divide created by members' existing political and spiritual beliefs. It seems as if you are the man for the job."

"Thank you. My wife and I would love the challenge of a new start here in the Highlands – regardless of the difficult climate."

"Before you get too excited, I should point out that, as with everyone else with responsibilities on this project, your field of endeavour has a tendency to get somewhat wider. Besides being the Padre here, you will be required to coordinate the activities of the ladies and liaise with the appropriate directors involved. I know that, traditionally, ministers tend to be involved in ladies' committees regarding social events, but this is rather more than that. Some of the ladies will be engaged in commercial activities such as producing and marketing Highland herbs, pottery, artwork, horn and wood carvings and so on; it would be too unwieldy and time consuming for these activities to be dealt with on a case by case basis. Your job will be to coordinate their efforts, giving support and encouragement, arranging for the production of suitable packaging and publicity through the Commercial Department so that these products can be marketed. Because the other directors are primarily concerned with the employees of the corporation, the ladies need an avenue of communication to get things done without interfering with the project development. You are that avenue."

"Not content with that; Sam continued, 'you will also be expected to take a leading roll in the provision of entertainment and sporting activities throughout the community; this will require liaison with the Personnel Department and the Commercial Department. Housing problems will best be dealt with through you to the Property Department. In other words you will be providing an across-the-board social service. You will be the first port of call by anyone experiencing any difficulties. You will, of course, have direct access to myself should anything arise that you feel falls outside the domain of the other directors. I hope this resume – which I am sure is not complete, hasn't overwhelmed you too much."

"I must admit, the requirement is rather broader than I envisaged but I have had experience of community entertainment through carnival organisation, being a member of a drama group, and a local choir, as well as being president of a tennis club; so feel that it is all compatible with the basic task of uniting the community and becoming the focus for personal consultation."

"I take that as an acceptance; welcome to the team. Will you attend the policy meeting at the big house tomorrow? Although you do not have the status of a Director, I would expect you to sit-in at such meetings and draw attention to any social problems you perceive."

"Thank you, I shall be there."

"I should add," said Sam, "that it is the policy here to allow the ladies to be observers at these meetings but I must ask that they refrain from speaking. If something troubles anyone, they can raise it after the meeting with the appropriate executive. So, Dorothy, you too would be most welcome."

After they had gone, Sue commented, "I was watching Dorothy's face during your list of duties and I could see her eyes getting wider with every addition; I thought for a moment that she was going to say it was too much."

"If you think about it, it isn't much more than a good vicar would do; it just sounds a lot when it is formally presented as a list. Anyway, tomorrow everybody will discover they are not the only ones with much to do – it applies to us all."

CHAPTER 13

While all the newly engaged executives of Glenquoich Development Corporation had been serving their notice from previous employment and making preparations for the move up to Glenquoich, Sir Richard had been down to London canvassing his fellow peers and members of the cabinet so as to oil the wheels of power in an effort to achieve his ultimate objective. All the while stressing the need for confidentiality at this stage, he was taken aback, after a few days, to read tabloid press headings such as:

THE BEAUTY OF THE HIGHLANDS OF SCOTLAND TO BE DECIMATED
and
POWERFUL PEER RIDES ROUGH-SHOD OVER LOCAL INHABITANTS.

Reading the articles, he found he was being accused of carrying out clandestine developments in an area of natural beauty and using his position to short-circuit planning authorities. A campaign was to be mounted to bring an immediate halt to all activities at Glenquoich. It was quite obvious that one of his many contacts had opened his big mouth; but to whom, and why was there so much belligerence?

Despondently he returned to his beloved Scotland to collect his thoughts. Going through his messages with his secretary Miss Fitzroy, she mentioned that Morag Matheson had telephoned seeking an opportunity to speak with him. "I certainly wish to speak with her;" he exclaimed, "make an appointment as soon as possible."

Two days later Morag arrived – accompanied by the local special constable, Malcolm McInnes.

"What is this then?" Sir Richard interjected, as Miss Fitzroy announced them, "I don't recall you mentioning that there would be police present. Before we go on," he said, reaching into his desk drawer to operate a switch, "I must advise you that everything that is said is now being recorded – this may be used in any legal proceedings that might ensue."

"Why do you consider that necessary?" the policeman challenged.

"Because, at a previous meeting with Miss Matheson, outrageous claims were made regarding my activities here at Glenquoich and I have just cause to believe that she may be running a vendetta against me. I must ask Miss Matheson; why are you here?"

"I am here to establish whether or not you were responsible for obscene telephone calls to me about two months ago," she demanded.

Highland Haven

"Obscene telephone calls? What on earth are you talking about?"

"It would appear," answered Malcolm McInnes, "after Miss Matheson's previous visit to you, she started to receive these calls which were quite suggestive; Miss Matheson found them so very distressing that she felt it necessary to go away overseas."

"Are you suggesting that I made those calls?" Sir Richard challenged, indignantly.

"Maybe you didn't but I'm sure you paid somebody else to do your dirty work for you," Morag insisted.

"You, my dear lady, are leaving yourself wide open for a charge of slander – in front of your own reliable witness."

"I'm afraid that is true," confirmed Malcolm, "I must ask you to withdraw that remark."

"Oh very well; but it seems too coincidental. Who else would choose that moment to verbally assault me?"

"I cannot help you there; although you verbally assaulted me with your unfounded accusations, it is not in my nature to retaliate with such unreasonable tactics. If the police and the telephone authorities cannot track down the culprit, there is nothing more to be done."

"I'm sorry Morag; but I must agree we cannot make unsubstantiated charges;" said the policeman formally, then added, "I'm sorry we troubled you Sir Richard, we shall leave you to carry on with your business."

"Before you go," interjected Sir Richard, "I must ask Miss Matheson a key question and seek an honest reply – bearing in mind that the tape recorder is still running and that Constable McInnes is a witness. What I am asking is; have you had anything to do with statements in the press denigrating me and my activities here in the Highlands?"

"I told you when we last met that I have contacts with influential people and that I would see to it that you would not run rough-shod over we highlanders. I intend to ensure that we do not have a repeat of the Highland Clearances of yesteryear."

"I suggest to you Miss Matheson that you arrange for your so-called influential people to see to it that these statements are withdrawn in print, otherwise they – and you, will find yourselves on charges of libel to add to the slander I have already suffered."

"Do you deny that you are planning to desecrate Glenquoich?" she fired back at him.

"I most certainly do, in fact we are going to great lengths to ensure that we do not interfere with the wild life, merely enhance it and make it accessible to a wider public."

"Ha, so you say, but I don't wish to wait until the damage is done – it would be too late."

"You have no idea what you are talking about. Our plans have been kept confidential up to now simply to avoid commercial concerns moving in to ruin what we have in mind. I have no intention to submit to your tirade, I shall not demean myself by countering your attack on me. As far as I am concerned the matter is closed. However, I will say this, that in accordance with good business practice, we shall be giving a presentation of our intentions to the local community at a social gathering in the Tomdoun Hotel. You, along with everyone else will be advised of the date and time."

Seeing her about to make some retort Constable McInnes interjected: "I think, Morag, Sir Richard is being quite fair and reasonable and suggest we should leave now and await the public information night."

"Very well;" she agreed with reluctance, and then as a parting shot, "it had better be good."

After they had gone, Miss Fitzroy was called into her boss's office. "Make a transcript of the conversation on this tape, and then preserve this in the safe. Bring me a new cassette for the machine. As soon as Mr Jackson is available, arrange for a meeting with me here." These curt, demanding instructions were quite unlike Sir Richard's normal attitude which was usually firm but pleasant.

When Sam Jackson duly arrived, Sir Richard reviewed the situation of the conflict with Morag Matheson. I want you to do two things; arrange for a presentation at the Tomdoun Hotel, and I suggest we provide a supper and a glass or two of wine – nothing elaborate or it will look like bribery. At the same time see if you can have discreet enquiries made around the village, to find as much as possible of Miss Matheson's background and her contacts here at Quoich, in the rest of the glen and further afield – perhaps down in London. To win a battle one must know one's enemy. I hope you find there is no contact at Glenquoich; I abhor quislings."

Having established a good relationship with the company pilot, Ted Evans, Sam sounded him out about others employed at the big house. "I'm absolutely certain that nobody here has any connection with this Morag," Ted assured him; "but I will keep my eyes and ears open down the glen. There are one or two with whom I am quite friendly and perhaps they can give us a lead."

Sam also engaged a very discreet Private Detective he had met through Rotary, down in Yorkshire. He was briefed to follow back through the media articles to find the source and also to check on the background and activities of Hamish Gordon, the failed Commercial Director, to see if he felt he had any axe to grind and whether or not he was in contact with Morag. In the meantime he arranged for the presentation evening and saw to it that residents throughout the district were made aware of the date and time.

It wasn't long before the enquiries yielded positive results; it was found that the person who contacted the press was a Marcus Matheson, a cousin of Morag. Marcus was an Under Secretary on the Cabinet staff. There was no ground for doubt regarding the linkage. Local enquiries had also been quite fruitful; when tongues were loosened with a few drams, conversation down at the Invergarry Hotel had turned to gossip about Morag accusing Sir Richard of obscene telephone calls, it wasn't long before Malcolm Ferguson was boasting that it was he that had made the calls. Since they had been found guilty of violating Customs and Excise laws he didn't hesitate to explain the reason why Robbie McIntosh and he had decided on the scheme to deflect Morag from stirring things up at the big house.

When Sam reported his findings, Sir Richard recalled that Robbie McIntosh had been present at the original meeting with Miss Matheson. He called in his secretary. "Take down a letter to Miss Morag Matheson;"

Dear Miss Matheson,

As a result of making enquiries to determine the source of the recent press articles, it has come to light that your cousin, Mr Marcus Matheson was the person feeding the media with these libellous statements. We have also found that he is employed as an Under Secretary on the Cabinet staff.

You must realise that if you persist in your antagonistic attitude towards me and the Quoich Development Corporation you will be putting your cousin's position in jeopardy. I would not hesitate to bring charges against you both

I trust we will hear no more of your unfounded accusations.

Sincerely

Sir Richard Blaisdale

Also take down two letters, one to Mr Robbie McIntosh and a similar one to Mr Malcolm Ferguson;

Dear Mr McIntosh,

As a result of making enquiries into the reason for false allegations made against me concerning obscene telephone calls, I find that you were the perpetrator of this vile act along with Malcolm Ferguson. I understand the reason you planned this disgusting verbal attack was to prevent her from causing investigations in the area which may have uncovered your illegal activities for which you were subsequently arrested.

Your actions have caused much distress, first to Miss Matheson and then to myself; I will provisionally resist taking further action provided I experience no further problems created by either of you.

Should charges on this matter be laid, I am quite sure you would not escape with suspended sentences.

I hope this is the end of the matter.

Sincerely

Sir Richard Blaisdale

"When Miss Fitzroy has prepared these, and I have signed them, I would like you to take them and personally present them just before the community meeting; I want them to be aware that we know what has been going on but not give them the opportunity to respond before hearing what we have to say regarding our plans."

On the due date Sam took Sue to the Tomdoun for an early bar meal so that he could check the arrangements before Sir Richard and Lady Blaisdale arrived, and also to present the letters as Morag and the others arrived. During their meal, they became conscious that the normally quiet hotel was filling up with visitors - the message had obviously got around.

About 15 minutes before the meeting was due to begin, Sam saw Morag talking with Robbie and Malcolm; it was the ideal moment to hand each of them their sealed envelopes. Although he moved away as soon as he had handed them over, he kept a close watch as each ripped open their mystery letter. He saw expressions of surprise followed by anger then nervousness; as they discreetly moved away from each other. Then Malcolm Ferguson caught up with Robbie McIntosh and was heard to say; "How did *he* find out; neither the police nor the telephone people could find out anything?"

"You must have been blabbing in the bar, you stupid drunken fool"

"I heard everyone talking about Sir Whatnot getting it in the neck from Morag and joined in; that was all."

"Nobody else knew; you must have opened your big mouth."

"It's alright though; he says he isn't going to do anything."

"Not until it suits him. It means we've got to toe the line or we are in trouble."

"I bet he's found out how those articles got in the paper and has written to Morag as he has to us."

"It looks that way;" confirmed Robbie, "so we all have to behave ourselves."

The two principals arrived just before the appointed hour, so Tom took them through to the dining room which was to serve for the meeting.

"Ladies and Gentlemen," Sam announced, "my name is Sam Jackson and this is my wife Sue. I am the Development Director of Glenquoich Development Corporation. This meeting has been called in order to inform you of our plans and how they will bring benefit to you all."

He quelled the mutterings and verbal rumblings, "on my right, may I introduce Sir Richard and Lady Blaisdale. Sir Richard is the Chairman and founder of the company and the originator of the vision for the Highlands. Sir Richard will, first of all, explain that vision, I will then give some indication of how we are planning to turn that vision into reality. Ladies and gentlemen - Sir Richard Blaisdale."

He stood up and waited patiently for total quiet. "I love the Highlands and, contrary to the mistaken opinion of some, am very sad that, not only was this area largely depopulated in the 18th and 19th century Clearances, it has failed to repopulate since. In fact, in modern times, the tendency is for young people to leave for better education and improved job prospects; and the older people leave to find easier living in their fading years. My vision is to reverse that trend. With the development of modern communications, and computer technology, there is no reason why many industries which are based on these technologies should not operate in the peace of the countryside. Additionally tourism can become a much more attractive proposition if the facilities offered are up to present day standards of comfort and convenience. This area of outstanding natural beauty is ideal for companies to send their executives for rest and recuperation while engaging in further training by attending seminars. Sports other than shooting and fishing

Maurice Duffill

should be on offer for selection as competition venues, while being available for training purposes. However, it requires a dedicated team of people to bring all this about while still preserving, or perhaps even enhancing the environment. These people and those needed to staff the various facilities will become the nucleus of a new community here at Glenquoich; but this will be no ordinary community. This plan to bring together capable, like minded people presents a great opportunity to test out a new philosophy of company and local government management. The residents of our township have all agreed to a different set of rules for the social structure of this community which is based on harmony. We are only just getting started; there's no knowing how successful we shall be but the increased activity around Glenquoich can only be beneficial to the rest of the area. Let us work together in mutual support."

As he sat down once more, the whispered comments became a general hubbub. After a short pause, Sam Jackson rose to his feet and thanked Sir Richard for his informative address. He then outlined in general terms the planned work; the creation of an Alpine style village, with hotel and conference centre, the concealment of the communication tower and restaurant as a highland castle, the introduction of a narrow-gauge railway to Mallaig, as well as the planned commercial activities of hydroponic and fish farms, the publishing and printing house, the Community Bank, all backed up by retail outlets, medical clinic, primary school, secondary and tertiary education facilities, and the necessary administrative offices. He then pointed out that to keep the area safe and so prevent thugs and other villains infiltrating and causing problems a security corps would be established which would monitor all traffic movements in and out of the area. "This, I must point out;" Sam explained, "will not interfere with the free movement of residents in Glengarry. However, for convenience, we ask that anyone wishing to frequent Glenquoich should enquire for a pass to stick on the windscreen of their car. This will avoid irritating delays."

"How can you take control of the glen road like that?" called an anonymous voice from the audience.

"A bill has been passed allowing the privatisation of the road from the dam to Kinloch Hourn," Sam replied; and then continued before arguments started, "in order to staff all these enterprises and to assist with the construction, all residents are invited to apply for employment. Since a wide range of positions will become available, it is suggested that anyone interested make a general application stating what type of work would be of interest and what skills or qualifications you have that you think appropriate, we will then advise as and when suitable openings become available. Local contractors and tradesmen are also invited to solicit for business. Although we shall necessarily employ contractors from further afield, suitable local services will be selected in preference."

136

"It must be quite obvious that, from all that has been said this evening," continued Sam, "great benefit to the locality will stem from successfully developing Sir Richard's vision." After a suitable pause, Sam drew the meeting to a close. "Unless there is any urgent question, I suggest we leave it at that; giving yourselves time to consider the prospects. If you have any questions, special requests or suggestions, you can contact my office by letter, Email, fax or phone via the contact details on the leaflets distributed to all. From time to time a newsletter will be circulated giving progress with the development and advising of any new work coming up. With that, I suggest we all relax with the supper provided; there are soft drinks, glasses of wine or tea and coffee to wash it down. Thank you all for your attention."

Sir Richard and Lady Blaisdale left the hotel but Sam and Sue remained to circulate in an effort to determine reactions – either positive or negative. A handful of people spoke with Sam regarding the various proposals but it was obviously just out of general interest or sounding out possible future employment. Two or three contractors presented their business cards; which was to be expected. There was no nastiness, Miss Matheson and the two villains giving them a wide berth.

As they drove the lonely single track road home in the crystal clear February night, with frost on roadside shrubs sparkling in the moonlight, Sue commented, "From what you've been telling me, I'm surprised Morag Matheson did not take the opportunity to stir up trouble."

"That was the point of those letters; and that's why I didn't hand them over until just before the meeting; Morag and company didn't have time to think about the content or get advice from anybody. They probably thought it better to keep a low profile. I've no doubt that Robbie and Malcolm will keep their mouths shut from now on but Morag might seek outside advice. If we don't hear any more from her, we'll know what that advice has been."

"If the rest of the glen is in favour of what is happening because of the prospects on offer, the three offenders would be afraid of alienating their fellow residents," suggested Sue.

"That is true, my learned one. I think we have heard the last of it."

"But wasn't it blackmail; to threaten them with further action unless they toed the line?"

"I dare say, but that is life; if you cause trouble, you can expect some retaliation – causing conflict never solved anything in the long run."

The next day the 'Press and Journal' and 'The Scotsman' both displayed much more favourable headings:

THE HIGHLAND CLEARANCES RECOMPENSED
GRAND PLAN FOR REMOTE AREA

The following day, when the papers finally arrived in the glen, Sam read the reports that had been written based on their public meeting. With varying degrees of accuracy they seemed to capture the main thrust of the project – completely reversing the mood of the previous publicity.

"It's good to read that we are not villains after all," he commented to Sue, "but I'm not sure I like the idea of the project being in the public eye, it adds further pressure."

"I didn't notice any press at the meeting."

"Since we don't know everybody, you wouldn't be able to judge whether they were press or residents. I know one thing, we are going to have to frequently update the outside world as to what we have achieved and the measures we have taken not to spoil the wildness of the general area. Ah well; just another rod to my back"

"You poor thing," mocked Sue, "you thrive on it."

"You often accuse me of being an octopus with its eight tentacles, I wonder if there is an animal that has one body but eight heads," Sam shot back, "there seems to be so many aspects to be considered, and I could certainly do with them."

CHAPTER 14

Everyone gathered at the big house before the appointed hour for Sam's inaugural meeting; anxious to show keenness and eager to learn what was to be presented.

With the appearance of Sir Richard and Lady Blaisdale, Sam rose to his feet, took a position at the head of the large dining table and announced, "Gentlemen, please take your places, as marked, at the table. Ladies please be seated on the chairs provided around the room and be reminded that you are here as observers and may not participate in the proceedings. Sir Richard and Lady Blaisdale are also here as observers although the meeting will close with a short address by our host. Miss Fitzroy will take minutes; these will be circulated to the participants within 48 hours."

Sam then formally opened the first project meeting of the Glenquoich Development Corporation.

"We are here today to officially launch this project by reviewing everybody's roll so that all can discover how they fit in to the team, with whom they will be mainly working, and to whom they can turn for professional assistance. Before we begin this process I wish to introduce new members of the team who were not present at the original briefing. Bill Bates, there, has been appointed Commercial Director in lieu of Mr Hamish Gordon who decided our organisation was not for him. We have also just appointed a Community Padre, Doug Grant, sitting at the far end of the table. To take some engineering load off myself we also have with us Arthur Brown handling electrical supply and distribution, and Harry Shaw who will be our computer and communications buff. We'll hear more from them later in the meeting."

"As a small preamble to the proceedings, I would like to point out that, whereas we have much serious business to discuss, it need not be done stiffly. I am not advocating flippancy, but I do believe a conversational approach leads to friendly discussion and more positive results. However, I wish to clarify a point of etiquette; during formal meetings such as this, we will address each other formally – not only does this maintain the significance of the occasion; it helps the minutes secretary to properly record the event. At other times I am quite happy to use first names to generate the informality which I believe leads to more fruitful discussion." declared Sam.

"To get down to the business in hand, I will summarize my position. As Development Director, I am responsible to Sir Richard for the prosecution of the whole project in order to achieve his vision for Glenquoich. This is a massive task and the only way I'm going to succeed is to delegate *all* the work to the other Directors and the subordinate staff. I shall try to organise myself out of a job;" as an aside, he added, "in that I am sure I will fail. However, I urge you all to be fully

Maurice Duffill

open with what you are up to and be prepared to discuss problems in your sphere, others may be in a position to offer help; that practice will provide cover should anyone be absent. None of us should feel the need to engage in empire building, I think you will find your empire is large enough as it is." Murmurs of confirmation could be heard all around the room. "Besides general management, I shall have overall responsibility for engineering services, these being basically divided into three spheres; energy supplies will be delegated to Mr Arthur Brown who has just arrived and hardly had time to collect his thoughts. Perhaps he would stand to give us a brief summary of his work."

"Good morning everyone; not being a director, my sphere of activity is perhaps not as wide as others but it will embrace the whole area geographically; this probably means I shall come into contact with everyone on the team – at some stage or other. You will notice that Mr Jackson referred to my domain as energy supplies rather than electrics; this is because electricity - albeit a very convenient form of energy for distribution, is not necessarily the most efficient; consequentially I shall be looking for alternatives wherever possible. The use of gas is an obvious possibility; solar energy is not to be ruled out even though, in these parts, we see that golden orb only on the days following a blue moon. I will look into the use of thermal energy except that, unlike New Zealand, our springs seem to issue forth icy waters rather than steam. In that connection, I do have a novel idea I wish to discuss which may put a new slant on the possibility. Having said all that, most of my work will be concerned with the generation and distribution of electricity and being an essential feature of most developments I ask to be consulted as early as possible in any aspects of the project so that cabling and power supplies can be sized correctly. Thank you."

"Thank *you* Mr Brown. "Now then, to continue my delegations; also newly arrived, Mr Harry Shaw is responsible to me for engineering the system of communications, computing, and any automation systems, so I invite him to take the floor and elaborate."

"Being situated, as we are, in the shadow of mountains;" began Harry, "radio, micro wave links and television reception are not possible directly; as a result we shall be building a communications tower atop Sgurr a' Mhaoraich; at well over 3,000 feet, this gives us line of sight with other transmission towers outside our area. We will also install satellite dishes to enable world-wide communication via that medium. From this tower and these dishes, the system will be disseminated throughout the area by broad-band cable, and by radio to mobile phones. In your homes you should receive good quality digital TV from a large number of channels; you will also have available good facilities for connecting your own PC to the Web and for Email. Within the system we shall have our own network – QuoichNet, for passing information from one office to another which will also be available to the householder; a system of security codes will limit who can see what. Local banking and other personal business such as booking seats in the restaurant or sessions on the tennis courts will be available through QuoichNet. A central computer will be installed for use by all departments which will also be available to any householder via QuoichNet. With regard to automation, I will be responsible for developing an appropriate system using our central computer and our system of communication whenever a requirement emerges. Control of the telephone exchange is an obvious application, but a notable requirement will be the automated tramway system which, I am sure you will hear more about from our Civil Engineer. I will be working closely with Harry Brown on this and other power distribution needs. Just to finish my introductory speech, I would like to say that my wife, Liz, and I are very pleased to join in this project and have found – so far, a very friendly association with everyone we have met. Thank you."

"Well that was clear and concise," complimented Sam; "and now we move on to civil engineering; this is delegated to Angus MacKay. Mr Mackay, please give us your briefing."

"Good-day to you all," Angus boomed out in his broad Highland accent. "My job is straightforward," he lied, "I provide the transport infrastructure, the drains, the pipelines for water, the foundations for buildings and any of the difficult things, the others can't manage," he jokingly stated, causing much amusement around the table. "I have made a start on two interesting projects which, apparently, are most urgent. The first of these is a narrow-gauge railway to Mallaig to carry passengers and goods; the route survey is well in hand and earth-work will start this week. Because of the mountainous terrain, some of the track will have an Abt rack fitted as commonly used in Switzerland to enable trains to climb or descend steep inclines. The other project is the tramway serving the area around Quoich, already referred to by Harry Shaw. This will be the prime means of passenger movement from home to office, shops, entertainment and sporting facilities – thereby overcoming the environmental objections to the motor car. This will be based on a unique concept in that, to avoid unsightly overhead electric cables, large, high speed gyroscopes will be installed under the vehicle floor; used to store energy, these will be boosted at each tram stop where contact will be made with the power supply. A second exciting feature of the system is that there will be no drivers; the air conditioned vehicles will be fully automated, being called for on demand by the intending passenger operating a push-button at the stopping place – just as you are used to doing with modern lifts. Also, as with automatic lifts, the passenger will then select the desired destination by push button on the vehicle causing it to move off in the appropriate direction. Between stations there will only be one track, so the system will rely on Harry's computers to establish that the line is clear to the next station where there will be double track allowing vehicles to pass each other.

Maurice Duffill

For added safety, not only will the central computer – and its back-up system, monitor and control all movements; each vehicle will have its own data processor double checking the safety of its movement; sensors front and rear will act as a further safeguard against collision with debris on the track. So, although we appear to be in the wilds here, the most modern and sophisticated system will be available to us. A third project, which is at the evaluation stage at the moment, concerns a transport link to the Property Director's pet project but I'll leave him to introduce that to you. As a finale to my address, I must point out that, it is not only I that is employed here; my wife Fiona has been engaged as the school teacher although, at the moment there is no school building, however classes for young children will be accommodated here in the big house for the time being. Here endeth my first sermon," Angus jokingly concluded.

"Our young civil engineer seems to revel in the various challenges laid at his door. It is just as well since there is much to do," added Sam. "The whole area is the concern of the Property Director; so we will now hear from Mr Alan Fraser how he sees his domain."

"Good housing is of prime importance for everybody and since there is virtually non available, I have assumed this to be my first priority. I have already discussed with the Development Director the merits of creating an Alpine style rather than the traditional Highland stone cottage; as a result various designs of houses and apartments have already been prepared. Work is now in hand to prepare the structures in piecemeal form so that speedy construction can begin in the spring as soon as foundations and basic services have been laid. It has already been decided that a transport station – for train and tram, will be constructed alongside the lochan at the head of the steep hill from Loch Quoich down to Kinloch Hourn where we are now. It is appropriate, therefore, that the shopping village along with certain other facilities - such as a hotel and guest house, gymnasium, and squash courts, as well as some admin offices, should be constructed there. From this transport centre, a cable car system will run up to the summit of Sgurr a' Mhaoraich where my pet project will be built – as referred to by Angus, sorry – Mr MacKay. This project is the communications tower required by Mr Shaw. The special feature of this tower is that it will be designed to overcome the potential unsightliness – it will be built to look like a Highland castle." After a pause to let that concept soak in to his captive audience, Alan continued, "However, not only will it accommodate all the aerials and dishes together with their associated equipment, it will be a conference centre and restaurant with grand views of the surrounding panorama.'

"My concern is not limited to buildings; agriculture, forestry and fish farming come under my umbrella. Thinking of umbrellas reminds me of an interesting suggestion I have to make which has not yet been discussed. Most of you will not

142

Highland Haven

yet have had time to study Loch Quoich, but the main dam is at the eastern end from where the loch bends – somewhat like a banana, towards the west cum south. There, are constructed two small dams to stop the water flowing into the next glen. Although the dams face west, rather than south, being set in two steep valleys, they form natural sun-traps and would be an ideal location for our hydroponic farms. Better still, if our engineers could build a glass canopy to span across each valley we would have a superb glass-house in which to grow all manner of produce. One valley is 100 metres across, the other is 150. The arched roof would be a low profile so would not intrude on the wild surrounding country. The location is on the route of the railway; thereby providing ready access for personnel as well as incoming materials and outgoing produce. It could become Glenquoich's larder. On that optimistic note I shall end my resume." concluded Alan.

"Well, *collectively*, we do seem to be full of bright ideas; but it is up to the team, *collectively*, to see to it that these ideas bear fruit," Sam expounded. "Now then, none of this will succeed unless we generate income *collectively*; it is the task of our Commercial Director, Mr Bill Bates, to ensure that does occur – over to you, Mr Bates."

"What a challenge; such a broad spectrum of potential but all starting from nothing. We have just been hearing of probable output from hydroponic farms, mention was also made of forestry and fish farming, but the output from these will largely be consumed internally – I don't mean we will eat trees; I mean the community will absorb the bulk of production albeit there will be some surplus for export. The reduction of our imports by these enterprises does equate to a sale in that we do not have to spend so much off campus. However, the real earners must be tourism, sporting activities and conferencing. It is sound policy when trying to generate income from people that they be attracted by different objectives; we will then receive trade from different sectors. For instance, the hotel could receive trade from corporate organisations, possibly taking all the rooms for a three day series of seminars; tour operators could make a substantial booking for a couple of nights to accommodate their coach tours; travel agents and individuals may book one room for a number of days. Sporting events will also generate demand for accommodation; this will tend to be of a lower standard – targeting the guest house or the chalets. The benefit of this spread – each element of which needs a different price structure, is that when one sphere is in the doldrums another may well fill the gap. International trade is essential for the same reason. So the sooner the hotel is built, the sooner we can get started; of course I shall begin publicity in advance in order to establish trade the very next day after the workers pull out," he declared, confidently; and then continued, "with publicity in mind I have proposed an enterprise which will help in that direction while earning an income."

143

Maurice Duffill

"Initially we shall produce an in-house magazine featuring articles of Highland interest while focusing on the progress of developments here at Glenquoich. Besides keeping everyone informed regarding this great project, it will be publicising what will be on offer later and any new developments as they come on stream. A prime object of this publication is to gain publishing experience and develop our editorial team in readiness for the real earner. "British Scene" will be a new type of journal containing very reliable articles interlinked with each other - building to an encyclopaedia. This will, of course, carry advertising features related to Glenquoich." Completing his proud exposé, he then changed tack, "In support of the corporate strategy to bring trade to us, anyone with craft skills is encouraged to submit items for sale to the visitors; however, I must stress that we do ask for a high standard; we do not wish to sully our image with anything tacky. Supplemental to the obvious money earner of tourism and other visitors, we will be looking for other exportable products and services; computer programming, financial services, project management, anything in which we have developed an expertise that may become available when our own development has largely been completed. In summary, I think we have great potential and so look forward to some of the facilities being up and running."

"Salesmen are renowned for being optimistic but," said Sam think Mr Bates is certainly on the right tack. To do all that has been mentioned, we need staff to plan, and staff to do, and someone to manage the staff; that someone is the Personnel Director, Mr Stewart Slater."

"I am, at the moment, in a somewhat odd situation; traditionally it is the function of the Personnel Director to seek for and select applicants for vacant positions but, apart from the Padre – from whom we will hear shortly, all the Directors and other staff members were selected without any assistance from me. Don't misunderstand me; I am not complaining but I make that statement in order to explain why I shall be seeking details from all of you – including the Development Director. Not only will it be necessary for me to establish basic details of all employees, I will seek family details – this is so that we have a complete community directory; this is more than the establishment of a company – here we will have a township with all its attendant administrative requirements. In due course I shall, for instance, be inviting nominations for positions on a Community Association Executive Committee; this will be the funnel through which any common needs, or considered desires, of the residents can be channelled to the management. This same committee might choose to organise social functions or raise funds for some charitable purpose. Knowing the details of resident families will also enable proper arrangements to be made for medical services and educational facilities." Having dealt with the staffing aspect of his portfolio, Stewart then diverted to support services, "we will be establishing a

144

clinic to deal with medical matters and a primary school; secondary and tertiary education will initially be provided by tutorials, and by computer based lessons – in the manner of an up-market version of Australia's School of the Air. Your housing needs, will be dealt with through my department, although the actual construction will be by the Property Department."

"In due course," Stewart continued "I will be sending to all employees a detailed explanation of our salary policy which, briefly, is based on a system of points allocated to each person based on his education and experience. This will show how, by improving your education or adding to your experience, you can reasonably expect an increase in remuneration. It will also explain how those points are converted into cash by a variable factor decided according to the success or otherwise of the company – taking note that the variation affects all of us in the same proportion. Another information leaflet which will be circulated as soon as possible will explain to all how your investment in the enterprise we are all engaged in will be offset by the lack of income tax."

As an afterthought, Stewart added, "I almost forgot to mention a very important responsibility allocated to me and that is security. We will be establishing our own security force that will also double as the emergency service; as a result we should all feel very safe here. Finally, I must claim credit for introducing and engaging at least one member of staff, a most remarkable person – your Padre; who is not really your minister but a totally non-denominational councillor very able to deal with your personal and private matters, however, I will leave him to explain his position within our community."

"Thank you, Mr Slater; you gave a good lead to the Padre, so we will now hear from Mr Doug Grant."

"I am not used to being called Padre; I am a lapsed Reverend and, therefore, **have** been trained in theological matters, but have had a change in my outlook on life. However, it appears that this background is a suitable basis for the position of Padre within this emerging community. It is important for all to be aware that, in my maturing years I have developed a view which transcends all forms of religious doctrine. I do not wish to denigrate the Church, but I now see this as a man-made institution albeit with strong spiritual links. If, as most people do, you believe there is a God – whether you admit to it or not, He must be regarded as the pinnacle of all. Your existing religious approach, whether it be Catholic or Protestant Christian; Jewish; Muslim; Hindu; Buddhist; or whatever, must be based on the same origin – the creation of the universe, however you view it. My current philosophy was to start there, then work forward to the creation of matter, followed by living plants, then animals, and so to humans. However, I didn't stop there; I entered the human mind and discovered – in principle, how it works, how we learn, how our character develops and how this is influenced by the environment of our experience. I then discovered the relationship of the soul and where it 'resides'. It was then I realised that the pathway back to the creation was via 'The All Enveloping Influence' which is generally referred to as God by western religions or philosophies; but has an actual physical presence which requires explanation."

After a pause for reflection on the brief introduction to his well considered appraisal of humanity, Doug moved on to his immediate plans, "Although we will be establishing a church in which you may pray or simply have peace to reflect, I have no intention of preaching to you, I will not be holding traditional church services, but will have gatherings in which we might establish common purpose. In these meetings I would be most pleased to have the opportunity to discuss with you my findings and, through my maxim of 'consideration for others', to see how this philosophy can lead to harmony within one's self, within the family, in the workplace, in international affairs. My brief is to actively deal with problems of the heart and mind rather than the physical problems we have just been hearing so much about. Please treat me as your councillor with whom you can discuss – in absolute confidence, any problems be they large or small." Changing course once again, he led into his other duties, "Hoping that nobody has any problems in this unique environment, my time will largely be spent arranging social opportunities for us all. If then you have any thoughts of particular activities, I would be grateful for your suggestions. Personally, I do enjoy tennis, I was a member of a drama group, and a local choir; I was also active in the organisation of an annual carnival supported by sporting competitions, as well as dances and the like; so my wife Dorothy and I hope to be able to bring the lighter side of life to offset your busy activities developing Glenquoich. Thank you for your attention."

"I, for one, will be most interested to learn more of your thoughts on life and how they lead to creating harmonious relationships," declared Sam. "We have one final member of the team to enlighten us, the man who will be keeping his beady eye on the finances; let's hear from Sir Richard's accountant, Mr James Donaldson."

Unaccustomed to being in the limelight, he rose to his feet and began hesitantly, "Er, gentlemen and er, ladies, the only time I have ever spoken at a meeting such as this is to present the accounts at a company Annual General Meeting; to talk of oneself is somewhat different. I have worked with Sir Richard for many years dealing with his affairs on behalf of my employers. I was flattered to be asked to join his organisation to work directly and surprised at the significant increase in the salary offered; naturally I accepted. I now know why I was offered so much; my duties have been revealed to encompass so much more than simply monitoring income and expenditure." His biographical revelation over, Donaldson then set about explaining the scope of his responsibilities, "besides keeping account of all the financial transactions within the company, I am required to make

Highland Haven

myself available to assist the project planning by providing cost analyses for specific projects and to estimate profit potential for any exportable products in conjunction with Mr Bates. I will, of course, administer the unique salary system in cooperation with Mr Slater. On a more personal front, I shall be establishing a Community Bank operated by competent members of our community, backed with the financial expertise of one of the major banks. Not only will this be available for the various enterprises to handle their incomings and outgoings, it will provide the service to all members of the community. Through this, I shall make available internal investment options so that every one has the opportunity to capitalize on their tax free income whilst supporting this great enterprise. I can assure you of absolute confidentiality in these matters which will not be considered part of company operations; nobody – including Sir Richard, will know of any details of your affairs. As a closing comment, although I have not yet been party to any of these arrangements, I have considered the unique features of the remuneration package we will all enjoy and believe them to be most beneficial."

"Thank you Mr Donaldson, I'm confident that your financial services will be well received," commented Sam, and then continued, "we have now heard from all the current key players in this exciting adventure and it is quite clear that we have a good crew; this should make my job of melding you all into an effective team a pleasurable task. It is obvious that all of you seem to be sufficiently keen to have started planning your projects even before you started employment here – that's a good sign. Although it is not my policy to burden any of you with producing mounds of paper, I now ask you to set down the principal details of the various aspects of your work so that I can combine them into a Critical Path Analysis. I will then be in a position to combine the planning of all your projects, and to set priorities; this might call for adjustments to be made to your programmes. When Harry has got communications links set up, we will exchange information electronically on our local network; this is much more effective than paperwork since one can readily extract sections from each other's documents to incorporate or amend as necessary."

"One final word; at this stage, we do have an element in the Glengarry community which has been the cause of some difficulty due to misunderstandings and/or misinformation. We had a public meeting last week which it is hoped has set that aside but care must be taken not to cause unnecessary problems with local residents. Please do not discuss our affairs outside our team; should you feel there is a need to make public statements, let me know and we will agree what form it should take. And now, I will ask Sir Richard, who has been patiently listening to our deliberations, to perhaps say a few words."

"Thank you Mr Jackson. I must say that you all seem to have got into the spirit of this venture already; which is most gratifying since we are not simply

147

constructing buildings, laying down a railway, and carrying out commercial activities to generate income – we are building a community, a community with a difference, one based on a harmonious society structure. This is a great experiment with potentially far reaching consequences – make no mistake, there is more to this than is apparent at present. As Mr Jackson commented earlier; you have the makings of a great team – I look forward to great results."

Sam thanked their Chairman for his confidence in them then formally closed the meeting. As they broke up, Sue joined him commenting, "Well your first meeting seemed to go down very well, and I must say it is exciting the way everyone seems to have got stuck in so early. I can't wait for the castle to be built and the hotel and shops to be open."

"Well I'm afraid you are going to have to wait a while; until this winter weather breaks, progress is going to be slow."

"In the meantime;" Sue suggested, "we ladies can get on with the business of creating a community – with the help of Padre Doug."

Sue was not the only one discussing the meeting on the way home. "I'm not sure I like the padre's approach to religion," declared Janette Bates to her husband Bill. "One needs the discipline of dogma to focus minds on spiritual matters."

"I know what you mean but you must admit there are many approaches to what individuals or groups consider the Ultimate Being. Doug does have a point, the differing religious 'rules' do often lead to conflict."

"But who is he to tell us we shouldn't worship? The point is that I, for one - and I'm sure there will be many others, would like to attend a traditional church service on a regular basis – even if, because of the lack of great numbers this was only once a month, rather than once a week."

"Well look dear, when you ladies get together to discuss the social aspects of the project, you should raise the matter to determine what the others feel."

CHAPTER 15

The following day the ladies called their own meeting; it was Mhairi who initially set the wheels in motion by contacting every wife in the village. "Ladies;" she began, "although we witnessed a very interesting meeting yesterday which covered most things that are planned for Glenquoich, we were pretty well left out of the picture. I suggest that we organise ourselves to deal with matters concerning we ladies."

"I thought that was what the padre was going to do when he moves in," countered Elizabeth Shaw.

"I don't think he is expected to get us organised, merely help coordinate our activities with the various divisions. I think we should show the men that we too can do a good job and not wait for them to tell *us* what has to be done. Initially, we should formalise our committee by electing a chairperson, a secretary, a treasurer and perhaps three others in support."

"You seem to be doing the leading; so I nominate you for the Chair," declared Janette Bates.

"I second that," interjected Sue.

"Would anybody else care to offer themselves?" asked Mhairi.

After much shaking of heads, she declared herself as chairperson.

Sue was nominated as secretary but she declined; pointing out that she was very busy in a similar capacity as secretary to the whole project. She did suggest Janette Bates for the post. This was seconded and agreed by the others. Ann Slater became treasurer and the remaining three all agreed to serve on the committee.

"That takes care of all of us," observed Fiona Mackay, the school teacher.

"It does for the moment;" conceded Mhairi, "but there will be many more ladies as the staff builds up. Now for the first major suggestion, I propose that we take it upon ourselves to establish and run the hydroponic farm."

"That sounds like a big job;" complained Elizabeth, "I for one know nothing about hydroponic farms – I don't even know what that word means."

"Well I've learned something about it from reading agricultural journals and talking with my husband, but have never been involved," admitted Mhairi, "however, it is really the growing of plants in water that has had all the necessary nutrients added, rather than in soil – where the nutrients are not controlled to the same degree. Generally, seedlings are put into open pipes or troughs which have a slight slope on them; the nutrient rich water is then arranged to flow through, continuously. The benefit is that the plants always receive what they need when they need it and there are no weeds. As a result they grow quickly and consistently so that good quality crops result which are all the intended size. The modern

Iceberg lettuce is the classic example of clean well developed produce which can be cultivated in this way."

"That sounds very good," offered Ann, "but the climate up here is not very good for growing such things, surely."

"If you remember, at the project meeting my husband suggested that it might be feasible to build glass canopies across two small valleys at the head of the loch; well they've already looked into the practicalities and have decided that it would not be too difficult – so they are going ahead. I wondered if we could grow vegetables under the big one and flowers under the small one."

"You can't eat flowers."

"No, but you can sell them. I'm going to ask Alan if blinds and lights can be fitted to control the day cycle; this is what is done in professional horticultural houses so that the moment of blooming can be arranged to suit delivery."

"That sounds very elaborate," Fiona suggested, "we'll have to learn to walk before we can run."

"True; but we may as well aim high; we can always pull our horns in if we have to."

"Is it known when the canopies will be installed?" Ann asked.

"I can answer that;" Sue offered, "on the provisional programme, the first is scheduled for the beginning of May and the second to follow two weeks later."

"That means we have three months to learn what we need to know so that we can get started straight away," declared Mhairi. "I suggest we all search for as much information as possible by surfing the Web, searching the library, and telephoning possible contacts. In four weeks, we will meet again to exchange notes and decide how we are going to proceed."

"Agreed; let's have a cup of tea," Elizabeth insisted.

"While we do, we should also decide what other enterprises we can engage in. I know that Sue knits toys, and I will make perfume and creams from wild herbs; these we can sell in the tourist shop when it is built, to raise money for decorating the church or other charitable-type needs. If by our next meeting you could each consider what, if anything, you can contribute then we can think about brand names or other means of marketing the products to have a common thrust." Sensing a waning of interest, Mhairi concluded, "I can see that we have talked enough so hereby declare the meeting closed."

Whilst enjoying the inevitable tea and biscuits, Janette raised the matter of the padre's intention not to hold traditional church services. "I like going to church on a Sunday to sing hymns and join in prayer, even to listen to boring sermons; it provides a platform to re-look at life." She declared in a sudden bluster, without any preamble. "I think it is wrong that this padre fellow should declare his new-found philosophy as a matter of policy."

Highland Haven

I agree entirely," enjoined Anne Slater. "Those of us who have been brought up in a Christian household can't be expected to toss aside all we have learned, all we believe. So much for his maxim 'consideration for others'; he doesn't seem to have considered others at all."

"Ladies, ladies," Mhairi interjected. "I think we are getting a little heated before we have examined the facts. Mr Grant said *He* wouldn't be holding traditional services; he didn't say there shouldn't be any."

"Well, I suppose that's true," admitted Janette, "but I don't think I would care to listen to someone who is prepared to discard the very basis of so many people's lives."

Morag Donaldson joined the debate, "I am a writer and, as such, I'm always looking for angles. I don't want to offend anyone here since we are only just getting to know each other, but what I see here are blinkers. Janette and Anne feel very strongly about their religious upbringing which is fair enough but that doesn't preclude them from hearing what others might have to say. The padre stated clearly that he has a fresh view of life that he would like to convey to us; let's listen – without preconceived bias, to what he has to say, maybe his philosophy will deepen our understanding. He certainly didn't seem to be a dogmatic type of person - quite the opposite, to me he came over as a very understanding, deep thinking fellow who might have something new to consider."

"Well ladies, on that note of consideration I think we should call a halt to our discussion," suggested Mhairi, "We seem to have had more to say after the formal meeting than during. Perhaps we should delay any further discussion, formally or informally, until we have met the padre and had time to gain a more full impression of his views."

All agreed, they would invite Doug and Dorothy Grant to a meeting with them the following week.

Having welcomed the padre and his wife to their meeting room in the big house, Mhairi then explained their concern regarding Doug's policy not to hold traditional church services – adding that some ladies were very upset and disappointed.

"Oh please don't misunderstand me; you must realise you are basing your views of my views on the very brief statement I made at the inaugural meeting. I am most certainly not advocating that you should not follow your chosen religious calling; I merely pointed out that *I* wouldn't be the one to conduct such services. Besides my newly developed philosophy, there is the problem of the coming together of residents having differing religious backgrounds. More than likely we will have Episcopalians, Catholics and members of the Wee Free, all of which choose to worship in a different manner. What I have in mind is that, when we have established a church, we would invite ministers of each religion to conduct services, perhaps once a month so that one could select which week to attend for service. Perhaps some would care to sample the alternatives to widen their thoughts on pathways to God."

"If you will allow me," Doug continued, "to convey my thoughts on spiritual matters, I'm sure you will find that my pathway is wide enough to allow any and all religions to come along with me – given that one exercises an open mind. What I am proposing is that everyone should continue to enjoy their chosen church but that, hopefully, you may consider a wider view which can lead to greater understanding. Regardless of your own upbringing, I'm sure you will agree the world is suffering due to the differing approach to spiritual needs, causing conflict leading to war particularly in the middle-east – the seat of many of the principle religions of the modern world. I think this is due to misunderstanding created by tunnel vision. Whereas there is nothing wrong in gaining support from particular dogma; that should not prevent taking a wider view."

"Please give me the chance to show how my approach to the All Embracing Influence we call God not only encompasses all spiritual avenues, it leads to a greater understanding of each other – how we become who we are. I cannot do this in one quick session; that would imply triviality. Please be patient with me."

"Well," said Mhairi, "you do seem to have allayed our fears. We appear to have been guilty of misunderstanding due to tunnel vision; we jumped to conclusions based on very limited knowledge. Please accept our apologies."

Murmurs of support confirmed that she had conveyed the sentiments of all present, prompting the immediate serving of tea and biscuits.

During the ensuing months, there was much activity throughout Glenquoich. With the improvement to the weather pattern, contractors with much extra labour had taken full advantage of the pre-planning by Sam, Alan and Angus, backed up by the rest of the team. The foundations of houses were appearing on the loch-side, the village was taking shape at the head of the loch, and even the castle had got its toe-hold on the mountain-top. The railway was snaking along the north-western shore, heading into the next glen on its way to Loch Morar and Mallaig.

Arthur Brown's idea for the use of thermal energy was being tested out by drilling down into the earth's crust at selected points adjacent to the housing and the village. The hope was that water could be pumped down into a drilled loop such that the water emerging from the rising bore would be warm; it was not expected to be at high temperature but sufficient to provide under-floor heating as a background warmth. If they were successful in finding a heat pocket, once started, the circulation would be naturally convective – requiring no pumps, and therefore energy efficient.

Arthur's piece of brilliance was the manner in which he planned to distribute the warm water. He devised a water-driven diamond drill at the head of a flexible pipe having external, longitudinal ribs bringing the outer diameter up to that of the drill bit. Driven by a high pressure pump, which was arranged to act as the reaction base, the water-flow would drive the drill bit while the return flow would carry the spoil down the outside of the tube, between the ribs. With this arrangement, they would be able to drill horizontally through the granite to join up the main bore to the foundations of each building, keeping the resulting bored pipe below the frost line without having to excavate the rough terrain. The pipe being flexible enabled the bore to be steered to the required target. From this bored pipe, a convoluted system of plumbing laid in each floor would, with the aid of a small pump, take the water from warm up-flow to cool return. This form of under-floor heating would be energy efficient; removing a possible heavy burden on the electricity supply network.

Angus had given initial priority to the first section of the tramway running along the northern shore of the loch – from the main dam to the village. This would become the busiest route, bringing visitors from the outside world to the hub of the development at the village as well as providing residents with a service to and from their homes to the shops and other facilities. Most of the housing was being built along this course, overlooking the loch from the south-facing slope to take advantage of the greater exposure to sunshine. The transport network could then be extended into other areas as and when it became necessary after the system had proved itself. A large, multi-storey car-park will be built just below the main dam – so that the profile does not intrude on the skyline and to protect the vehicles from the harsh weather conditions. Residents would drive in at the bottom, off the lower dam service road. The tram station would be on the top floor, roughly level with the dam top. Lifts would be provided for pedestrian interchange. Casual visitors would leave their vehicles on the top floor adjacent to the main security gate entrance to Quoich in order to utilise the tram or minibus Residents would be able to collect their cars from the car-park when leaving the township for the outside world.

While all this heavy construction was in hand, Harry Shaw had established a basic communications system from a temporary transmitter, pending the completion of the castle; Bill Bates had opened the bank and essential shops all housed, for the time being, in a group of portable site huts. Stewart Slater, the Personnel Director, had ceased to be a nuisance to all and sundry when he completed his survey of resident's details so that the unique salary points system could be inaugurated and allowing for the assessment of immediate facility requirements this being essential for planning by other members of the team.

With the men-folk being so engrossed with the multitudinous activities; working excessive hours to take advantage of the long daylight hours of the summer season, the ladies had turned their attention to the social aspects of the fledgling community. They invited Doug Grant to address the whole community – small as it was at this stage, as a diversion from all the tasks in hand.

Now having settled in, the Padre made good use of the enthusiasm of the ladies' committee to establish the basis of a spiritual meeting room in the big house pending the construction of a purpose built church. At the first meeting, attended by virtually the whole staff, Doug was pressed to elaborate on the philosophy he had mentioned at the inaugural meeting.

"There are many aspects to my developed thought train but perhaps if I ask *you* to think; to think about harmony, this may be of immediate help." He then went on to discuss how waves of musical notes could be made to harmoniously combine to give a pleasing result or, if the tones were not tuned in to the appropriate frequency, they made an unacceptable noise. He then likened this to human nature by suggesting that if we showed tolerance towards other's viewpoints by retuning - adjusting our own attitude a little, conflict would be avoided and harmony would ensue. He continued by restating his maxim of 'consideration for others'; "this does not mean you must always give in to the other person's demands, but you should consider the situation from his/her point of view. If we all took that path through the maze of life's conflicts, we would surely arrive at the most equitable solution to all our problems. The very fact that you have arrived at a satisfactory agreement will give personal satisfaction; you will then experience fulfilment. It is fulfilment that leads to happiness; not, as most people seem to think - materialism. Materialism is like a drug; one becomes used to the level of input and then develops a desire to have more. A family on a low salary would just love to own a new car instead of the 'banger' currently used, but a middle class family's desire is to have not one modern car but two or even three. And so it goes on; 'if only we had this or that we would be happy', but no – there is always something else. It is important that everybody has ambition – to drive us forward, but this should be based on something more meaningful than material gain."

"The Chinese philosopher Lao-Tzu, way back in the 6th century B.C., advocated living in a simple and honest manner. He rejected righteousness and benevolence because they imposed on others. Rank, luxury, and glamour, he considered as empty values. He suggested we should return good for good, and good for evil; returning evil for evil breeds chaos. This we have witnessed so often in these modern times. I believe these maxims are as valid today as they were so long ago – perhaps even more so."

"Just to finalize, I would ask you to think how, in conducting your daily business, you can apply the thought process aiming at harmonious relationships, through considering the viewpoint of others. If you can truly see the situation as the other person does, you can more readily solve the problem which was creating conflict; this surely leads to greater efficiency as well as a more amicable relationship between you. This, in turn, develops a better day for you and generates that feeling of fulfilment. The fundamental requirement is to *think* - think of others. Well, that is my contribution to productivity for today," Doug jokingly concluded.

As chairperson, Mhairi thanked Doug for his thought-provoking comments and invited anyone to pass comment.

"I would like to say something," responded Fiona, the young school teacher. "Have you noticed how all the philosophers of the past are men? We've just heard of Lao-Tzu and most of us know of other ancient thinkers such as Aristotle, Plato and Socrates, then more recently Locke, Hume, and Kant, to name a few. Now we have our own Doug Grant, philosophising before our very own eyes, but where are the thinking ladies? May I offer a humble contribution from the fair sex?"

"Most certainly," Mhairi confirmed. "All contributions are most welcome."

"Very well then, let me explain. My husband Angus and I enjoy the social intercourse of playing cards in an evening; to us it is more uplifting than most television programmes. It is not easy to find a game for only two players that can hold interest and does not become dominated by one player; but we have found *Chinese Challenge*, a game based on patience. Please be patient with me, I will get to the point – eventually. Each player begins with a complete pack of cards – perhaps pink for the girl and blue for the boy. The object of the game is to dispose of all one's cards. There are, of course rules to be obeyed while cards are placed in descending order, in alternate colours, on eight initial cards on the table. The eight aces – when they appear, are progressively placed in the centre of the table, followed in correct sequence by the 2s, 3s and so on up to the kings. There are two crucial rules; firstly, only one card can be moved at any one time, and secondly, a card *must* be placed on the appropriate suit in the centre - if this is possible. The combination of these two rules results in much rearrangement of the table display in order to reach a valid card trapped behind others in the descending black/red sequences - particularly when one or more spaces have been created."

"Although I have not fully explained the play or penalties that can be imposed, I hope you can imagine the complexities that develop which causes the fortunes of the players to swing backwards and forwards, as with a pendulum – sometimes even to the very last card in a player's hand. Now we come to the crux of what I wish to say; *Chinese Challenge* emulates life. Nature deals each of us a problematical set of cards which we have to play while adhering to the discipline of a set of rules (laws). Life is full of ups and downs (pendulum swings) so one should not give up until the very end. The skill needed for a successful life is to make as few mistakes as possible. Not taking an opportunity is a mistake. Contain your anger when things are not going well; don't blame your opponent for your own mistakes. Finally, it is not so much winning - as not losing, which brings success."

"These lessons, Angus and I have learned, are constantly being repeated during games. These games are sometimes tense, sometimes funny in the way that the turn of a card reverses the trend of the game, but always intriguing. Each game mirrors patterns in life. So endeth my first, and possibly last, sermon."

"Well, I must say that we do appear to have a lady philosopher in our midst," acknowledged Mhairi. "Perhaps we should all ponder the lessons displayed in *Chinese Challenge;* Thank you Fiona.

"I would like to add my comments to Fiona's observations," Doug offered.

"Please do," agreed Mhairi.

"Fiona mentioned that one should not blame your opponent for your own mistakes. This is a very important point. My observations of life have shown me that, generally, anger – although directed outwards, should be directed inwards. A bad situation can often be traced to one's own failings; minor they may have been, but these failings are then aggravated by subconsciously apportioning blame elsewhere. Conscious effort should be applied to avoid deepening the crack appearing between both parties. Fiona's maxim *it is not so much winning as not losing,* strikes me as being excellent advice. Playing a game, such as that described by Fiona, can be very good training of one's attitude. Attitude is so very important; our reaction to life's hurdles will result in fulfilment or failure."

During the inevitable tea and biscuits afterwards, the general feeling was of comradeship based, not only on Doug's suggested thought process and Fiona's philosophical observations; but on the fact that they were making great strides with all aspects of the project even though they had only recently come together as a team. Everybody was finding a new, uplifting sense of purpose which completely off-set the other-than-ideal climate of the region. Spells of sunshine did not, at this time of year, bring warmth; but it did bring pleasantness to the outlook, adding to the aura of optimism.

Mid April saw the first significant milestone – the opening of the railway from the village station as far as the small twin dams where the canopies were to be built.

Much progress was made beyond; but it would be many months before Mallaig would be reached; however, this initial section was important in that it would serve the housing developments along that shore and give access to the proposed hydroponic farm. Since this section did not involve steep inclines there was no need to have any sections of rack; consequently Angus had acquired two diesel railcars and some flat bed rolling stock so that a provisional service could begin.

Sam arranged a formal opening to which everyone was invited. Sir Richard, under the guidance of a qualified driver, took the controls to drive the railcar through a ribbon stretched across the track leaving Village Station. Returning into the passenger compartment, he joined the rest of the directors and their wives to sip champagne while the driver took them to Twin Dams station. On the way he congratulated the team for their success in achieving this much in such a short time and commented that the availability of these first ten kilometres would be a great asset in the development of the housing programme and the hydroponic farm.

On arrival at Twin Dams, Angus announced that work had already started on the foundations for the two canopies over the small valleys – referred to as North Valley and South Valley. The station had been sited midway between the two valleys so that there was ready access for supplies to, and output from each of the growing-halls; either to the village or outward to Mallaig for 'export'. Alan added that, between them, they had designed a system of reflecting shutters – similar to enlarged Venetian blinds, so that sunlight could be reflected into the growing-hall or that the whole roof could be closed off, to preserve warmth, whichever was required. He pointed out that this facility would take advantage of the fact that the valleys were orientated east to west – which was originally considered a disadvantage.

On the return trip, Alan drew attention to the foundation work of the clusters of houses to be seen at intervals along the route. Arthur Brown declared that warm water *had* been the result of his trial bore; consequently the foundations could now have the heating pipes installed and the upper surfaces laid. Convenient to each hamlet, Angus had prepared a platform as a rail halt; this would be available on demand by the residents. A proper intermediate station was constructed – complete with double track passing loop, at Gleann Cosaidh where the railway crossed the large burn by way of a graceful bridge. It was thought that access to that glen would be required by walkers and stalkers as well as for the hamlet being established at the mouth of the burn. Arthur then added that provision had been made so that this first section of more-or-less level railway could become an extension to the tramway system should it be considered desirable.

During the latter part of their return journey, there was much discussion between the ladies and Sir Richard regarding their plans for the hydroponic farm. They had studied the various techniques and had decided that graded granite from the quarry would be the prime growing medium and that initially they would produce lettuce to gain experience then widen their expertise with other vegetables including tomatoes. The first target would be to supply all the needs of the community then start to 'export' to surrounding districts. They also told him that Liz Shaw had volunteered to take a specialist course on the management of hydroponic farms; as a result, when she had completed the course Liz would be made the manager. Sir Richard was very impressed by their professional approach commenting that it looked as if the ladies would be the first to generate an income for Glenquoich.

When Mhairi discussed their plans with her husband Alan that evening, he commented that she should have gone on the hydroponic management course. "I had thought of it;" she replied, "but I didn't want to get bogged down with the management of the farm. As I have said all along, I want to branch out into preparation of herbs as perfume as well as for medicinal and beauty treatment."

"If that is what will make you happy, my cuddly one, but you'll need help."

"Sue said she wanted to get involved with me; and we do get along nicely together; besides which, we do have the Padre to liaise with the Commercial Department."

"Talking of the Padre, when is his next natter?"

"He's going to have them once a month – the first Sunday at 10 o'clock in the morning."

"Next Sunday is the first of the month," declared Alan, "I'm interested to hear more of what he has to say."

"In the meantime, we've been invited by Sam and Sue to have a walk around their home at Alltbeithe with dinner to follow; Angus and Fiona are also invited." Mhairi announced, "I'm looking forward to it; too much work and no play leads to all sorts of nasties," she added.

The weatherman in the sky was being cooperative the day Sam and Sue welcomed their guests to their expanded cottage. After showing them around, they all went for a leisurely walk along the track leading up Easter Glen Quoich.

"This is quite a sun-trap;" noted Angus, as they enjoyed the abnormally good spring weather. "You could build more houses on these south facing slopes Alan."

"No shop talk," demanded Sue, "we're here to relax and unwind."

"What a peaceful place it is too," contributed Fiona, "it's even emptier than down at Kinloch Hourn."

"Empty? It's far from empty;" Alan protested, "that hawk wouldn't be circling if the area had no wild-life hiding in the heather; he's busy at nature's supermarket selecting his next meal."

158

Highland Haven

"Well I didn't mean empty of wild-life – just of people and their trappings; I know there are many deer around but what else would there be?"

"I'm not particularly familiar with this particular area but probably stoats or weasels will be scurrying around; pine marten will be resting awaiting sunset before starting their nightly vigil, and I know there are wild-cats around – those big vicious beasts with rings around their tails."

"Now then Alan:" Mhairi interjected, "don't try to impress these sweet young things with your country knowledge, that's almost as bad as talking shop."

"Hear that;" Sam joined in, "poor Alan's as henpecked as I am. Beware Angus, keep firm control over your lovely lady; don't let her gain the upper hand: your life will become a misery. You can tell, just by looking at us, how brow beaten Alan and I are after years under the thumb of our better halves."

"Somebody will be going without dinner tonight:" Sue suggested, "you, trying to kid Angus and Fiona that you are hard done by."

"There's no danger of that," said Fiona, "not now that we are going to be Mum and Dad; all our attention will be towards the wee bairn."

"Oh, congratulations," chorused Sue and Mhairi simultaneously, "how soon?"

"In six months."

"Oh isn't it lovely, Sam, Glenquoich's first born?"

"Yes; congratulations, we'll bring out the champagne when we get back to the cottage."

"Add my congratulations," interjected Alan, "it's odd that it is the school-teacher that sets the ball rolling. Are you trying to ensure that you have a job for at least the next ten years?"

Fiona responded, "for all there is a lot going on here, the environment is so relaxing compared to where we were in the Middle East, making a baby just came natural."

"I must admit," added Angus, "I was so busy with my work out there, I hadn't realized just how difficult Fiona was finding the unfamiliar environment; she never really settled, even though we were amongst an enclave of expats."

"I can understand that," Sam offered, "spending your formative years developing your character based on those around you then transferring to a world based on a totally different culture, must be a shock to the system. I must ask Padre Doug how such matters fit into his philosophy – he claims it covers all situations."

"I even found it strange coming to Scotland from England;" admitted Sue, "I've never lived out of my country of birth before and thought Scotland was just an extension to northern England; but it isn't. It truly is another country with different laws, different traditions, even a different language in remote parts. Although this area is absolutely beautiful and the people are great, I don't think I would like to have come alone, but I'd follow my handsome hubby anywhere."

"That's good to hear," Sam declared, "'cos my stomach is demanding attention so follow me home and into the kitchen and get cracking with the dinner."

"Now who's brow beating? A woman's work is never done," bleated Sue.

After a most enjoyable meal, they all settled in the lounge with coffee and a malt whisky.

"I was talking to Janette Bates the other day," Fiona confided, "and she, being perhaps a little more church-orientated than most of us, was rather keen for the construction of an actual church to be started sooner rather than later. She suggested a very good location which has a special character."

"This sounds intriguing," Sam commented.

"Well, where Loch Quoich kinks like a banana there is a small island just off the northern shore, it is where the tramway meets the railway before running towards the village. Janette felt, if a bridge was built, this would make the ideal site for the church because of its peaceful situation and yet close to railway, tramway and road. What do you think?"

"It sounds good; just a minute," Sam said, "I'll pop through to the project office and get a detailed map." A moment later he was back opening the appropriate chart on the coffee table for all to see.

"It seems ideal to me," commented Alan, "if Angus gave us a tram stop right on the junction, it would be accessible from all directions."

"A don't see a problem in that," admitted Angus, "and a bridge from the nearest point to shore is but a short stroll away."

"Would there be room for a memorial garden?" Sue enquired.

"Just about; if the church was say 50 metres by 30 metres, it would be half as long and half as wide as the island, leaving room for a small walk all around. Memorial plaques could be affixed to the outside wall to be readily seen whilst strolling along the pathway."

"Oh, this sounds exciting," Sue exclaimed, "can we get started soon?"

"Patience dear," Sam retorted, "we need to consult Doug for his thoughts on the matter and then, if he agrees on the basic idea, we'll consider alternative designs from Alan while Angus designs the bridge. I must admit though, it does seem like an excellent situation."

"I've just been cogitating while you were talking," offered Alan, "a church of that size would hold about 300 people, allowing plenty of space for a foyer and a platform area for an alter and rostrum, as well as an office/vestry. We probably would not normally fill so many seats so should arrange a partition to reduce the size for regular meetings, but open up for special occasions such as a choral concert or perhaps an Easter play."

"Right then," declared Sam, "try to find time to prepare one or two designs for consideration and, Angus, you consider the station and the bridge. Although we mustn't indulge in over elaboration, both designs need to be a bit special in view of their purpose. Perhaps the designs can allow for future adornment by community volunteers over the years."

"Although I said we should not have any shop talk," Sue admitted, "we seem to have developed something really great for the future of the community. I can't wait for it to be completed."

"Women!" declared Sam, "no patience, no concept of what is involved – just lovely to look at."

CHAPTER 16

At the beginning of May, Sam had called a progress meeting for the Friday to review work in hand as well as future developments; and so all the heads of departments gathered at the big house.

"I really feel we are on our way," opened Sam, "now that the railway is operating as far as Twin Dams. How soon can we expect the housing along that stretch to be finished, Alan?"

"Because we have prefabricated the frames, and a great deal of the detail work is done, we expect the first one to be complete by the end of May. Given we find no hidden snags; we expect to complete one per week thereafter."

"What progress with the commercial buildings?" Sam enquired.

"As you have seen, the main building in the village is beginning to take some form now that the foundations are complete. For everyone's benefit, I should explain that this building is a combination of transport terminal for trains, trams, and mini buses, together with a small shopping mall at ground level. At first floor level we have some administrative offices and the terminals for two cable car systems; one to the castle on Sgurr a' Mhaoraich and the other down to Kinloch Hourn. The floor levels above this constitute the hotel and main conference centre. It will not be just a large slab of concrete; as this artist's impression shows, we have broken up the profile by incorporating wings and features such as large eaves on pitched roofs to continue the Alpine theme. It is expected that the shops and offices will be ready for occupation by July; the hotel will not be completely fitted out until next year."

"What about the tramway, Angus?" Sam asked.

"The route from Village station to Car Park station at the main dam is now complete. We are awaiting delivery of the first tram so that trials can begin; this is expected at the end of May. Given that the trials are satisfactory, we need a decision regarding whether or not we should extend the tram system to cover the initial part of the railway as far as Twin Dams."

"Well;" said Sam, "I've given quite a bit of thought to this idea and feel we should. Bearing in mind that the residents will not be running around in their private cars, I want them to have a good, flexible means of travel between each other as well as to the community facilities. If we have separate systems from Twin Dams to Village as opposed to that from Car Park to Village, it would mean having to change from one to the other. Those living on the western limb, towards Twin Dams, would also be disadvantaged since they would have to wait for a scheduled service rather than calling on demand. I also thought that to give a frequent service on the rail line would be inefficient, requiring more manpower whether there was a need or not. Does running trams on the rail line, as well as the mountain railway trains, present big problems?'

"From my point of view," interjected Harry, "I can alter the programming of the master computer to add that section without too much difficulty, but we must then decide how much control we should have on the trains to avoid conflict with the trams."

"I suppose," interposed Angus, "that it would be necessary to have loop lines at each stopping point, rather than just at the midway station of Gleann Cosaidh, so that trams could readily pass."

"Well that would certainly help;" agreed Harry, "to keep them short, we could always arrange that the tram went in the loop, leaving the straight-through track for the longer train."

Sam commented, "I know of a system in Manchester where trams change from ordinary railway track to tram-track laid through city streets. At the transition, the control system changes mode so as to be compatible with the different circumstances. Can we install such a dual system in the locomotives for the mountain railway?"

"Yes we could; we can make it inhibit the driver's controls if the next section of track is not clear. The movement of the mountain trains is already going to be monitored by track circuitry, so this information can be fed into the tram control computer to complete the system. If we wish to go ahead with this modification, I could arrange trials on the two railcars we already have."

That's a good idea;" confirmed Sam, "but why were we monitoring the mountain trains when they are manually operated, not computer controlled?"

"Well, Angus and I felt that, since the route was over rugged, uninhabited terrain, it would be wise to always know where the train was – particularly in the event of heavy winter snow."

"A very sensible precaution. Arthur, what about the additional requirement of power supplies for the trams along this added section?"

"No problem; the mains distribution cable to the houses and the hydroponic farm runs alongside the railway and has spare capacity, so it would be just a matter of tapping into it at the recharge points."

"Very good then, we'll do it:" declared Sam, "the system will be much more complete. If the experiment with the two railcars proves completely satisfactory, we'll retain them as supplementary rolling stock for use in very busy periods or in the event of mains failure. What can you report, Angus, regarding progress with the rest of the railway?"

"We've already laid track from Mallaig to Morar, along the existing British Rail track and are progressing well with track laying up the side of Loch Morar since we are just, in effect, notching into the shore. Provisional work has been started on the more difficult section between Loch Morar and upper Glen Dessarry. We then have a 500 metre long high level bridge to construct over Allt a' Ghiubhais before entering the 1200 metres of tunnel. The tunnelling is now under way from the northern end - utilising the completed concrete viaduct across the hillside of Coire nan Gall to remove the spoil. Barring unforeseen problems, I estimate completion by the autumn."

"Perhaps you would explain for everyone why you constructed the concrete viaduct instead of simply cutting a track into the hillside."

"Two reasons; firstly there are many burns running down the slope which would have had to be bridged – so we constructed, in effect, a continuous bridge. Secondly, it was felt that we would be causing too much interference to movement of deer and other wildlife; by raising the track they can pass underneath which, incidentally makes it safer for the trains. We have, by the way, dyed the concrete brown to merge with the landscape."

"I hope the deer learn that it is safe to go under the structure," commented Alan, "they are naturally nervous of strange happenings."

"They seem to be alright with it when there is no actually activity," Angus assured him.

"What news from your domain, Arthur?"

"Besides the cabling to the housing under construction, the tramway from Car Park to Village and the hotel and shops, which is now all done, I'm looking into a pumped storage installation utilising Loch Fearna. It's certainly technically feasible; but the question of costing versus the benefit has yet to be addressed."

"What does our Commercial Director have to say to match the promising progress on the engineering front?"

"I must say that building and civil works   are progressing faster than I expected and I am conscious of the challenge presented to keep my domain up to speed. With that in mind I feel that now is the time to have a positive publicity push. How about that; a P.P.P.?" he light-heartedly interjected. "If there is no objection, I would like to invite members of the press, radio and TV to a gathering here to show off what we have achieved in this short time and point them in the direction of where we are going. The highlight for them could be a train trip from Village to Twin Dams during which they would be subjected to our briefing. If we coupled both railcars together, I presume intercom between them could be arranged. I would limit the invitations to the capacity of the two cars."

"I don't want to appear negative," replied Sam, "but don't you think we should wait until more of the facilities are ready?"

"Really effective publicity can be gained if we convey to the press the dynamic situation we have here; they will be keen to return – perhaps every couple of months, to witness the progress. Our own publishing department has, as you know, launched its first journal "Highland Highlights", which has, of course, featured Glenquoich; this is creating interest in the scheme." Bill Bates continued, in an enthusiastic manner, warming to the attention he was gaining, "I'm keen to start bringing in day visitors this summer; they can take train and boat trips, fishing and roe-buck stalking must also maintain its continuity. We now have facilities for sailing, wind surfing, and water skiing. I have arranged with a fellow who lives down Loch Hourn to take passengers on boat trips out to the Sound of Sleet, this we might develop with a view to arranging ferry trips from Mallaig and/or Kyle of Lochalsh. We can offer sight seeing flights in the Widgeon. I also thought it would be an attraction for day visitors to be taken on a wild terrain ride in an Agacat. So you see we already have plenty to offer during the summer season and should take advantage of it to start developing an income."

"Right Bill; let's have the press, but keep them on a tight rein, whereas I agree that publicity would now be beneficial, we do not want to attract undue pressure. Might I suggest that, before the press visit, we invite a similar number of locals from down the glen and subject them to the same treatment; this would serve as a good public relations exercise as well as being a practice run for the media bash."

"That's not a bad idea, I'll do that."

"Now then Stewart, how is the personnel department?"

"I've got the records up to date; procedures initiated; and the basis of a security corps established. A check-in gate is being constructed where the road passes the main dam so that any vehicle entering or leaving can be logged and directed to its destination within Glenquoich. All the men engaged for the corps are proficient in first aid and two of them are qualified paramedics. We are currently establishing a clinic and have fitted out a couple of Land Cruisers as emergency vehicles. I have discovered that a district nurse lives down the glen; although she is due to retire, she has agreed to work for us at the clinic on a part-time basis, mainly for routine treatments, particularly of children and ladies. A link has been established with the doctor at Fort Augustus for medical advice. The primary school is established in the big house, under the direction of Fiona Mackay, but further educational developments, although being planned, are pending the completion of corporate buildings. In principle, we visualize developing a college as a remote annex to the Inverness High School, with a particular emphasis on environmental, computer and business studies. The Padre has taken quite a load off my shoulders with his active involvement in ensuring the provision of adequate leisure activities; he is doing this with positive support from the ladies of the community"

"You seem to have matters well in hand," praised Sam, "but, regarding the educational developments please keep me fully informed; I'm anxious that whatever we take on should be to the highest standard, I want Glenquoich to become renowned for excellence."

"Absolutely. I too believe that educational standards are of prime importance; students must be set on the right path at the outset."

"Now then James, how is the accountancy field, are the residents taking up the investment opportunities offered?" enquired Sam.

"They certainly are, I was surprised; they have really taken to the spirit of this remarkable venture. Although there is significant risk involved, some have sold shares on the stock exchange to provide more funding. Personally, I don't understand what is really happening; there appears to be such a buoyant mood, it is almost like a disease infecting everyone – but this infection seems to be bringing enthusiasm rather than malaise."

"Perhaps I can help you to understand," began Sam, "those working directly on the various projects are boosted by the underlying principle that this is not just a money-making business; it is a scheme to improve the lifestyle of the community whilst binding us closer together. Residents have discovered that, as the padre pointed out, happiness does not come through gaining material objects but through fulfilment. This fulfilment is gained from the satisfaction of successfully completing each of their tasks on time or even ahead of schedule. This has an ongoing effect; each of us sees around us the rapid progress being made and can realize how that will make life here better – all want to be a part of that progress."

"In my field of accounting, I have never come across anything like this before," admitted James, "it is like opening the door from a dark room and moving into the sunshine – it's changing my outlook, I must admit."

"Well, on that philosophical note, I wish to thank everybody for the effort being applied to these demanding tasks – please keep up the good work, the sooner we get to the stage of fully opening our doors, the sooner we can start generating an income to balance our payments."

As they were leaving, Sam called the property director back. "Alan, Can we give some thought to creating a college campus? I've been looking at this map of the south side of the loch and have identified a possible site. I am aware that in the winter months the mountains put that side in shadow; I think generally the north-facing shore will be without sun from early October to the end of March – you can check on that. However, not all of the south side runs east-west; see here, towards the dam there is this island, Rubha Dubh nam Fiadh, and to the south of it the mainland shore is running north-south even facing south-west slightly. This will surely receive sun for the greater part of the year."

"I think you may be right," confirmed Alan.

"Is it too much to ask that college buildings be built on piles, half in the loch and half on the shore with an access bridge from the south? This way we would have a stylish feature to be seen from the more active north side. Accommodation could be built along the south shore where it runs north-south. An extension of the tramway from Car Park station, across the dam and along that shore would link staff and students to the rest of the community or readily to the outside world."

"I think your idea could work; it's certainly worth looking into. I'll have a word with Angus to see what he thinks from the civil engineering point of view. I do have one thought though; it might be worth considering swapping the concept around."

"How do you mean?"

"Since the colleges don't need sunshine particularly, but housing does, why not build the collages ashore and the accommodation on the island which will certainly have greater direct sun than the mainland shore. Your architectural thoughts can still be a feature with the colleges half in and half out of water and the accommodation units, flats and houses, could have prominent patios projecting over the water. Occupants could even take advantage of the fact that the marina is not far away on the other side of the loch; they could have their own boat as a ferry."

"I think you have a good slant on the general concept Alan, so pursue it with Angus and then let me know the outcome."

CHAPTER 17

Sunday; the clouds were low, cropping off the mountains; not just the tops but almost down to road level – in fact one felt almost able to touch the solid base of the rain-laden overburden. It was quite oppressive, almost eerie since it wasn't actually raining; just thoroughly dismal with what should have been day, turning to night. It was in this sombre mood that many of the residents met at the big house to hear what the padre might have to say during his second gathering.

"Welcome to my house of thoughts;" was Doug's greeting, "I'm sure we are all in a rather sober frame of mind during a morning such as this; how then can we find some joy, some enlightenment, under these circumstances? Well, I imagine that you are all probably thinking that there must be a better place than this; The Riviera, or the Greek Islands, perhaps even Australia - anywhere that the sun brings brightness and comforting warmth. Well there *is* some joy for you, some enlightenment; we are all thinking on the same lines – we are in harmony. As I mentioned on a previous occasion, harmony is so important; while we are making 'music' together, we are all pulling in the same direction. Notice how, in days of old, the oarsmen of galley ships would sing together creating a common rhythm for a more effective combined effort; their ship would move along much faster. The Afro-Americans were renowned for their singing whilst working in the cotton fields, or pulling boats up the Mississippi; the harmony eased the burden of their working day. Harmony is of fundamental importance in achieving fulfilment."

"Although I stated at the outset that I would not preach, I do seem to be preaching, preaching to the converted since you all seem to be working very effectively as a harmonious team; making great advances with the various projects here at Glen Quoich. I wonder though whether or not you had thought how this has come about. I believe Sam Jackson is, himself, in complete harmony with Sir Richard's ambitions and has managed to convey that aura to you, his team. I use the word 'aura' quite deliberately since we each have a personal aura of electromagnetic vibrations stemming from our thoughts – both conscious and unconscious. This is a fact, not some wishy-washy myth; actual electromagnetic signals are generated by the brain activity of pulses transferring energy via the synapses from cell to cell. This activity is very much akin to the operation of the early spark transmitters and crystal receivers which were common in my early days. Individually these are quite weak but can be received by others who are close. When I say close, this can be physically close, since its strength drops off by the square of the distance away, or emotionally close due to the persons being tuned to the same wavelength. Collectively, if we are all on the same wavelength we will generate a much stronger signal due to resonance – one signal reinforcing another which, in turn, reinforces the original. This becomes more apparent when we are physically close together say at a meeting – such as this. The aim of the leader of that meeting should be to focus everyone's attention on a common aspect – which is what I am attempting to do."

Janette Bates interjected with a supporting observation. "Some years ago, I attended a rally conducted by the evangelical preacher, Billy Graham. I wasn't sure that what he might have to say would agree with my existing religious outlook; however, he galvanized the whole congregation into a common thought train, and one could feel a tremendous atmosphere developing; we all felt warm and loving towards each other. I, like most everyone, left the stadium feeling quite uplifted."

"Thank you for that input Janette, "Doug acknowledged, "that is an excellent example of the resonance effect of common thought taken to a highly emotive state. It should also serve as a warning; a skilled leader can generate resonant support not only of beneficial vibrations, but of immoral and/or illegal activities. I'm sure we have all read of weird sects being established – particularly in the USA, in which sensual activities take place, often to the financial benefit of the organizer. The skill of the leader in these cases has been applied to pseudo-religious activities so that satanic vibrations reverberate causing his followers to cast aside their inhibitions and indulge in many deviant practices – even the taking of life."

"For good or for bad, this coming together of human psyche is possible due to finding oneself in a common physical and emotional environment. Those around you are performing in a certain manner with general approval – it must, therefore, be okay then for you to join in this activity; extra moral strength is necessary to challenge what all those around you believe to be the norm."

"I see," said Fiona, the school teacher, "this is why teaching in class is so effective; the children all start to think in the same way, as directed by the teacher, and their thoughts affect the thoughts of those nearest to them. I realize now how a teacher with a bad attitude creates an unsettled class. It makes me a little nervous to think of the power one can have over other people's minds – particularly youngsters."

"I don't wish to aggravate your nervousness; I'm sure that your attitude is most satisfactory, but you used the correct word when you referred to the *power* that collective thinking can generate. Propaganda during a conflict, such as in World War 2, is a very powerful tool. Germans were encouraged by the Nazis to believe that they were the superior race and that inferior strains should be eliminated. This leads to an understanding of how the holocaust was able to take place; officers and men were progressively introduced to the notion that the presence of Jews was a hindrance to the development of the 'master race'. Slowly, insidiously, minds were warped into believing that it was for the greater good to annihilate the whole Jewish race. Be warned; think about what you are being told – compare it with your own moral code; don't allow antisocial tendencies to infiltrate your character; build on the good, reject the bad."

"At a future gathering, I would like to elaborate as to how your character is actually formed and why environment is so important; as on this day, we were all influenced by the oppressive clouds and our own close association. However, my underlying theme is to think; think about what you see, and what you hear. Think about why things are the way they are; if nothing else, I believe it adds much interest to our lives but, more importantly, it can prevent one from doing undesirable things."

"Thinking can even save you money; lack of thought allows TV advertising to penetrate our psyche and cause us to needlessly spend money on items which are not necessary. If we extend that notion, we can begin to realize how the unthinking masses can be seriously influenced not only by commercial promotions but by political propaganda. The natural tendency is for people of a particular stratum in society to frequent clubs and other venues attended by like-minded persons. This being the case, the general aura unconsciously reinforces the individual's mind-set; he or she becomes a staunch Socialist, or a firm Conservative, even though no real thought has ever been given to the details of political policies."

"If we think about such matters as basic political opinion, it becomes apparent that democracy is flawed; the vote of the unthinking carries as much weight as that of the professional politician. This is made even worse in such countries as Australia where penalties are enforced on non-voters; making every Tom, Dick and Harry apply his mark alongside meaningless names. Let's be radical with our thoughts and consider, in the light of such problems, whether or not each voter should be made to pass a validity test designed to establish the candidate's basic understanding of current affairs as they relate to social management. The point is that just thinking about the problem leads to the development of understanding. To make decisions without understanding is totally irresponsible."

"If, as you say, democracy is flawed;" interjected Alan, "what system would you substitute in its stead?"

"A dictatorial democracy seems to fulfil the requirements as I see it; the leader dictates the policy but his decisions are subject to a veto by his supporting committee. To choose who should lead or who should represent your area, I believe a three-two-one system of voting would yield a more representative result. To explain, if you select your preference from the list of candidates by giving three votes, your second choice two votes, and your third choice one vote, the end result will be weighted – showing the true support. As mentioned earlier, I believe a voter should have to attain a certain qualification; let's face it, you do not allow the tea lady to have a vote at your management meetings. I am aware that this violates the now well established principle of one man, one vote but – if you think about it, with one vote you are effectively saying you support 'A' but have no support for 'B' when, in fact, you are often having great difficulty separating your preferences. This suggestion is a variation on the system of proportional representation.'

"Well ladies and gentlemen, I have dashed through a number of important matters which are really deserved of deeper treatment, however, I hope my deliberations have given you some food for thought since that is what I am suggesting; let's *think*, let's think about what makes the world tick and maybe go even further and think what makes the universe tick. I'd like to pursue that wide avenue at our next gathering. Thank you all for your indulgence. By the way, your input is most welcome – if only to stop me preaching."

They had all been so engrossed in the subjects being highlighted that, until they broke up for a social chat over tea and biscuits, they had not noticed the weather. It was now absolutely pouring with rain; to combine two common phrases, the cats and dogs were coming down in buckets. It really was appalling; where there was a hard surface, the rain was rebounding more than half a metre. As they watched through the great bow window, the drops, which had virtually merged into a wall of water, began to separate into the icy balls of hailstones.

"Cumulonimbus," Alan declared.

"I beg your pardon;" Sue retorted, "are you swearing?"

"Certainly not. Cumulonimbus is the large, violent, unstable cloud that generates hailstones and, judging by the size of the icy missiles bouncing off the driveway, we have the granddaddy of a beast overhead right now."

"How come we now have such an unstable cloud, creating these great squally winds," Sam enjoined, "when an hour or so ago we had that very stable oppressive cloud mass overhead?"

"It must be an occlusion;" Alan replied, "the heavy cloud we had when we were coming here this morning was probably Nimbostratus, this is a very thick stable cloud, rising sometimes thirty to thirty-five thousand feet; that's why it was so dark and oppressive. Such stable cloud is typical of a warm front. On the other hand, unstable cloud is typical of a cold front. If an active weather system is fast moving around a deep depression, the cold front catches up with the warm front – this is called an occlusion. The cold air, being heavier, pushes – like a wedge, underneath the previously stable air mass, with its moisture laden cloud, lifting it into colder air, this causes heavy rain. As we have just seen the heavy downpour is then replaced with the turbulent rain and hail of the large, unstable Cumulonimbus."

171

"You can see all that, just from the change in rain-drops?" queried Sue.

"Most certainly. This is such a clear-cut case that I can go on to say that shortly there will be a lull then a change of wind followed by a lightening of the sky as the cloud breaks up to give separate showers. If it doesn't, and the turbulent conditions continue for over an hour, it will indicate the merging of two or more Cu-nimbs, making a pretty rotten storm front."

"I tell you what; "Mhairi declared, "I've no intention of going out in this, and if two or more of your horrors have merged, you can forget your Sunday lunch."

"Let's see if Pat Evans can rustle up anything," Sam suggested, as he went in search of the housekeeper.

"I could prepare a cold smorgasbord, if you decide to stay;" she declared, "give me about half an hour's warning."

After watching the weather for a while, it was decided that the situation out there was not improving and so they all agreed to make an event of it by having a social lunch of whatever Pat could provide. It turned out to be most enjoyable, particularly after a couple of pre-meal drinks from the now well established club bar.

It was about half-past two when the clearing weather allowed the lunch party to break-up and consider going home. Some had already left when a phone-call changed the whole mood; it was from the contractor's foreman working on the railway bridge at the southern entrance to the tunnel.

"The storm has washed away the temporary scaffolding-trestle-bridge;" he declared, "men are lost – we need help."

Sam immediately notified their untried emergency crews, instructing them to meet at Twin Dams.

"What access do we have to the southern portal Angus?"

"From here we can get by train to the northern portal then – if we're lucky in this weather, use the helicopter to ferry men and equipment over the ridge. To do that last bit on foot could take about five hours."

"Where's the chopper now?"

"Being Sunday, the pilot is on standby with his machine parked on the flat not far from here."

As they spoke, Ted Evans came through from the private wing.

"I've just heard; can I be of help?"

"What is your assessment of the conditions?"

"I need to check with the Met. Office, but there is some sign of easing although it is still very turbulent."

Highland Haven

"Okay, you get yourself briefed," instructed Sam then, turning to Stewart Slater, who had also appeared in order to coordinate his emergency crews, "contact Mountain Rescue and get them to send a team up Glen Dessarry and another to be picked up by our train from Mallaig – we shall then have a three pronged attack from the north, the south, and from downstream. Better alert the RAF rescue chopper to supplement our own – but warn them of our presence. When you contact the team to come up Glen Dessarry, be sure they are on the look-out along the river for survivors who may have been washed down by the flood. You will be the central control, coordinating movements; myself, Angus and Alan will go to the scene."

As Stewart dashed away to carry out his instructions, Ted Evans returned to declare that heavy showers were still to be expected but they would progressively be dispersed. He went on to declare that the Sikorsky Spirit's normal capacity was twelve passengers but with help, he could soon remove the seats to make way for casualties, leaving just four seats.

"Grab any help you can get; we three will get rigged up in wet gear and boots to come with you. Your gear is fairly close to hand;" Sam declared, "but mine is too far away; I'll borrow some from Sir Richard while I inform him of the situation."

"I'll stay here until you get back:" Sue decided, "Maybe I can be of help to Stewart, on the radio or the telephones or something. I'd prefer to be actively occupied rather than sitting alone at home brooding."

"Janette and I will assist at the clinic should it be necessary," contributed Mhairi, "I'll ring the district nurse to get her here to prepare for injured."

"Fair enough," agreed Sam, as he left the room in search of his boss.

By the time the three directors had got to the helicopter, eight seats had been removed and a basic assortment of ropes, spades, crowbars and some first aid equipment had been loaded. Ted started the engines as soon as they climbed aboard.

"How many men were working there?" Sam asked Angus.

"Harry Jackson, the foreman told me that besides himself there were twelve men working on the shuttering for the bridge piers, in preparation for the big concrete pour starting tomorrow. A couple of men escaped with minor injuries but the rest went down with the steelwork."

"What about the men working in the tunnel?"

"Work on the south portal had been halted pending completion of the bridge concreting; the two regimes interfered with each other. The men had been temporarily transferred to the northern entry, providing round the clock working. There is no ready access for them to help – unless you want to lift them over the ridge by chopper."

"We'll bear them in mind should we need extra manpower," Sam decided.

As they flew above the western limb of Loch Quoich they were relieved to find that a clearance in the appalling weather had occurred. Although it was still very blustery, the turbulence was not too much of a problem, and they could clearly see the two four-wheel-drive emergency vehicles negotiating the rough track along the north shore.

Sam went forward to have a word with Ted at the controls. "Take us straight to the scene and then come back to Twin Dams to pick-up and ferry the men and equipment in. Can you also radio back to Stewart and arrange for both rail-cars to be at Twin Dams to bring back casualties. The ladies could help by being travelling nurses"

"WILCO." Ted acknowledged, and then radioed the two rescue vehicles, and Stewart to advise them of the plan.

While Sam was sitting in the co-pilot's seat, they passed over the roofs of the hydroponic farm. It was like falling off a ledge; the turbulence struck with dramatic force. All Ted's skill was required to stabilize the aircraft as they now flew over the rugged terrain rather than the level surface of the loch. Following the new railway south from Twin Dams Station, they gained more height as the slope of Druim Buidhe slid underneath. The face of the ridge being fairly consistent, Ted managed to hold the chopper fairly steady but, after about five minutes, they had to pass over the rough terrain under which the tunnel was passing; they were immediately tossed about violently. Another minute and they came in sight of the tangled mess that was once a temporary high-level bridge.

"Good God, look at that; its like a smashed Meccano set. The poor devils must have fallen about 250 feet," Ted observed as he struggled to bring the chopper down on a vaguely level area about 150 metres downstream – just clear of the debris.

They leapt out as soon as Ted set her down and then unloaded the limited amount of gear they had brought with them. Before Ted took off again, Harry Jackson appeared reporting that there were two men with minor injuries, and two with back injuries, just a few metres away.

After a moment's thought, Sam instructed, "we're not equipped to move those with back injuries; the RAF will be here shortly and can transfer them direct to Raigmore Hospital in Inverness. We'll stick to the plan; Ted, you go and pick up our emergency teams. I'll have a word with the injured fellas while Angus and Alan start an assessment of the situation."

Amongst the mass of bent and twisted steel tubing men could be seen trapped but it was unclear how badly injured they were. Harry told them that he had been in the site hut when this wall of water and boulders came down the glen; there had been no time to warn the men on the bridge. "The rain must have caused a landslide blocking the burn," suggested Alan, "the build up behind would then push the whole lot down to the bridge."

"I've brought a couple of spanners down to release the scaffold joints so we can get to them," the foreman said.

While they set about trying to release those that were trapped, Sam had got to the four injured men and reassured them of the help that was imminent. The two with back injuries were about 100 metres apart and, sensibly were being helped by the two with minor injuries. By the time they had got them as comfortable as possible without moving them, the chopper had returned with one of the teams and their equipment.

Sam ordered the two walking casualties to return with the chopper and to take the first railcar back to the clinic. Then, drawing attention to the approach of another heavy downpour, he got the rescue men to rig temporary covers over the injured before covering them with blankets. Leaving them to care for the casualties, Sam and Harry Jackson started to survey the immediate downstream area in case there were any injured men lying helpless in the wet.

After a while, "Over there!" the foreman shouted.

Sam came to his side to see what he was pointing at. On the other side of the swollen river was a crumpled heap alongside a large rock. They repeatedly called out but there was no response. Just when they were wondering how to get across, the chopper returned, carrying the second emergency crew. Sam signalled frantically to prevent Ted from landing and directed him across to the heap. There wasn't a suitable landing area but, while hovering close to the ground, two of the three-man team climbed out and dropped alongside the mystery bundle.

Locked together, in a freezing grip, two men were found to be unconscious. They both had facial injuries but other problems could not be readily determined. Exposure was obviously a problem so blankets, a tarpaulin and a medical kit was dropped to them before the chopper moved away to reduce the problem of down-wash. It was then that they noticed a body wedged between two rocks, about five metres away.

Sam returned with Harry to the tangled mass that had so recently been a bridge.

"There are three men trapped in the steelwork;" revealed Angus as he and Alan worked feverishly to unbolt the twisted joints, "the two halfway up are talking but don't know how injured they are. The one trapped low down appears to be a goner – probably drowned."

"That makes two losses and two missing," Sam revealed.

Just as the heavens opened to bring torrential rain once more, the train from Mallaig arrived with the mountain rescue team and cautiously stopped before the broken bridge. Above the noise of the wind and the rushing waters of the river, the sound of the RAF helicopter heralded *their* arrival but, in the increasingly turbulent conditions, two attempts had to be made to land on the limited flat whilst avoiding Ted's chopper already parked there.

When all was safe, Sam called a brief conference but before he had time to propose their course of action, the Flight Lieutenant pilot reported they had picked up a radio message from the mountain rescue team approaching up Glen Dessarry. "They have found a man suffering from exposure about three kilometres downstream from the bridge and are currently giving him treatment; they have requested a pick-up."

"There's still one missing;" Sam declared, "we need to search for him. I suggest that you, Flight Lieutenant, should take charge of the two casualties with back injuries and the two from the other side of the river. Ted could pick up the exposure victim and on the way search for the last man if he takes two of our emergency crew members. The rest of us should concentrate on releasing the men still trapped in the steel-work. When that is done, we will reassess priorities for transfer."

"That sounds like a practical plan – given that the weather eases a little," replied the RAF pilot.

As if the weatherman was listening, the rain eased and the squally wind dropped as the skies cleared – at least temporarily. Whilst the two with back injuries were being carefully eased into the RAF rescue aircraft, Ted took-off with two men and a couple of stretchers to search downstream as far as the Fort William Mountain Rescue Team. About a kilometre down the glen they spotted the still form of a man washed up on some rocks; he was unconscious but still alive. CPR was applied with positive results, they then checked him over finding broken ribs, a broken arm and many lacerations. He had received a severe blow to the head causing concussion, but they managed to lift him aboard and then settle him on a stretcher.

Further down they came upon the Fort William team and managed to land close by. The casualty was lifted on his stretcher into the chopper. Ted suggested to the leader that, since all the men had now been accounted for and that there was plenty of help up at the bridge, they could be released. However, he replied that, as a matter of course, being a Police team, they should establish exactly what had happened to ensure there had been no negligence. With that, they continued on foot while Ted flew back to land near the bridge just as the RAF helicopter was leaving to take the four most injured men directly to Inverness.

By now the light was beginning to fade and so a new pressure was applied to complete the rescue. The men had been freed from the steel; the two survivors suffering multiple injuries but none life threatening. Sam made the decision that they should be taken immediately by Ted to Twin Dams, along with the two already on board, and the two emergency crew members. They would all board the second railcar to be taken to the clinic, while the chopper returned to ferry the remaining men back. The team from Mallaig would return on the train taking with them the two bodies. Ted told Sam about the police investigation so, when the chopper returned they had to wait while the Fort William team arrived.

By the time they came into view, Sam was becoming concerned regarding the lack of light. The leader quickly explained that they would camp overnight where they were and then commence a full assessment the following day. With that Sam joined the rest in the helicopter for an immediate take-off. They dropped off the emergency crew members at Twin Dams to collect their vehicles and then Ted flew back towards Kinloch Hourn.

"It's always fairly dismal at the head of the loch: by now it will be pretty dark down there. I don't know if I shall be able to see well enough to make a safe landing," Ted admitted to Sam sitting alongside him. "I will descend over the loch to the west and then approach the landing pad cautiously."

They crested the ridge and started a gentle descent aiming to the west of the helipad when, quite suddenly, a ring of light appeared. Cars had been positioned in a circle, facing inwards. As soon as the sound of the returning chopper's engines had been heard, headlights had been switched on to illuminate the landing pad.

"Thanks for that – whoever you are," said Ted with relief, and then changed course and angle of descent to make a direct landing without any difficulty.

Willing hands took charge of the equipment to be offloaded and the weary passengers, together with pilot Ted, made their way to the big house for well earned refreshment. They were soon joined by Stewart, who reported the safe arrival at Raigmore hospital of the four seriously injured men taken there by the RAF.

"What news from the clinic? Sam enquired.

"Doctor Haig, from Fort Augustus, came at the request of Nurse Jones, and he has set the broken bones and generally stabilized the injured men. He recommends that they all should be taken to Inverness for X-rays and a thorough check-up - particularly in view of the head injuries; but feels this would be better done tomorrow after they've rested," Stewart reported.

"Was it your bright idea to illuminate the helipad?" Ted asked.

"No; that was Bill Bates. He's been of tremendous help, rustling up extra beds and organizing the ferrying of casualties down from the station to our temporary hospital here in the big house."

As if on cue, Bill came in to the room to join the group reviewing the events of the afternoon and early evening. Ted immediately went to him and shook his hand, as he thanked him for his forethought.   Sam took the opportunity to thank everybody for their efforts and then left the room to visit the injured in the ad hoc hospital. He found, not only the doctor and nurse tending medical needs but the Padre busily taking down contact details so that loved ones could be notified.

"Thank you for that, Doug," Sam commented, "could you extend your services to Raigmore and establish the condition of the four men there, and whether or not their relatives have been notified. We also need to establish the identity of the two deceased who were taken to Mallaig and advise the next of kin."

"I've already had a word with Harry, the foreman, and have got their names, but we will not have access to their details until the contractor's office opens tomorrow. I shall follow through this task with regard to all of the men."

Sue and Mhairi came into the room, wearing aprons covered in plaster-of-Paris. "We're about done, how about you?" enquired Sue.

"There's nothing more to be achieved by me tonight, I just could do with a nice relaxing meal to relieve the tension," Sam declared.

"Well Mhairi has suggested we both go to their place, she and I will share the task of preparing a meal then we can have a quiet evening together."

"That is just what the doctor ordered," sighed Sam.

CHAPTER 18

At a hastily convened meeting the following morning Sam again thanked everybody for their best efforts and then stated that all should learn as much as possible from the unfortunate incident.

"One observation I will make, is your position in such circumstances," Sam addressed Stewart. "It seems inappropriate for your title to remain Personnel Director - your sphere is rather wider than that, I propose that you be henceforth referred to as Director of Administration. A small, upwards adjustment to your salary may also be appropriate."

He then went on to request the preparation of a formal review, by Stewart, of all that had happened, together with observations and any recommendations for procedures in the event of emergencies.

"I have already had some basic thoughts on the matter and would ask each department to prepare a risk assessment to assist me in future planning. I feel we need to grade possible accidents on their potential degree of consequences. This incident was obviously a one-off but we might have a potential drowning due to a boating accident, or a severe road accident such as a collision of two mini buses loaded with passengers; a cable car might come to grief, or the hotel may catch fire. On the other hand there are sure to be less critical accidents such as hand injuries from tools, or a broken leg due to a fall. Whatever, we need to have a response code appropriate to the perception of the incident so that more or less people become directly involved; the code can always then be upgraded or downgraded according to need."

"That is a sound approach to the problem," agreed Sam, "we need also to be prepared to accept a revised change of command in the field according to one's area of expertise and detailed knowledge. One lesson we have already learned, thanks to Bill, we need proper illumination of the helipad, that's your domain Arthur, please give it high priority. When you have dealt with that, you might consider how we could help Ted land the Widgeon in the dark – bearing in mind there may be night fishers on the loch."

"Why are the police investigating the incident?" enquired Stewart, "surely it was just an accident."

"It was truly a matter of routine procedure but, with the two deaths, it will now assume greater importance since there will be an inquest. Will you arrange with Ted to take photographs of the wrecked structure both from the air and from close-up at ground level; this will also give you an opportunity to witness the scene first hand. While there, go up stream and take shots of where the landslide started, just for the record."

"Actually, I have already initiated that because of insurance claims, both by us and on behalf of the injured. Ted is preparing to leave at 10.30 this morning. It is also expected that the injured men we have here will be fit enough to be transferred by helicopter to Raigmore as sitting passengers immediately after lunch. I have arranged for the nurse to travel with them just in case there is a problem."

"I suggest we look into the cost of modifications to the helicopter to make it more suitable for emergency use," Angus proposed, "a winch arm for picking up people when a landing is not practical is an obvious consideration, and perhaps conversion to ambulance mode is another. I would imagine the manufacturers would have such designs readily available as options."

"That's a good suggestion;" agreed Sam, "I shall pursue that myself. What effect will the accident have on your schedule, Angus?"

"We need authority from the insurers – and, I suppose the police, before we can clear away the debris. I have already contacted the scaffolding contractors to prepare them for our re-ordering, they can move in as soon as we say. The big pour of concrete scheduled for today has been cancelled and could be rescheduled for one week after the clearance date if Harry can get a team together, and if the shuttering is okay. I think I will re-visit the site this morning with Stewart to assess what damage, if any, was done to the work in progress."

"Might I suggest," interjected Alan, "that when any significant work is being done away from the village, that a stretcher be on hand. We suffered through lack of stretchers on this occasion and, with the terrain being as rough as it is, it is very risky moving casualties."

"I'll arrange that," agreed Stewart.

"Well gentlemen, I think we have covered the matter sufficiently, pending Stewart's formal assessment, so we'll get on with the job."

Just as they were breaking up, Sue came into the room saying the press were on the telephone wanting to know what happened yesterday. "Simply tell them that floods demolished some scaffolding while men were working on it but, because two men were killed, they had better check with the police at Inverness for any official statements."

On the Wednesday following the accident Sam had a visitor; it was Detective Chief Inspector Hamish MacLeod from Northern Command Police at Inverness. After initial greetings and the provision of a pot of tea, the DCI launched into the reason for his visit; I have to inform you that our investigations into the incident on Sunday have revealed that it was *not* an accident. As a result, the forthcoming inquest will either be postponed pending further enquiries or will declare it a case of manslaughter/murder by persons at present unknown."

"Good heavens; how can you conclude that, surely it would be classed as an act of God?" Sam suggested.

"Under the circumstances of the heavy downpour that had obviously occurred, it would be a reasonable assumption. Whereas it was initially thought that an avalanche had caused a temporary unstable dam to be formed which then burst, our team could find no such evidence and believe that rocks were hand placed to form a rough dam. We need your full cooperation, Mr Jackson, since we have now opened a criminal investigation."

"You will certainly have that;" Sam assured him, "how can we help?"

"Do you know of anyone who would have a grudge against your company?"

"Inevitably, when developments are taking place, particularly in an area of natural beauty such as this, there are objectors; but I wouldn't think anyone would go as far as sabotage," Sam responded.

"Passions can get out of hand," the DCI suggested.

"Although we had publicly announced our intention to build a railway from Glen Quoich to Mallaig, very few people would know the details of what we were actually doing up the valley beyond the end of Glen Dessarry – it is quite remote and rugged."

"Quite so; this narrows our enquiries quite significantly. Presuming that the only way anyone would know about the scaffolding across the river would be by observation. Can you tell me when it was erected?"

Picking up the telephone, Sam said, "I'll check. Angus; what date was it that the scaffolding was erected? I see, that's fine, I'll fill you in later, I have the police with me." Replacing the receiver, he relayed the details.

"So it has only been in position some ten days; that limits our enquiries still further. In that time somebody has seen the steelwork, realized an opportunity to interfere and carried out the disastrous act."

"Perhaps they only intended to wreck the scaffolding, not to kill anybody," suggested Sam.

"That's as maybe. It is the difference between the two possibilities that differentiates between manslaughter and murder. Do you know if any hill-walkers or stalkers were seen in the area during construction?"

"I doubt there was anyone stalking; the Red Deer season doesn't start until the 1st July, and there are no Sika or Roe Deer up there. However, I shall make enquiries with my staff. Perhaps you will be interviewing the work crew?"

"I definitely will. Do you have any data on the actual rainfall?"

"We certainly do. As a matter of fact, because our Property Director is particularly interested in climatology, a rain-gauge was set up quite near to the work site. I'll fax you the figures when they are recovered."

"That's excellent; they will help our consultant to assess the flow rate of the river and determine pressure on the rock dam etc. Do you have any other information that might help with our enquiries?"

"Our Admin Director is in the course of preparing a full report on the incident, mainly to analyze our own responses, but also to assist the insurers. We have also taken photographs from the air and close-ups on the ground. They'll be included in the report; in fact I have a set here you can see now."

"Oh these are very comprehensive and very professional. I see you have also taken shots of the rock dam, I see our men carrying out their assessment. Thank you Mr Jackson, you have been most helpful. I'll keep you informed of our progress."

"Before you go, I must ask; is there any reason why we cannot clear the site so that work can be resumed?"

"You carry on; these photographs are most suitable as evidence. I look forward to your report as soon as it is ready."

"By the way, added Sam, as the DCI was leaving, "I've already referred the press to Northern Command HQ for any official statements."

Sam called Bill Bates on the telephone. "In view of the accident, I suggest you finalize arrangements for the public and press visits as soon as possible."

"Oh, I thought you may wish to postpone them; the public visit was set for Saturday and the press for next Tuesday, but I was just about to cancel it," Bill replied.

"Let them go ahead; I think it might forestall gossip resulting from Sunday's drama. In any event, they won't get to see the accident site. However, don't engage in any discussion about what has happened – it is now a case of manslaughter. Simply state flood waters washed away some scaffolding with men on it. If there are any further questions, refer them to the press releases from the police."

"Manslaughter; who is being charged with manslaughter?"

"Don't worry; none of us are in the frame. The police think the flood was deliberately caused as an act of sabotage. They are making detailed enquiries."

Sam then called Angus and asked whether he knew if hill-walkers or stalkers had been seen in the area of the bridge. "As a matter of fact, now you mention it, I remember Harry Jackson had to stop the scaffolders working when they were building it, because of pony trekkers walking right underneath."

"I never thought about pony trekkers," admitted Sam. "When was that? Do you have any details of how many there were and which way they were going?"

"I'll contact Harry and find out. What is the relevance?"

To Angus's amazement, Sam explained about the sabotage theory, stressing that we should be careful not to start rumours in view of the police investigations.

It wasn't long before Angus rang back to say that the trekkers were travelling upstream on their way from Kingie to Inverie and that there were approximately a dozen of them.

"How do we know where they were from and where they were going?" queried Sam.

"Harry chatted with them when he stopped the men working."

"What day was that?"

"He said it was about lunchtime on the Wednesday – ten days before the accident."

"Thanks Angus; that information is going to be most helpful."

He then rang Ann MacDonnell, who took them pony trekking when first they came, to ask who might be the person taking a string of ponies from Kingie to Inverie.

"Oh, that'll be Robbie McIntosh," she replied, "he often takes a party on that route and then, perhaps the following week, after the ponies have rested, he will bring another party back. It is a popular dramatic trek which takes about three days."

Realizing he had already crossed swords with him, Sam immediately rang the police at Inverness to convey this new information to DCI MacLeod.

Saturday came and Bill, meeting the expected visitors at the security gate by the main dam, found that additional people wanted to come on the trip but he refused them, judging that they were only here because of tittle-tattle due to the accident. He did, however, include them in the initial briefing regarding the car-park, now under construction and the tramway under-going trials. He explained that if and when any of them wished to visit when the facilities were open, they would be required to park their cars and then make use of the automatic tramway. Purchasing a one-day travel ticket would give unlimited access from Car Park to Village, Twin Dams and Kinloch Hourn. To travel by rail from Village to Mallaig would be a separate charge.

The agreed party boarded mini buses each accompanied by one of the executive staff giving a commentary as they proceeded along the loch-side to the village. Bearing in mind that the visitors, being local, were all familiar with Glen Quoich as it was before the project started, they were keen to see how the scene had changed. Particular interest was shown in the automatic tramway, so the method of use was explained. The only construction along this stretch of the single-track road was foundations for some houses on their right and the addition of a marina on the left in the bay formed by the old quarry from which the dam wall material was originally excavated.

Rounding the peninsula where the old radio-telephone shack still stood, a distant view of the village under construction presented itself and the work on the castle atop Creag a Mhaoraich could be seen. This caused much chatter since nothing of the sort had ever been seen in this area. It was pointed out that the mountain top construction would appear as a stone castle when complete and that the village buildings would all be of an Alpine style. This caused a further heightening of interest.

As they approached the bridge across the limb of the loch which went north to Alltbeithe, the passengers could see the new houses, in clusters, along the north western shore, beside the railway to Twin Dams and beyond. The style generated by the roofs having large eaves and the upper, dorsal story projecting beyond the ground floor, together with the shuttered windows met with general approval, although there were comments comparing them with Swiss cuckoo clocks and music boxes.

The buses pulled up at a newly opened café in the village for a break with morning coffee and the opportunity to ask questions. Bill Bates apologized to all for the incomplete state of the village which, due to the very active construction, was not yet suitable for a walk about. He declared that all except the hotel would be ready for business in July. From the café, all could clearly see the cable car climbing to the castle construction where, Bill explained; a restaurant would give a magnificent vista over the mountains and out to the Isle of Skye. He also pointed out that there was to be a second cable car from the terminal down to Kinloch Hourn, but this was not yet constructed.

After the refreshment break, the combined party boarded the two railcars, linked together for this occasion so that all could travel as one group. As they travelled parallel to the road they had just motored along, Bill explained that subsequently, the automatic trams would run along this route as well as the longer distance diesel electric trains to Mallaig, and that the latter were fitted with the mountain railway rack system to ensure full traction on steep slopes. By the time he had finished his explanation, the railway had veered towards the south and then around to the south-west, giving views of the loch and mountains from an angle that had never been seen by the majority of the locals.

As they travelled towards Twin Dams, they had close-up views of completed Alpine-style houses forming little hamlets by the rail-side. Already landscaping of frontages was taking place, making quite attractive settings. As they rounded the bend into Gleann Cosaidh, a glimpse of the ultra slim high level bridge they were about to cross presented itself; and then, as they traversed the valley, the sensation of being on a knife edge caused considerable excitement. As they continued, and the end of the loch came into view, Bill explained about the roofs over the valleys below the two small dams and pointed out how, being a very shallow profile, they did not intrude on the surrounding wild scene.

At twin Dams, they all alighted for a brief look at the developing hydroponic farms. Bill pointed out that production was at a very early stage but that it was anticipated fresh produce would be exported via the mountain railway to Mallaig and Fort William – perhaps much further afield when the project becomes fully developed. Explaining how the adjustable shutters would direct controllable sunlight into the buildings, he also predicted the production of out-of-season cut flowers designed to provide an income, again by export out of the area, but they would also be used in the hotel and restaurant.

"What happened on Sunday?" a voice from the group called out.

"There is a police investigation, so I cannot say too much, but I can explain basically what happened. As you can see, the railway continues south across the hillside. You may be able to just see that, about three kilometres from here it enters a tunnel – not yet complete. On the other side, as it exits the tunnel, it is due to cross a bridge similar to the one we crossed coming here from Village Station but much longer and much higher. We built a temporary scaffolding trestle bridge from which to work while building the concrete bridge. On Sunday the very heavy rain caused flood waters to bring down a lot of rock which smashed into the steelwork and collapsed it. Unfortunately, men were working on it at the time and two were killed. I'm sure you will be reading more about it when the police finish their investigations."

"Oh my God; I didn't know anyone was killed," shrieked a female voice. As Bill turned to face the voice, the lady was seen to collapse. She was lifted into a seat on the railcar while smelling salts from the first aid kit were used to revive her. She soon recovered her composure but was then suffering embarrassment at the fuss she had caused.

"How are you feeling; are you alright?" Bill asked, and then after an affirmative nod, "Could I have your name please?"

"Oh it's alright. I'm feeling well enough now; it was just a shock to learn men were killed."

"That's as maybe, madam; but it is company policy to record any incident as a matter of routine."

"What if I don't wish to give my name?"

"I must insist; this train is not moving off until I know who you are."

"Come on Morag, tell him who you are, *we* all know."

Maurice Duffill

"My name is Morag Matheson," she reluctantly revealed, "I live a couple of miles beyond the Tomdoun Hotel."

"Thank you madam," Bill acknowledged. "If everybody will re-board, we will now commence the return trip."

During the return journey Bill introduced the general activity plan of conferences and seminars at the hotel, a great increase in sporting activities, and the future development of college facilities. He went on to remind the locals that there would be many opportunities for employment and that they should apply according to their experience.

After transferring to buses at the village, the run back to the car park was subdued as the visitors were deep in thought about all they had seen. As they disembarked, they thanked Bill for their most interesting morning visit.

Unaware of any special significance relating to Morag Matheson, Bill simply entered the details in the computerised incident log, on his return to the office.

It was the next day that Sue opened the Incident Log to update details relating to the accident when she noticed Bill's entry. She immediately drew Sam's attention to it, knowing what had occurred before. "Why would she be so shocked?" mused Sam, aloud; "unless she had something to do with Sunday's catastrophe. Get Bill on the phone, I wish to know exactly what was said."

After hearing Bill's account of what he had told them and how she had responded, Sam rang Inverness Police HQ and drew DCI MacLeod's attention to the known previous association between Morag and Robbie McIntosh. He also explained about the enquiries made on Sir Richard's behalf which revealed details of the obscene calls.

"If they're in this together," cogitated the DCI, "why were they making obscene telephone calls to her before?"

"Initially they thought our developments here would upset their nefarious activities, so tried to raise objections which – they hoped, would stop our work. When they realised that pressure from Miss Matheson might cause official investigations, they dreamed up the telephone scheme to take her mind off what we were doing."

"I understand; now it appears that she's moved into the realms of sabotage – probably paying McIntosh to do the dirty deed. I wonder if his colleague Ferguson or McGilvery were called upon to assist; two men were sighted on horse-back in the area - going upstream at dusk on the Wednesday and returning during the half light of dawn on the Thursday. I'll put further investigations in hand."

The press arrived on Tuesday morning; journalists, photographers and TV film-crews, all eager for news related to the accident now that they had been advised of

186

the two deaths. They brought with them copies of their respective publications bearing dramatic headlines:

MURDER IN THE MOUNTAINS

SABOTAGE BRINGS DEATH TO THE HIGHLANDS

WAS IT MANSLAUGHTER OR MURDER?

Bill had considerable difficulty in focussing the group on the intended purpose of the visit, only succeeding with the promise of a full briefing later in the tour. With that, they settled to a repeat of Saturday's public viewing.

While at the village for the coffee break, one of the journalists raised a question regarding the manner in which members of the community traded.

"I noticed that your residents here don't use money at the shops," he said, "I asked one of them about the card they used and she said they spend GQPs from their smart-cards. Could you explain?"

"Certainly: A GQP is a Glen Quoich Point, this is the in-house currency – the currency in which everyone is paid. Salary is credited to the employee's account at the Community Bank; when cash is required for general purchases, the account holder takes his/her smart-card to the bank and the required amount is electronically embedded in the card and the account debited by the same amount. At all the retail outlets, shops, café, restaurant, hotel, railway, and tramway etc the card is scanned and the appropriate amount removed electronically. This removes the need to carry cash for anything, without the involvement of credit cards – just the one, smart-card."

"That sounds fair enough; but why GQPs, why not our normal currency?"

Bill then explained the points system and how the rate of exchange can be varied by the executive in keeping with the trading success of the Glen Quoich Development Company.

"While the value is retained as points, the company has the use of that capital to assist with the financing of the various projects – I think it is called seigniorage; this way everybody is contributing to the wellbeing of the enterprise."

"Isn't that like stealing the employee's money?" countered another journalist"

"Not at all; the account holder receives interest on the points value held at the bank, just like normal interest bearing accounts; in fact the interest rate is quite generous – normally ½% above the bank rate for the rest of the country."

"How can the company afford to do that?"

"By encouraging all residents to keep their funds in GQPs, this reduces the need for the company to borrow capital at an even greater rate."

"What if, as in the early stages of your development, the company is not making a profit; wouldn't the value of the GQP be held down?"

"Yes; but this doesn't matter too much because everybody is treated the same so the price of all internally produced goods is held down. This encourages everyone to buy home produced food etc and it will mean that the cost of exported goods and services will be attractive to outsiders."

"What do the residents think of this cash-less system?"

"They like it because they find they can control their household or personal budget readily by having separate cards, and they enjoy the benefits of the interest being earned while the money is not actually being used."

"Isn't it a bit risky though, what if the company goes bust?"

"Firstly, the pound value of the GQPs paid in salaries etc is put into a trust account kept independent of the company finances so that, in the event of a total crash, the salaries are secure; it is only the interest gained on a spread of investments made by the trust that is used to finance development. Secondly, everyone is free to hold monies outside the glen, in normal banks or investments on the stock exchange as a safeguard – we are not a fascist dictatorship. But, in fact, many have done just the opposite; they have invested capital in the company, or directly in particular projects within the development. This shows their confidence and determination that this enterprise will succeed."

"Perhaps you can understand;" Bill continued, "how, by this monetary policy, our society is developing as a subtle combination of Capitalism and Communism – not a wishy-washy half-way house, but taking advantage of the better features of both systems. Similarly on the political front, we have a Dictatorial-Democracy. The Chairman dictates the basic philosophy of the development which is carried out by the executive but safeguarded by having the power of veto when greater than 67% raise an objection. This option has not been applied as yet, and we don't visualize doing so; but it is there as protection against unreasonable demands."

"This is very interesting; I thought you were going back to the feudal system where everyone had to buy from the company store, but it appears there is much more to this project than just grabbing profits from tourists. Going back to the practicalities of GQPs, if I was a visitor to Glen Quoich, how would I buy anything?"

"The bank will supply a temporary smart-card carrying whatever value you choose to pay in pounds, dollars, and francs, whatever. When you leave you will receive the balance remaining on the card, in the currency of your choice. A change bureau will be operating at the entrance by the main car park to issue these cards."

There was much note-taking and mumblings within the group while all this was being absorbed, as they boarded the railcars to continue their tour.

Highland Haven

At Twin Dams, where they were in view of the railway leading towards the tunnel, Bill elaborated on the incident rather more than with the local visitors. Their disappointment at not being able to see the destroyed bridge was eased by presenting them with photographs taken by Ted Evans.

Notwithstanding the interest in the topical news item, they were suitably impressed with what they had seen and expressed interest in future visits when developments would be further advanced. Bill provided each with a portfolio containing a written summary of the Glen Quoich Development Plan, illustrated with artists' impressions of completed buildings, sketch maps, and drawings.

They left happy that they had plenty of material to work on.

Sam took particular interest in the following day's newspapers but, instead of articles describing developments at Glen Quoich, what confronted him was more reference to the sabotage:

TWO MEN AND A WOMAN HELPING POLICE WITH THEIR ENQUIRIES

SABOTEURS LIKELY TO BE CHARGED WITH MANSLAUGHTER

"It looks as if the police have picked up Morag and her accomplices," Sam commented to Sue, over the dinner table.

"It's awful, isn't it; I wonder why they went to such extremes?"

"The fellows probably did it for money, but Morag was obsessed with what she imagined. It is a clear case of shouting before one is hurt or, as Doug Grant would say – tunnel vision, no pun intended."

"Yes but why go so far without finding out for sure what was actually going on?"

"As she said in my office, she was afraid if she didn't act quickly, damage would be done that couldn't be undone."

"But you explained to her that you were taking great care not to spoil the region."

"You've got to understand that people with passionate views become blind to other possibilities; being focussed can make a person very narrow-minded. She was demanding that we should consider the viewpoint of nature lovers while she was not prepared to consider the viewpoint of ourselves as developers. We have completely reversed the tragedy of the Highland Clearances by attracting people back into the area, bringing prosperity with them – but, through her glazed eyes, she couldn't see that."

"I suppose," concluded Sue, "it is that blindness to the views of others that causes wars."

"It certainly is," affirmed Sam.

CHAPTER 19

The first Sunday in the month saw the gathering of Padre Doug's regular clientele awaiting, with interest, his latest deliberation. After general conversation relating to the stupidity of those responsible for the sabotage, and the lack of understanding which apparently led to the act, Doug's opening words came as something of a shock.

"You dumb cluck: You've got the brains of a bat: You stupid goat: You're as dopey as a donkey. These derogatory remarks," Doug explained, "are the sort of comment one hears in connection with bad decisions such as the fateful plot leading to this recent terrible act. Notice how these statements all imply that animals have no intelligence; but let's think, are animals quite as dim as they appear? If you watch a flock of sheep grazing in a meadow you will observe that they tend to eat on the hoof; they're for ever moving from where they are to somewhere else – the grass further afield always seems greener. Do they go in different directions to seek the juiciest grass? Not generally. The leader moves in a particular direction and they all follow, they stick together – *like sheep*. Why would they do that? Maybe they are too lazy to think for themselves, but then perhaps they are wiser than we give them credit for. It could be they have realized, with their limited brain power, they are better off thinking collectively."

"How can they think collectively?" challenged somebody from the audience, "they are not able to converse so how can they have committee meetings," he added scathingly.

"You are quite correct, they don't talk as we humans do, but they can communicate – and do it decisively, so long as they are close together. Let's examine a modern marvel familiar to most of us - the personal computer. The fundamental ability of a basic computer element is simply a choice of one from two; yes or no; on or off; go or stop - 0 or 1. It is only when this ability of one element is linked with other elements that its decision making ability widens to YES, IF; or YES, WHEN. Linking *this* ability with others widens the capability still further until, by repeated interconnections and feed-backs, we have something quite sophisticated – this is the function of a silicon chip. I believe many animals work in this way; their individual brains are not sufficiently sophisticated to develop to the degree of the human brain, but collectively they achieve a level suitable for their needs. Individually their decisions are limited to eat, walk, move left, move right, and so on; but subconsciously they are feeding input to the flock regarding the quality of feed available, impending dangers, and other matters of concern to them all. Notice how, if you are driving along a lane with sheep on both sides, just as you arrive, they run across in front of you to be together with the others – this, I believe, is so that they can share their thoughts about the potential danger you are presenting."

"This notion brings us to the question, how *do* they communicate? The answer to that lies in waves – brain waves, not the sort of hypothetical brain waves that we attribute to inventors, but the actual electromagnetic waves that emanate from all brains, particularly human brains as they respond to action between active cells. If you are close to someone – emotionally, or close physically, these waves can be detected by another brain. Called Extra-Sensory Perception or ESP for short, this ability is somewhat cloudy in the case of humans due to the myriad of thoughts which are going on at any one time. It takes great concentration or a special closeness for the particular transmissions to be separated from the clutter of signals from all around and from those within one's own brain. In days long gone by, when life was much simpler, we humans could think much more clearly, because there was so little distraction from everyday matters; hence we had the seers of the past with brains able to lift thoughts to much higher planes. Thinking clearly, as is generally realized, is also much easier for a human if one is alone – preferably well away from other active brains."

"Animals do not concern themselves with the effect on a mortgage of the latest rise in the bank rate; the tragic loss of life in the Middle East; the problem of avoiding a bottleneck on the trunk route to the office; or any other such man-made encumbrances. Their minds are free to receive relatively uncluttered signals from those around them and to re-transmit these thoughts – possibly slightly modified, back into the flock or herd. In the event of a threat, this feed-back creates a resonant feed-back, generating a wave of concern resulting in action such as a stampede. Collective brain power is convincingly demonstrated by shoals of fish, or flocks of birds, reacting as one body in order to change direction instantaneously – particularly as danger threatens."

"So what can we - supposedly clever, humans learn from all this? We should *think* for ourselves; we are not totally dependent on the brains of others but we should also learn from the animals and communicate effectively in order to make considered decisions. In other words – don't be an animal but learn from them. The perpetrators of the sabotage to our railway bridge were totally lacking an understanding of what was going on here and allowed their animal instincts to direct a course of action having disastrous consequences."

"What I can't understand," interjected Ann Slater, "is, what did they hope to gain by destroying the bridge, it would only delay progress, it didn't solve anything?"

"I suppose," offered Alan, "as with other violent protests we hear of, they hoped to gain publicity with a view to raising support for their cause."

"It's a misguided policy;" insisted Ann, "people tend to distance themselves from trouble-makers."

"I agree; but some people's passion gets the better of them, it shows the shallow nature of their character," Alan added.

"That's a good leader to further thoughts, I'd like to talk about how character is formed," Doug declared, "but I think we've had sufficient serious contemplation for this session."

"I was going to ask you about that," admitted Sam, "Does environment affect one's character?"

"It certainly does, particularly in the formative years, so I look forward to our next get-together discussing this very revealing aspect of human behaviour which, again, depends on wave transmission. Thank you all."

Early June turned out to be the beginning of a record summer of sunshine with only very occasional refreshing showers. Was this to be an omen? With the tramway operational between Car Park and Village stations and the railway as far as Twin Dams, Glen Quoich was opened to general visitors for the first time since the development project was started.

To add attraction, the cable car to the yet-to-be-completed castle was opened to the public, giving access to a view point on one of the turrets, and the marina was operational offering a variety of boats for hire for rowing, sailing, fishing, and water skiing. For those that could afford it, sight-seeing helicopter rides were available, and there were boat trips by Angus McGilvery down Loch Hourn into the Sound of Sleet for a close-up view of the Isle of Skye.

With the weather being so favourable, the daily numbers of visitors increased as the weeks went by, most came just for a day to explore the facilities, and took advantage of the all-day tickets for unlimited rides on the tram and the rail-cars. The few who took advantage of the offer to rent the newly completed apartments for longer stays enjoyed the lengthy days of sunshine for relaxing, fishing, hill walking, and general enjoyment of what was on offer.

Sam remarked to Alan that if the weather was always so pleasant, they would have no difficulty in gaining the tourist trade they were looking for. "But, but, but," replied Alan, "it won't always be like this and, come the winter, the trade will evaporate."

"I am fully aware of that, so I am pushing Bill to publicise other activities that do not depend on the weather, and Stewart is aware that our scholastic ambitions need to be established as soon as possible. Of course, the opening of the hotel next year will make a big difference. Bill tells me there is already advance interest being shown in booking for seminars, conferences and corporate symposia. I'm hoping that the castle will be completed *early* next year so that we can open the high level restaurant."

"If we are blessed with a good summer, the basic structure will be complete by the autumn – as will the hotel, giving us the winter months to complete the fitting out ready for staffing in the spring."

"That's good; Angus tells me that, with the success of the cable car system up to the castle, he has started making detailed plans for the similar cable run down to Kinloch Hourn. We will then be able to offer a very interesting tourist trip from the Highland Railway at Mallaig to the Highland Railway at Kyle; Bill is already negotiating with the rail companies to offer package deals. Just imagine the novelty of travelling from Fort William by train – preferably steam hauled, to Mallaig, and then by our mountain railway to Quoich Village. After savouring panoramic views during lunch in our Castle Restaurant the visitor then enjoys a double cable-car ride down to the sea loch for a cruise to Kyle in order to take the train into Inverness - it's a winner. I shall look forward to sampling it myself."

"By the way," offered Alan, "my exposure meter project is developing nicely; Harry Shaw has incorporated a comprehensive programme in the main computer to map the whole area."

"I'm sorry Alan, you've lost me; with having so much on my plate, I must admit to having forgotten all about your special project – just run it by me please."

"Actually, it is my fault that you are not in tune, I realize now that I haven't been keeping you up to date, so I will recap. As you know, my earlier research – prior to coming here, resulted in a method for monitoring micro-climates, that is the climate at specific locations in an area such as a farmer's field, or different locations in a town or village. With help from a specialist company, we have now developed an inexpensive chip to carry out this task, and combined with an equally inexpensive radio transmitter, its data can be sent to a central point for evaluation. I have set up quite a large number of these sensors throughout our development area, and they are now sending data back to Harry's main computer. His programme combines all this information and presents it as a series of climatological maps. We can view these maps on any of our PCs throughout the network."

Turning to Sam's PC, Alan, with a few keyboard operations produced a variety of maps showing the variation over the area, at any one time, of temperatures, rainfall, wind, and other parameters.

"That's marvellous," declared Sam. "I suppose, with these you can best select what to plant where and when`"

"That's exactly it, but then having planted one's chosen crop, the system monitors progress and can give warning of the approach of critical conditions. We are just about at the stage where we can produce a demonstration CD so that we can market the system and its individual components. There are many applications for its use in agriculture, viticulture, water catchments, health-care, tourism, pollution control, forestry, and so on. The odd thing with this product is that although it concerns the climate it does not depend on the climate for us to produce it, we can produce and sell the various components at any time of the year."

"That's good; it sounds great, let's get on with it."

It was midsummer by the time the inquest was held on the fatalities resulting from the bridge catastrophe. The Coroner conducted a thorough enquiry into the circumstances leading to the deaths by drowning, compounded by injuries received during the collapse of the scaffolding forming a temporary bridge over Allt a' Ghiubhais in upper Glen Dessarry. Taking advice from experts and from photographic evidence, he found that there had been no negligence on the part of Glen Quoich Development Corporation or their contractors. He did declare that, although there had been abnormal rainfall immediately prior to the incident, the sudden surge was not a natural occurrence; a dam of rocks had been built upstream of the scaffolding. As a result he directed that the police should endeavour to bring charges of murder, or manslaughter, as soon as practicable.

The police immediately arrested and charged Morag Matheson, Robbie McIntosh and Malcolm Ferguson with sabotage and with murder/manslaughter. At their preliminary hearing bail was refused since it was felt they might continue to display hostility to the developers.

This caused a sensation throughout the glen among the traditional inhabitants and the newcomers. This was further heightened by the press having a field day. The locals who had known Morag for many years could not believe that she would be involved in such behaviour; they felt very sorry for her predicament. Many believed she would not survive a jail sentence; the ignominy of being labelled a criminal would be more than her pride could stand. On the other hand Robbie and Malcolm, although not previously considered as criminals, were known to be into a variety of nefarious activities; it wasn't too surprising that they had overstepped the mark. Morag's contacts in high places sought the best lawyers money could buy but their choice was limited by the fact that the case was to be tried under Scottish law which differs from English law and that of most countries. This point was picked up by the media.

While enjoying one of their many social evenings at their community club, Sue noticed the article referring to Scottish versus English law and asked Mhairi what the difference was.

Highland Haven

"Well I'm not a lawyer so don't know the subtleties but the main difference I am aware of is that, whereas in English law a person is declared either guilty or not guilty, in Scottish law there is a possible third verdict – *not proven*."

"Why ever do they have that?"

"I think it is a very good feature," offered Doug who had joined them, "if in an English court it is found that there is insufficient evidence, or that the evidence is considered inconclusive, the only verdict allowed is not guilty. The person cannot then be retried under the same charge. Whereas in Scotland, the verdict of not proven allows for the accused to be retried at some future date if and when more evidence is gathered."

"Canny these Scots." Sue muttered to her husband Sam.

"I don't know why England, or any other country for that matter, doesn't adopt the third verdict, I can't see anything against it," suggested Mhairi, "it tends to stop fancy lawyers getting their clients off when they are really guilty."

"Scotland leads the way once more," preened Alan. "What Scotland does today, the world does tomorrow; years ago it was our sensible approach to law with the three possible verdicts, today it is our fundamental approach to genetics with Dolly the cloned sheep."

"Ups! He's on his high horse, we'd better change the subject," suggested Mhairi.

"How are your scents and creams coming along Mhairi?" Sam asked; eager to avoid pointless conflict.

"Oh great. We have now got quite a range of cosmetic herbs developing, and Doug is helping with the design of labels and the packaging. We are keeping clear of medicinal products because the marketing is a minefield of rules and regulations which require years to obtain approval. However, we are growing comfrey, fennel, sage, thyme and others to sell as potted plants for anyone to plant in their own gardens and use for medicinal purposes. Our garlic beds are already looking very productive but we will use them as our own parental stock so that next year we can produce a much greater quantity. More excitingly, the shelves of our village shop are stacked with all manner of products to counteract dry or oily skin, cleansing lotions, skin refreshers and much more. There are formulations to improve nails, help tired feet, and oils for the hair."

"All this - just from herbs?" Sam challenged.

"Certainly, there are actually many hundreds of herbs available for a multitude of purposes but the trick to marketing herbal products is to establish ways of preserving their properties until needed for use."

"Do you think you will be able to expand your market outside of Glen Quoich and the visitors?"

"I'm sure we shall; we are using the village shop as a market test. With the number of visitors increasing we are keeping a detailed account of sales so that we know which type of product is most popular with various nationalities. We will then concentrate on exporting them on a preferential basis. Those working in the shop are briefed to solicit possible agents if particular interest is shown."

"I think the lassies are doing a great job," contributed Doug, "they've certainly kept me busy devising appropriate packaging."

"A man of many talents," observed Alan. "Raising our thoughts to a higher plane," he sarcastically continued, "tell me, what is the basis of your philosophical view of life? You seem to be able to tie everything together."

"Well, it is rather radical, but I believe it links everything in the universe, be it the expansive domain of the cosmologist, or infinitesimal field of the quantum physicist; be it animal, vegetable or mineral, even spiritual matters - before or after death."

"That is quite a claim. Is this something you've studied from the ancient philosophers?" Persisted Alan.

"No, I developed the concept as a result of giving consideration to an anomaly in physics."

"Could you explain?"

"Certainly, but it will take some while and I may bore the ladies too much."

"Oh Doug, don't treat us as if we were a cluster of bimbos," cut in Sue, "I'm sure others besides myself would be fascinated to listen to your dulcet voice explaining how you see everything linked together."

General approval of the rest of the group sealed his fate. Sam suggested that they adjourned to the dining room to enjoy their evening meal and then, over coffee and the usual malt whisky, Doug could give them an after-dinner speech.

"If you insist," agreed Doug. "Your reactions could be of considerable interest to me, so can we make a bargain? Would each of you scribble an honest note as to what you think of what I have to say? It is important that you do not consult with each other; I wish to discover how ladies react rather than men."

With their curiosity raised, they all agreed and eagerly sought sustenance. Some three-quarters of an hour later, and now in a receptive mood after a very pleasurable meal, Doug's audience settled with their after dinner drinks to await his deliberations.

"It all started some years ago in this very glen. Dorothy and I rented a cottage here for a year or so when I first retired, this was a deliberate attempt to unwind from the stresses of commercial life and to seek a new direction. I love to spend time on my own in the peace and serenity of such an environment; just to let my thoughts have free rein. Spending time in the evenings at my favourite knoll, I marvelled at the vastness of the skies; the great distances between heavenly bodies and the incredible numbers involved. My thoughts went back to the creation of everything – the big bang. This phenomenal burst of energy expanded in the form of electromagnetic waves and then, by a complex process, progressively formed protons, neutrons and electrons; as conditions changed, these basic 'components' formed all the elements with which we are familiar and combined to create galaxies of stars, some with attendant planets. I have deliberately avoided going into detail as to how all of this occurred – it took me many hours of study to learn the rudiments, sufficient to say that all these elements resulted from the original electromagnetic waves of pure energy."

"That seems a fair postulation," interjected Sam.

"Just think," continued Doug, "if all the elements are formed from waves, all materials - be they organic or inorganic are made from waves."

"Surely you don't mean to imply that *we* are made of waves," challenged Fiona.

"I certainly do. This, I believe, is a fundamental fact and ultimately leads to my whole philosophy."

"I find this very difficult to accept," Alan admitted.

"I know it is hard to think of one as being just waves," Doug agreed, "but you have to bear in mind that we have developed through a very complex, multilayered process. Just think of this table for example, it is nowhere near as complex as we, but it once was a tree – or a part of one. What makes a tree? Sunshine, rain, and soil; but those three are nothing like a tree. Sunshine is composed of waves, but what about rain? Water is H_2O - hydrogen and oxygen, these are elements composed of waves. Soil is more complex since it comprises many different materials processed by worms and insects, but if we trace back through its structure we will arrive at the elements from which it is created – and these elements are also composed of waves."

"Maybe we are a bit dim," suggested Sue, "but a tree, or a table, is never as complex as the human. Surely there are more than waves in our make-up?"

"The difficulty we all have in appreciating the truth of such a matter," suggested Doug "is the vast number of stages of development through which the human being has travelled. Let's, as an analogy, consider a man-made example of complex development - the computer. Without concerning ourselves regarding the technicalities of electronics, I think we are all aware that this modern marvel is based on a silicon chip – basically a piece of sand that has been manipulated. Yet daily we see examples of colourful, moving images displayed on our TV sets, or we are aware of a PC's ability to carry out complex calculations. Many of us use them to process words on a screen before triggering a printer to produce faultless documents. This wondrous device relies on a complex series of layers of programme development – crude beginnings becoming progressively more sophisticated. We too have developed from crude beginnings and, by a complex sequence of development, have become sophisticated biological beings."

"I begin to see what you are driving at," conceded Sue, "we are the latest animal to develop on this planet, so have taken the most steps in our evolvement."

"That's exactly the point I am making, but the link with electromagnetic waves is not complete; the most fascinating has yet to be revealed. I think, however, that perhaps it is too much for me to expect that, in one session, you should follow my reasoning when it has taken me years to arrive at my hypothesis. I will give you time to dwell on what, I hope, we have established; that everything in the universe – including us, is comprised fundamentally from electromagnetic waves. I suggest that the relevance of this can best be pursued during our next monthly session."

"You've certainly got us intrigued," Sam declared, "I, for one, can't wait to hear your 'next thrilling instalment' of - *The Thoughts of Doug*". I've just had an idea; we are about to open the Castle Restaurant for the first time, let's launch it with a charity dinner – with the proceeds going to the Raigmore hospital, in Inverness. Doug could give his talk as the after dinner interest."

"Oh, I don't know about that," Doug replied, "if you wish to raise funds, I suggest the entertainment should be somewhat lighter – music and dancing perhaps, with a comic emcee."

"Maybe you are right," Sam conceded, "I'll leave the details to the entertainment department – that means you, Doug. Perhaps we will reserve your deliberations for the opening of the College of Philosophy at our soon to be established Highland University."

"By the way," said Sam, turning to Alan, "thinking of the university and our established style of construction, your various designs of Alpine style buildings are worthy of promotion. Let's consider capitalising on the expertise gained building such a wide range of housing and offices by using the principle of common features that are exportable."

"Yes," agreed Alan excitedly, "If we could develop a market outside of the glen, it would make good use of the manufacturing facilities we have built up and provide another source of income to the community. I'll raise the matter with Bill Bates to look into the commercial aspects."

The party finally broke up in an uplifted mood; not only had they absorbed a thought-promoting intellectual talk by Doug, they had also witnessed the birth of a new project and an appealing social event.

CHAPTER 20

It was mid winter when witnesses were called to appear at the Sheriff's court in Inverness to give evidence in the case against the saboteurs. It dragged on for nearly three weeks but the outcome was inevitable. Although it was obvious what had happened, there was insufficient evidence to definitely prove that Robbie and Angus actually built the temporary dam. Morag's payment of £800 to them was dismissed as an overdue payment for previous services rendered. The jury had no alternative but to return a verdict of not proven.

As the court closed, Sam met Detective Chief Inspector McLeod. "I suppose you are frustrated by the outcome Sam offered."

"Not really, I always knew we would have difficulty actually proving *they* had done it. I believe the plot was to do damage but, because the men worked in that appalling storm to meet their schedule, they got caught out. It was an accident triggered by a felonious act. Their spell in custody will teach them a lesson, at least Morag Matheson will take a long time to overcome the social slur, and all three will be worried that we will be able to find positive proof in the long run; that possibility will hang over them for ever – a *just* sentence. We will, of course, be keeping our eye on them for a long time to come."

Driving home from Inverness the Jacksons and the Frasers suffered torrential rain and howling wind.

"Who would want to live in a place like this?" Sam mused.

"I would!" Mhairi declared. "Regardless of the weather, we have created a harmonious, productive community in an area of outstanding natural beauty. Many would welcome the opportunity to live in Glen Quoich."

"Great speech," Sue agreed. "It has been so exciting seeing the various developments getting under way. I'm sure when it is all finished; we will be the envy of the world."

"Talking of getting finished, I see that the holiday chalet park on The Point is coming along fine," Sam observed, "you'll be needing to find a manager soon Alan."

"Stewart has been working on it for some time and we have a strong candidate coming next Monday; James Miller, who has had related experience in Australia. Would you have time to meet him so that you can give him the basic policy briefing?"

"As far as I can remember without looking at my diary," Sam confirmed.

"I'm just looking," Sue interjected, "I have it here. Yes, you are clear. What time should I book?"

"He will be under the directorship of Bill Bates," informed Alan, "so we've set up an interview for 10.30 am with Bill, together with Farquhar Henderson, the Tourism Manager, Stewart, you and I, if that fits in with your day."

"That's fine by me but I'll let Bill do most of the talking."

"If he appears to be suitable, we would like him to start as soon as possible so that he can take charge of furnishing of all the units, arrange for cleaning staff and take on a maintenance person. We are hoping his wife will act as receptionist/secretary/general assistant. Preliminary 'sales' promotion has gone out ready for the coming summer season so she is needed to handle the enquiries instead of Bill's office."

"I notice a possible conflict of responsibilities between the new couple and Farquhar," Sam observed.

"This is at the top of the agenda if we find the new man is to our liking."

"I like it when wheels continue to turn without my involvement," Sam commented, "there'll be no need for me in a while."

"Don't kid yourself; we have it arranged that if anything goes wrong, you take the blame. Then again, if something good occurs, the rest of the executive staff will gladly take the credit."

"See what I'm up against Sue? It's all a vicious plot."

"Bill and I have had our heads together," announced Alan. "We have set a provisional date to launch the Castle Restaurant by having a special dinner for executives and their invited guests. This, if you agree, will be three weeks on Saturday. We also thought that prior to that event, we would have one or two preliminary 'thank-you' meals for all those tradesmen who have worked so hard to get the job done; these would act as training and test sessions for the kitchen and serving staff. By the time we have the executive dinner, the system should be in top form."

"Oh! I am looking forward to that," Sue interjected. "I'm dying to see what it is like up there – looking out over the mountain peaks; but I admit to being a little apprehensive about the cable car ride up to the castle."

"You have no need to worry," reassured Alan. "It has been well tested and much used during construction; carrying heavy loads of materials as well as people."

Sam gave his approval of the plan as they pulled up outside his home, inviting Alan and Mhairi in for supper and drinks.

Highland Haven

The applicant for the position of Holiday Park Manager, together with his wife, arrived at the Quoich Village Hotel just before 10 o'clock; giving themselves time to freshen up and relax after their drive from an over-night stop at Fort William. With five minutes before the appointed time for interview they presented themselves at the enquiry desk to be directed to the interview room on the third floor. Somewhat surprised by the size of the interview panel he introduced himself. "James Miller, commonly called Jimmy, and my wife, Mary."

"Welcome to Quoich," Sam replied, extending his hand for a friendly shake. "I am the Development Director, Sam Jackson. On my right is Bill Bates, the Commercial Director, and Farquhar Henderson, General Manager, Sports & Tourism. If successful, he will be your immediate boss. On my left is Stewart Slater the Director of Administration who, amongst other matters, is responsible for all personnel employed by Quoich Development Corporation. Later I will explain some special principles regarding our policy here but first Mr Bates will open the interview"

"My responsibilities cover all commercial activities here; the sporting activities and accommodation being under the direct control of Mr Henderson. If successful, you would be responsible to Mr Henderson for the chalet park and the holiday apartments. In your c.v. you stated that you had had previous experience in this field. Please tell us about it."

"In Australia, I carried out the maintenance of 40 chalets including arranging for the weekly cleaning by an army of ladies. This was at a waterside park on the Myall Lakes where we had available a small fleet of boats for fishing, sailing, water-skiing, or just simply for fun. I maintained these and supervised the letting. My wife was the receptionist, taking bookings and dealing with enquiries from punters – er, I mean customers."

"You do realise, Mr Miller, that this position is rather more responsible," interjected Farquhar Henderson. "You would be responsible for the success or failure of this branch of our enterprise."

"Exactly," Jimmy retorted. "Since my wife was so involved with the bookings and customer relations aspect and I had all the practical experience of providing services; water, sewerage, cleaning, repairs and general maintenance, we are confident that we can raise our game to management – knowing what is actually involved in running such a development. This is the underlying reason why we have come to the UK – to raise our sights."

"Very well," acknowledged Farquhar. "I will take you to see the chalet park and show you some of the holiday apartments in the village and, at the same time, enumerate the particular responsibilities involved. We will all meet back here after lunch to finalise matters."

Maurice Duffill

After a walkabout in the village to see the apartments and other facilities, Farquhar drove them out to The Point to see the layout of the chalet park and the limited boating facility. He explained that publicity was already in hand in readiness for completion and that the pair of them would need to take over all bookings. Although the chalets were almost ready, it would also be their responsibility to furnish and equip them all to the standards set by the directors. They would have to canvass the labour force in the general locality for cleaners, maintenance workers, and staffing of the bar-restaurant. The Director of Administration would prepare advertisements and assist in coordinating the recruitment. It would be up to them to ensure that the annual costs (including their own salaries) did not exceed the income from the lettings, bearing in mind that trade was rather fickle in the autumn and winter.

Returning to the interview room after enjoying a complimentary lunch in the hotel bistro, Jimmy and Mary found all the directors ready to confront them once more.

"I take it that Mr Henderson gave you a good grounding in what is expected of you; do you think you can handle it? challenged Bill Bates.

"We certainly do. It will be a natural extension to our previous experience."

"I'd like to hear Mrs Miller's comments," Sam requested.

"We love what we have seen and the area is absolutely beautiful. Please engage us; we are sure you have provided the right environment for us to make this venture a success, plus," added Mary, "I'd love to spend any spare time painting these dramatic mountains and the lake."

"Loch," prompted Sam light-heartedly; "we don't have lakes in these parts, only lochs, or lochans if they are small."

"I'm sorry, I've made my first mistake already and I have only said a few words." She sheepishly admitted.

"Don't worry about it I was being rather pedantic. However, I must point out that this is not just another job; the appointment requires your commitment to a unique lifestyle." He then explained the philosophy underlying the development of Quoich and invited Stewart to explain the salary policy as well as the tax and investment arrangements."

When the details had been reviewed, Bill declared, "All the points raised are set-out in this contract and I am pleased to say we are prepared to sign if you are."

"We trust that the small print is in keeping with all we have learned today and gladly sign." replied Jimmy. "Thank you for the opportunity to show our worth."

"Welcome to the team," Sam concluded.

Highland Haven

It hardly seemed three weeks had passed when wives of executives were to be found excitedly preparing themselves for the formal dinner to be held in the unique venue sitting aloft and aloof on the highest peak in the area. The exuberance was not solely due to the dramatic setting but the significance of the event; although all facilities were not yet complete, effectively this dinner was acting as the major opening event of the whole Glen Quoich project. Dignitaries were invited from London's parliamentary world, local government, the tourist board and, of course - the press. It was to be a gala occasion.

Prior to the dinner, the invited guests were given a presentation, in the Village Hotel conference centre, by the commercial director, Bill Bates, and the property director, Alan Fraser. This summarised the achievements so far and reviewed the current work in hand to bring the project up to a viable level of development. Before transferring to the cable car for the uplifting journey to the Castle Restaurant, all were offered free reign to explore the facilities by being given day-tickets to travel the tram/train system at their leisure the following day.

Without exception, all guests were overawed by the unfolding vista as the cable car lifted groups to the newly built castle sitting atop the conical Sgurr a' Mhaoraich. From its location in the high central tower, the restaurant offered unrestricted views over what is arguably the most dramatically beautiful highland scene in the whole world. To the north, range after range of mountains could be seen forming a rugged carpet to the distant horizon. To the east, the glens fashioned extended fingers pointing to the softer, yet still dramatic Great Glen which severs north-west Scotland from the rest of Britain. To the west, the Rough Bounds – Europe's most barren mountain region, provided the foreground to the Cuillin range across the Sound of Sleat on the Isle of Skye. To the south, distant Ben Nevis – Britain's highest peak, beckoned one's attention sitting, as it does, as a proud guardian of Fort William, the tourist Mecca of the Highlands.

During the five-course, wine-laced dinner, the setting sun cast spectacular, red tinged shadows of multiple peaks upon multiple peaks. Diners' attention was torn between the sumptuous food and the ever-changing scene being witnessed through plate glass windows – an experience destined to live-on in the memories of all present.

As the dessert course gave way to cheese and biscuits, malt whisky was served for the guests to savour during the inevitable speeches.

Keeping the formalities short, Sam thanked everyone for their presence then briefly outlined where progress of the development project stood and the targets yet to be achieved. He then introduced Sir Richard as the father of Glenquoich Development Corporation.

Sir Richard drew attention to the socio-political aspects of the venture highlighting the experimental nature of the procedures adopted by the community;

and how the inhabitants of Glen Quoich appeared to be enjoying a harmonious, inspired way of life. He referred back to the unfortunate, disastrous historical period known as *The Clearances* when peasant crofters were ousted by absent landlords in favour of sheep grazing – causing a mass exodus from these lands. He hoped that *this* venture would show how the tragedy could be reversed to the benefit of new residents, visitors and the nation as a whole.

Not wishing to let these hopes be unanswered, a prominent newspaper editor rose to his feet to give an impromptu vote of confidence in Sir Richard's great initiative.

With that, the evening drew towards a conclusion with entertainment provided by a traditional Scottish accordion band whilst guests mingled to exchange excited comments related to this most memorable evening. Many articles appeared over the next few weeks in newspapers and magazines which could only help draw attention to the activities at Glenquoich;

MAGIC MEAL IN THE MOUNTAINS

HIGHLAND HISTORY REWRITTEN
People takeover from sheep

As a result of the publicity, the commercial department was inundated by freelance journalists seeking complimentary meals and overnight accommodation in return for them writing articles promoting the venture; most were turned away in favour of direct contact with selected journals in order to have some control on the quality and content of future publicity. Visitor numbers were increasing as a result of the media coverage, causing a further rise in buoyancy of the general mood of residents – the launch had been successful.

CHAPTER 21

The next eighteen months seemed to be filled with opening ceremonies, each accompanied by media visits bringing the Glen Quoich project very much into the public eye. The big event was the completion of the mountain railway across much uninhabited terrain to link the Highland Railway and the harbour at Mallaig with Glen Quoich. This gave ready access not only for tour groups and those who just loved railways, but much needed freight handling both in and out.

More or less coincidently, the completion of the second cableway, to take passengers down from the Village terminal to the shore at Kinloch Hourn, opened up a very interesting tourist route from Mallaig to Kyle of Lochalsh via a dramatic ferry-boat trip up Loch Hourn and along the Sound of Sleat. Although this made the route fairly expensive, it became an increasingly popular method of planning for holidays at Glen Quoich; visitors would be able to come via Mallaig and leave by Kyle, or vice versa.

The Property Director, Alan Fraser called at Sam's office to introduce a piece of exciting news. "Have you noticed that the owners of Knoydart, the adjacent estate, have put it up for sale?"

"I'm afraid I don't find time to scan the property journals but I'm sure you are going to tell me all about it," he jokingly prodded.

"How did you guess? Actually I made a formal enquiry and have received a portfolio of details. The estate consists of all the Rough Bounds and the surrounding coastline; amounting to over 17,000 acres. It includes the small village of Inverie, the hamlets of Airor and Inverguseran, as well as a number of isolated cottages. I believe it would make a perfect addition to our existing property and I'm sure could be acquired for a modest price since this is the third time it has been on the market without attracting a firm buyer."

"Sounds interesting," admitted Sam, "but what would you do with it?"

"It already hosts a fantastic area for shooting, fishing, hill-walking, climbing, pony tracking and would provide a great area to develop adventure activities for groups – particularly youth organisations such as the Boy Scouts or the cadets. Many of the village cottages already provide holiday accommodation while Britain's most isolated pub, *The Old Forge*, boasts entertainment in the form of a ceilidh virtually every evening whilst its restaurant provides a top quality menu. The existing isolated cottages would make superb lettings for people seeking a period of solitude: The small clusters could accommodate those seeking peace and quiet without total isolation: but most importantly, our control of the estate would protect us from possible unwelcome developments"

"What sort of developments do you envisage?"

"There has been talk of using the vicinity as a military training area. If we owned Knoydart we could prevent its misuse although we might choose to rent out certain sections for occasional military purposes but with tight controls over the activities in which they might engage; no tanks or live ammunition, for instance."

"I must say, it is worthy of further investigation. You prepare a presentation and we'll set it before Sir Richard for his blessing, or otherwise."

"I'm a jump ahead of you," admitted Alan, "I have it all on disc; we just need a date."

About a week later, Alan, slightly apprehensively, made his presentation to Sir Richard and was somewhat dismayed by his response.

"I must admit to having already made an expression of interest in the Knoydart estate to their lawyers. I didn't reveal this to you since your own initiative seemed as if it might answer the question of how best to make use of the asset. This you have ably done. I am, therefore, happy to say that this acquisition should proceed. There are, however, one or two points I wish to raise. For political reasons too complicated and, for now, too confidential to reveal, the purchase will need to be done privately by me. If negotiations are successful both with the purchase and with certain authorities, the property can then be brought under the umbrella of the Glenquoich Development Corporation. This is why, Mr Jackson, I had not involved yourself in these matters. The second aspect I wish to raise is that, given we are successful on both accounts, I do not wish that the Knoydart estate be developed. Apart from making necessary repairs and minor improvements to the existing residences, I wish to retain the character of this unique area. Accordingly, any plans will require my personal approval before any work commences. I am aware this appears to be a contradiction to my giving carte-blanche to you Mr Jackson but this acquisition must be seen as a special addition to our development plans."

Barely two months passed when Sir Richard advised Sam that the Knoydart estate now belonged to him and that political complications could be avoided if the estate was treated as an external asset. "Accordingly", Sir Richard declared, "you are to keep separate account of all matters relating, treating any direct involvement of the Glenquoich Corporation as a chargeable service. Having said that, It must be policy to generally follow our established principles of consideration for residents and employees even though they will not be personally included in our salary/tax scheme. Perhaps, at some future date, we might – with their agreement, bring them fully into our unique lifestyle."

"You may feel that these restraints mitigate the advantage of the acquisition, which – to a degree they do, but I am anxious not to upset our political status which, I appreciate, I have withheld from you. In the meantime, the broader base of our combined assets will give us greater inertia in the region which might ultimately lead to achieving the political aim of my ultimate ambition. The time is still not right for this ambition to be revealed to the public."

Sam immediately called a meeting of the executive to reveal this new development and explain the restraints. The disclosure caused much excitement since it underlined that Sir Richard had enough financial clout to make this very large investment. All were now also keen to explore the estate which they had eyed to their west but had been too busy to indulge.

"Alan and I have been plotting," Sam confessed to Sue when he returned that evening. "We've organised a day out for the four of us, plus Angus and Fiona – tomorrow."

"Oh, that's short notice. Where are we going? What should I wear? Why didn't you let us know?"

"Amongst other things, we are going on a boat trip, but I wasn't sure that it would be available until Alan rang a short while ago. We left the final arrangement until he was pretty sure the weather would be kind to us. The boat skipper, Angus McGilvery, and the weatherman have agreed to cooperate so it is 'A' ok for lift-off as 'they' say."

"A boat trip – with that criminal fellow, is that wise?"

"Forget about his involvement in the nefarious activities with the Russians; he was only doing a job for which he was being paid. He must be a pretty good skipper with a reliable sturdy boat to do that sort of thing."

"Where is this boat trip to, and why is it so special that you've arranged for the six of us to go?"

"Your travel executive will now give you a résumé of the itinerary so skilfully arranged by your ever-loving husband on your behalf."

Putting on a formal-official tone of voice, Sam revealed the plot. "Departure for the village is at 08:30, where our travelling companions await. We then board the brand new cable car for the descent to Kinloch Hourne. There will be ample time for a short walk to the pier to board the Highland Queen by 09:30. Your skipper, Angus McGilvery, will then pilot the boat the length of Loch Hourne into the Sound of Sleet. Turning south-west the cruise will continue to the village of Inverie on the Knoydart peninsula - E.T.A. 11:00. There will be time for a stroll through the village before a 12 o'clock lunch at Britain's most remote pub, *The Old Forge*. Your versatile tour of Scotland's most beautiful rugged area continues after lunch with a ferry trip to the harbour at Mallaig. Departure by train from Mallaig Station is scheduled for 14:00 hours (2 o'clock to you) – not by the usual British Rail tourist train to Fort William, but by the recently opened narrow-gauge mountain railway. During the journey alongside Loch Morar - while searching for the local monster Morag, and the scenic climb over the uninhabited terrain to the wild Loch Quoich, afternoon tea will be served. Arriving at the fascinating new development of Glen Quoich, your journey will terminate at Quoich Village with cocktails in the hotel lounge."

"Darling!" Sue exclaimed. "This sounds marvellous; you are a clever little outing organiser. At least, if you lose your current job, you could always become a travel agent. I can't wait for tomorrow – oh but I must get organised; I need to sort out what I am going to wear."

"Never mind all that. Where's my dinner? If I can set up the whole trip as well as carrying out other duties – all in one day, then you can do your sorting out *after* your master has been served."

"Any more of that, and it will be served in your lap – oh superior one who has an army of slaves to carry out his bidding while he sits with his feet up," Sue retorted, as she made an over-elaborate bow.

During the meal, Sam revealed Sir Richard's acquisition of the Knoydart Estate and that this trip was Angus's original idea to show off his new cable car, as well as the completed railway, to Fiona. "Alan and I expanded it to include the six of us to make the trip viable for Angus McGilvery whilst carrying out a circuit of Knoydart."

Meeting at the transport terminal, the following morning, the ladies were most excited at the prospect of their trip.

"All aboard for the descent to the 'Loch of Hell'," Sam announced as they stepped into the cable car.

Although, by now, they had all become familiar with the narrow road down from the village, this was – except for Angus, the first time they had glided between the soaring peaks without having to twist and turn while the driver strained his neck to be sure nobody was just over the next brow, driving up. As the sea loch came into full view, Fiona couldn't help but marvel at the dramatic beauty of the scene unfolding before them. "This is awe-inspiring – I do wish I could paint, I'd love to have this view hanging on my lounge wall."

"Maybe Mary Miller can oblige," Alan suggested, "she is an artist in her spare time."

"Spare time – spare time!" teased Sam, "Nobody should have spare time."

"Oh shut up, you scrooge, let's bask in the beauty revealed by Angus's brilliant piece of engineering."

Further conversation was drowned by the sound of a gorgeous waterfall directly beneath them as their plunge between the peaks eased to a less dramatic gradient for the approach to the bottom terminal. A pleasant winding walkway had been constructed for the transfer to the pier. Early signs of landscaped native flora developing alongside made the walk most pleasurable.

Angus McGilvery was waiting by the gangway leading onto the Heather Queen, giving each passenger a welcome handshake on arrival.

"He seems quite pleasant," whispered Sue to Sam.

"Did you think he would attack you with his wooden leg, or wave his hook as his parrot screamed?" Sam sarcastically replied.

Before she had time to respond, Angus made an announcement. "In accordance with good safety practice, I must ask each of you to put on a life jacket. I am not expecting my dependable boat to spring a leak but should something unforeseen occur, and someone fall overboard, it would be too late to wish one was being worn. Various sizes are available so help yourselves," he said as the engine was started and mooring ropes cast free. Turning west, the Heather Queen passed between the narrow shoulders which almost closed off the head of the loch, and entered the loch proper, which became well over half a kilometre wide.

"Now that the loch has widened, it doesn't seem so oppressive between these great mountains," observed Fiona. "In fact they now appear quite dramatic. It is like standing back from a painting to appreciate the whole picture."

About half an hour later, they passed through another narrow 'gateway' to reveal an even greater widening of the loch to something like two kilometres shore to shore.

"What was it you were saying about standing back Fiona, to admire the picture," Sue commented. "This is absolutely magnificent. We are cruising effortlessly amongst such rugged terrain – just like the Norwegian fiords."

"I had no idea this loch was so large," Fiona responded. "We've now been cruising for quite a while and not yet got to the end. How long is it Mr McGilvery?"

"Angus, please. In modern measure, it's over twenty kilometres from Kinloch Hourne to the Sound of Sleet."

Alan interjected, "I understand this is the greatest incursion of tidal water in the whole of Britain."

"That'd be right," confirmed Angus

"I see there is a village on the north shore; does anyone live to the south?"

"Only me - at least on this side of the Rough Bounds."

"What are the Rough Bounds?" Mhairi asked.

"The mountains to the south of you now, which are the most rugged in the whole of the country. There are small settlements on the other side but otherwise it is an uninhabited area. You'll be seeing quite a bit of it all as we go down the sound, with the Isle of Skye opposite."

As they cruised around the bend the scene opened up even more to reveal the famous island on their right rising up to the red Cullin Mountains.

"This panorama is absolutely unbelievably beautiful," observed Sam. "No wonder there is so much poetry and so many songs born in the highlands."

A road could be seen on Skye which, Angus informed them, connects the main road to the ferry from Mallaig at Ardvassar. On their left side – just rugged mountains could be seen with clouds clipping the tops which seemed to emphasise their height. "Knoydart," Sam declared; "the estate that Sir Richard has just bought. We are cruising around its boundary until we stop for lunch."

"What, all those mountains? He must be a very wealthy man. Oh look," Marie declared, "there are a few cottages near the shore. I wonder if anyone lives there?"

"They were crofters' cottages," skipper Angus obliged, "but they were unable to sustain themselves after The Clearances. They are now let as quiet holiday retreats."

"How do people get there, there doesn't seem to be a road."

"Some hike there but usually a boat is used. *I* drop people off from time to time."

"It certainly would be a quiet retreat – no TV, no electricity, no noisy neighbours."

"That is one of the main attractions of the area," volunteered Alan; "besides hiking, stalking, pony-trekking, and other adventurous pursuits."

Another cluster of cottages came into view which, the skipper informed them was Airor and connected by a rough road to the village of Inverie, where they would be calling for lunch at the pub. Various small hamlets could be seen on the other side where the road on the Isle of Skye came close to the shore. The Sound of Sleet, down which they were cruising is, at this point, about four miles wide but ahead it was widening still further. Angus swung the Heather Queen in a great curve to the south, revealing the harbour of Mallaig ahead of them, but he continued the turn, passing between a couple of small islands and headed for a narrower passage leading back into the mountains.

"We are entering Loch Nevis," their skipper called out, "which ultimately reaches back toward Loch Quoich, where you started."

"Which of those mountains is Ben Nevis? Sue enquired.

Highland Haven

"Oh that would be some thirty miles away from here, more or less straight down that stretch of this loch," Angus said as he turned even further towards the northeast to approach the landing at Inverie.

They were all pleased to be stretching their legs as they stepped ashore to find themselves in an old world village of stone cottages with pitched, slated roofs. Like Glen Quoich, there was little sign of motor vehicles, just the occasional local person going about their daily routine and happy to give them a cheery greeting. Although they were blessed with a fine day, the air was a little chilly, which accounted for the smoke spiralling from the many chimneys.

"Laing may your lumb reek," Alan declared.

"I beg your pardon?" Sue retorted.

"Long may your chimney smoke," Alan translated. "It's a greeting which means *I hope you have a long and happy life*."

"Oh isn't that sweet? Just when I thought you were swearing at us."

"Don't encourage him," Mhairi enjoined, "he'll only continue to exercise his limited gaelic vocabulary – to the annoyance of us all."

"That, my dear, was not Gaelic; it is an old Scots greeting; the language of Robby Burns – typical of the lowlands and the east of Scotland rather than the Highlands and the Western Isles."

"Pardon my ignorance," Mhairi replied in mock humility.

Angus led them to *The Old Forge* where they found a table set for six in front of a lively log fire. "This is Janet," he said, as their host appeared from the kitchen. "I'll be going about my business. You have an hour before Bruce will take you on to Mallaig on his ferry. Enjoy your lunch."

"Will you be having a dram, afore ye go?" enquired Alan, demonstrating his rusty Scottish accent.

"Well just a quick one," Their skipper replied as he downed in one gulp the whisky Janet had automatically poured. Then he was out of the door with a "slàinte-math" tossed over his shoulder.

"Some character," Sam commented as the door closed behind him.

"Just look at this menu," Fiona declared in amazement. "Sea foods galore plus venison and salmon, not to mention home made stew and soup."

"Being lunchtime, stew will do me fine," announced her husband, Angus.

General agreement made the landlady's task very straightforward.

"A bottle of red for the ladies and three beers for we fellas, I think," Sam ordered, receiving approving nods from the rest.

"Looking at all those musical instruments, there must be a band here." Mhairi observed.

"Not really," commented their hostess as she was about to disappear through the kitchen doorway; "they are for anyone to have a go at. We have fiddles, and

211

guitars for the musically adept and Jew's harps, or spoons for the beginners, as well as pennywhistles and mouth-organs for intermediates."

"I imagine visitors could have quite a gay old evening around the fire with that lot, but what is that drum thing?"

"That's a bohran. It's good if you've got rhythm."

"Why don't we arrange to spend a weekend hereabout," Sue suggested. "We could enjoy walking and then let our hair down here in the evening."

"The weather here is not usually so pleasant," Alan interjected; "The south-westerlies come howling in bringing rain by the barrel full. The ground will be sodden as the run-off washes over the peat bogs."

"Just listen to old misery; trying to spoil the image," Mhairi scolded.

"Tell me this then, why has the pub got those large clothes drying racks by the fire?"

"Well we will just have to come prepared, "Sue persisted.

"Sam," Alan declared, changing the subject. "Now all this land has been added to our existing territory, I think we should engage a keeper to manage the deer shooting over the whole area. I don't know if you are aware, but we have an obligation to maintain the herds even though they are nominally wild."

"It is probably a matter of coordinating the existing stalkers; maybe they do already cooperate. Get Farquhar Henderson to look into it but stress he must be careful not to tread on anyone's toes."

"That's enough shop-talk," Sue insisted.

After a most relaxing meal they bade farewell to their host to walk back to the landing in time for the ferry. Bruce Watt's boat *Western Isles* turned out to be quite large; having room for about eighty passengers. They joined a cluster of hikers returning home together with a handful of part-time locals going to Fort William to catch the overnight train south.

The short boat trip seemed even more pleasant now they were all wined and dined. Doubling back the way Angus had brought them, they were confronted with the great entrance to the Sound of Sleet - the mountains on either side acting as a great funnel from the North Atlantic. They realised the likely truth of Alan's dramatic climatological exposé. Still, it didn't take away the delight of the magnificent panorama presented to them on this most beautiful day. Entering the bustling harbour of Mallaig just after the arrival of the fishing fleet caused Fiona to remark, "It's just as well all the boats were going in rather than coming out as we arrived."

CHAPTER 22

While the executive party were enjoying their informative but relaxing tour, the recently appointed chalet park managers, Jimmy and Mary Miller, were enjoying a working day doing something which most people would love to do but rarely get the chance. They were spending money as if it was about to go out of fashion; but it wasn't their money, it was company money. They had travelled to Inverness to equip the chalet park with all the furniture and equipment necessary to make some 25 chalets habitable – as dictated by a profile set out in a company document.

They were making the most of spending time selecting matching double and single beds, only at the last minute asking the assistant for a price for 25 doubles and 100 singles. This would cause a big intake of breath followed by, "You did say 100 single beds and 25 doubles?" The manager is then brought to negotiate special terms. They then added, "Of course, we will need bedside units for them all as well as sets of drawers, bedside lamps and rugs."

"As the manager is excitedly making notes in his book, the list would grow; do you have suggestions for dining-room suites and associated lounge chairs and/or settees?" Then, just to keep him on his toes, "We will, of course obtain alternative quotes from your competitors."

This unfamiliar exercise of power was repeated at a kitchenware supplier with enquiries for 150 settings of cutlery, crockery and glassware. Added to that would be jugs, bowls, pans, electric kettles and toasters together with an array of cooking paraphernalia.

They realised that suppliers would be used to catering for the needs of hotels with multiple rooms but they amused themselves by only admitting the quantities required late in the enquiry to shock the sales person. Entering a television shop, they answered the usual bored question "Can I help you?" with, "Yes, we are looking for an inexpensive TV which is able to receive a digital signal."

"Oh yes sir," would be the condescending reply. "If you wish to keep the cost down, the old format is cheaper and it will be good for many years yet."

"Not where we are. Oh, by the way, we need at least 25."

The change of tune which came as a response to that revelation was so amusing.

"This reminds me of the prank I played at that shoe shop in Luton," Jimmy recalled, "do you remember?"

"I can't say I do – remind me."

"I must admit you were not there so it won't stick in your memory as it does in mine. Anyway, you and I had been larking about and I accidentally laddered your best stockings. The next day that I was in town, I went into a shoe shop to buy a replacement pair. I chose your favourite brand and colour then, just as I was about to pay the £1.00, the lady assistant said that if I would buy two pair there would be a replacement guarantee. I said "Oh yes, what sort of con-trick is this?"

"It's not a trick Sir; the design has a special stitch to reduce laddering. Hidden in the top band is a code number which can only be seen using a UV light. If both stockings of a pair become laddered, they will be replaced free. In any case, having four identical stockings means your wife will have six possible pairs."

"Alright, you've convinced me. I'll take the box with two pair."

"Do you not remember? When I gave the box of stockings to you, you said 'Oh thank you, a new pair of stockings. Oh two pair, oh *three* pair."

"What? The assistant must have put the single pair in the box, believing it was one of the two. Now we don't know which the matching couple are"

The next day, on the way to the office, I noticed the shop had just opened; I would be their first customer. I stormed in with a bit of a scowl on my face and said to the senior of the three assistants, "Yesterday I came into this shop to buy a pair of stockings for my wife."

"Yes Sir?"

"But, having chosen the required make and colour, I was persuaded to buy a box of two pair."

"Yes Sir?"

"When I got home and my wife opened the box, there was not two pair in there."

"*No* Sir?"

"No! There was three pair. So here is the £1.00 for the extra pair. I then turned and stormed out of the shop, glancing over my shoulder to witness the startled expressions on their faces. It was worth the money just to see them so flabbergasted."

"I remember the three pair of stockings," Mary recalled, "I thought you were being very generous. I think shop assistants are programmed for what should be normal; it shocks them when something out of the ordinary happens."

"I'm sure your right. Let's have some more fun buying all the bed linen; sheets, pillow-cases and blankets by the hundred. By the way, did you know that, in Australia, they call all that sort of stuff *Manchester*?"

"What, bed linen?"

"Yes. When there is a sale on, TV adverts announce 20% OFF MANCHESTER. It makes me think that about a dozen suburbs are being relocated to some other district."

"Why on earth do they call it Manchester?"

"I think it must be because Manchester used to be the cotton spinning capital of the world - not that it is now; virtually all bed linen would be made there"

214

Highland Haven

"I've just had a thought; where are we going to get all this linen laundered every week?" Mary queried.

"A commercial laundry has been built in the village to deal with all our needs and that of the two hotels as well as cafés, restaurants, and anyone who wishes to use it. Of course we will have to pay for the service to make the laundry a viable business. The directors have just signed up a Chinese family to run it, so it should be ok."

"It is peculiar that laundries are usually run by Chinese, but they do seem to be good at it."

After negotiating their long list of wants with three linen suppliers, Mary was beginning to feel weary. "Jimmy, I hate to admit it but I'm getting a bit tired of all this money spending and we still have 60 miles of highland road to drive. Let's pack up for today, go home and compare prices so that we can make decisions on who should supply what."

"I agree - enough is enough. We'll just make one more call."

"Oh not another round in the stores, I really think I'm done for the day?"

"I'm sure you will enjoy the call I have in mind. How about a meal at Fort Augustus, on the way home – The Lovatt Arms, I think."

"Now you are talking, let's get at it."

CHAPTER 23

Stepping ashore at Mallaig, the tour party found it was but a few strides to the railway station where they were to begin the next stage of their round trip. Seeing a smart new train adorned with the words GLENQUOICH DEVELOPMENT CORPORATION, Sue remarked, "it looks smaller than the train at the other platform."

"That is because it runs on a narrow gauge railway," engineer Angus advised. "The rails are only one metre apart instead of the four foot eight and a half inches of British Rail's tracks."

"Why make them smaller, everything has to be special?"

"It keeps costs down because we can turn tighter bends in the mountains than standard track."

Sue then joined the question and answer session; "I thought mountain railways had three rails, there are only two."

"Further along, when the gradient becomes too steep for normal traction, there *is* a third rail – with teeth, which are engaged by a gear on the locomotive to transfer the pulling power or the braking force. You will also notice," Angus eagerly explained, "that there is a locomotive at both ends; this is so that we do not have to rely on the couplings to stop carriages from rolling downhill."

"These engineers think of everything," Sue said to Mhairi.

"We have to – to keep you ladies safe," Angus added, gallantly. He then took the opportunity to introduce the driver and his supporting crew to their Development and Property directors together with their wives, stressing that this was a Very Important Party in his charge. Having completed hand-shakes all around, the guard made the traditional call of "All aboard" whereupon they all obliged by taking seats in a plush new carriage. Following the sound of a whistle, the train moved smoothly off accompanied by a pleasing hum from front and rear.

"Oh look," Mhairi called out, "there are stacks of our cartons of produce from the hydroponic farm just being loaded on the Fort William train by a fork-lift truck."

"It appears you have been productive," Sam commented.

"You will notice," Angus declared, diverting their attention to the inside of the coach, "a large LCD display screen at each end of the coach compartment. The one at the front is coupled to a wide-angle digital movie camera mounted on the front locomotive, giving a view forward – as seen by the driver. The one at the rearmost partition is similar – looking back down the track, the way we have just travelled."

216

Highland Haven

"That's marvellous," Alan enthused, "I often wished I could travel up front in a loco, to get the driver's view. This is even better, we can see forwards, backwards and sideways while sitting in comfort with friends."

"Well, it was obvious that most people would be travelling in this area to witness the scenery and, like you, would wish to be up front. This was the solution. Of course, since we have a loco at each end, you have views forward and backward.'

"That beats British Rail," Sam declared.

"There is also a very practical purpose," Angus continued, "a movie picture of each journey is recorded on to disc which is then downloaded at Village Station to our main computer. This provides us with a visual track inspection every trip. Each month we will randomly choose a recording to vet; if all is well we will delete all except that one. However, if there appears to be a problem we can check through other recordings to determine when it began and so establish a rate of development which will set the priority for action. There is another benefit of the system; if – God forbid, there was an accident such as a derailment due to a landslide, we would have recorded visual evidence of the circumstances – like an aircraft's black-box."

"Well, it does appear that the system to improve passenger's enjoyment has been made most cost effective." Sam observed.

The new, narrow-gauge track was laid alongside the British Rail track for the first three or four miles to take advantage of the level corridor without interfering with existing operational schedules. Just after the station at Morar, the Glenquoich track parted company to follow along the north shore of Loch Morar.

As the 18 mile long stretch of water came into view, Angus gave them a bit of tourist spiel. "It is reputed that the monster of Loch Ness, *Nessie,* has a cousin living in this loch. Her name is Morag. Some people believe that there is a subterranean passage joining the two lochs. However, I'm sure you do not wish to listen to me telling you dubious legends or boring you with the many points of interest so I draw your attention to the earphones by each seat; if you switch them on you will be able to listen to a prepared commentary related to the current position of the train. As you will hear, it gives historical, geographical and geological information as well as other tantalising titbits which some will find of interest."

"This is amazing," Sue said, adding "I've never travelled on a train like this one before; it has all mod-cons."

At that very moment, the connecting door opened to admit an attendant offering refreshments.

Maurice Duffill

"You can't whack it," Sam confided to Alan; "Angus has done a first class job here. I engaged him as an engineer but he has certainly extended his expertise to customer relations."

Sitting there, in the comfort of ergonomically designed seats, sipping coffee and gazing at the views forwards, backwards and sideways, was a most relaxing pastime. Two stops were made while on the shore of Loch Morar, at the hamlet of Bracore and at the almost non existent Swordland. Angus told them that, since the railway happened to pass by these places, they had provided a 'halt' to pick-up or drop-off people and parcels. The driver has to be notified in advance if a drop-off has to be made. "It's just a little public service we are able to provide at virtually no cost," Angus added.

"That seems very considerate," Fiona commented, "but why the stop at Swordland, there doesn't seem to be anything there?"

"If you look at a map, you would see that it is also very close to Tarbet, on the shore of Loch Nevis; there's just a narrow neck of land between the two lochs. By stopping – on demand, at Swordland we provide access to the isolated communities on both shores and, via a ferry, we can even get to Inverie; where we had lunch."

"The people there surely use the Mallaig ferry."

"Yes but now, holiday makers can make a pleasant round trip; Inverie to Tarbet and Swordland, then Mallaig, and back to Inverie – or any variation. Of course everyone also has ready access to Glenquoich."

Five or six miles further on and the train slowed, gave two little jerks and then carried on, now climbing away at the head of the loch.

"You will have noticed the slight irregularity just back there," Angus declared. "That was caused by each loco engaging the rack; the third rail. From now on we are on either steep climbs or steep descents until we reach Loch Quoich at Twin Dams. We are truly a mountain railway."

"I notice there was a section of double track, just before the start of the third rail," Alan commented.

"Yes; that's the only part that is wide enough and flat enough to allow the passage of trains."

Leaving the loch at Kinlochmorar, the prepared commentary began spewing out unintelligible gaelic names of features to be observed in the increasingly rugged terrain. Gleann an Lochain Eanaiche turned out to be the name of the glen up which they were climbing. The stream, or more correctly – burn, carving its way down issued from a small loch locked away between towering peaks. Close by the track, waterfalls tumbled down which probably caused a display of leaping salmon every year as they climbed to the calmer waters of the lochan above for spawning.

218

Highland Haven

"Oh look – on the front display screen," exclaimed Alan, "there's an osprey circling over the lochan ahead of us, no doubt looking for the opportunity for some fishing. I wonder if the train will scare him off?"

"There he goes," Sam confirmed the suspicion, "he's just zoomed down the glen, on our right-hand side. What a pity, it would have been great to see him catch a salmon."

"Oh you morbid thing you," moaned Sue.

"Not at all. That's nature's way; it's one species job to feed another. Whatever; it would have been a great sight to witness for real. I've only ever seen it on documentary films."

As the train continued up, above the lochan, twisting and turning ever tighter, the mountains seemed to close in as the glen became quite narrow.

"I can quite see your concern Angus, regarding possible land-slides," Mhairi commented. "Whatever will happen when the snows of winter come?"

"We do have two snow blowers that can be hitched to a loco – one in front and one behind to avoid it becoming trapped on the single track. Oddly, we do not expect frequent heavy snow in this area; the warmth of the Gulf Stream penetrating the sea lochs tends to keep the temperature up. However, when conditions are right, the heavy moisture sweeping in from the southwest could be lifted and cooled by the mountains to give us a heavy dose."

As they climbed ever higher, the burn alongside became smaller and smaller until there was just peaty heather to be seen, and then a new streamlet started – flowing the other way. They had obviously crested the summit, although mountains still towered above them.

"I've asked the driver to stop just around the next bend," Angus announced. "From there you will be able to see the high bridge which was the subject of the sabotage attack. We will then cross it and immediately enter the half-mile tunnel."

As the train slowed to a stop, they all looked first at the forward looking display and then out of the right-hand side. There they saw the slim span with two tall columns supporting the rails as they dramatically crossed the deep valley and then disappeared into the portal of the tunnel.

"That is some bridge," Alan expounded.

"Did the scaffolders fall all the way down into the water?" Mhairi enquired.

"They certainly did, along with tons of steel tubing," Sam confirmed.

"It is a wonder that anyone survived."

"Far from being an intrusion, I think the bridge is quite beautiful," Fiona offered. "The slim modern lines contrast spectacularly with the rugged background. I must compliment my husband on a job well done."

"Thank you my dearest one." Angus retorted. "I bet that remark will cost me."

"What about wind," asked Sue, "could the train be blown off?"

Maurice Duffill

"Well spotted," Angus replied, "it is a matter of concern because of the funnel effect of the valley we are about to cross. Consequently, we have set-up a weather station which sends its data out by radio. The train driver has to interrogate the base computer for permission to cross; failure to do so and the train will automatically stop."

"Very clever."

At that moment, the train moved off to curve its way onto the bridge. As they crossed, the passengers were very conscious of the narrowness of the structure. They had no visible sight of the supports as they went apparently into space over the tumbling waters beneath. Before they had time to become concerned, they entered the darkness of the tunnel. Instinctively, they all looked at the forward display to watch the growing circle of light as they approached the exit; an experience not normally available to rail travellers.

As they burst out into the sunlight once more, Mhairi exclaimed, "there are the two hydroponic farms, I can see the curved roofs."

"They are not an intrusion on the landscape," Sam observed. "In fact, if you were not looking for them, they would probably go unnoticed."

"Oh look. There is a string of horses passing under the railway and one of them has a deer on its back." Sue noted.

"That'll be stalkers from Kingie," Alan offered. "They take paying visitors out on the shoot and then sell the kill – mainly to Germany I understand."

"How beautiful they look. It is like times long passed; before the days of motor cars. It brings out the arty side of one's character; maybe a poem or even a painting could result from observing such a sight," Sue declared.

About a mile further on, Angus announced "We are approaching Twin Dams Station where we disengage from the rack and join the electric tram route. The track running off to the right leads to the Quoich industrial area where we have a quarry, a concrete batch plant, a joinery works, and our rail & tram maintenance depot."

Leaving Twin Dams, everyone was once more on familiar territory but it was still a pleasurable experience to travel along the loch-side in the great comfort afforded by the diesel electric train rather than the more basic tram. Twice they met trams coming in the opposite direction which were parked in passing loops to give priority to the more long distance train.

"Now that the housing has developed, along with chalet accommodation," Sam proffered, "is it worth considering doubling this section of track which is shared by train and tram?"

Angus said he would look into the costs involved and then report back. "I would also like to discuss with you a further extension to the tramway; giving a complete circuit of Loch Quoich. Perhaps I could have a meeting with you and Harry Shaw next Friday to consider the merits."

"I'll get Sue to set a time and let you know," agreed Sam.

It seemed like the end of a grand journey as the train slowed for its approach into Village Station. Just before they alighted Sam announced that he had booked a table for six at the Castle Restaurant to follow a tour of Harry Shaw's computer and communications set-up, so the most enjoyable day was not over yet; once more they were treated to the drama of the cable car ride. Harry, the 'bits-and-bytes' brains of Glenquoich, was at the top terminal to greet them as they emerged from the tremendous trip up the mountain to the castle sitting atop.

"Having had, what I'm sure was a most revealing round trip – no doubt a beautiful visual exercise, I now wish to introduce you to the electronic world of Glenquoich Castle which – I hope will be an illuminating mental exercise. Come in to the hub, where we monitor all that is going on with the various systems"

"Good heavens! Look at all those screens," Sue exclaimed, as they entered Harry's control room. "Why ever do you need all those?"

"At the central desk, the main screens are used to look at any part of any system. If problems have developed, it is here that we examine the conditions and the options for action."

"When you say 'if problems develop', do you mean with your systems, or do you mean outside problems; with the railway, power distribution, weather, security, or whatever?" Alan enquired.

"The quick answer is both. That is why there are a number of screens available to the controller; he can, for instance, investigate why power has failed to the tramway and, at the same time establish the positions of all the vehicles. One of the screens is showing a log of the sequence of cause and effect. Another is linked directly to our own computer system, acting like an x-ray machine, in case we have internal failure."

"I see, on the main panel, there are sections devoted to all the various systems you are involved with," observed Fiona.

"Yes; a wide range of functions are either monitored or directly controlled from this room. Most systems are, of course, automatic. Besides having a supervisory role of the cable-car, tram and train operations, we monitor banking systems – not the content of actual accounts I hasten to add. All the systems in the hotels – environmental control, purchase and sales account management, staff management, maintenance planning, etcetera, are all centralised here. Security monitoring throughout our whole area of responsibility, both internal and external, is centralised here along with coordination of emergency services. We monitor the climate at many points throughout the area by utilising radio linked monitoring stations developed by Alan. This information is fed onto QuoichNet for use by the agriculturalists, building services, event planners, and by the population as a whole. Communications as well as Internet and television distribution are obviously controlled from here. It is in the mainframe computer here that all our developing university's research papers are held, together with the necessary administrative records. Teaching programmes for the school pupils are made available from here – not only to the school, but to each home. There are a number of other functions centred here but, I think that résumé should suffice to illustrate how very important we are," Harry concluded, with a deliberate stress to blow his trumpet.

"With all that lot going on, it's no wonder that you have flashing lights all over the panel. I just hope the controller understands it all," added Sue.

"Of course, all this costs money," continued Harry. "We offset the costs by selling our services to a variety of clients. On the floor below we have programmers and technical writers devising systems akin to those developed for use at Glen Quoich. These computer-based systems, along with Alan's climate monitoring system, are of value to resorts, tour operators, forestry, construction projects, developers, transport authorities, and others. We have been called upon to write programmes for special projects – some quite alien to us, for such spheres as the North Sea oil rigs, and even aircraft control systems. These are quite profitable and widen our sphere of expertise, making our services more attractive to future clients. The total cost of running all the services we provide is more than met by our software sales so that I can declare we are now making a positive contribution to the Glenquoich Development Corporation."

"Quite a speech," Sam declared. "I must commend you, but don't apply for an increase in salary just yet."

"Although I wouldn't say no to your offer to double my income, I must declare that my exposé was not so motivated – it was for the interest of all present," Harry replied in the same light-hearted manner. "However, just to finalise my explanatory blurb, I will introduce you to Arthur Brown's domain, which is also situated in the castle," he announced, leading all of them along passageways to the electrical distribution department. "We work quite closely together to ensure that the power requirements of the whole community are adequately met. In Arthur's absence, I will explain that we are coupled to the North of Scotland Hydro-Electricity Board's system so that they can provide all our needs. However, we have installed a number of small generators of our own to minimise the demand or even to export power to *them*. In this connection we have a couple of pumped storage systems where, during our high demand periods, we let water out of high-level lochs through generators to reduce the power intake from the hydro-board. During the night, when demand is low, we pump the water back up again – out of the main loch. The power required when pumping is purchased at a much lower rate of charge than when we sell the generated power."

"Isn't that cheating," challenged Mhairi, "buying cheap at night and then selling dear during the day?"

"No, we are providing a service to the hydro-board – even when we are buying from them; because the demand we make during the night helps them to keep a more even loading on the system as a whole. It would be bad economics to maintain expensive generating and distribution equipment which is under utilised."

"Electricity is not the only form of energy provided by Arthur's department. As you know, gas is found to be the most economical means of water heating. Initially bottled gas has been provided wherever required but, progressively, this will be upgraded to a piped supply from bulk storage as centres of demand are established. The castle and the village commercial premises are already coupled to a bulk storage facility located in a redundant tunnel. This is re-supplied by road tanker but ultimately we hope to feed this from a ship supply terminal to be established in Loch Hourn; thereby cutting down vehicular traffic according to the general policy of our development corporation."

"The third form of energy – the low level heat extracted from rock borings has proved to be quite worthwhile since it provides basic background heating during the winter for residences and commercial premises. So you can see that, besides being a magnificent location for a restaurant and hotel, the castle is a vital centre of control for the whole community."

With that, they all moved to the restaurant to relax with a pleasurable meal in the unbeatable location in the clouds.

"It seems incredible," Fiona expounded, "that from a position that would have previously required mountaineering skills to enjoy, we can sit and sip while anticipating the joys of cuisine prepared by a top chef. Whoever it was that dreamed up this castle with all its attributes should be congratulated."

"Thank you most kindly ma'am," Alan replied, "I must admit I had something of a problem convincing our boss-man here that the idea wasn't as crazy as it first appeared."

"Well I'm glad you did," Sue commented, "it's so beautiful here even though we can't now see very much with those heavy clouds blocking the setting sun."

"Actually," Alan volunteered, "in the daytime, this would be a great place to watch a big weather-front approaching – particularly if it was accompanied by a good show of lightning."

"Oh I don't fancy that," Sue admitted, "we've got to use the cable-car to get home. I think I'd rather spend the night here than risk storm and tempest suspended from a bit of wire."

"It's rather more than a bit of wire," Angus pointed out.

Maurice Duffill

"Of course it's all part of the plot," Sam offered. "Invite people to the restaurant, summon up some bad weather, and we have increased occupation of hotel rooms."

CHAPTER 24

"Excuse me, Mr Jackson," a waiter leaned over the table, "there is an urgent telephone call from Mr Slater. I will plug-in an extension near your table."

"Hello Stewart," Sam said cheerfully, "what's the problem?"

"We've had a bank raid."

"What! Who would be stupid enough to raid our bank, there's hardly any regular cash kept there?"

"It wasn't cash they were after; it was the safety-deposit boxes."

"But how, with all our security provisions?"

"They took over the bank just at closing time. That's not all, Sir Richard's private office was also broken into – shortly afterwards."

"I presume you have closed off the entry gate to the whole complex and notified the police?"

"Yes, but they escaped down the road to Loch Hourne where a high speed boat was waiting."

"When was this?"

"They got to their boat about five minutes ago."

"Get on to Angus McGilvery; see if he can head them off until the police zero in. I'm coming down straight away. Meet me at the cable-car terminal."

Sam quickly told his dinner guests of the trouble and then, making his apology, dashed out of the restaurant to catch the next cable-car down to the village terminal. Stewart was waiting, as arranged.

"Did you manage to contact MacGilvery?" Sam asked, as soon as they met.

"Yes, by radio," Stewart replied, waving a hand-set in further explanation. "He was just arriving at Arnisdale – for a night out, and says that no boat has passed by in the last 15 minutes so has turned back and is now lying in wait – in the dark, in mid-water."

"Good for him. Tell me, how did all this happen?"

"I haven't had time to obtain all the details; I've been too busy responding to the problem. However, as far as I can tell, it seems that a Mr Foster engaged the bank-manager in some business discussion just prior to bank closure and, when the counter customers had all left, the manager instructed the staff to lock-up as usual. It was then that Mr Foster's associate took control by following the key-holder behind the counter and disabling the alarm button. Foster demanded the list of box holders. Between them they burst open selected boxes chosen from the list."

"Do we know which boxes were chosen?"

"Not yet. I left the bank after telling the manager not to touch anything but to allow the staff to recover from the shock until the police arrived."

Maurice Duffill

"How did they get down to Loch Hourn; visitors are not normally allowed to drive in by car?"

"They stole yours. It was all planned quite thoroughly; about the time the two left the bank and alarms were being raised, two apparent hikers gained entry to the club at the Big House and then forced Sir Richard's desk drawers open – taking everything."

The radio in Stewart's hand burst into life; "there're coming – just abreast of my boat-house. I can see the fluorescence of their bow-wave. I'll wait until they are a little closer then hit them with my spotlight. Ah, that shook them. They've turned back but there is nowhere for them to go; I've blocked the narrows. I'll just keep my beam on them and see what they do."

"Angus, it's Sam Jackson here. You keep them occupied but don't get too close; we don't know how violent they may be. There is a police chopper on the way; I can hear the engine now. I will redirect them to you. Hopefully they can re-tune to this frequency to communicate directly with you."

"They'll not get past me Mr Jackson; you can be sure of that."

"Let's not have any heroics; it's not worth it."

The police helicopter landed on the hotel roof making good use of the illuminated pad provided for the purpose. By the time it had settled, Sam and Stewart had arrived by lift and dashed across before the pilot shut down the engine. Sam shouted his news about the escapees and gave them the radio frequency. Two men leapt out; Detective Chief Inspector MacLeod and a forensic investigator, DS Jones – complete with a bulky black bag. The pilot immediately opened up again to take-off with the remaining crewman.

As the chopper climbed away to the north-west, the group left on the roof could hear the crewman making radio contact with Angus to determine his position. After some interchange which established that they had about eleven kilometres to fly, they estimated they would be with him in just over five minutes.

Having welcomed Hamish Macleod and his colleague, Detective Sergeant Jones, Sam briefed them on what basically had transpired and complimented them on their quick response.

"You were dead lucky," Macleod commented, "we were just on our way down to Glasgow where Taffy here was due to demonstrate his techniques. Hearing your alarm call, I thought I would poke my nose in before the team arrive by road."

With a crackle, the radio interrupted further conversation. "We can see your spotlight, Angus. Ah, there they are. We'll drop down close to them to make it clear we are here."

As the police helicopter neared the fugitives, Angus saw a powerful airborne beam stab the darkness right into the power-boat. Five men could clearly be seen but they made no attempt to surrender. Instead, the boat turned south – heading straight for the shore.

"What in hell's name do they think they're doing?" Angus called, as the boat ran aground at high speed. Seeing the men leap out and run alongside a mountain stream, he added "unless they've got some help, they'll not survive, they're heading into the rough bounds – and the weather forecast isn't good either."

As if his comment was the cue to the heavens, heavy raindrops started sheeting down.

"We won't be able to hang about too long in this," called the pilot. "While we keep an eye on them, can you disable their boat so they can't escape?"

"I can that," confirmed Angus, who had powered up to the little estuary of the stream. A moment later he reported "Their spark-plug is in ma pocket and the boat was damaged when they ran aground, so they won't be going anywhere in that."

"Good. I'm returning to Quoich Village now and will arrange for search parties to commence at first light. Good luck Angus – don't get too wet."

"And good luck to you. I'm away for a wee dram to wet the inside."

Hearing the conversation between the chopper pilot and Angus, DCS MacLeod called the chopper on Stewart's radio to establish the coordinates of the landing point. He then asked to be taken to a telephone. They quickly descended by lift to the hotel foyer. After consulting a small book from his pocket, the DCS dialled a number.

"Fort George; can I help you?"

"Connect me with your commanding officer."

"He is not present at the moment. Who is calling?"

"This is Detective Chief Inspector MacLeod, Northern Command Police; it is most urgent that I be put in contact with Colonel Morrison – without delay."

"Please bear with me a moment Sir; I will see if contact can be made."

After a pause for perhaps half a minute, the voice of James Morrison boomed out of the ear-piece, "Hamish, my friend, what can a do for you, what's so urgent?"

"We have five fugitives entering the Rough Bounds, we need to find them before they escape or die of exposure in this dose of weather which is currently inflicting itself upon all and sundry. We need teams equipped with night-glasses and the resilience to cope with Britain's toughest terrain."

"It's a bit short notice; we are on exercise at the moment off Glenelg."

"Excellent. You are not far away from the scene and you are obviously equipped with boats. Why not treat this as a rapid response anti-terrorist exercise."

"You have a crafty way of twisting one's arm. Where exactly were these fugitives last seen?"

"Our chopper pilot gave the National Grid Reference as NG 8525 0625 which is the estuary of a mountain stream where they crashed their boat. They were last seen moving south from there, on foot."

"We have a ground support helicopter here, fitted with night vision equipment, which is capable of all-weather flight – somewhat superior to your little whirlybird," he mocked. "I'll mobilise him to seek out the targets while a platoon shoot round to the coordinates in an assault craft; they'll take the best part of an hour. Do we know if they are armed?"

"We must assume so. They waved guns about, but they could have been dummies."

"Right. The wheels are in motion. You owe me one – I'll send the bill to Northern Command HQ in Inverness. Tell me, what means of communication is preferred?"

"Best to use radio. The local frequency is 107.6 megahertz. Contact here is Stewart Slater who is responsible for security at Glenquoich."

"Very good then, we'll use that frequency for all communications concerning this operation so that Slater can be aware of what is happening."

After leaping ashore, the five fugitives took temporary cover behind a rocky outcrop to avoid the glare of the airborne beam and to take stock of their situation. Suddenly the beam was switched off as the helicopter, and the boat were heard withdrawing. The total darkness - made more intense by the heavy cloud overhead, was soon accompanied by a demoralising quiet only countered by the sound of incessant rain driven by a strong wind.

"Where the hell are we?" burst forth Frank Bolton, leader of the two bank raiders, "we're stuffed."

"Keep your cool, Franky," the driver asserted. "They've given up on us, at least for the time being. By the time they come back – probably tomorrow, we'll be gone."

"Gone where?" joined in Phillip Mars, one of Sir Richard's office raiders. "You smashed the boat, you stupid bastard. We ain't going anywhere – and they know it."

"Give over, Phil. 'arry couldn't take on their bleedin' air force *and* the navy. At least we've got time to think." It was Phil's mate John Brady getting his six-penn'orth in.

"We've got to think a bit bloody smartly," said another voice from the dark – it was James White, normally called Snowy, "we'll all die of exposure out here. I copped a map before we set off, all there is is mountains and more mountains; nobody lives 'ere, there's no roads nor nothin'."

Highland Haven

"Look, when we ran for cover, we crossed a bit of a track;" Harry observed, "it must lead somewhere."

"Yeah, when we was coming in the boat to do the job it wasn't dark; I saw a cottage back up towards where we did the job, and a bit further on there was another," Observed Brady. "We could shelter in them and work our way back to the village where the lads raided the bank."

"That's an idea; they'd never think to look for us in their own back yard," Frankie agreed, "and there's a little train runs from there to that fishing port. We can catch a regular train south from there."

"Do you know how far it is from here to the village?" Harry, the boat driver challenged, "it's about five miles to the pier where I picked you up, then you've got to get up the hill to the village."

"At least we'd have shelter and per'aps get some food at the two cottages."

"It's the first place they'll look."

"'ave you got any better ideas?"

"I have. It's not too far from here to a boat house I saw when we were coming. It's probably where that boat came from that copped us with his searchlight. If we follow this track *that* way, it'll probably lead us there."

"What then?"

"If he's in, we'll nick his boat; if he ain't, we'll wait in comfort then ambush him."

"If we get 'is boat, where are we going with it?"

"Instead of going back to Mallaig, we'll go to Kyle of Lochalsh where we can get a train to Inverness and then away south." Harry suggested.

"I think they'll nab us in the boat; I'm going the other way – to the village." Frankie declared.

"I'm with you." Brady agreed.

"It's too dodgy. Are you with me?" Harry asked of the other two.

"I reckon. Just so we can get out of this bloody rain; I'm soaked."

"We'll see you two back in London." Harry commented as the party split up to go their separate ways.

Stumbling along the narrow track in complete darkness, the fugitives made very slow progress; sometimes even reduced to crawling up slopes on all-fours feeling for rocks. Although all of them came from rough backgrounds, this situation had reduced them to snivelling children struggling to find their way in the dark. They were not trained SAS Commandoes; their domain was the streets of London where they could smash a door down if they needed shelter. Here they were at the mercy of nature's angry moods – and she seemed to be pretty angry this night.

It was about an hour later that Harry's party stumbled upon the boat-house with its associated cottage. There was no light to be seen so after a brief survey which established that the boat was not there, Harry tried the cottage door. Finding it not locked, they crept in and searched the two rooms. A log-burning stove gave out much needed warmth although it had obviously been shut down to await the return of its owner.

They stripped off wet clothes and dried themselves on blankets from the bed. They then sat in front of the stove, in their underwear, in the dark, wrapped in anything they could find. Although they had discovered an oil lamp, they didn't dare use it for fear of showing they were there.

"I 'ope nobody comes until me clothes dry out; I don't fancy getting dressed again in that cold, wet clobber," Snowy moaned.

"Ideally," Harry agreed, "I hope we can stay just long enough to get some food in us while we are drying out then grab the boat when he returns."

"How are you going to see where were going, if we get his boat?"

"It'll not stay this dark forever; when we get out into the water, we should be able to see the outline of the coast. We'll have to take it easy but I have a pretty good impression of the route we need to take."

"While you were talking, I've been feeling about and have found some bread and some cheese. We can at least have a bit of a feed," Phil declared.

"Did you find a bottle of Whisky, these Scots always have one?" Snowy challenged.

"There's all sorts of bottles here but I can't tell what's in them."

"I'll come over and use my sniffer."

Just then, the sound of an engine caused a rising of their pulses.

"He's coming back," said one.

"No. That's a chopper," decided Harry. "They'll be using infra-red, or ultra-violet, or whatever; to see in the dark."

"Well they'll not see us in here; the heat of the stove will fool them."

"Maybe so, but don't move about. Any movement will attract their attention."

"Well, I'm putting my bloody clothes on just in case."

"Search-One to base. I can see a heat source down at the boat-house cottage but it looks more like a stove. I'm not sure whether or not anyone is there. I'll continue down the loch to the position given for their landing. Over."

"Roger Search-One. Go as far as the cottage marked on the map as Runival; they'll probably follow the track along the shore."

"Search-One from Assault Team, we are about ten minutes away from the boat-house so will investigate."

Highland Haven

Much to the relief of the occupants of the cottage, the sound of the chopper faded as it travelled further up the loch – but their relief was short lived.

"Listen," Harry said, "there's another engine; sounds more like a boat.."

"It must be the boatman from here," Phil suggested, "better get ready to nobble him when he comes in.'

They listened as the sound drew closer; it was definitely a boat and it was approaching the boat-house. Finally the engine died. The intruders tensed as they heard the boat bump against the landing stage; and they waited for the boatman to tie-up and come to the cottage.

Suddenly, the door burst open and two commandos burst in armed with sub-machine guns and backed by a third wielding a powerful spotlight. The assault was accompanied by much shouting – designed to put fear in the hearts of the occupants. The squatters almost died of fright. Instead of *them* overwhelming an unprepared boatman, *they* were staring down the barrels of murderous weapons.

"Where are the other two?" demanded the leader.

"Th-they went the other way, along the loch-side path," stammered Harry.

"Face the wall. Spread your legs. Keep your hands up," they were ordered.

Cable ties were used to bind their wrists behind them before being roughly thrown on to chairs and the bed.

"Who are you? Who are you working for?" demanded the leader, as their pockets were rifled for wallets and any other identification evidence.

"Harry Smith, James White, and Phillip Mars," stated the lamp holding soldier as he pointed to each in turn; "all from the Big Smoke – London," he added.

"What are you doing up here?" the Commando leader challenged.

"We saying nothing without a solicitor," Harry moaned.

"Forget it lad. You're not in a police station. You'll tell us what we want to know or you won't see tomorrow."

"You can't treat us like this; we have rights."

"Oh? And what rights would they be?"

"The right to a fair hearing, for one," Harry pleaded.

"Look matey; you gave up your rights when you stole that boat, raided a bank, broke into an office, commandeered this cottage. Who the hell do you think you are – little Hitler?"

"You can't do anything to us," Harry persisted, "you'll get yourself into hot water."

"Is that so? Nobody knows we've found you so, if you are never found, nobody will accuse us of anything. We can easily arrange for you to perish due to exposure in this remote, wild terrain – particularly on a night like this. Get up! Let them out; we'll frog-march them up the hill separately and listen as their calls for help fade away – one-by-one."

As the cottage door was opened, the sound of the rain pounding on the nearby rocks was challenged by the sound of a howling wind; they wouldn't last the night out there.

"Bring one of them out. Cut off his bonds and make sure there are no marks. There's bound to be a steep drop around here where he can 'accidentally' stumble to his death."

Two soldiers grabbed Phil Mars and dragged him to the door.

"Harry, do something," Mars pleased.

"Ok, ok, you've made your point." Harry conceded.

"Well then, what are you up to?"

"We were briefed to rob the bank and raid a particular office."

"But you didn't just rob the bank, did you? You went after particular safety deposit boxes."

"Well yes. We were to look for personal documents of the directors of this Glenquoich Development Corporation and the office was of the President, Richard Blaisdale."

"*Sir* Richard Blaisdale. So where are these documents you nicked?"

"We've each got some. We shared them out between us in case one of us got caught and to ensure we got paid."

"How was that to be?"

"We are due £1,000 for each useable document."

"Well, now you are going to hand them over for free. Search their clothing," he barked.

'Now for the nitty-gritty. Who arranged all this? Who was going to pay you? What was in it for him?"

"I don't know what it was all for and I don't think we were dealing with Mr Big," Harry confessed.

"Who *were* you dealing with? Come on, don't try my patience."

"All we know is his name – Bill Braithwaite."

"Where does he live?"

"I've no idea. I got a phone call one day from this bloke who said that me and my mates had been recommended for a special job. If we were interested we should meet in the Crown and Anchor the following night. He warned us that we would meet only this one time whether we took the job or not. If we agreed to go ahead, he would brief us there and then and then, he would contact us after the job was done."

"How are you to be paid?"

"He gave us £5,000 as a deposit. When the job was done, we should hand over the documents; he would have them checked out and then pay us £1,000 for each good one. Of course there's no way we will hand them all over – we might never hear from him again."

"This is Search-One. We've spotted two bodies moving towards Runival but can't see the other three."

"Search-One from Assault-One, we have apprehended the other three fugitives in the boat-house cottage. Take note, the other two are carrying documents which must be retrieved before they destroy them."

"Roger Assault-One, we will drop two men ahead to ambush them."

Frank Bolton and John Brady heard the chopper coming and ducked down behind a large rock. As it flew by their hearts sank as they supposed that the cottage they were heading for was the chopper's object of interest.

"What do we do now?" Brady asked.

"Let's listen to decide if they land there," Frank suggested.

After listening as best they could over the noise of the wind and rain, the beat of the rotors came closer once more, then passed by.

"I don't think they landed," Frank offered, "the rotor noise never shut down. They probably just had a look to see if we were there."

"How could they see in this weather?" Brady queried.

"Night glasses. They'll have these fancy binoculars that can see in the dark."

"I'm glad they didn't land; I'm dying to get out of this God awful weather. I'm soaked, and I'm cold, and I'm hungry, and I'm tired. I wish we'd never agreed to come up to this miserable place. At least in the city we can always get a roof over our heads."

"I'm just as wet and cold as you, so let's get on with it; the faster we move, the sooner we will be under cover."

"HOLD IT RIGHT THERE," demanded a voice from the dark.

The two fugitives almost collapsed with shock as the two commandos thrust sub-machine-guns in their ribs. "What the hell? Who are you?"

"Never mind who we are, take your coats off."

"What, in this weather?"

"And your pants, and your shirts."

"You must be mad, you sadistic bastards."

"We want those documents you've got; so the sooner you strip for a search, the sooner you can cover up again."

"How did you know we had some documents?"

"We just know, so if you don't want to die of exposure you'd better hand them over."

"Here's mine," Brady quickly said, rather than suffer the elements while in the altogether.

"And mine," Frank added, not wanting to prolong their agony any further.

"Frisk them," the leader ordered, "they may have more hidden."

While his colleague obliged, by roughly pulling open their clothing, the leader called up the chopper to report they had apprehended the two villains. The sound of rotors once more heralded the approach of the airborne battle-wagon. With guidance from the ground, the pilot managed a tricky landing in appalling conditions on a small knoll. The soldiers bundled their captives quickly onto the aircraft so that it could take-off again before the blustery wind caused any problems.

"Search-One to base, we have captured two fugitives and secured the documents they were carrying. Request instructions for delivery."

"You are to proceed to the head of the loch where an illuminated landing pad awaits."

"Roger. ETA five minutes."

"Assault-One to base; we have loaded the other three captives – complete with documents, do we proceed to the head of the loch?"

"Roger. Police will await your arrival at the landing stage."

"Roger. ETA 10 minutes."

CHAPTER 25

As the police had been going about their task of securing evidence from both crime scenes they had been monitoring the radio traffic between the commando units. Pleased with the result, a small army of constables was sent down to Kinloch Hourn to receive the captives.

"What is important is that we establish who engineered these raids," DCI MacLeod declared, "there is something quite unusual in the way they largely only took documents, leaving cash untouched – bar the odd handful due, I suspect, to uncontrolled temptation."

Sam enquired as to whether they had yet discovered what documents were taken.

"Yes. After interviewing all the staff at the bank, my officers have established that all the contents of boxes held by each of the directors was removed and, strangely, fresh printouts of account holdings, again of each of the directors."

"I'm bloody glad they've managed to recover them," Sam declared. "We pride ourselves on complete security of private matters. It wouldn't do to have our personal affairs passed around willy-nilly."

"Is there likely to be anything of special interest to an outsider – or to another insider for that matter?" Macleod asked.

"Are you suggesting that it was an inside job?" Sam exploded.

"It is a possibility we must not overlook; it would appear that they had no difficulty in extracting the financial statements from the computer. Access codes must have been used."

"Oh bloody hell; this puts a new twist to the whole thing."

All five fugitives were taken, by police van, to Inverness for further questioning. The bank staff was re-interviewed, this time to concentrate on establishing connections with friends and relatives as well as checking on their financial state to determine whether any pressure existed to seek extra income. The Manager's background had been thoroughly checked out before being offered the position, so he seemed to be cleared. The rest of the staff members were the wives of employees of the corporation and had a good standard of living whilst enjoying the unique social environment of the Glenquoich community so were unlikely to jeopardise their position. There was, however, one exception. Agnes Turnbull, one of the tellers, was a local woman who travelled daily from her cottage at Inchlaggan a few miles down the glen. She was unmarried and lived alone.

Hamish Macleod reported his findings to Sam Jackson, adding that they would carry out further checks on her, being the odd-one-out. Hearing this, Sam suggested that his staff might be able to help due to their local knowledge. Macleod agreed, so long as it was done discretely so as to avoid future trouble if she was found to be quite innocent.

"When are we going to have our documents returned?' Sam asked.

"We need to hang on to them while we establish the motives behind the operation, but don't worry, the content will be kept completely confidential; we have a special unit for this sort of situation."

Northern Command Police interrogators were briefed to concentrate on finding out who Mr Big was and where the intermediary, Bill Braithwaite, could be found. Repeated questioning – without sleep, of the five individuals made no progress. It was concluded that the villains really did *not* know who he was or where he lived. It was decided to carry out what American crime films call a 'sting'; the prisoners would be taken back to London and made to act as if the raid had been successful so that the hand-over of documents could be monitored.

Having returned to Inverness to supervise the enquiry, Hamish MacLeod rang Sam to ensure that nobody revealed the five had been captured; it was important that the contact – whoever it was, should believe that all had gone according to plan. Sam confirmed that only he and Stewart Slater were in the picture and they would imply the men had escaped down the loch.

As soon as he rang Stewart to explain the situation it was admitted that he had already told his wife. "We must stop it there," Sam insisted, aware that he too had explained the evening activities to Sue. "Get Anne to swear secrecy until the matter is closed. We'll pretend that the raiders escaped down the loch; which they did – initially. 'Police are continuing their enquiries' is a good stock comment that should satisfy inquisitive minds for the time being."

Within 24 hours Ted Evans reported to Sam that Agnes Turnbull was a friend of Morag Matheson. In fact, it was suggested there maybe some sexual association between them. "Now there's a coincidence," Sam declared. "Anything to do with Miss Matheson has proved to be bad news."

Sam promptly rang Hamish MacLeod in Inverness to give him this latest tit-bit and remind him of Miss Matheson's previous use of her cousin Marcus Matheson – in London. "Is that too much of a coincidence?" Sam suggested.

"We'll monitor him while we track the documents. It looks as if we are going to have a pincer movement going for us on this caper. Thanks for that," he concluded.

Highland Haven

MacLeod immediately contacted his opposite number in the Metropolitan Police explaining the background and to point out that the sting would have to take place in two days time – when Braithwaite was due to contact Harry Smith. In order to follow through, they would need to put a tap on Smith's telephone so that a trace could lead to Braithwaite's whereabouts. Smith and his merry men had agreed to cooperate in the understanding that they would only receive nominal sentences for being the pawns in some dastardly plot. It would also be necessary to witness any contact between Braithwaite and Matheson – if indeed he was Mr Big. Phone taps were authorised on both Matheson's home and his office.

The party of five were put on the Inverness to London sleeper train so that they would arrive at Euston Station as per plan. Of course, a discreet escort of plain clothed officers also made the trip. They were joined at the terminal by two more from the Met. Who informed them that the telephone monitors were in place and, if the villains didn't try any funny stuff, they expected to bring the matter to a successful conclusion quite quickly.

The next evening Harry Smith received the expected call. "How did it go?" Braithwaite asked.

"Ok, no sweat. Where do you want the exchange to take place?"

"You put the documents in a large plain envelope and then take them to a locker at Victoria Coach Station. Post the key to yourself in an A5 sized, red envelope; on the back write 'from number …' quoting the number of the box."

"If I post it to myself, how will you get it?"

"Don't worry your little head about such details." Braithwaite scoffed.

"I don't like this; what about our money?"

"You'll have to trust me."

"I'm damned if I will," Harry retorted. "I'll put half the papers in the locker but keep the rest – including the bank statements and some of Blaisdale's papers, until you've coughed up."

"You cross me mate, and you'll suffer."

"I've no intention of crossing you; I'm just safeguarding our interests. Some papers will be there before the day is out and you'll get your red envelope tomorrow." At which Harry promptly slammed down the receiver – knowing the police would have had ample time to trace the call.

When the telephone conversation was relayed to their chief, he was less than pleased. "Blast," he said; "there'll be no phone message from Braithwaite; it's going by mail. Send someone to keep an eye on the locker that Smith uses," he ordered, "and tell Smith to use coloured sticky tape to seal the envelope of documents."

Calling at a stationers on the way – to buy a greetings card in a red envelope, Harry took the Tube to Victoria Coach Station and, as instructed, left the package of documents in a locker, Putting the key between the folds of the card and, sealing the envelope, addressed it to himself and wrote on the back "FROM NUMBER 152". As the envelope slid into the mouth of a nearby post-box, Harry mused about his presumption that some corrupt employee of the post-office would be used to divert his red envelope to 'Mr Big'.

A watching Detective Constable glued his eyes to the post-box until the usual red van arrived and the postman emptied the box as normal. His report came as no surprise. How could anyone in the post-office know into which box the red envelope would be posted? No, the pick-up would have to be by Harry Smith's delivery man or someone at the sorting office in which he was based. Smith's post-man would be too obvious so it was more likely that another employee would scan Smith's mail and then steal the red envelope.

The Detective Constable at Victoria was relieved by another around mid-night with instructions to keep the locker under constant surveillance. It was at about 2 am that a uniformed post-man came to the block of lockers and, after looking furtively around, opened number 152. He took out the contents and hurriedly returned to his waiting Post-Office van. The constable noted the registration number then reported in. Unseen by the watchers, the postman stuck a pre-paid 'official' address label on the package – Holburne Creations, 233 Holburne Street, London SE3. On returning to his depot, just half a mile from Harry Smith's home in Battersea, he introduced it into the stream of mail being sorted; it would be delivered in the normal manner the following morning.

As dawn broke, the observers of Marcus Matheson's residence - at 235 Holburne Street, kept a keen watch as the postman came down that side of the road, posting hands-full of mail into front-door letterboxes. At 235, powerful binoculars disappointedly witnessed only a couple of window envelopes disappearing into the waiting slot. Unobserved, a package, sealed with yellow sticky tape slid clumsily into number 233's slot. Within minutes, the package was passed over the low wall at the rear from 233 to 235; it was a common occurrence – 'people often mistook a 3 for a 5'.

"No package delivered here," reported the observers. "Check the lunch-time delivery," they were ordered.

A conference at the Met decided that discreet surveillance was required at the Battersea Postal Sorting Office. Having confided in the Operations Manager, it was discovered that the driver of the 2 am pick-up van was Bradley Blake and that he was tasked to make an early morning collection of post-boxes in a large area to the south of the River Thames. It was noted that the Victoria Coach Station was just north of the river and, therefore, off his route. From now on, Blake would be trailed whenever he went out on his rounds.

Highland Haven

A day or so later, Mrs Matheson left their home at 235 Holburne Street to do some local shopping. She towed a two-wheeled bag trolley in which to carry her purchases. 'Nothing odd there', thought the observers as she disappeared up the street. Between buying fresh vegetables from a green-grocer and bread rolls from the nearby bakery, she called at the post office to send off a small packet; it was addressed to Bradley Blake.

By lunchtime the following day, the packet was in Blake's hands. Removing the outer wrapper revealed further instructions along with twenty £10 notes, enclosing an inner packet. On his way to work that evening he crossed the Chelsea Bridge to call at the coach station. He put the inner packet – unopened, into box 152, then the key into the same red envelope previously used and already addressed to Harry Smith; this he would post at the sorting office as soon as he arrived.

To receive his own red envelope after the delay of these few days came as a surprise to Harry Smith. Slashing it open revealed the same greetings card with the key inserted – no message. It was presumed that he was required to reopen the locker in order to progress the complex procedure. Another trip to the coach station resulted in some considerable satisfaction. It came from the discovery of a £5,000 payment together with a note demanding the rest of the documents; particularly the bank statements. Harry let the police know about the note but claimed that only £1,000 was contained in the packet.

"Go ahead, send the other documents," he was instructed; "we now know who the link is, so should be able to follow it through."

Harry repeated the procedure of a few days ago, putting the documents in a large envelope sealed with yellow sticky tape and placing it in locker 152. Resealing the key in the self addressed red envelope – which had escaped the franking stamp, he posted this in the same box used the first time.

That night, observers were not surprised when Blake deviated from his route to cross the Chelsea Bridge and retrieve the package from the locker. On his return to the sorting office, his every move was being watched. Having unloaded his van, his supervisor ordered him away on an errand to rescue bags of mail from a broken down van on another pick-up route. As soon as he was out of harms way, the contents of all his bags were searched until a packet sealed with yellow sticky tape was found. It was addressed to 233 Holburne Street – not 235; here was the answer to a puzzle. The packet was re-introduced to the sorting process

The following day, observations were made at the front *and the rear* of 233 as well as 235 Holburne Street. Those at the front warned those at the rear that a delivery had just been made – and the yellow sealed package had been posted into number 233. Cameras with telephoto lenses had been clicking away to record the event. Within minutes, the occupant of 233 appeared at the back door carrying the target package. He reached over the low wall separating his garden from that of 235 and placed the package on a garden table, handily situated close by. The back door of 235 immediately opened and the package was collected. Every action had been recorded on camera.

Reporting in, the observers were instructed to do nothing other than to send their film to control and continue the watch. The films were developed and printed then compared with file photographs of the suspect. It was confirmed that Marcus Matheson was the collector of the package.

At a summary conference, it was agreed that they had hard evidence against the intermediary, Bill Braithwaite due to the original telephone conversation with Harry Smith. They had photographic evidence against the postal worker Bradley Blake and they now had photographic evidence linking in Marcus Matheson. However, two points remained; the link to Matheson was weak – he could claim that mail was often passed between the two houses due to address errors and that he had no prior knowledge of its content. Furthermore, all were anxious to learn to what use Matheson was planning to put the documents and why. To prevent leakage of personal details related to innocent parties, the documents passed to him had all been doctored – they were pure fiction. Not only did this protect the directors' privacy, and that of Sir Richard, it provided the basis of a trap should any of the information be used.

Matheson spent hours scanning the documents, finding property leases, contracts of employment, insurance policies, and the like but, until he consulted the bank statements, there was nothing he could use. Pouring over a file of bank statements found in Sir Richard's desk – all from an overseas bank, under the heading 'South East Asia Trust', he suddenly spotted an irregularity. Every three months there was a payment of £25,000 made to Mr Sam Jackson. Quickly he sought the printout from the Quoich Bank under Sam Jackson's name. There he found a regular monthly salary input along with various ins and outs but no sign of the quarterly payments. Puzzled, Matheson skimmed through all the documents taken from Jackson's deposit box and realised he had passed over a series of statements from Barclays Bank; *there* was the £25,000 every three months. He had originally thought that this was Jackson's normal salary and expected that the local bank would be used for minor transactions but finding that his salary was deposited in the Quoich Bank, this meant that the Barclays input was an extra payment – probably for special services rendered, or hush money for something Jackson had discovered. "I've got them," he declared to himself; "it has all been worthwhile".

Highland Haven

A letter arrived in Sam Jackson's mail, printed by a word-processor on plain paper; it simply read 'Who's been a naughty little boy then? I reckon Sir Richard's £25,000 a quarter has been sent to the wrong account; I'll be giving you instructions shortly as to where to redirect the funds' and was signed 'X'. It was obvious that the extortion letter was originated by Marcus Matheson, but how to prove it; he'd been very careful to cover his tracks so far. Sam called Hamish MacLeod at Inverness police HQ.

"We'll have to go along with his plan," the chief of detectives advised, "he'll slip up sooner or later. We have the edge because he does not know that we know who he is and how he has been communicating so far. To put this case firmly to bed, we need to establish a direct link between him and the documents; we can do that through you."

"Understood," Sam confirmed. "I'll let you know when he contacts me again."

With the increase of permanent residents as the project developed, the primary school, run by Fiona Mackay and now in its new building at the village, enjoyed a swelling register, as did the various colleges of further education which were attracting considerable interest from outside the area.

The chapel situated on the small island had been completed for a little while giving time for the ladies to incorporate some of the decorations they had been preparing. It was decided to have a formal opening to which ministers from the various denominations would be invited to attend and contribute. In lieu of a sermon, it was agreed that Doug would give his promised further talk which would emphasise the non-denominational nature of the establishment.

Beginning with a review of points covered in his casual talks so far presented, Doug then expounded on the fundamental conclusions he had drawn from considering the common physical link between all forms of matter, whether animal, vegetable, or mineral, created by the electromagnetic wave.

"Since we humans have very active brains which radiate signals to other brains, it becomes quite apparent that every individual's development will be influenced by those around him or her. This evolutionary path begins in the womb, initiated by the combination of genes from both parents, but straightaway, influenced by the mental activity of the mother since she is in direct close contact as the infant brain develops. This process continues through childhood with, hopefully, the added influence of the father and other close relatives. Parental attitude to life, developed in their social environment, is transmitted to the evolving character of the young person. Unless the youngster receives alternative input, he/she will, quite naturally, adopt the standards of those closest. The establishment of a code of conduct depends entirely on how firm the surrounding environmental aura has been. The 'superior' attitude created in well-to-do sections of society stem from the success of forebears whereas the 'survival' mentality generated in less fortunate city areas naturally leads to opportunism frequently based on crime."

"Environmental influence is not restricted to the human brain, our harmonious feelings for our pets is obviously transmitted to the brains of the animal in question – and, in some cases, reciprocated. It doesn't stop there however, even inanimate buildings can be influenced; churches and cathedrals become holy. The resonant aura of worshippers is progressively absorbed by the very fabric of the building which then re-radiates the electromagnetic waves back to receptive brains. I have even experienced the homely radiation of a hotel, run on a harmonious basis, where the aura of contented staff and satisfied guests has penetrated the structure and furnishings. This contrasts with the superficially clinical international form of contemporary hotels. Such situations of holiness, or homeliness, are self perpetuating since the aura resonates between the receptive living subjects and the inanimate fabric."

"Taking this concept of harmony to another level, we realise that our involuntary mental radiations and receptions interact with the complete surrounding environment. The cosmos, built up as is everything, from the electromagnetic energy waves of the creation, is a very complex vibrating 'structure'. There are many interrelating patterns of waves creating unique points of intersection – just as waves on a pond after dropping a number of stones into the otherwise calm surface. Similarly, each of us has a unique characteristic built up from waves of experience; that characteristic keys into the pattern of cosmic waves at the equivalent intersection. This combination of waves is what we refer to as one's soul; it is independent of body and consequently remains after bodily death."

"The link between the hardware of the brain and the ethereal soul is the software of the mind. The soul - or the established characteristic of the individual, acts as the programmer of the mind; setting the format of one's actions and reactions. Minds of true lovers become harmoniously sympathetic; growing together; linking with souls in close formation. Bodily demise need not be of great concern to them since their union will live on in the interlinking waves stemming from the creation."

"On this comforting note I will leave you to cogitate on this brief excursion into my hypothesis which, I am sure, you will need time to allow some of the radical aspects to be appreciated. If I have given you food for thought, I will have achieved my objective."

"Doug," a voice from the audience called out. "You claim that these electromagnetic waves are the link between everything but you have made no mention of God."

"A good point, particularly in view of this occasion – the opening of our chapel," replied Doug. "There are many aspects and examples of the universal link concept I have not covered in this introductory talk but, since spiritual beliefs are rather fundamental, I will briefly touch on this particular sphere of interest. Before proceeding I must point out two basics; firstly, I do not wish to advocate any particular religious calling and seek to respect everyone's right to follow their own spiritual impulses; and secondly, I ask you to try to set aside the concept of God as a bearded man wearing sandals. If God is the creator of all things His influence extends beyond earthly matters to the whole universe – including any extraterrestrial beings that may - or may not, exist; earth-bound forms are, therefore irrelevant."

"In the concept I introduced earlier, God is the name we have given to the pure energy which, as a result of the Big Bang, led to the creation of everything. The pure energy waves which have emanated from that momentous event are the All Enveloping Influence linking everything to everything. This concept does, therefore, indicate how 'God is in all of us' - since we too are created from waves. It also explains how we come to be 'made in His image'; *we* are made from *His* energy waves – not the other way around; it is very presumptuous to interpret the biblical quote to infer that *He* looks like *us*. Not only we, but all animals – even plants and inorganic matter, are made in His image, due to the All Enveloping Influence of the Electromagnetic energy waves stemming from the Creation."

"Realising that most religious beliefs are focussed on a supreme being, this concept can lead to an understanding of the commonality of Christianity, Islam, and Judaism, even Confucianism, Buddhism, and Hinduism. We do need to attempt to set aside the different interpretations in order to accept the common basis of the All Enveloping Influence."

"Most energy waves which reach our planet have been deflected by, or absorbed and re-radiated by, the many cosmic bodies; they too were created by the waves emanating from the Big-Bang. To commune with God it is necessary to filter the extraneous, indirect electromagnetic waves and focus primarily on the unadulterated waves radiating directly from the creation. This is the purpose of prayer, aided by an environment enhanced by those of like mind, preferably in a building which has already absorbed similar 'vibes'. The alternative is to seek an isolated natural location - not having interference from human presence, which will be largely free of extraneous waves."

The anonymous voice from the audience acknowledged Doug's reply adding, "That concept of God certainly gives much room for thought."

"One can relate this general hypothesis to many aspects of life," continued Doug, "the academic world, the criminal world, international conflict, sporting contests, and more; those particularly interested might like to read *"The Link –*

from Big Bang to Brain and Beyond", which examines this whole concept in more detail. This will be the focus of the philosophy course here at the Highland University. With that I must close by thanking you all for your interest and attention, and by asking you to *think*, think about matters rather than simply accepting the status quo."

The appreciative response displayed by the audience suggested that the forthcoming course would be well attended.

CHAPTER 26

It was about a week later that Sam received his second letter from the extortionist. "Wrap £24,000 in used notes in a parcel. Wrap this, and another £1,000, in an outer parcel. Place this in a storage locker at Inverness Station. Put the key between the leaves of a greetings card in a red A5 sized envelope. Address the envelope to a non-existent local address. Write on the back FROM BOX… (Stating the number of the locker) and then post it in the nearest box to the station. You have seven days;' the letter concluded. Sam immediately contacted Police HQ and relayed the details to the chief of detectives.

"This is a similar pattern as that used to obtain the documents," Hamish revealed. "Leave it to us; we'll make up the parcel. A provisional arrangement has already been made with the Bank of Scotland so that English Pounds could be made available at short notice. We'll have them all marked with a UV sensitive inscription to positively identify these particular notes." To conclude, he said that MacLeod must have established a contact in the Inverness post-office. "I wonder if your Miss Matheson had anything to do with *that*"

"She's not *my* Miss Matheson – she's *my* pain in the neck," Sam retorted.

"The only way we are going to link her in to the post-office worker is to get him to identify her. I have an idea; we'll get his back up to make him more susceptible by only putting £500 in the outer parcel. We can do the same with Matheson in London by only sending half the asked for amount. If we need to prolong matters, that would persuade him to contact you again. In any event, it saves us £12,500."

Post office worker, Malcolm Fraser, on the late shift at Inverness, had been approached while going out for a smoke. A woman, who refused to give her name, asked him if he would like to earn extra cash – tax free, every three months. Post-Office pay not being overly generous he showed immediate interest. "How much extra cash?" he inquired.

"How would £1,000 suite you?"

"Very well," Fraser eagerly replied. "But what do I have to do to earn it?"

"There's no danger; all you have to do is collect a parcel from a station locker and post it. I will give you pre-printed, officially pre-paid labels to put on."

"Sounds too easy. Why pay £1,000 for me to do something you could do yourself – for nothing?"

Maurice Duffill

"I don't know which locker. You'll have to look-out for a particular envelope; the key will be inside."

"Ah, now I see, you want me to steal a letter to find out which locker has the parcel in."

"Well, are you on or not?" she angrily retorted.

"Count me in. How do I get paid?"

She explained to him that he would have to remove the outer wrapper of the parcel to expose his fee. He must not open the inner parcel – just label it and post it. She added, "the envelope you are looking for will be A5 sized, coloured red, and will state on the back 'FROM BOX ...' giving the locker number. The first one should come in the next couple of days and then every three months. The address on the envelope will be false so destroy it.

"You're on." He confirmed.

"Here are the labels. Now repeat your instructions so I can check you understand what you have to do."

He read the address – Holburne Creations, 233 Holburne Street, London SE3, and then dutifully went through the procedure, thinking carefully with closed eyes, to be sure not to make a mistake then concluded by asking; "How do I contact you?" But she had gone; evaporating in the darkness of the night. He went back into the building wondering if he'd been dreaming or was he now due to have a three-monthly tax-free boost to his income. He would have to watch out for the red envelope.

The police prepared the parcel, the inner being wrapped in distinctive paper contained only half the asked-for amount and then put £500 in the outer wrapping. The parcel was placed in locker number 139 and the key inserted in the red envelope and posted to a fictitious address. They then advised London to look out for the delivery – presumably to 233 Holburne Street.

It was quite a task for Malcolm Fraser to scan all the incoming mail over a period of days without drawing attention to himself. Two or three days had passed without spotting the target envelope but then he had the idea that since it had a false address on it, it would be directed to the reject bin. Low and behold, there it was – it was Fraser's red-letter day. 'The crafty woman', Fraser mused, 'she had specified a false address for that very reason'. He eagerly opened it to reveal the key to locker number 139. During his smoke break, instead of standing in the alley beside the sorting office, Fraser quickly walked around to the station and retrieved the parcel. With excited haste he ripped off the outer wrapping and extracted the envelope containing his fee. As soon as he returned to the sorting office he put the pre-printed label on the inner parcel and secretively introduced it to the general

246

flow of mail to be sorted. Only then did he open the envelope to reveal £500. 'The bastard,' he inwardly cursed; 'she promised me a thousand quid. I wonder what was in the parcel I sent. Next time I will open it to find out'.

36 hours later, watchers in London observed the procedure at numbers 233 and 235 Holburne Street; clicking telephoto cameras recording the arrival and transfer of the distinctively wrapped parcel. As instructed, no action was taken.

With delight, Marcus opened the parcel to reveal piles of £50 notes. "on the nose," he exclaimed to his wife, "this is proof that they are up to something. I'll do the same to Sir Richard and see if he coughs up just as readily. Just a minute – this isn't 24,000 it's only 12,000. The rat-bag; I'll have to turn the screws again."

"I wonder if the postman opened the package," his wife suggested, 'then kept half for himself".

"That's a thought; I'll ring Morag and get her to tackle him". In a moment of anger, he immediately dialled her number to give her the news.

"I'm reluctant to expose myself to him again," she retorted, "at the moment he has no idea who I am but if I tackle him, he will be on guard and may follow me."

"If you don't sort him out, there will be nothing in this caper for you. Look, he's on a good thing; he won't want to spoil his new found easy money."

"I suppose you're right," she conceded. "Leave it with me, I'll see what can be done."

The conversation was listened to with great interest by the telephone monitors as they recorded it for use as evidence. As soon as it was reported back, wheels were set in motion. MacLeod at Inverness was notified that London was preparing to arrest everyone involved as soon as Northern Command confirmed that Morag Matheson and the postman had been arrested while actually in contact. That very afternoon she was seen leaving her home by car and heading for Inverness. A state of alert was initiated with special attention being paid to the sorting office.

At about 11 pm, the unsuspecting Morag approached the sorting office back entrance. With some trepidation, she took up a position where she could observe the rear door and awaited Fraser's smoke break. As soon as he appeared she gritted her teeth and approached him – all hell was let loose; police appeared out of the shadows from both directions, blocking off any attempt of Fraser to re-enter the sorting office. Morag virtually collapsed in genuine shock as she was bundled into one of the cars which arrived with sirens screaming; the drama was too much for her.

The success of the operation was transmitted down to London triggering raids on the Mathesons at 235 Holburne Street, then the homes of the intermediary, Bill Braithwaite: The five raiders previously arrested in Scotland were also rounded up: The postman, Bradley Blake was arrested as he came out of the south London sorting office to go on his pick-up round: The occupants of number 233 were brought in for questioning. About this time, the Quoich bank teller, Agnes Turnbull was taken – shaking with fear, from her home in Glengarry to Northern Command Headquarters in Inverness.

Two days later, Detective Chief Inspector Hamish MacLeod rang Sam Jackson to give him the news that all had been arrested or taken in for questioning and to confirm that Marcus Matheson was the Mr Big in the operation. He also commented that as a result of a search of 235 Holburne Street and Malcolm Fraser's effects, all the marked money had been recovered.

"Why did he engage in such an operation," Sam enquired.

"As soon as we made it clear that we had ample hard evidence, and that the five villains had agreed to cooperate, he capitulated and informed us of his motivation. As a result of his previous involvement with his cousin Morag, when he arranged a Press attack on your corporation's activities, he lost his position on the Cabinet secretariat. This cost him a serious salary reduction as well as loss of prestige. It appears that when he backed off as a result of pressure from your end, the press poked their noses further in, causing some embarrassment. The last straw was when Morag was arrested in connection with the sabotage. His superiors demoted him pretty dam smart. He was obviously very aggravated by his reduced income and loss of face and, due to the continuous prompting by Morag, sought recompense. He honestly believed, because of Morag's brainwashing, that your operation was a cover-up for something sinister, that's why he had only documents stolen. Finding – on our planted bank statements, that you were receiving a big quarterly kick-back from Sir Richard, he thought his ship had come home. Not only would he be able to hurt you and Sir Richard to gain revenge, he would more than recover the loss to his income. In fact, he would be very nicely in profit if he could get both of you paying-up on a regular basis."

"Well that's quite a story," Sam admitted. "Are you sure you can link him to all that happened?"

"Certainly; although he was careful not to establish links, he overlooked an important detail. Choosing to not use the telephone, fax, or email, but to write his few instructions on plane paper using his personal computer so that the type could not be attributed, and taking care to delete each document as soon as he printed it out, he obviously was unaware that details were still lodged within the innermost bowels of his PC: our technicians were able to recover all the evidence we needed."

"The wonders of modern technology," commented Sam. "And what about Morag, will she escape the arm of the law this time?"

"I'm afraid not; we caught her red-handed with the postal worker and, because he felt he was cheated, he revealed all. Her friend Agnes Turnbull is considered a minor cog in the overall mesh so should get away with a nominal sentence although she will suffer the loss of Morag and her job."

"Well, you all seem to have done a good job," Sam declared. "I take it that I can now reveal all to the rest of the directors. We may take another look at our security arrangements regarding staff being engaged in sensitive areas."

'Will you thank Angus McGilvery for his cooperation; it was his blocking of the escapees that gave us the edge in this whole affair."

Sam called a special meeting of directors to which all wives were encouraged to attend. Somewhat apprehensive regarding the purpose, they all gathered at the appointed time to be relieved, yet intrigued by what their Managing Director had to tell them regarding the extortion case. The Personnel Director, Stewart Slater, expressed regret that he had not instigated a vetting procedure capable of identifying the potential threat of Agnes Turnbull. He was, however, reassured that nobody could have foreseen any danger in such a quiet, clean living person.

"On an entirely different matter," Sam announced, "Sir Richard has been in touch to advise that we are to have a very important visit which will require our very best efforts to create the right impression."

He quelled the general murmurings to explain, "virtually the whole Cabinet together with the Shadow Cabinet and a fair selection of peers from the House of Lords are to spend two or three days here in just over a month's time. I have not been informed of the objective; merely that the whole future of Glen Quoich depends on us generating a favourable impression."

Much discussion took place between everyone in the room. Sam allowed it to continue for a while as a natural reaction to his announcement before continuing. "Not knowing what they are looking for, it seems obvious to me that we must highlight the achievements and special social benefits of our society. This is not just the physical developments that we have managed to introduce but the harmonious nature of our lives together, aided by the ready access to modern facilities. Let's not put on a false face but honestly display the advantages of living here. They are to be treated as normal paying guests; and I stress the word *paying*. It is likely that the press will get to hear of this great influx of officialdom and come snooping around – there must be no hint of corruption by giving favours."

"This explains something," the commercial director, Bill Bates, revealed, "we have had an abnormal level of bookings for overnight accommodation from the press for the weekend of the 25th and 26th of August."

"That is the weekend in question," Sam admitted. "How the hell did they get to know before we did? I hope they have not taken too many rooms because, as this list shows, we are being inundated."

"Good grief." Bill exclaimed, "I'm going to have to do some jiggling to ensure that they are accommodated to a good standard."

"Surely *all* our guests are accommodated to a good standard," Sam retorted – with tongue in cheek. "They will be arriving by various means so Stewart, make sure that your security personnel are on the ball to check each person and issue the appropriate day tickets without being overawed by their status. And let's all ensure that the press do not make a nuisance of themselves."

Glen Quoich was certainly receiving plenty of free publicity; the press was having more than one field day regarding the bank and office raids since cases were being brought both in Inverness and in London. The revelation that the Development Corporation were not up to any 'funny business', whilst drawing attention to the state of the development of their Highland domain, brought renewed interest - accompanied by increased bookings. The end result was, therefore, quite the opposite of the Mathesons' intentions.

August 25th saw the arrival of political dignitaries and press by all available means. They came in twos and threes by car, by train, by boat, and by plane; it was as if it had been orchestrated in order to review all the facilities available. Members of the security staff were kept on their toes in order to ensure all were booked into the complex and issued with their tickets. It was important that it be seen that every effort was made to keep reasonable tabs on who was on the estate; this being the basis of Glenquoich's secure environment which has led to the relaxed lifestyle.

The following day some of the visitors sampled the available water-sports while others roamed the trams and cable-cars, taking pictures and chatting with residents and holiday-makers. Everywhere the press followed – at a reasonably discreet distance, checking on who said what to whom in an effort to glean the overall purpose of the visit.

While holiday-makers responded with favourable comments regarding the facilities available and the courteous service received, residents reported that they were being asked many questions about their financial involvement in the development, the use of Quoich money, the tax benefits, and other aspects of the regime.

By special arrangement, Harry Shaw held court in his control room for the benefit of those dignitaries seeking a good general summary of technical services provided. There were some mumbled favourable comments regarding the comprehensive linking of television, Internet, computer based information, education, and other services available to all households as well as business.

During the afternoon of the second day all the political dignitaries attended a conference in the Village Hotel – without the press, followed in the evening by a banquet in the Castle Hotel.

On the final day, some left early while others absorbed more of the atmosphere before making their way south, by the diverse means of their arrival. At no time did any of the visitors make any formal or informal statement to directors, or to the press, as to the reason for the survey.

Everyone felt a little flat after their departure, knowing they had been the subject of very high level scrutiny but not knowing why.

"Ah well," Sam declared at an ad hoc meeting, "I'm sure we will discover, in due course, what it was all about. In the meantime we look forward to Doug's inaugural lecture at the launching of the Department of Philosophy."

CHAPTER 27

Having welcomed the audience to his opening university lecture, Doug gave some background to what was to follow. "In this course we will examine the philosophies of the great minds of the Greek and Roman empires as well as some more modern great thinkers. Students will be required to study these in order to determine the relevance today. However, to do this, one needs to establish a base from which to work. With this in mind, I ask you to consider the thoughts and proclamations of a contemporary thinker – Myself."

"The most important requirement is that you should *think* for yourself. As a basis, let me take you back to fundamentals; the fundamentals of time and space. Please allow *my* mind to take you on a journey that led me to a great revelation. I am not a physicist but have a great interest in the fundamentals of how things came to be as they are. All material matter we know is made up of molecules. In their turn molecules are made up of atoms. A water molecule is, for example, made up of one oxygen atom and two hydrogen atoms – this is elementary but more complex molecules are comprised, in the same way, of various combinations of atoms. Originally, it was thought that an atom was indivisible; it was considered the smallest particle of matter. We now know that the atom *can* be split; it is not truly the smallest particle of matter. So, of what is an atom made? Scientists have established that there is a nucleus surrounded by electrons – originally thought of like the Sun and its surrounding planets, all held together by gravitational forces."

"This, it turns out is not entirely true; the nucleus, or 'Sun', is composed of a number of positively charged protons, normally matched by a similar number of neutrons – all together as a clump, while the 'planets' we call electrons are formed as a negatively charged cloud around the nucleus. The number of protons varies according to the element; for example hydrogen has only one, whereas oxygen has eight and Uranium has 92 - the number of electrons matches the number of protons."

"Please do not lose heart; these basic facts of physics are not intended to tax the brain of non scientific persons – I mention them merely as a foundation to what follows. Being the kind of person I am, these facts have long been known to me – as I am sure they have been to many of you. However, what intrigued me was, of what are protons, neutrons, and electrons made?"

"I turned my mind, first of all to electrons – probably because they form the 'shroud' around the nucleus through which one must penetrate to progress further into the heart of the matter. I had read that, strangely, electrons sometimes perform as particles and sometimes as waves. I reasoned that if they *were* particles, then we would need to know of what *they* were made – and so on ad infinitum. Let's,

Highland Haven

therefore, consider the possibility that they are waves; waves of what, you might ask?"

"It is now fairly conclusive that the universe began with an 'almighty' explosion of pure energy – now referred to as the Big-Bang. The next logical question is, in what form was the pure energy released? The answer turns out to be electromagnetic waves. Is this then the answer; electrons are electromagnetic waves?"

"Starting at the simplest element; that of Hydrogen, where there is only one electron, I can show that this is consistent with the formation of one wavelength of electromagnetic energy bent around to form a sphere – vibrating somewhat like a soap-bubble. The next simplest element is helium – having two protons, and therefore two electrons. Now then, if we think of any wave, its amplitude passes zero twice – once on the way up and then on the way down. We can interlock two identical waves at right-angles to each other by synchronising the two zero positions. This means that two electrons can vibrate around a nucleus at the same radius."

"More complex elements - requiring more than two electrons, can be established by having another wave at a greater radius; a bubble around a bubble. I can show that this can be achieved utilising two wavelengths as a unit. Two wavelengths wrapped around in a circle have four zero positions, allowing the interlocking of two, four or six waves. Similarly another concentric bubble can be formed from four sets of three waves. Continuing this process we can explain the structure of the electron cloud for every existing element and any theoretical element."

"My conclusion is, therefore, that electrons *are* waves of electromagnetic energy. It is also probable that protons and neutrons have a similar character but at a much smaller radius due to a much higher frequency of vibration – resulting in far greater energy values."

"If electrons, protons and neutrons are waves, what then is a particle? My hypothesis suggests that if a single wavelength of electromagnetic energy was to form a sphere *without* being centred on a nucleus – this would be a particle. It is not too difficult for this to occur; if an electron is physically knocked from an atom, or drawn from an atom by a strong magnetic field, we would have a free electron. This is commonly achieved in the electron gun which forms the heart of most television sets. A free electron is a particle formed of a wave which can revert to being a wave when combined with a nucleus."

"I repeat my apology for indulging in this technical excursion but we now are able to make a grand – very fundamental statement. *Since the components of an atom appear to be composed of nothing more than electromagnetic waves, and all matter - whether organic or inorganic, is built up from atoms, we can conclude that everything is made of waves."*

"Now I realise that this might well come as something of a shock but there is nothing else from which anything can be made. During this course, I will show that this has even greater implications than one might at first think; it can explain animal communications, love and hate, fantasy and religious aura, it leads to the explanation of the workings of the mind and its relationship to the soul, it generates an understanding of 'life' after death and, most importantly, explains our relationship with God – how we are made in His image, how He is *in* all of us."

"These explanations – and much more, must wait for further study, but what I ask of you now is that whatever you study you would do well to consider the reasoned logic just presented as a basis from which to work. The use of reason and argument to seek the truth *is* the definition of philosophy."

"Thank you, ladies and gentlemen for your attention. May I wish you happy pondering."

As the audience dispersed from Doug's talk to take trams back to their homes, gentle light snow was falling but, typical of the fickle Highland weather, by the time they were disembarking a howling gale had created a face-smarting blizzard. Within minutes, returning residents were like walking snowmen due to the rapid build-up of the wondrous white deposit from the heavens. It was with multiple sighs of relief that the sanctuary of heated homes was finally achieved.

By morning the wind had eased but the coming of sunlight revealed a changed landscape. The deep snow had covered all roads and tram tracks causing all sharp shapes to become rounded and indistinct. Drifts climbed against walls as if trying to reach the heavy layers drooping from roofs. It was quite difficult to realise what was what. Residents bold enough to open front doors found a wall of snow at chest level.

The telephone system was put to maximum use as friends and relatives rang each other to determine if all were safe. Officials initiated the as-yet untested snow clearing plan thinking that nature could have at least offered a more gentle covering for the initiation. Trams could be fitted with snow ploughs but this fall was too great for them to achieve an initial clearance. One special locomotive, fitted with snow-blowing equipment was put into action, directing the discharge towards the loch in order to reduce further build-up which might blow back. This rail mounted vehicle was supplemented by a jet powered road vehicle known as a Snowerific, which uses the heat of the engine to convert the snow to water-vapour.

Highland Haven

When the tramways had been cleared the snow blowing locomotive set-off on the more remote mountain railway to Mallaig. Two trams fitted with ploughs were used for scheduled runs around Quoich so as to ensure continued clearance.

The children of course enjoyed the resulting sparkling play ground. Snowmen appeared in what had been front gardens, snowball fights ensued whenever groups gathered, and enterprising youngsters were seen sliding down hills on tin trays. This triggered a suggestion from the sport & tourism manager, Farquhar Henderson, to Sam Jackson that they should build a permanent bobsleigh run – in fact a number of them; one for novices, one for intermediates and one for the experienced; the last being to a standard similar to the Cresta Run. "If we develop a technique of creating an icy surface – as is done for indoor ice rinks, we could offer a unique sporting facility all the year around which would assist Britain in training for the winter Olympics as well as providing a great attraction to Quoich."

"Sounds like a good idea to me," Sam acknowledged, "I'll have a word with the other directors to see how we can incorporate the proposal in our next budget period."

The snow clearing provisions proved to be quite effective, which was just as well since wind blown snow and further overnight falls continued to cover the transport routes. The remote mountain railway was, however, not so troubled as one might have expected; the section across the open hillside being raised was automatically cleared by nature and the tunnel of course was immune. The only section seeming to suffer was alongside Loch Morar due mainly to snow slides from the hill above, but the snowfall in this area was lower than further inland due to the proximity to the warmer water and the prevailing wind. "It might be wise to build snow tunnels at one or two critical points," admitted Angus to Sam, "but the blower can cope with it generally."

After a few days the weather eased and snow deposits started to reduce, returning the panorama to normal. Activities had not been seriously interrupted and the arctic conditions had been received as an acceptable diversion from the sometimes drab winter days. The children were, of course, sorry to lose their winter wonderland, trying to see who could keep their snowman for the longest period.

Although the weather could be pretty atrocious at times, the glen did enjoy periods of bright sunshine even in the winter, making it ideal for the sporting fraternity to enjoy the challenging outdoor life. All in all Glen Quoich was proving to be a most desirable place regardless of season; making it a busy and prosperous area. The young, ever growing community had knit together well, developing a pleasant social life in a crime-free environment; the inhabitants were becoming the envy of those in less fortunate districts.

Would this Eden last?

CHAPTER 28

Sir Richard, having just returned from a visit to London, called for a meeting with Sam. After listening with great interest to a review of progress and the immediate development plans, he raised an alarming topic.

"For some time now, I have been aware of personal medical problems," he confided to Sam; "that was one of the reasons for my trip south. Exhaustive tests have revealed that I have inoperable cancer of the liver."

"Oh, Sir Richard, what can I say? I'm so terribly sorry; I'm shattered by your news. What is Lady Blaisdale's reaction?"

"She too is very distressed, but we have known for some time that I had a problem and we suspected the possible outcome, so it does not come as such a shock to her. We decided not to mention our concern until the consultants confirmed that nothing can be done. I apologise for shocking you in such a manner but felt the time had come to reveal the situation."

Sam sank into his chair, still struggling to come to terms with what Sir Richard had just revealed. "I'm sorry," he said, "but having dealt with many difficult problems concerning this project, I feel totally inadequate to face up to your disastrous news. Just when it seemed that the dawn was breaking over Glen Quoich this great cloud has descended."

"I realise I have dropped a bombshell, and that you will need time to consider the implications. However, that is the point of this meeting. I wish to brief you on my plans for you to continue in my stead; apparently, we have four or five months in which to ensure that my dream can be realised – even if it is to be posthumously. I must say that you have risen admirably to the challenges that my ambitions have set you. As a result, I have no hesitation in declaring you as my successor. However, I have never revealed to you my ultimate objective; *I wish to change the world*. I know that sounds all very dramatic but, in essence, that is my aim; well at least to set that change in motion."

"I am a much travelled person," Sir Richard continued, "not just as a visitor to various countries but as a resident, or as an involved businessman, discovering the many variations of social hierarchy. Whether the culture is based on Christianity, Islam, Buddhism, Hinduism, or whatever, it is clear that any nation has to have some overall policy of control. I'm not thinking of policing; I'm referring to political control. In these more enlightened times we are all aware that many countries have massive problems due to abject poverty and yet their ruling classes are bathed in luxury. This can't be right. Equally, it would be unreasonable for those displaying the talent of leadership, or inventiveness, or shear drive, to be held down to the level of the laziest, uncaring, weak individual. What I believe to be the

256

ideal is a subtle blend of the supportive communist approach with the initiative displayed by the capitalist system. The question arises; how can this be achieved?"

"In our venture here at Quoich we have introduced elements of control borrowed from various regimes: we have a dictatorial democracy in that *I* have prescribed the form that this community should take, we have the caring elements of a communist society by establishing our social security system and our regimented pay scale, and yet we have the incentives required by a capitalistic order with our various methods of passing the business success or failure to those most involved. These all combine, I believe, to create the foundation of an ideal brotherhood which manifests itself in social harmony which, I'm pleased to say, has quite definitely evolved here."

"In order to achieve this I have been able to isolate our settlement from the general demands of Britain's tax laws and business rules, but our community is not large enough to be totally independent. Any state needs overall foreign policy; we cannot function as an independent state, we need defence forces to prevent predators from taking over, we need foreign representation to establish trade links and to deal with cross border disputes, we need the established higher level of legal ruling, and many other services outside the scope of our limited province."

"In my position as a member of the House of Lords I have been able to persuade influential government sources to agree to carry out an experiment in an effort to seek a balanced system of political management. The experiment is the Glen Quoich Development Corporation. Supporters of my views have been keeping a close watch on what we have been developing here and are now ready to take the next step. A bill is scheduled before Parliament to declare Glen Quoich an independent state; a dominion – with myself as President."

"Good heavens, why would they do that?"

"They – like me, feel that none of the current political options properly fulfil the need of world society. If our policies prove to be workable and demonstrate a greater balance between the haves and the have-nots, developing a more harmonious culture, it would lead the way to adjustments in government policies worldwide."

"This is awesome. I presume it was in preparation for the debate on the bill that we had the recent visit of politicians."

"Quite so; that is why I never revealed the ultimate aim for fear that it would influence your outlook with a less than beneficial effect. However, my health – or lack of it, has intervened; it is unlikely that the bill will be passed before my demise. In any event, I need you to develop the concept in order to make all this worthwhile. If nothing else - successful development of Glen Quoich will demonstrate that a viable community can be established in remote areas reducing the burden on city development. Similar projects could be established in deserts or other improbable sites which could lead to the curtailment of the growth of urban sprawl. So we have two objectives; a political one and a practical one."

"I have already formalised my will and have had your succession drafted into the bill in order to facilitate a smooth transition whether or not I survive to the passing of the act of Parliament. I suggest you make no mention of these arrangements and the ultimate ambitions to anyone, other than your wife, until after my passing. I will announce that I am suffering ill health and will be increasing your responsibilities accordingly. This should suffice until independence is granted. I suggest you go home now and take time to absorb your new outlook. We will settle details progressively in the ensuing weeks."

Sam left Sir Richard's office in a daze. Walking to his car he literally pinched himself to be sure he wasn't dreaming; pain of the pinch caused a flutter of the heart with the realisation of the mega implications. Arriving home without being conscious of the drive up the tortuous hill from Kinloch Hourn – his mind was in a whirl. Tom had great difficulty in containing himself while Sue completed the preparation of their evening dinner. Having said to her during the meal that he had something very important to discuss, he refused to enlighten her until the table was cleared and they had settled with coffee and a malt whisky so that the matter could be dealt with in a relaxed manner.

"So, come on then, tell me what is so important that you need my full attention. Has Sir Richard given you your marching orders or has he arranged a great fat bonus for all your hard work?"

"If, dear lady, you would let me get a word in edgewise, I will enlighten you. Firstly, you must, and I mean **must,** keep this entirely to yourself; don't discuss it with anyone – including your close friend Mhairi. Others will be informed as and when appropriate."

"Yes, yes, ok, don't keep me in suspense – get on with it," Sue urged.

Sam revealed the dramatic news of Sir Richard's terminal cancer and that he had only about four or five months to live.

"Oh darling, how shocking; whatever is going to happen now?"

"That is the point; I am to take over completely, but that's not all." Sam summarised Sir Richard's plans and then explained about the bill being introduced in Parliament. "If this all goes through and Glen Quoich is declared an independent dominion, with Sir Richard's death I will become President."

"I don't believe it, I don't know what to think; it is fantastic, it's exciting, but it's scary."

"Scary is certainly the right word. When you persuaded me to write for the job as Engineering Manager in this unknown-to-us place we could never in a million years have imagined to where it would lead. Becoming Development Director was a big leap, but this is something way out of my experience; I'm not sure I'm up to it."

"Of course you are, my love. You always rise to the occasion."

"This is different; it is political. It's all about persuading people - not solving physical problems."

"I must admit, I never thought I would be the President's wife."

"Sue, don't develop any grandiose ideas; this is a very serious development."

"Don't go all pompous on me again."

"I'm sorry but we've got just a few months to prepare for a major change in our lives and can only discuss it with Sir Richard. As you said a moment ago, it's scary. What we must do is simply get on with the current job in hand while we allow the new prospect to sink in. The hard part will be to avoid changing our attitude to all those around us."

A couple of weeks later, Sir Richard addressed one of Sam's regular project revue meetings. He revealed to the heads of departments the shocking news of his terminal cancer. The announcement that he had only a few months to live caused a babble of awe-struck comment. He went on to state that, progressively, Sam would take on increased responsibility so that the whole project would be able to continue without intervention from outside the current organisation. "I trust that you will all give Mr Jackson your full support. As I move into the next world, I would like to believe that this great enterprise will continue to flourish and that my ultimate ambitions will be realised – albeit posthumously."

With this remark he excused himself and left Sam to continue with the meeting.

As soon as Sir Richard was out of the room, the level of excited chatter increased until someone raised the question; "What did Sir Richard mean when he referred to his ultimate ambition?"

An ominous silence awaited Sam's reply. "I'm sorry but I have been asked to keep that under my hat for the present; to release details at this stage might jeopardise the objective but, rest assured, the prospect is very exciting and potentially beneficial to us all."

"Sir Richard asked that you support me as I progressively take on the overall responsibilities for the whole venture. *I* ask, that you all show your support of our Chairman's great vision by bringing your various projects to the next stage as soon as possible. It would be a great boost to him if, in the course of the few months left to him, we could declare success in as many aspects as possible. I propose therefore to modify today's agenda to explore how we might speed development in each sphere of your responsibilities. This is short notice but perhaps by temporarily applying resources in particular directions we can achieve specific goals in the next three months."

Having insisted that he be transferred from hospital in London to the big house at Kinloch Hourn for his last days, Sir Richard was keenly aware that his demise was imminent. Sam had frequent brief meetings to reassure him that all was well with the project. He was able to confirm the completion of the tramway extension giving access to the developing college campus and that the colleges had received official support to be eventually united as The University of Quoich with departments of computer studies, climatology, philosophy, and political reform.

The conference facilities in the village and at the castle were proving to be quite a draw, leading to a most satisfactory occupation rate for the hotel and the guest houses during the winter as well as the summer months. With the completion of the second cableway which gives easy access from Village to the head of Loch Hourn, the tourist route from Fort William via the Highland Railway, the mountain railway, the boat link to Kyle of Lochalsh, and onward by observation train to Inverness was also proving to be in great demand. Many were taking a break at Quoich to enjoy the facilities and for sight-seeing. This also added to the success of the available accommodation. The hydroponic farm had now established itself as a reliable supplier of fresh vegetables to Quoich's own market as well as to commercial outlets in Fort William and further afield. Sporting facilities on the loch and the hillsides have developed into a major attraction. Quoich's computer services were gaining a foothold in the programming market and publishing was widening its field, based on the success of the journal *British Scene*.

On top of these successes Sam was able to report that the community had developed into a close-knit society enjoying good health and a happy, prosperous lifestyle. Most importantly, the indications from Westminster were that the Quoich bill was about to be passed by both the Lords and the Commons. Sir Richard could end his days with great satisfaction.

Sam had just completed one of his regular executive meetings when he received a call from Sir Richard's secretary conveying a request from Lady Blaisdale for him to attend immediately at the big house. On arrival, he was shown directly to Sir Richard's bedroom where he met Lady Dorothy. She declared that her husband was very weak and agreed with him that Sam should be present. By the bedside, the attending doctor confirmed that his patient was in his last hours.

Highland Haven

In attempting to make his passing peaceful, Sam reassured his Chairman that all was well and that the Quoich community was looking forward to a prosperous future thanks to his great foresight.

At that moment Miss Fitzroy knocked and entered the room with some haste. She passed a fax message to Lady Dorothy who read it with great care and then, after a pause declared to her failing husband "Congratulations Mr President." A glow of understanding came over Sir Richard's face.

As Sam read the confirmation of the passing of the act of Parliament, giving Dominion status to Glen Quoich, his newly elevated Chairman, satisfied that his work was done, slid peacefully from this world.

Lady Dorothy bent over to give him her last kiss then straightened up and said, in a very formal voice, "The President is dead" – and then, turning to Sam, "long live the President."